P9-EED-210

DEEP
IS THE
FEN

BOOKS BY LILI WILKINSON

A Hunger of Thorns
Deep Is the Fen

Pink
The Boundless Sublime

Wilkinson, Lili, 1981-author.
Deep is the Fen

2024
33305256209937
ca   06/11/24

DEEP
IS THE
FEN

LILI WILKINSON

DELACORTE PRESS

This is a work of fiction. Names, characters, places, and incidents either are the product of the author's imagination or are used fictitiously. Any resemblance to actual persons, living or dead, events, or locales is entirely coincidental.

Text copyright © 2024 by Lili Wilkinson
Jacket art copyright © 2024 by Lindsey Carr

All rights reserved. Published in the United States by Delacorte Press, an imprint of Random House Children's Books, a division of Penguin Random House LLC, New York.

Delacorte Press is a registered trademark and the colophon is a trademark of Penguin Random House LLC.

Visit us on the Web! GetUnderlined.com

Educators and librarians, for a variety of teaching tools, visit us at RHTeachersLibrarians.com

Library of Congress Cataloging-in-Publication Data
Names: Wilkinson, Lili, author.
Title: Deep is the Fen / Lili Wilkinson.
Description: First edition. | New York : Delacorte Press, 2024. | Audience: Ages 14+ |
Summary: Merry is determined to stop her best friend Teddy from joining a men's-only secret society that specializes in backward thinking and odd traditions, even if it means teaming up with her archnemesis, Caraway Boswell.
Identifiers: LCCN 2023016201 (print) | LCCN 2023016202 (ebook) |
ISBN 978-0-593-56270-3 (hardcover) | ISBN 978-0-593-56271-0 (library binding) |
ISBN 978-0-593-56272-7 (ebook) | ISBN 978-0-593-80923-5 (int'l ed.)
Subjects: CYAC: Secret societies—Fiction. | Magic—Fiction. | Best friends—Fiction. |
Friendship—Fiction. | Fantasy. | LCGFT: Fantasy fiction. | Novels.
Classification: LCC PZ7.W652 D44 2024 (print) | LCC PZ7.W652 (ebook) |
DDC [Fic]—dc23

The text of this book is set in 11-point Baskerville.
Interior design by Michelle Crowe
Leaves illustration: Oleksandra/stock.adobe.com

Printed in the United States of America
10 9 8 7 6 5 4 3 2 1
First Edition

Random House Children's Books supports the First Amendment and celebrates the right to read.

Penguin Random House LLC supports copyright. Copyright fuels creativity, encourages diverse voices, promotes free speech, and creates a vibrant culture. Thank you for buying an authorized edition of this book and for complying with copyright laws by not reproducing, scanning, or distributing any part in any form without permission. You are supporting writers and allowing Penguin Random House to publish books for every reader.

For every girl who refused to be a damsel in distress

A billion little lights

A multitude can make a sun

Here we are to save the world.

—FOURTH FLOOR COLLAPSE, "LITTLE LIGHTS"

1.

TEDDY HAS FILCHED A BOTTLE OF WASSAIL FROM HIS da's cellar. He pours it out like it's liquid gold, and we each take a thimble-sized glass.

"To us," he says, smiling at Sol and me. "The three best friends that ever were. To unshakable loyalty and unbreakable bonds. Happy Whitsuntide."

Sol drums the floorboards with his heels, his cheeks glowing.

I love them both so much. I want to stay in this moment forever. The three of us, together and young and happy.

I look threadwise, refocusing my eyes slightly to see the mettle floating around us, silvery strands of life-force. I'm no witch, but I can see mettle, and recognize who or where it came from, in the same way I can track a rabbit or a fox in the woods. The mettle between the three of us is connected—intricately braided together over the years of our friendship. We're inseparable, and that's the way I want it to stay.

They're waiting for me. I clink my glass against each of theirs, careful to make eye contact as I do so.

The wassail is as strong as it always is, all cloves and hyssop, and we each wince and gag, swallowing it like medicine.

Teddy holds out the bottle. "More?"

Sol makes a face. "Ugh, no."

"Merry?"

I shake my head. Even that one thimble-sized glass is enough to make me feel warm and a bit blurry around the edges. But Teddy refills his own glass and downs it in one gulp.

We are ensconced in the sitting room in the house where Sol lives with his aunt, surrounded by open chip packets and cans of fizzy drink. We've been playing twlbwrdd—an enchanted Ilium set where the king piece crumbles to dust when he is captured and the maidens stain red if they get captured by a liegeman. We've been here since midafternoon, and Teddy and Sol have filled the air with the musky scent of teenage boy. I get up and open a window, breathing in the sweetness of the night. In the distance, I hear the faint jingling of bells, and the tramping of feet.

Whitsun Eve is *our* night. Our families are always off celebrating, either at the Rose and Crown, or in Da's case at the Frater House with the other Toadmen. It's a night steeped in ancient tradition, and we have our own traditions too. Battered haddock, scampi and scallops with chips and mushy peas from Branwyn's fish shop. Cans of redcurrant fizz and packets of cheese puffs. We play games and just generally flop around and enjoy knowing that school is over and we have the whole glorious summer stretching before us.

"We should go camping," I say. "Up to Dryad's Saddle or farther, to Fish Creek. We could leave the day after tomorrow."

"Watch your king," Sol murmurs to Teddy.

"I can't go until after next Thursday," Teddy says, moving his king piece behind the shield wall.

"Why not?" I slide another maiden into position.

He hesitates for just a moment before answering. "I'm needed at the forge."

Something in his tone is off. Teddy's a terrible liar. I look over at Sol, who is busy studying the board, and I get a sudden, awful feeling that they're hiding something from me.

"I thought Wayland was giving you the whole summer off?"

Teddy shrugs. "It's just a few extra days."

"We can go next Friday," Sol says. "Forecast says it'll rain this weekend anyway. I vote for Dryad's Saddle—we'll see if the damson plum is fruiting this year, and we can explore more of the cave we found behind the falls."

"Sounds good to me."

Teddy turns another of my maidens red, and Sol slips his black raven around the edge of the board where there's a gap in Teddy's shield wall.

The tension leaves my shoulders as I remember last summer, our lips and fingers stained purple from damson, lazing by the banks of the Mira and falling asleep under the stars.

"You'll never get through," Teddy informs me, capturing another maiden. "Admit it, I win."

I glance at Sol, whose mouth twitches in a suppressed smile.

"Never," I tell Teddy. "A shield maiden fights to the end."

He laughs. "Oh, Merry," he says. "Always so competitive. Is being joint dux of our school not enough for you?"

He leans on the word *joint,* because he knows it rankles. Never before in the history of Candlecott School have there been two duxes. I'm certain that I'm the rightful one, and that Caraway Boswell's father increased his endowment because he couldn't stand the idea of his precious son coming second.

Teddy takes advantage of my brief moment of seething resentment and turns my last maiden red. He lets out a shout of triumph. "Bow before your king!"

I curtsy theatrically. "A mighty show of strength, my lord. Just not quite mighty enough."

Teddy looks back down at the board as Sol moves his raven into the castle. Teddy swears good-naturedly as his king crumbles into glittering black dust.

"Again?" Sol asks, sweeping the pieces back into the box to reset them.

Teddy leans back and stretches lazily. He's effortlessly handsome in jeans and a slouchy pullover, square-jawed and hazel-eyed, his golden hair swept over his brow. Something catches in my chest when I look at him. We were seven years old when I made the rule. We swore a blood oath, the three of us, to be best friends forever. And I made Teddy and Sol swear that they would never fall in love with me. I knew that any romance would upset the balance between us—the perfect harmony of three friends. And I was seven, then. Romance was the furthest thing from my mind.

But now I'm seventeen, and Teddy is the leading man in all my nighttime fantasies.

One of the twlbwrdd maidens slips from Sol's fingers and tumbles to the floor.

"Curses," he says, picking up the broken pieces. "Why do they make them so fragile?"

"I can fix it," Teddy says.

4

He takes the pieces from Sol and frowns at them, concentrating. I look at him threadwise to see ghostly hands manipulating the mettle of the little stone fragments, pulling them back together, drawing on energy from other things in the room—daffodils in a vase, the rising bubbles from his can of redcurrant fizz, the fingerprints in the clay statue on the mantelpiece. He whispers to himself as he works, muttering song lyrics or a nursery rhyme—there is mettle in oft-repeated words.

The stone maiden clicks together, good as new. Teddy hands it back to Sol and then turns to me, already defensive.

"What?" he says.

I shake my head. "You know what. You should be more careful."

"I'm not the one who dropped it."

"Was that a covenant spell?" I ask.

Teddy shrugs.

"Teddy."

There are one hundred legal spells in Anglyon. Covenant magic. All other magic is illegal, unless it's being done by one of the big magic corporations. But Teddy knows it's not the legality of magic that upsets me. It's been four years since Ma died, but it still hurts. Some days the grief is as sharp as if it were yesterday.

Sol puts the piece back in the box. "Probably enough twlbwrdd for one night," he says brightly. "Shall we play cards?"

Sol is always trying to make peace between Teddy and me. But I'm just so *angry* at Teddy. At how carelessly he flaunts his magic. At how *hungry* he is to experiment, to learn more. When he *knows* how I feel. He knows what happened to Ma. There's a reason why there are restrictions on magic. It's dangerous. People die.

"Post and Pair?" Sol says, shuffling a deck of cards with nimble fingers. "Or Bone-Ace?"

Sol can't see mettle the way I can, but he says he can hear it, strings vibrating at different frequencies, forming complex harmonies as they wind together. These are the secrets we whispered to each other as children, secrets that bound the three of us together. There's no magic in Candlecott, or at least there isn't supposed to be. Not since the witches tried to take Mwsogl Hollow and the good people of Candlecott drove them out. Nobody else in town knows what we can do—that I can see mettle, Sol can hear it, and Teddy can use it in his forge. Even though we're not witches, people might not see us the same way if they knew. That's why the three of us are as close as close, bound by love and secrets.

But soon we won't be three anymore. Sol is heading overseas—he hasn't been home to Habasah to see his sisters since primary school, and then he plans to travel for the rest of the year.

I'll miss Sol, of course. But . . . a little part of me is glad to have some alone time with Teddy. It's different when it's just us. Last time it was just the two of us—when Sol was in Scouller for a school music competition—Teddy kissed me behind Goody Bhreagh's milking shed. We didn't talk about it afterward. Didn't tell Sol. That was two years ago, but my stomach still lurches every time I think of it happening again.

Teddy doesn't exactly look like he wants to kiss me right now. His jaw is still stuck out pugnaciously, ready for the fight that he knows is coming.

I pick up a newspaper from the coffee table and brandish it

at him. "Did you see?" I say. "The auditors rounded up another coven of witches in Fishgate. Sent them off to a recovery center. Is that what you want?"

Teddy rolls his eyes. "I'm not a resistance witch," he says. "And there are no auditors in Candlecott."

"Because we don't do magic here."

"*You* do," he says. "Tracking magic with your witch sight."

"It's not *witch sight*," I reply hotly. "Looking threadwise isn't magic. It's just . . . looking."

But I know that isn't true. I know that my ability to see mettle isn't normal. It's all part of the witch's curse that killed my mother. I glance back at the newspaper, at the photo of the witches in grainy black-and-white. They look terrifying to me, unglamoured and raw and full of rage. Only criminals and celebrities have their photos taken. Celebrities because of their natural beauty, and criminals so we can see them as they truly are. A camera can't capture a glamour, so everyone else just has their picture drawn or painted. Even here in Candlecott, where glamours are only for extra-special occasions.

"Come on," Sol pleads. "It's Whitsun Eve. Don't fight."

There's a moment of tension as Teddy and I engage in a battle of stubbornness. But then Teddy shrugs.

"I vote for Bone-Ace," he says.

"Only because I always beat you at Post and Pair," I reply.

He punches me lightly on the arm, and Sol beams.

A heavy knock at the door makes us all jump. Teddy and Sol both look to me, even though we're in Sol's house.

I glance at the clock. It's eleven-thirty. A bit late for social callers.

"I'll go, then, shall I?" I say. "Neither of you brave knights wants to step in?"

Sol's cheeks stain pink, and Teddy shoots me a rueful grin. "You're much more threatening than us, Merry," he says.

He's not wrong.

I extract myself from the couch and make my way over to the entrance, lifting the latch and stepping back as the door swings toward me.

There's a monster on the doorstep.

A huge, leering skull stares in at us. Not human, it's too big and too wide, with gaping eyeholes on either side of the head, amber glinting from within them in the dancing light of a guttering torch held by one of several robed figures standing behind the monster.

It's a toad.

Nearly seven feet tall, wreathed in a gray shroud that hints at broad, bony shoulders. Scraps of ribbon and lace float from the gray fabric, along with garlands of bells and smaller bits of bone.

I'm not sure why they have come here—is it because of me?

I look at them threadwise and see the familiar strands of Da's mettle, swirling around one of the figures. I recognize the others too—the usual Toadman crowd. And my stomach twists as I catch a glimpse of a brownish tendril weaving in among it.

I've seen this before—glimpses of it around Da when he returns from the Frater House. It's not silvery bright like regular mettle. I've never quite been able to focus properly on it, but I know it's got something to do with the Toadmen. I can't ask Da, of course. He doesn't know I can look threadwise and see mettle.

He doesn't know that I can recognize a curse when I see it.

Behind me, I hear the scrape of a chair, and Teddy's voice calling out.

"Do your damnedest, you old devil!"

The creature's skull swings wildly, the diaphanous robe floating around it like ghost tatters. Teddy appears at my shoulder, his eyes bright with excitement.

The Toading happens every year on Whitsun Eve. Toadmen going from door to door, exchanging taunts and rhymes. They'll end up at the Rose and Crown, and all the adults will have sore heads tomorrow. It's a Candlecott tradition.

But it isn't *our* tradition.

One of the robed figures bangs a staff against the ground once, twice, three times, and the monster's huge grinning jaws snap in reply. Bells jingle, and from behind the creature, someone starts to play a fiddle.

Two robed figures step forward to flank the monster, each one masked and hooded. The first has sharp horns curving upward from behind its bulging yellow eyes. A black mouth gapes from ear to ear, studded with sharp teeth. The Howling Toad.

A deep male voice emerges from behind the mask.

We are the toads o' Deeping Fen
Come to greet you, gentle friend.
The year is old, the night is deep
Wake him now from listless sleep
The bramble-frog of Morgendagh
He who rises with the stars.
We'll chase away the spirits old
Let us cross your fine threshold.

The Order of Toadmen is supposed to be a secret gentlemen's society, but it's pretty hard to keep secrets in Candlecott. Maybe the other chapters are better at it, in bigger towns and cities. They meet once a week in the Frater House and eat biscuits and play backgammon, and then a few times a year they put on silly costumes and do rituals like this. But they don't usually come here, because Da knows I don't like it. He's been a Toadman practically his whole life, and when I was younger I didn't think much of it at all. I used to love the shiver of fear when the Toadmen would bang on our door on Whitsun Eve, back when Ma was still alive.

But since I learned to see mettle, it feels like maybe the Toadmen are something more than old men playing dress-ups. There's something about those brownish mettle wisps that makes my stomach churn with unease.

Teddy elbows me aside, his cheeks as red as apples. His voice is extra loud, emboldened with wassail.

Begone, you toads, you slimy frogs
Back to your fens and to your bogs
Our house is warm and good and bright
It welcomes not beings of the night.

I frown at him. Since when did Teddy know Toad rhymes? Can't he just tell them to bugger off?

The second robed figure steps forward, and I recognize it as the Ghost Toad, its mask blank white and featureless save for two black holes for eyes.

About one toad the bards do sing
So bold and brave they made him king
Let us in and tap the cask
It's cold, and twice you've made us ask.

I move to close the door, but Teddy elbows his way in front of me.

Begone, O king of mucky courts!
Your breath does stink
Your face is warts.

The words come out of his mouth as smooth as butter. Like he's been practicing. Then the monster—the King Toad—steps forward and speaks in a deep voice that is quiet but commanding.

We are the Toads of Deeping Fen.
And we will not ask you again.

The fiddle cuts off abruptly, leaving silence breached only by the sputtering of the torch. The air is suddenly heavy with the threat of the King Toad, the looming malice of it all.

Teddy looks over his shoulder at me. He's beaming, delighted to have played his part in the ritual.

I scowl at him—he knows I don't like the Toadmen. I've told him and Sol about how I think they do secret magic. Illegal magic. Dangerous magic.

I want to slam the door—whatever's going on with Teddy,

I don't like it. I hesitate, glancing at the familiar stoop of Da's shoulders, and in that moment Sol steps around me, opening the door wide to welcome them into his house like the traitor he is. I shoot him a murderous glare, and he shrugs.

"It would be rude not to," he murmurs.

Sol has always been too polite for his own good.

The robed figures cross the threshold and the air in Sol's cozy sitting room suddenly feels colder. But then the tension of the moment is broken, and the fiddle starts up again as the Toad-men reach up to remove their hoods and masks. I know them, of course. Harry-the-Bus and Creepy Glen are the two masked toads. There's my lovely da, helping to extricate Gruffydd Thomas from the King Toad costume, laying the papier-mâché skull carefully against the doorframe, its beer-bottle eyes still glinting. And Huw Jones with his fiddle tucked under his chin.

"Sorry, love," Da says under his breath as he comes in. "They insisted on coming here."

His eyes flick to Teddy as he says this, and uneasiness throbs in my gut. I help Sol set out bottles of beer and thimblefuls of wassail, and a platter with speckle bread, stone cakes and goose-berry tarts.

Huw comes over to ask Sol a question about their set list for the fair tomorrow, and Creepy Glen and Gruffydd Thomas usher Teddy over to the window, where they bow their heads and speak in low voices. I desperately want to go over there and find out what they're talking about.

But before I can move, Harry-the-Bus digs me in the ribs. "Heard you'll be off to Staunton come September," he says with a grin.

I feel Da's eyes on me. "I'm not going," I tell him.

"Sure you are," Harry-the-Bus says. "A university scholarship like that—it's a once-in-a-lifetime opportunity."

I want to slap the bottle of beer out of his hand, but I manage a polite smile instead. "I've made up my mind."

Sol catches my eye, and I scowl at him. We've had this conversation before. It feels like the only thing people want to talk about. Candlecott is my home, and I can't leave Da all alone. If Ma were still alive, then maybe things would be different.

The Toadmen drink their beer and wassail and eat the speckle bread. Then they sing "Little Saucepan" for us before pulling their costumes back on and heading out the door.

"Ready for tomorrow night?" Gruffydd Thomas says to Teddy as he crosses the threshold.

Teddy glances guiltily at me, but nods.

Da tells me not to wait up. I watch them traipse up the street to harass the next poor unsuspecting household. Then I round on Teddy, and he shrinks away from me, holding up his hands in defense.

"What was all that about?" I demand.

"Just a bit of fun."

I throw a leftover scallop at him, and he ducks too late. "It's Whitsun!" he protests, wiping grease from his cheek. "The Toading is traditional."

"It's not *our* tradition," I fume. "Our tradition is to stay home while everyone else goes to the pub and gets drunk. Our tradition is fish and chips and twlbwrdd. Just the three of us."

"Well, things change."

Teddy isn't quite meeting my gaze.

13

"You're not . . . joining, are you?" I ask.

"I'm thinking about it."

The uneasy feeling in my gut explodes into anger. I turn to Sol. "Did you know about this?"

His eyes slide from mine, and he nods, abashed.

"I can't believe you've been keeping secrets from me! Both of you!"

Sol's cheeks go pink. "I said we should tell her," he mutters to Teddy.

"And I said she'd react exactly like this!" Teddy pours himself another thimble of wassail, and I screw up my nose.

"You *know* how I feel about them. They do magic," I say as a realization hits me. "That's why you want to join, isn't it? You think they can teach you more magic."

"What if it is?"

"I've *told* you what I can see. The brown shadows on their mettle. I think their magic is cursed. It can't be legal."

Teddy snorts. "Since when did you care about *legal*?" he says. "What about when you stole Bill Gaffney's prize pig and put it in the staff room at school?"

"That's different. Bill Gaffney got his pig back. It was just for fun."

"The Toads is just for fun too."

But I know this isn't true. I can see it in his eyes. There's a lot more going on here.

"You think it's going to be *fun* to wear those silly robes and dance around under every fish moon jingling bells and muttering rhymes? You think it's *fun* to sit in that fusty damp hall with all those boring old men, eating stale shortbread and playing backgammon?"

"Make up your mind, Merry," Teddy says. "Is it dangerous magic, or boring old men?"

"It can be both."

"Your own da is a Toadman," says Teddy. "Nearly all the men in Candlecott are."

I can't talk to Da about any of this. I've tried to explain to him the weird feeling I get about the Toads, but it's hard to explain without telling him about those glimpses of strange mettle. And I promised Ma I wouldn't tell him that the witch's curse got me too.

"All Da's friends are Toads," I say hotly. "It's the only social thing he does. But not you! You have us."

I glance over at Sol to see if he's willing to chip in, but he's just watching us, his brow creased. He hates it when we fight.

"Not for long," Teddy says quietly. "Sol's going overseas and you're off to the university. I'll be left here all on my own. What else am I supposed to do?"

"I'm not going to Staunton, I told you."

Teddy snorts. "Of course you'll go. As if you're going to let Caraway Boswell be the only one from Candlecott to take up that scholarship."

He knows that any mention of Caraway Boswell will distract me, and he's right. Horrid Caraway Boswell with his perfect hair and his equally perfect academic record. Caraway Boswell, who stole my dux glory. Caraway Boswell, the haughty, insufferable snob. And a Toadman to boot. I can see it in his mettle.

"Caraway Boswell," I start, my voice dripping with disdain, "is *not* from Candlecott. He's a boarder."

"He'll still be the only one going from our school if you don't," Teddy says.

I hate the thought of Caraway Boswell beating me. Being the only one to go to Staunton. But I just can't leave Candlecott and Da . . . and Teddy.

"Don't let this spoil our night, Merry," Teddy pleads. "Or our summer."

He slings an arm over my shoulder, and I duck and wriggle away.

"You stink of cloves," I tell him.

"It's the wassail."

"I hate it."

"You love it."

"I hate you."

"You love me."

My cheeks grow hot. "Shut up."

"You're just cranky because Harry-the-Bus mentioned the *U* word."

"And here you are mentioning it again!" I retort.

"You know what's really great?" interrupts Sol desperately. "Ice cream. Ice cream solves everything."

This kind of logic cannot be argued with, and we head into the kitchen to pile bowls high with creamy scoops of blueberry and honeycomb and pear, drowning them in caramel sauce and Sol's aunt's rhubarb syrup.

We end up playing Knave Noddy, and Sol wins every time.

Teddy drinks more wassail and eventually falls asleep on the couch, his snores so loud they make the windows rattle.

"Why didn't you tell me?" I ask Sol, keeping my voice low. "The *Toadmen?*"

Sol shrugs. "It's what he wants."

I shake my head. "He doesn't know what he wants."

"That's not fair, Merry," Sol says. "Teddy is as grown as you are."

But that's why it hurts. Teddy knows exactly what he's doing. He always does. Which means he knows this will hurt me and has decided to do it anyway.

"Teddy's feeling like he's going to get left behind," Sol says, as calm and sensible as ever. "You and I are leaving." He catches my warning look and corrects himself. "*Possibly* leaving. And . . . they came asking for him. Telling him how great his smithing skills are. You know how ambitious he is. They've promised him things. Opportunities. You're not the only one who has dreams, you know."

What kinds of opportunities could they offer him? What promises have they made? "I just wish he weren't ambitious about magic."

"Teddy is special." I can see the fondness in Sol's eyes as he says it. "It's not often you get magic talent like that in a man. I think the Toadmen will be able to help him use it safely."

Sol is always so kind and sensible, it's impossible to argue with him. I nod, and he nudges me gently.

"Also," he says, "he's going to look *great* in those long flowing robes."

I snicker at the thought of it. "And the little bonnet?" I say. "The one with the frill around the edge?"

"He'll have to learn the Haycorn Dance," Sol reminds me. "The one with the bells and the ribbons."

Teddy lifts his head and looks blearily around. "Whadid I miss?"

Sol and I exchange a look and dissolve into giggles.

TEDDY WALKS ME HOME at around two in the morning. Sol invites me to stay the night, but Da will be out late doing Toad stuff, and I want to be there first thing in the morning to help him get ready for the poultry show. Sol parcels me up some leftover speckle bread for breakfast.

The night is crisp and clear, scented with woodsmoke and night-blooming phlox. Stars carpet the velvety darkness of the sky, and a fingernail of moon glows blue above us. I link my arm through Teddy's, and we walk in amiable silence through the empty cobbled streets of Candlecott.

We pass the forge on the edge of the village green, and I feel Teddy's chest swell slightly, and I know he's thinking about his apprenticeship, and his dreams of becoming one of the great smiths of history. Tomorrow he will be demonstrating his skills before the whole town at the Whitsun fair, and I know he's going to knock everyone's socks off.

The sound of alcohol-soaked merriment drifts across the green from the Rose and Crown. I hope Ken Lanagan has plenty of his famed hangover dram available tomorrow at the fair. I've never had it, but I've heard it includes pickle juice, coltsfoot and a dash of laundry detergent.

Houses are replaced by fields and furrows, and I look up the hill to Candlecott School. I can see lights on in the dormitory, and my stomach twists as I imagine horrid Caraway Boswell there. Probably studying, even though school is over for the year. Why hasn't he gone home to his mansion in the city, or sauntered off to spend the summer on a yacht somewhere?

I can only imagine how insufferable he'll be at Staunton. The university is probably full of people like him. People from big cities and wealthy families who look down their noses at simple countryfolk like me. There's a part of me that burns to go. To take up the scholarship and show them all how wrong they are. To be the best at everything. To prove that your family's name or how many butlers you have is meaningless. But another part is afraid that I'd become one of them. That I'd return to Candlecott and people would treat me the way we treat people like Caraway.

We turn down the lane that leads to our little farm, and I see the porch light burning cheerfully to welcome me. Out of habit, I glance up to the window where I used to see Ma sitting, waiting for me to come home from Sol's, and for Da to come home from the Frater House. Another Whitsun tradition.

But Ma isn't there, of course.

The hens inside the chicken coop greet me in their creaky, sleepy way. Out of habit, I look threadwise to check for any fox mettle that might be lurking nearby. But all I see is chicken, and little gossamer-thin streaks from moths and other small night creatures. An owl passes overhead, swift and silent, its mettle streaming silver behind it like a shooting star.

We stop outside my front door, and Teddy gently turns me to face him.

"Don't be mad," he says. "About the Toadmen."

I am mad, but I remember what Sol said and bite my tongue. "Just . . . promise me you'll be careful," I say. "And stay away from Creepy Glen. And don't let it take up any of our time together."

Teddy flashes me his dimples. "No fear," he says. "Nothing is going to keep the three of us apart this summer."

He gives me a hug, and I breathe him in, iron and woodsmoke. My heart beats a little faster.

"Good night," I murmur, but I don't turn to go inside.

"Merry." He keeps his hand on my arm.

It's going to happen. He's going to kiss me again. I tilt my chin up to him, and he lays a finger on my cheek. The night around us seems to hold its breath, waiting.

"It's Whitsuntide," he says gently. "Your da's out, so you're first foot in the door."

The perfect moment slides away, and I feel a sting of disappointment. "You know I'm not superstitious."

Teddy frowns. "You want Jenny Greenteeth to snatch you in the night?"

I sigh and rummage in my pockets. "I've got a silver coin already. And the speckle bread from Sol."

"Here." Teddy passes me a blackened bit of charcoal.

"Where did that come from?"

"I always carry coal," he says. "Nothing luckier for a blacksmith. You still need salt. And evergreen."

I snap off a sprig of lavender from the bush that grows by the front door. "Surely that's enough."

Teddy shakes his head obstinately. "Salt is the most important one! Protection."

I snort. "And what exactly do I need to be protected from in Candlecott?"

"You're not going to stay in Candlecott forever."

"Says who?" The thought of leaving here . . . I don't know how Sol is doing it. How can he leave? Where else could possibly be as perfect?

My treacherous mind shows me an image of gray spires and oak-panelled lecture theaters, but I shake it away. "Brutus has a salt lick. In the barn."

Teddy disappears and returns a moment later with a sliver of salt that he's chipped off the large block. I slide it into my pocket with the lavender and the bit of charcoal.

"Enough?" I ask.

"A coin for wealth," Teddy recites. "Bread for nourishment. Salt for protection. Coal for warmth. Evergreen for a long, healthy life. Ideally you'd have whiskey as well, for good cheer. I should have brought the wassail." He hesitates, like he's considering running back to get it.

"I get enough good cheer from your breath," I tell him. "And anyway, I drank some of the wassail, so I'm still carrying it through the door."

"I suppose so."

I hesitate on the threshold for a moment longer. Just in case.

"Happy Whitsuntide, Merry," Teddy says cheerfully over his shoulder as he turns and makes his way back down the garden path.

2.

THE WHITSUNTIDE FAIR IS ALWAYS HELD ON THE VIL-
lage green from midday, and today is no exception. Colorful
bunting is strung from every tree and lamppost, and strains
of cheerful music rise to greet me, as well as mouthwatering scents
of spiced lamb skewers and cinnamon-dusted doughrings. All of
Candlecott is here, the town square bustling with energy and excitement as people chat and laugh and pass judgment on who has
baked the lightest sponge, stitched the neatest quilt, brewed the
finest ale and grown the largest marrow.

I pass pens containing black-faced sheep, their wool scrubbed
snow white for the occasion, and glossy-coated cows with enchanted bells around their necks that chime on the hour. Da is
still at home, putting the finishing touches to the three birds he'll
be entering in the poultry show this year.

I buy a griddle cake from Kasun Gamage and burn the roof
of my mouth on a lava-hot currant. It's worth it, though.

The band is playing on the wooden stage, boards shaking
under the stamping boot of Laura Cotton as she marks time.

Huw Jones coaxes a merry melody from his fiddle, and beside him Sol grins at me from his stool. He's got his crwth on his knee and is bowing away at the strings, tapping his foot in time with Laura Cotton as she steps forward and starts to sing.

Here be a fine tree
Standing fast at root
Bearing well at top
Every little twig
Bears an apple big
Every little bough
Bears an apple now
Hats full, caps full!
Threescore sacks full!

The crowd joins in for the last two lines, and everyone cheers.

I spot Teddy coming out of the forge, where he's demonstrating making horseshoes and pokers. He's wearing duck canvas trousers that are singed around the edges, and a heavy leather apron. His face is smudged with sweat and soot. Someone stops to talk to him, I can't make out who, but assume it's one of his adoring fans. Girls and boys alike flock to Teddy, especially when he's all greasy and dirty, with his muscles on display, highlighted by the showers of glowing sparks from his anvil. It's enough to make anyone swoon, myself included.

He makes his way over to a drinks stall and accepts an earthenware mug from a pink-cheeked woman who's too old to be moon-eyed over a teenager. He downs the whole thing in one, then grins at her as she refills the mug, giggling. I roll my eyes fondly and start to work my way through the crowd toward him. Someone else is at the drinks stall, talking to Teddy, a girl who can't be older than ten or eleven. She has a sweet face, pretty and childlike, but there's something about her firm expression that doesn't seem to match her age. Teddy shakes his head in answer to her question, and he looks up, straight at me, his brows drawing together in concern.

Someone is calling my name, a voice that makes the skin prickle on the back of my neck.

Caraway Boswell.

Dark hair sweeping elegantly over his forehead. Thick brows slanting in a permanent frown. Mouth always a little puckered, like he's sucking on a sour gumdrop. His skin is alabaster, with cheekbones that could cut glass and eyes like remote glaciers.

He's glamoured, of course. The rumor at school is that he always wears a glamour. Even while he sleeps. Never lets anyone see him without it. I can only assume that this means he's hideously ugly without it, which is a satisfying thought. Even so, why choose a glamour so cold? He's not exactly handsome now. He's still weirdly shaped, with those cheekbones and that chin. He doesn't look like a real person. A bit elven, perhaps, but not in a sexy way.

Nobody in Candlecott wears a glamour every day. We had dress-up ones when we were little kids, and people use them for special occasions like weddings or school dances. But every day? Too expensive. Too . . . *witchy.*

He lifts a hand to get my attention, but I don't have time for Caraway Boswell. Not today.

Teddy steps forward to envelop me in a hug. I feel a wave of smugness as his fans scowl jealously at me.

"Did you see Sol?" he asks, beaming with pride. "He's killing it up there."

"Of course he is," I say with a grin. "I assume you are too."

He puffs out his chest. "Naturally. Gaffer Rhees said my pokers are worthy of Gofannon himself!" He checks his watch. "Nearly time for your da's show?"

"I'm going in there now," I say. "But, Teddy, what did that little girl say to you?"

His face clouds over, and he puts down his lemonade mug and takes both my hands in his.

"She was asking about the Spitalwick Hag," he says, lowering his voice so we can't be overheard.

The name is enough to turn the back of my throat sour. The merriment of the fair becomes discordant, and gooseflesh breaks out on my arms.

"Why?" I ask.

"She—she said the Hag escaped from prison. Merry, wait—"

But I'm already reeling away from him, searching the crowd for the little girl. I find her just as Caraway Boswell finds me.

"Morgan," he says. "I need to talk to you about something."

I ignore him and interrupt the girl, who is interrogating Bram Sealy. "Is it true?" I ask her. "The Hag has escaped?"

The girl turns her eyes on me. Brown with flecks of vivid green, and far too sharp to belong to such a young child. "Have you seen a woman around here?" she asks. "Tall, dark skin, dark hair? Bit witchy-looking?"

I stare at her. "You're asking me if I've *seen* the Spitalwick Hag?"

"The Hag?" Caraway frowns at the girl. "She escaped?"

The girl narrows her eyes as she takes in Caraway and his cold beauty. "That's a ridiculous glamour," she states flatly. "What are you trying to hide?"

"When did it happen?" he asks, ignoring her question.

But the girl has clearly decided that we are of no use to her, and disappears once more into the crowd.

The Spitalwick Hag.

The most powerful and dangerous witch in Anglyon.

People tell stories about Jenny Greenteeth, but they're just stories. A fairy-tale witch. But the Hag is the real thing.

She's been locked up for seventeen years, ever since she was arrested by auditors right here in Candlecott.

"Morgan." I'm surprised to see an actual crinkle in Caraway's perfect brow. He looks almost as unsettled by this revelation as I am. But he shakes it off. "We need to talk."

Caraway is dressed like he'd rather be wearing his school uniform—plain gray trousers (expensive, by the cut of them) and a white linen shirt buttoned all the way up to his chin. Who wears a shirt buttoned all the way up, unless they have to? At a fair? Why is he even here?

I glance at him threadwise and feel my skin crawl as I see brownish shadows on his mettle. There's a lot more than I've ever seen on Da. It seems to be wrapped around him, like he's being taken over by creeping ivy. I blink, and it's gone.

There's a *knowingness* in Caraway's eyes that I don't like.

It's as if he could tell I was looking at him threadwise.

"What?" I snap.

He's still looking at me in that infuriating way he does. Like he sees my every flaw and revels in it. I'm suddenly aware of my own crumpled flannel shirt with its frayed cuffs, my hair that's still in the braid I put it in yesterday. I didn't have a shower or wash my face this morning—it's entirely possible I have the remnants of last night's fish and chips still smeared all over me.

Not that I care. Why should I care what Caraway Boswell thinks of me?

I have more important things to think about.

Like the fact that the witch who killed my mother has escaped from prison.

"Listen, I know this is a bit . . . well, random, but there's this event I have to go to," Caraway is explaining. "And I need to take someone. It's like a family thing . . . kind of. And I thought—"

I blink. "Are you asking me on a *date*?"

"No," he says. "Not exactly. It's more of a—" He breaks off and rakes a hand through his silky dark hair. "I've been trying to figure out how to explain this for *weeks*," he mutters.

His words are almost drowned out by the great clanging of the town bell. It's one o'clock.

"I don't have time for this," I say. "Get out of my way."

"I really just need a minute."

"I don't *have* a minute," I tell him. "My da is about to win best bird for the fifth year running."

I stalk past him into the main tent.

There are many prizes to be won at the Whitsuntide fair. Biggest marrow. Best scones. Finest pickles, jams and preserves. But the one that everyone cares about the most is the poultry prize.

People are flooding to the tent, cramming in shoulder to shoulder, ready for the show.

Da has always been good with chickens. It's his gift. But after Ma died, he went all in. Over the last four years, the poultry prize has evolved into a theatrical face-off between Da and Peggy Ross. They each bring three birds and present them to the judges, who reveal their final score at the end. Da has been preparing for months, grooming, training and rehearsing for this moment. There's no way I'm going to let Caraway Boswell or the Spitalwick Hag herself get in the way of enjoying Da's victory.

"I'd really rather we talked outside," Caraway says into my ear. "I don't like crowds."

"Then don't *follow me into one*," I say, exasperated. "Can't you just go away?"

"I wish I could," he mutters under his breath.

Peggy Ross appears on the stage, carrying a handsome blue-crested langshan cockerel, to polite applause.

I let out a chuckle. "Nice try, Peggy."

"It's this weekend, you see. I have to bring someone . . ." Caraway is *still here*. This is more than he's ever talked to me since he first came to Candlecott.

"Shh," I say. "Da's next."

"Next at what?" Caraway asks, and seems to only just now notice the stage.

Da appears, his expression mild as always, his shoulders sloping and his head bowed almost apologetically. He's made a bit of an effort—he's wearing his best flannel shirt, which he may even have ironed for the occasion, and has trimmed his wispy gray hair and beard. He's holding Enid, a salmon-speckled totleger. He's lulling Peggy into a false sense of security. Enid is a sweet chicken, but she's nothing special.

"I have no idea what is going on," Caraway says. "Why is everyone clapping at a chicken?"

I scowl. "I miss the old Caraway," I tell him. "The one who was an aloof snob who never spoke to me."

"I'm not a *snob.*"

I snort.

Peggy looks smug as she produces a millefleur crevecoeur with a tremendous bouffant crest of silver-laced feathers. The judges mutter to each other and nod approvingly.

"You *never* come into town," I say. "You *never* talk to any of the local kids. You think you're so much better than us because you're from the city and your father is some fancy bigwig at a magic corporation."

For a moment, I see the muscles in Caraway's jaw clench, and he turns his head slightly away from me. But he recovers quickly.

"Morgan, I don't think I'm better than you. Better at differential equations, yes. But not *better.*"

Da emerges from backstage once more with Blodeuwedd, a dainty lavender-booted Serama, small enough to fit in the teacup and saucer that Da has placed her in. He sticks out his pinkie and raises the teacup to his mouth. Blodeuwedd gently pecks him on the nose, just like they rehearsed. The crowd loves it and cheers.

Suddenly I remember the brown shadows I saw in Caraway's mettle. Just like I've seen on my da.

"Are you a Toad?" I ask him.

Caraway looks startled. "Why do you ask?"

"You *are*," I say. "Admit it."

He shrugs. "Readily."

I didn't expect him to give in so easily. The Toadmen are pretty secretive. I mean, everyone knows which people in our town are Toads—Candlecott is too small to be able to hide that. But there's plenty Da won't tell me about what happens in the Frater House. All I know is the stuff they do in public—the Toading on Whitsuntide Eve, the Reaphook and Sickle dance, the harvest pantomime, which I always find an excuse not to attend.

"They do magic, right?" I say. "The Toadmen."

Caraway's lips form a thin line. "Yes," he says shortly.

I swallow. "Is it dangerous?"

"Yes."

My eyes stray to the door of the tent, where Teddy and Sol have just walked in, shoulder to shoulder. Sol spots me and gives a cheerful wave. Teddy smiles, but I can see he's still worried about me. Worried about what that little girl said.

"Ah," Caraway says, following my gaze. "You found out that Evans is joining."

Peggy is back, this time holding a leash. At the other end is a vicious-looking dong tao rooster, with legs as thick as a dragon's. She must have crossbred it with a kadaknath, because it is completely black—feathers, beak, wattle, comb, even its skin. It raises its hackles menacingly at the crowd. Peggy is right to look satisfied. It's a magnificent creature, and any other year, it would have earned her the trophy.

"Looks like your father is going to lose his crown," Caraway murmurs to me.

I give him a look so full of loathing that he shrinks away from me. "Don't be so sure," I say.

Da doesn't come out from backstage straightaway. The applause for the black rooster dies down, and there's a long silence. People start to whisper—has Da given up? Bowed to the undeniable magnificence of the dong tao?

Of course, I know him too well to doubt.

He emerges at last, but he brings no bird. Instead he's carrying a tall wooden stool—probably borrowed from the bar of the Rose and Crown. He places it carefully in the middle of the stage and then disappears into the wings again. He's taking his time. Letting anticipation build.

"What's the surprise?" Caraway asks. "Is his chicken going to sing us a song, perhaps? Strum a harp?"

I want to tell Caraway to shut his obnoxious mouth, but I can't resist showing off a little. "Three years ago Da won with a willow-bearded brabanter pullet that could play 'The Jolly Miller' on a glockenspiel."

Caraway raises his eyebrows. "You people really do take your chickens very seriously, don't you?"

I hate the way he says *you people.* I know what he means. Peasants. Common folk. I'm about to issue a heated retort, but Da is returning to the stage at last.

I know what's coming, and I hold my breath. Da is carrying Bran the Blessed, an Onagadori rooster that he has been raising in a specially built pen for the last three years, all in preparation for this day. He's carrying him tucked under his arm, angled away from the audience so all they can see is his reddish-golden breast and face and his bright crimson wattle and comb. He sits calmly in Da's arms, regarding the audience with haughty, detached disdain.

He reminds me a bit of Caraway.

Da places Bran the Blessed on the stool, his back to the audience so they still can't see him properly. Then he steps away, and the people of Candlecott gasp as one. The rooster's tail feathers stream down the length of the stool and pool on the floor, a waterfall of shining gold and brass and red.

"Bloody hell," mutters Caraway next to me. "Its tail must be six feet!"

"Nine and a half," I tell him, my chest swelling with pride for Da.

Bran the Blessed perches on his throne before his adoring subjects, his glorious tail making him look like a phoenix from an old fairy tale. I glance at Da, who is trying not to grin. Then Bran stands up, stretches his neck out and unfolds gloriously golden wings, letting out a full-throated crow.

Peggy Ross sighs and holds out her hand for Da to shake. Nobody bothers to hear the judges' final verdict. Bran the Blessed reigns over all.

"A very impressive chicken," Caraway observes. "Does it lay a golden egg too?"

I give him a withering look. "He's a *cock.*"

Caraway shrugs. "I don't know how these things work."

"Of course you don't. You're far too posh to know where your eggs come from."

"Look, Morgan, we're veering off topic. Like I said, I have to attend this event on the weekend. I need you to come with me."

There's an urgency in his voice that is . . . weird. It's the closest I've ever seen him come to losing his composure.

"Why?" I ask. "Why me?"

Laura Cotton claps me on the shoulder as she squeezes through the crowd. "He did it again!" she says with a grin. "Your da sure does have a way with birds."

Caraway looks around at the crowd uneasily. "We can't talk here. Come on."

He takes me by the elbow and drags me to the back of the tent, where several trestles are set up displaying the winning baked goods and preserves.

"I don't get it," I say. "Why are you so desperate for me to go to some family dinner with you? We're not friends."

He sighs and runs a hand through his hair. "Would it help if I offered to pay you for your time?"

I stare at him. "No. No, it would not."

"Hecate's teeth, Morgan." His voice is strained. "I don't know how to do this. I need you to come with me. I can't tell you why. But—I'll owe you. Big-time."

I am genuinely baffled. "I just can't think of any possible reason why you would want me to be your date at some Boswell family gathering."

"Then you don't have a very good imagination," he says. "There are heaps of reasons. Maybe my family wants to meet the girl who tied for dux with me. Maybe my father wants to offer you a summer internship. Maybe . . . maybe I like you."

I see his cheeks flush under his glamour, and he turns his gaze down to inspect Goody Bhreagh's prizewinning scones.

"It isn't any of those things, though," I say. "So why?"

Caraway coughs, still staring at the scones. "These look a little overbaked to me. I bet they're dry."

He loves passing judgment on us. He's been doing it since the moment he arrived in Candlecott, driven here by an expressionless uniformed footman in a big shiny black car that was definitely coated in some kind of enchantment, as no mud or dust from the driveway stuck to its wheels or hubcaps.

I had been scrubbing the stone steps of the school—punishment for some prank I engineered with Teddy and Sol. The footman dashed around to open the door, and Caraway Boswell stepped out, three years younger than he is now, but no less haughty and self-important. He looked around at Candlecott School with a disdain I couldn't fathom—the buildings were by far the grandest I had ever seen, built over a hundred years ago. The school had a reputation that stretched far beyond the borders of Pettavel, even beyond Anglyon itself. A world-class education, set among rolling hills and fields. What could be more wholesome? What better start for a young person? Clearly Thurmond Boswell agreed, because Caraway was sent here to board with the other fancy children when we were fourteen. The school tried to encourage the boarders to mix with us townies. They thought it would be good for the rich kids—the leaders of tomorrow—to see what real people were like. But it never worked that way. We sat side by side in classrooms, but the moment each bell rang, we separated like oil and vinegar.

Caraway Boswell was the worst of them all. He didn't even deign to rub shoulders with the other boarders. He was alone, aloof, the snobbiest of snobs. On that first day, when he got out of the shiny black car, he walked over to me, his black leather shoes crunching on the gravel. I looked up at his cold, glamoured face and instantly decided I hated him.

"Where is the headmaster's office?" he asked, in the clipped tones of someone born with a silver spoon in his mouth.

"Up there." I jerked my head up the steps to the front entrance.

Caraway waited. I don't know what he expected. A curtsy? For me to lead him inside, scattering rose petals before him? A round of applause? Whatever it was, he didn't get it from me. After a long moment, a frown had crinkled his forehead, and he'd turned away.

"Call someone to fetch my bags," he said over his shoulder.

"Carry them yourself," I retorted cheerfully.

He paused there with his back to me, his shoulders tense. Then he stalked inside without another word. And that was all I needed to know about Caraway Boswell. He was a total prat, and not worth my time.

He still isn't.

"My answer is no," I say vehemently. "I would *never* go anywhere with you."

He seems taken aback by the heat in my voice. "Did I say something to offend you?" he asks. "Are these"—he indicates the scones—"did *you* bake these, Morgan?"

He's trying to be funny, to break the tension. Well, I won't have it.

"No, I didn't bake them," I say hotly. "They're Goody Bhreagh's scones. And yes, they're overbaked. But she wins the blue ribbon every year because her husband used to win it before her, and she uses his recipe. Hers always turn out dry, but nobody tells her because Ben Bhreagh drowned in the Mira saving little Cam Thomas after he fell in, and around here we respect that kind of courage."

A silence falls around me, and even Caraway looks awkward. My stomach sinks, and I turn to see Goody Bhreagh, blue ribbon pinned to her cardigan, her eyes full of tears.

Oh no.

Goody Bhreagh lets out a little gulping sob, then flees the tent. A few people follow her. Everyone else just turns to look at me. There is an agonizing silence, and for the first time in my life, I want to swap places with Caraway. I want to be a stranger among these people, because then I'd just see disapproval in their eyes, instead of disappointment. But every one of these people knows me. They've known me since I was born. And they won't forget this.

Neither will I.

Ben Bhreagh may have died ten years ago, but I know that time doesn't make grief magically disappear. I know exactly how Goody Bhreagh feels right now, and I would give anything to take back what I said.

"And you say *I'm* the snob," Caraway murmurs quietly. "I think I'll leave you to it, Morgan. We'll talk later."

A white mist of rage descends. It's much easier to blame Caraway for all of this than it is to face what I've done. I never would have said those things about Goody Bhreagh's scones if he hadn't provoked me. I reach out to grab his arm, to pull him back so I can give him a piece of my mind. But the white mist gives me new strength, and I pull harder than I intended. Caraway trips and crashes right into me, and his weight sends me flying backward, arms windmilling, as we both tip inevitably toward the baked goods trestle.

It collapses beneath us, and we crash to the ground in an explosion of scones, jams and clotted cream. Caraway and I get all tangled together, and I find myself pressed against him, so close that I can smell bergamot and old leather through the overwhelming sticky scent of strawberries, cream and buttery pastry.

It feels like every pair of eyes in Candlecott is focused on me right now. Witnessing this humiliating moment. I glance up and see Da, who has just been handed the pewter trophy for the poultry prize, for the fifth year in a row. He's staring right at me, and all I see is confusion and disappointment.

I've ruined his big moment of triumph.

I've ruined Goody Bhreagh's scones, and broken her heart as well. Goody Bhreagh, who used to babysit me when I was little. Who brought us a pie once a week for six months after Ma died.

"Get off me," I growl at Caraway Boswell, shoving him away.

Caraway raises himself onto one elbow and licks cream and scone crumbs from his top lip. "You know, they're actually not bad."

He's tousled and flushed and splattered with jam and cream, but the glamour is still doing its job. His eyes glitter coldly.

I stand up and nearly fall back down again. Colorful bunting is snagged around my ankle, and I wrench it off savagely. Then I take a deep breath. I need to find Goody Bhreagh and apologize.

The crowd parts to let me through. Sol gives me a rueful smile. I can't see Teddy, though. Perhaps he went back to the forge.

Well, I guess I'm going to Staunton after all. It's not like I can ever show my face in Candlecott again. Not after this. On the other hand, Caraway Boswell will be at Staunton, so I can't go there either. Perhaps I could go overseas with Sol. Perhaps I'll run away and become a professional vagabond.

Goody Bhreagh is nowhere to be seen. She's probably gone home. I'll go and see her this afternoon. Take her some eggs and a bunch of flowers.

What I do see, though, is Teddy. He's talking to Creepy Glen, over by the apple-bobbing barrels. Creepy Glen says something, and Teddy lets out a laugh, his face breaking into genuine pleasure. I look at them threadwise and see those ghostly brown shadows on Creepy Glen's mettle. They're reaching out to Teddy, brushing up against him.

The Whitsuntide fair is one of my favorite days of the year, but all I feel is despair.

The Spitalwick Hag has escaped, and my best friend is being tempted by cursed mettle.

I clench my hands into balled fists to stop them from shaking.

I can't bear the thought of losing Teddy to a curse, the way we lost Ma. I have to do something.

I spot Caraway perched incongruously on a hay bale and march over to him.

"Tell me how I stop Teddy from joining the Toadmen," I demand. "Then I'll go wherever you want."

Caraway stares at me for a long moment. "Deal," he says at last. "Evans is going to be initiated tomorrow evening at the Frater House. There's a ritual tonight, though. He'll be at Mwsogl Hollow at midnight. Alone. You should try to talk some sense into him."

Mwsogl Hollow? I find myself lost for words, which I'm not used to. I don't like it.

"Good luck," Caraway says. "Evans doesn't belong in the Frater House."

Then he brushes jam from his shirt cuff. "I'll be in touch about the thing. Don't make any plans for this weekend."

And with that, Caraway Boswell glides away, leaving me staring after him, more confused than ever.

MWSOGL HOLLOW IS EERIE under the soft glow of the sickle moon. The color is leached from the silver-barked birch trees and the velvety moss underfoot, leaving everything looking wan and thin, like a dishcloth washed so many times you can see through it.

I never come here. Nobody does, not since the witches came.

They wanted the waters. Apparently the spring has some kind of power, useful in potions and witch drams. For centuries, they came under an ash moon, took their water, and slipped away in the dead of night. They didn't bother us Candlecott folk, and we didn't bother them. But then the prohibition years came, when the government banned magic entirely. The witches still came, and folk from Candlecott tried to stop them. We didn't want any trouble, but the witches would not go without their water.

My parents were there. There was a fight, and a witch was killed. Da says he saw the most powerful witch there—the Spital-wick Hag—raise a finger and point it at my ma, muttering some kind of curse. Ma was pregnant with me at the time, and she told me that's why I have witch sight. She made me swear not to tell

Da. *It'll just upset him.* Then, thirteen years to the day after that night, Ma collapsed in the kitchen while making dinner. After that, her mettle grew weak and wan, until her strings all broke and she died.

Seventeen years ago, auditors came and wrapped the Hag in iron chains. Stuffed wormwood and cloves in her mouth to stop her from cursing anyone else. Dragged her off to some prison, somewhere. These days, witches like her go to recovery centers, comfortable facilities where they stay until they are ready to put aside their wickedness and rejoin society.

But I don't think someone like the Hag could ever be rehabilitated.

The witches never came back to Mwsogl Hollow, and we don't go there either. There are rumors that piskies gather in the place where witch blood was spilled, and that they'll rip the fingernails from anyone foolish enough to disturb their pebble circles.

There's a decent-sized pool at the highest point of the hollow. The water comes straight from a spring deep in the hills, cold and clear. I startle as a glimmer moth flutters by, its soft wings brushing my cheek. A twig snaps on the path leading into the hollow, and I crouch down in the bracken.

She wouldn't come back here, would she? Not even for the water? But why was the little girl here, asking after her? For that matter, why was a little girl asking after her at all?

A figure emerges, just a shape in the darkness. I look threadwise and feel a wave of relief when I see Teddy's familiar silvery strands. My own mettle reaches out to him as he approaches, entwining to form the familiar connection between us.

He's wearing a heavy wool coat with the hood up. He walks

downstream, where the icy pool leaks out over slippery rocks and trickles noisily downhill to where it will eventually empty into the Mira itself.

He pulls a small packet from his pocket, something wrapped in a scrap of pale linen. I can't make out what it is, but he gently places it in the stream, among the rocks. Then he straightens up, tucks the linen scrap in his pocket and heads upstream to the pool. He hesitates at the edge and then slips off his boots. Then he looks over his shoulder and shrugs off the coat.

He's completely naked underneath.

It's been years since I've seen Teddy naked. When we were kids, the three of us would swim naked in the Mira all the time, but as adolescence crept upon us, we started to be more modest, keeping our shorts and shirts on when we went in the water.

Those hours slaving over an anvil with a hammer and tongs have worked quite the transformation, and my breath quickens as I slowly take in Teddy's moon-drenched form, pale and sculpted as a marble statue.

Damn, Teddy.

He dips a toe into the pool, and I hear him swear. The night is not warm—that pool must be as cold as King Badb's heart.

But I see him square his (extremely muscular) shoulders and stride into the water, pausing only to yelp and gasp when the water reaches the part of him that I haven't been able to see, due to him having his back to me.

The pool is deep, and Teddy is soon submerged, dipping his head under the water and then popping back up, swimming to the very center of the pool, where he treads water, like he's waiting for something.

He's staring at the rocky tumble downstream, where he placed whatever was in the bundle. I squint at it threadwise and see swirling threads, flickering with those strange brownish shadows.

Toad magic. I'm sure of it.

It's not just a glimpse this time. I can really see it, the brownish strands reaching out toward Teddy like grasping fingers. I creep forward so I can get a better look, and a bit of dry bracken crunches under my foot. Teddy's head swings toward me.

"Who's there?" he asks, his voice uncertain.

I hesitate for a moment, biting my lip. Then I stand up.

"Merry!" Teddy hisses. "What in Gofannon's name are you doing here?"

My brain comes up with a thousand excuses, but I settle on the truth. "Hopefully convincing you not to join the Toadmen."

Teddy glances around nervously, like he's expecting the Howling Toad himself to pop out and catch us.

"You shouldn't be here," he says. "This is secret stuff. I have to do it alone."

I push through the bracken to the edge of the pool. The moon is bright overhead, and the water is *crystal* clear. It doesn't leave much to the imagination. Teddy looks outraged.

"Whatever this Toad magic is, Teddy," I say, "it's bad. It's dangerous. Caraway Boswell even said so."

"And since when do you care about what Caraway Boswell says?" Teddy brings his knees up to his chest defensively.

I walk along the edge of the pool to look at what he placed in the rocky part of the stream. It's a little heap of yellowing bones. Not a bird or a mouse, that's for sure. The skull is about the size of a walnut, round and flattened, with two wide staring eyeholes on either side. It reminds me of . . .

"A toad," I say, realizing. "Of course it is."

Teddy mutters something, his tone resentful.

"I'm here now," I tell him, returning to the edge of the pool. "And I'm not going anywhere. You may as well tell me what's going on."

For a moment, it looks like he's going to argue. But then he sinks slightly in the water as he sighs. Teddy knows he's no match for me when it comes to a debate. And that water looks freezing, I bet he's dying to get out.

"It's part of the initiation ritual," he explains, his teeth chattering. "I caught a toad, down the boggy end of Alcock's cow pasture. Buried it in an anthill for thirty days."

"Thirty days?" This Toad business has been going on longer than I realized. How did I only just notice?

"The ants picked the toad clean until it was just bones. Then I dug it up and brought it here. *The Book of Anura* says if you put the bones in the stream under a sickle moon, then the toad bone will float upstream to be caught by a worthy acolyte."

The Book of Anura. A worthy acolyte. My Teddy. The thought of it makes me sick to my stomach.

"You're doing *Toad magic*," I say. "*Here*, of all places!"

He looks around at the hollow. "It's just because of the water," he says. "It's got nothing to do with . . . what happened."

I close my eyes for a moment. Hear the cries of good Candlecott folk, and the screeching of witches. The rasping breath of my mother as she wasted away to nothing in her bed.

"Do you think it's true?" I ask, my voice small. "That she's really escaped?"

Teddy shakes his head. "It would have been in the papers," he says. "That little girl was just a troublemaker. I've never seen her before; she must have been visiting the fair with her parents, and wanted to cause mischief."

Teddy sounds so reasonable. I want to believe him.

"Please don't do this," I beg. "I just . . . I think there's something about the Toads. A *feeling*. I know you're ambitious and you think they can help, but there has to be another way."

Teddy doesn't respond.

"Teddy, come on," I say. "Let's get out of here. I'll buy you a cider at the Rose and Crown."

He hesitates. "How about I meet you there in half an hour?"

"I've seen you naked before," I tell him. "If that's the issue."

The moon disappears behind clouds and a ragged wind makes the birch trees shudder. Without the moonlight, I can't see Teddy at all, can barely see my own hand in front of me. I'm gripped by a sudden fear that he will get too cold to swim, and go under, and I won't be able to find him in the icy blackness to pull him out.

"Teddy?"

"Shhh."

The wind drops as quickly as it came, and everything is suddenly very silent and still, save for the bubbling of the stream over the rocks. I can hear Teddy's teeth chattering. I look threadwise and can see his swirling mettle in the pool.

And I see something else.

The writhing mettle around the bones is growing more tur-
bulent, whirling like ribbons in the wind. A part of it breaks free,
wriggling, almost boiling, upstream toward Teddy, the brownish
shadows thicker than ever.

There is no way that this is covenant magic.

My heart quickens. The suspicions I've had, about the Toads
dabbling in magic . . . I was right. But *seeing* it is something else.
My heart hammers in my chest and my mouth is dry. How is it
possible? There are Frater Houses all over Anglyon. Surely people would know if the Toadmen were doing real magic. *Illegal*
magic. Surely the auditors would be on it, arresting Toads left,
right and center and putting them in recovery centers along with
all the resistance witches.

Wouldn't Da have said something?

I asked him about it only once. I'd only just learned to look
threadwise—the ability came on me at around the same time I
got my first period. Ma told me not to tell anyone about it, and I
hadn't. Except Teddy and Sol, of course.

When I looked threadwise at Da after he came back from the
Frater House, I'd seen a glimpse of that brownish shadow. Like
no mettle I'd ever seen before. Then it was gone.

"Da?" I asked. "Are you okay?"

He nodded with a slightly vague smile. "A little tired, duckling."

"Da . . . do they do magic? The Toadmen?"

A frown passed over my da's face. "Of course not," he said.
"It's just a club. A social thing. Nothing more."

There was something in his tone that made me sure I wouldn't
get anything more from him. So I didn't ask again. But over the

years, I've seen it again and again. Always just a faint shadow. Always after Da comes back from the Frater House.

It's a curse, I'm sure of it. Something the Toadmen do to their members—I don't know why.

But I know it's dangerous.

And now it's coming for Teddy.

I'm overwhelmed by a need to wade into the stream and snatch the bone from the water before it can get to him. But I find that I cannot move. Instead I watch, as the roiling mettle slowly makes its way against the current, up the burbling rocky stream and into the pool, where it swirls around a few times in its own current, then starts to head inexorably toward my Teddy, whose own bright mettle reaches and twines together with it.

Nothing good happens in this place. I want nothing more than to run away and forget about Toads and bones and witches.

And then it's done. The moon comes out from behind the clouds and I can see properly again, without looking threadwise. Teddy wades out of the pool, and I turn my back so I don't embarrass him any further. I hear the crunch of bracken under his feet, and the heavy fall of cloth as he puts the wool coat back on. Then he's by my side, and I turn to look up at him, the moonlight glinting in his eyes, a grin on his face.

He holds out his hand to show me the yellowing bone. It's a delicate, narrow horseshoe, no bigger than my thumb.

"I guess I'm in," he says.

"Is that it?" I ask as we wander up the path and out of the Hollow. "You're a Toad now?"

"Not quite."

I nod. "The ceremony tomorrow evening at the Frater House."

"How do you know about that?"

"Caraway Boswell told me."

"Why are you suddenly talking to Caraway Boswell? You hate him."

"I know," I say. "But he followed me around the fair all day today until I agreed to go to some family dinner with him this weekend."

Teddy looks at me, sharply. "This weekend? And you said yes?"

I shrug. "I don't know any details."

"Huh."

"Why?"

He shakes his head. "Never mind. Look, I get why you're concerned. But you have to trust me. I know what I'm doing. I'm not going to get into any trouble."

"I just wish I understood *why* you want this so much."

"The Toadmen know what I can do," he says. "The charms I make in the forge. They say they can teach me more."

"What do you mean, *more*? Are they going to teach you covenant magic?"

I already know the answer to this question. There's no way what the Toadmen are doing is covenant magic—the hundred simple spells still permitted after the Treaty of Goose Spring.

He shakes his head. "There's *so much more* to learn, Merry," he says. His eyes are shining. "I want to know it all."

We've left Mwsogl Hollow behind, but I feel more uneasy than ever.

Teddy's always been interested in magic, far more so than any good Candlecott resident has any right to be. But he never seems to worry about it, the way I do. People thinking he's a witch. Getting in trouble with auditors. I want to be a supportive friend, but I just wish he'd be more careful. I've tried to explain it to him— the way the thought of magic makes my skin prickle and my gut churn. The way it conjures the sound of cackling witches and Ma's rasping breaths, just before she died.

There's nothing in the world that scares me more than magic.

So why does Teddy want it so much?

Teddy wraps his arms around me. He's still shivering, and his cheek is fish-cold against my forehead.

"I'm worried about you," I mumble into his shoulder. "I just don't see why everything has to change."

"Change isn't always bad," Teddy says, his voice gentle. "Sometimes change can lead to great things."

But he's wrong. Nothing good will come of this. I'm sure of it.

3.

DA IS IN THE HENHOUSE WHEN I WAKE UP, FUSSING over his girls. Hot mash every morning, followed by dust baths and a series of enrichment activities that include a chicken swing and a xylophone. He's chattering away to each of them, and they cluck fondly back and follow him around, starry-eyed and adoring. Chickens are Da's gift.

The girls scatter as I approach, eyeing me suspiciously. I have no gift for chickens, and they know I'm the one who takes their precious eggs away every morning.

"Mornin', duckling," says Da, beaming at me. Clearly the glow from winning his tenth poultry prize hasn't worn off yet.

I kiss him on the cheek and then turn to pull the wire egg basket off its hook.

"Da," I ask carefully. "What made you want to become a Toadman?"

If Da is surprised that I'm asking about Toad stuff, he doesn't show it. He reaches down to the brooder and scoops up a fluffy chick, which peeps cheerfully at him. "I've been a member since

I was eighteen," he says with a shrug. "All my friends joined, and so I did too."

"What did Ma think of it?"

Da chuckles, gently stroking the chick with his thumb. "She never liked it," he says. "Said you could never trust a Toad. But they were so good to me after she left us. Like an anchor keeping me from setting adrift."

After Ma fainted that first time, she grew weak and pale. I could see with my thread sight that her mettle was growing dull and thin.

"It's the witch's curse," she muttered, over and over. "Nothing to be done."

Then one day I went up to bring her a cup of tea and I knew, straightaway, that she was gone. Her mettle was still there, but it was different. Broken, her strings snapped. Not living mettle anymore. It was the mettle of something that was once living. The mettle of memory. Of significance. Of things passed. Ma was gone.

I remember how lost Da was without her. How his eyes didn't crinkle in a smile, not even when he was in the chook shed. He turned all gray and limp, like a stranded jellyfish. But he smiled when he came back from the Frater House. It felt like being with his friends brought a little life back into him. So I kept my promise to Ma and didn't tell him about my thread sight. Didn't tell him about the brown shadows I saw around his mettle.

The chick in Da's hand has fallen asleep, its little head snuggled into the crook between his finger and thumb. The mother hen Gwenhwyfach watches on and clucks approvingly.

I take the basket over to the nesting boxes and grope around for eggs.

"Were you scared to join?" I ask over my shoulder. "I hear the initiation ritual is pretty intense."

Da's forehead crinkles apologetically. "You know I can't talk about that, duckling."

"You don't need to tell me what happened," I say, sliding two pale blue eggs into the basket. "I just want to know if you were scared."

Da's frown deepens, and he peers at me searchingly. "Who's been talking to you about Toads?" he asks.

"Caraway Boswell," I say.

The next nesting box is occupied by Gliten, a gorgeous golden-laced Barnevelder with a sharp eye and an even sharper beak. She growls at me in a most unchickenish way.

"You'd best keep away from that one," Da says.

"Gliten?" I ask. "Or Caraway?"

If Da has dirt on Caraway, I want to hear it.

Da chuckles. "Gliten is all bark and no bite. And she lays a lovely speckled egg."

I steel myself and reach under Gliten's fluffy bottom, and am unsurprised to find that Gliten's bite is, in fact, just as bad as her bark. I swear and suck on the injured finger.

Dad tsks at my language. "You'll turn the eggs rotten with that tongue."

"Tell that to Gliten," I say, glaring resentfully at the chicken, who glares right back.

Da slides a hand under Gliten to retrieve her eggs. Of course for Da, Gliten is as calm and serene as the moon.

Da carefully places the eggs in my basket, and I take a moment to admire them all together. Brown speckles, shell pink, pure white and pale blue. My stomach rumbles.

"You were going to tell me why Caraway Boswell is an untrustworthy weasel," I remind Da.

He takes the basket from me. "I don't think I was," he says. "What was it that caused that spat between you yesterday?"

My cheeks burn with shame as I relive it. I close my eyes and see the sardonic lift of Caraway's eyebrow as he licked jam and cream from his top lip.

"Nothing," I mutter. "Or at least, nothing important."

"It didn't look like nothing."

"He started it."

Da's expression grows serious for a moment. "The Boswells are a powerful family," he says. "Best not get on their bad side."

Thurmond Boswell is the director of thaumaturgy at Ilium, the biggest magical corporation in the country. Powerful doesn't even begin to cover it. Perhaps agreeing to go to the Boswell family dinner wasn't the best idea.

"Is Caraway's father a Toad too?" I ask.

Da doesn't answer. "I know Caraway might not be easy to get along with, my love. But if you can't speak to him without getting into a row for the whole town to witness, it might be best if you just stay away from him."

I had visited Goody Bhreagh the previous afternoon. Brought her a basket with eggs and flowers and a bottle of elderberry wine. I'd apologized profusely, and she had been gracious and kind, which made me feel even more wretched.

"I'm sorry I ruined your big moment, Da," I say in a small voice.

Da shrugs. "You didn't," he says. "The only moment I cared about was seeing Peggy Ross's face when I unfurled Bran the Blessed's tail."

He chuckles at the memory, and I decide that he's right. Caraway is bad news, and I'm definitely not going to his family dinner. Whatever sneaky, weasel reason he has for wanting me there, it can't be for my benefit.

In the last nesting box, Cigfa, a white silkie, is sitting proudly on a clutch of nine eggs.

"How's she doing?" I ask Da.

"Good," he replies. "As far as I can tell."

He crouches down next to her and gently strokes her fluffy feathers. She makes a contented croaking noise.

You can candle an egg with a torch in a dark room to see the baby chick developing, but I can tell a lot more from looking at the mettle. The insides of the eggs are swirling with it, coalescing around a dense knot of silver about the size of a walnut. I smile to myself. Of the nine eggs, eight are developing well—three cocks and five pullets. But in one, the mettle has turned limp and thin. It's still there—there is mettle in dead things too, in rocks and bones and dry twigs. But it's different, the way that Ma's was on the day I found her in her bed.

Once I figured out what I was looking for, it became easy to tell a male chick from a female, just by looking at the mettle. There's a different cast to it, a different energy. It's a useful trick, especially for breeds that are difficult to sex. With many, we wouldn't know otherwise until a bird either crowed or laid an egg. Da reckons I have a knack for chicks. I can't tell him how I really know.

It's harder for humans, of course. To see what makes us male or female or something else entirely. It's complicated—*everything* about our mettle is complicated. Take Sol, for instance. He was born with parts that made his parents think he was a girl, and they treated him like one until he was old enough to explain otherwise. But when I look at Sol's mettle, I can see that he is a boy. Perhaps if his parents had been able to see him threadwise, they might have understood him a little better. Even Teddy, who is as masculine as they come, is more complicated than he seems on the outside. The kind of affinity he has for magic—it almost never shows up in men.

"Time for breakfast, I think," Da says, straightening up. "What do you feel like?"

I laugh in response, because he already knows the answer. In our house, we eat a lot of eggs.

"Will you be home for dinner tonight?" I ask.

Da shakes his head. "No, duckling. You'll be okay on your own?"

"Of course."

I don't need to ask him where he'll be going. There's only one place that Da goes. It's the same place that Teddy will be going tonight.

THE PHONE RINGS AS we're eating our eggs.

Da answers, then hands the phone to me wordlessly.

"Hello?" I say into the receiver.

"Morgan." Caraway's voice is no less annoying through a tele-phone. "As promised, I'm calling with details for this weekend."

I glance at Da, then slide around the corner so he can't hear. "Deal's off," I tell Caraway. "Teddy is still joining the Toads."

There's a long silence on the other end of the line. "I held up my end," he says at last. "I told you what you needed to know. If you couldn't pull it off, that's your problem."

I remember what Da said.

It might be best if you just stay away from him.

"The *deal*," I remind Caraway, "was for you to tell me how to stop Teddy from joining the Toads. What you told me *didn't* stop him, so I will not be going to your family dinner."

Another long silence. Then a sigh. "Meet me outside the Frater House at seven," he says, and the line goes dead.

I return to the kitchen and sit back down at the table.

"What was that about?" Da asks.

"Nothing," I tell him. "Just school stuff."

THE FRATER HOUSE CROUCHES on the edge of town, squat, ugly and the color of a dried-up puddle. Like a toad, I guess. It has no windows, because good people forbid anyone should be able to get a glimpse inside. Six stone steps lead up to a bare wooden door under a portico supported by two gray columns. The carved stone crest of the Toadmen sits at the top of the portico—the Ghost Toad and the Howling Toad flanking the crowned king.

Caraway is nowhere to be seen.

I'm not really sure I should be here at all. Teddy would be

furious. He asked me to trust him, and I do. I just don't trust the Toadmen.

"No girls allowed, Morgan."

I reply without turning around. "Bite me, Boswell."

Caraway is dressed in the black garment that all the Toads wear when they hang out—buttoned broadcloth from neck to ankle, with frilled white sleeves spilling out from the shoulders. His cuffs are heavily embroidered and beaded with intricate designs. His head is bare of the silly bonnet that I've seen them wear, and it's probably the glamour, but he somehow manages to make the silly robe look elegant.

"So what's the plan?" I ask. "Am I going to burst in on Teddy's initiation ceremony like a jilted lover at a wedding?"

Caraway raises an eyebrow. "You won't stop the initiation," he says. "If he caught the bone last night, everything else is just a formality."

"Then why am I here?"

"I want you to see what they do. So you understand."

I stare at him. "You . . . just want me to watch?"

He nods.

"But how? You just said girls aren't allowed."

He winks at me. "There's a back door," he says. "Leads into the kitchen. Go through and head down the corridor at the end. There'll be some big wooden doors. Go past them and through the next door on the right. I'll meet you there."

I bite my lip. I want to see inside the Frater House. I always have. Then I'd know for sure what kind of shady business the Toads are up to. But . . . Teddy will be mad if he finds out.

It's like Caraway can read my thoughts. "Take this," he says, pressing a plastic packet into my hand. "Nobody needs to know you're there."

Then he glides past me and up the stone steps. His hand on the doorknob, he hesitates a moment, and then says over his shoulder, "Be careful."

Then he disappears inside.

I look down at the plastic packet.

It's a glamour patch. HUSH is stamped across the front, with AN ILIUM PRODUCT underneath in smaller letters.

We're simple, here in Candlecott. Glamour patches are for city folk—people who shop at giant malls and wear heeled shoes and do all sorts of other ridiculous things to pretend they're anyone but who they truly are. I haven't worn a patch since I was little, when you'd get novelty ones in children's birthday party bags.

I peel it open, remove the plastic backing, then stick the patch onto my bicep, underneath the sleeve of my T-shirt. I don't feel any different, but I'm sure it's working, making me unobtrusive, so that I blend right into the background of any scene.

THE BACK ALLEY IS deserted, save for a scrawny-looking cat perched on a fence. It hisses at me as I pass, and I scowl back at it. The rear of the Frater House is even more boring than the front—just a single door, which, judging from the exhaust fan on the wall emitting the sour scent of cheap coffee, leads to a kitchen.

I take a deep breath, then kick over one of the metal rubbish bins that sits outside the Frater House back door. The lid flies off as the bin hits the cobblestones with an almighty crash and goes wheeling across the alley before clattering down.

It really is very loud.

I flatten myself against the wall of the Frater House, on the hinge side of the door. And wait.

After a few moments I hear footsteps inside, and the door swings open. I catch it so it doesn't smash into my face and peer around the edge as a robed figure steps out into the alleyway. I instantly recognize the man as Jock Shirley, who works behind the bar at the Rose and Crown. I hold my breath as he strides past me and looks up and down the alleyway. He mutters a curse under his breath as he surveys the coffee grinds and eggshells that have spilled onto the cobblestones, and then bends to retrieve the bin lid.

I dart around the door and slip into the kitchen.

Luckily there's no one else in here. I scamper past a large hot-water urn and a rather battered-looking stove where a huge pot of soup simmers. Parsnip and ham, by the smell of it. Ugh. I'm not quite sure what I expected to find in a Toad kitchen— burbling potions, perhaps? Roast ox on a spit? All I see is soup and white rolls and packets of chocolate digestive biscuits. *This* is where Teddy wants to spend his summer?

The kitchen is long and galley style, with a swinging door at one end. I listen for a moment to make sure there's no one on the other side; then I slip out into what appears to be a dining hall.

I did it. I'm in the Frater House. The secret Toad sanctum, forbidden to women.

It certainly doesn't look like the kind of place that's dabbling in secret illegal magic.

Linoleum floors. Cheap fluorescent lighting. Wood-paneled walls hung with framed faded photos of Toads in their ridiculous outfits. Long tables set for dinner, plain white china and basic cutlery. I'd thought at least there might be fancy silverware. Goblets to drink out of or something. But no. It looks exactly like the dining hall at school. Is that the appeal? Old men wearing silly uniforms and eating bland dinners so they can pretend they're young again?

Everything smells like instant coffee and soup.

I head through the next door and find myself in a long, drab-looking corridor. There's a large, ornate set of doors opposite me, carved with stylized Toads hiding among leafy foliage. The door is open just a crack, so I peer through as I pass.

It must be the main meeting hall for the Toadmen. It's fairly large, the walls hung with rather moth-eaten pennants and banners. Wooden chairs are lined up facing a dais hung with more shabby-looking tapestries.

There are about thirty men seated in the room, all with their backs to me. They're wearing the silly Toad bonnets—embroidered gold with a glittering beaded toad eye on each side and a white ruffled frill all around the edge. But despite the bonnets and the fact that I can't see any faces, I still recognize Da at once by the slope of his shoulders. My heart catches a little to think of him in this place. I know all his friends come here, but . . . couldn't he have a less creepy hobby, like fishing, or bird-watching, or cross-stitch?

I see his face as he turns and talks to the man next to him. He's smiling. He looks comfortable. Happy.

Teddy isn't in the room.

Someone stands and turns. Creepy Glen, his face sourer than

a green gooseberry. My heart pounds as he heads toward the doors. The glamour I'm wearing might make me less noticeable, but I'm not invisible. I can't let Creepy Glen see me.

"Morgan!" Caraway's voice hisses from down the corridor. "In here!"

I scurry after him, closing the door behind me.

It's a small antechamber, dimly lit by a grimy clerestory window. There are various bits of Toad paraphernalia stacked along one side—the staffs they use for the holming dance, various gilt vessels and boxes probably used in their ceremonies. There are also less glamorous items—music stands and stacked chairs and crates of old paperwork. I can hear the burble of chatting voices through the wall—this room must run alongside the main meeting hall. There are three doors—the one I came through, one that I'm sure leads into the meeting hall, and a third, smaller door at the end that looks more like a cupboard.

Caraway pokes his head out of this third door and beckons to me. "Come on!"

I can hear footsteps approaching from the main hallway, so I follow Caraway into what turns out to be the large closet where they hang all the spare Toad robes. I gently close the door behind me, just as the door from the hallway opens.

I hold my breath.

"Anyone in here?" Creepy Glen says.

I back into the hanging robes, trying to move as silently as I can. It's pitch-black inside, and everything smells of old skin and mothballs. It's stifling. Robes brush my hands and my face as I burrow back into them, and I'm struck by an irrational fear that they might come to life and smother me.

The footsteps stop outside the door, and I hear a squeak as the handle turns.

I hold my breath, and time seems to slow down.

Creepy Glen leans into the closet, his eyes searching. At the same moment, an arm snakes out from behind me and catches me around the waist, drawing me silently back, deeper into the hanging robes. A warm body presses against my back, and a hand goes over my mouth to stop me from making a sound. Through the mothballs, I catch the scent of bergamot and old leather.

Creepy Glen's hand snags on a hanger holding some kind of elaborately embroidered apron, and he withdraws. The door closes again, plunging the closet back into darkness.

I try to bite the hand over my mouth, and it withdraws sharply.

"Hecate's teeth, Morgan."

Caraway's arm releases from around my waist, and I spin to face him. Not that I can see anything. I shove out to where I assume he is and feel him stagger backward.

"Get your hands off me."

"Gladly."

"What are you doing?" I ask.

"Saving you from another reputational calamity?"

There are a million things I'd like to say in response to this, but I manage to suppress them all. "Why am I here?" I ask instead.

"You'll see."

The murmur of chatter from the meeting hall suddenly falls quiet. Something bangs on the ground three times, and then I hear the sound of chanting voices, although I can't make out what they're saying.

"The initiation is about to start," Caraway says.

"Initiation?" I ask. "*Teddy*'s initiation?"

"It's too late to stop it," Caraway says. "So don't think you're going to leap out there and make a commotion."

I realize that I can see the outline of his horrid perfect head. The cupboard isn't pitch-dark after all. I push him to the side and see the source of the light. A little chink in the back of the cupboard—a crack in the wall.

"Look through," Caraway instructs.

I put my eye to the chink and see into an antechamber that must lead off the main hall. It's bare boards on the floor and walls, completely free of any ornamentation, save for a large, elaborately carved chair on a dais. A throne, really. The carvings are similar to the ones on the door to the main hall. The room is lit with oil lamps that flicker, giving the carvings the illusion of movement.

A figure is kneeling at the foot of the throne, blindfolded.

My heart catches.

Teddy.

He's wearing all white—the frilly shirt and loose cotton drawers that go under the main black toad robe.

A door opens and someone walks in. They wear the usual robe and bonnet of a Toadman, but with a richly beaded and embroidered cape over the top, open in front but fastened over the breast with a jeweled clasp. Their face is covered with a toad mask—not one of the mock-scary ones that go round on Whitsun Eve. This mask looks like it is carved from bone—black-eyed, colorless and unmistakably toadlike. The figure speaks in a deep, booming voice that is somehow familiar.

"Who art thou, come into our most secret and hallowed chamber?"

"I am Edward James Evans, apprentice blacksmith of Candlecott."

"And why hast thou come?"

"To become a Toadman."

My stomach churns at his words.

"Dost thou swear to keep the secrets thou wilt glean here on this day, and all other days?"

"I swear," Teddy replies.

"State thy case."

Teddy hesitates, then speaks. "I humbly present myself before the King Toad's throne, to offer my fealty to him, until the day I die."

I wonder if there is really a king—a president of Toadmen. Perhaps in the city.

"Make thy pledge."

"I swear to keep my secrets and perform my duties as a Toadman. If I break any of the Toadman's creed, then may my heart be torn from my breast by wild horses, my body quartered and swung on chains, and the wild birds of Uisnigh left to pick my bones, which should then be buried in the sands of Llanw Mawr, where the tide will bury and uncover them twice each day, to show my deceit and betrayal."

"Hast thou the Toad's Boon?" asks the masked figure.

Teddy doesn't look up, but he holds out a hand. I can see the curve of yellow bone from the stream last night.

The masked Toad takes it from him and drops it into a golden chalice, studded with red jewels. He lifts a golden pestle, set with a dull brown gemstone at the grinding end, and brings it down on the bone with a sharp crack. Then he takes a crystal decanter and splashes what looks like wine into the chalice, swirls it sunwise three times, then holds it out to Teddy.

"Accept the Toad's Boon," the figure commands. "Accept it with thine full heart. Take it into thine own body, and it will bestow upon thee the power and glory of the Three Great Toads of Deeping Fen."

Teddy rises to one knee and accepts the goblet. My fingernails dig into the palms of my hands as I watch him drink.

"Watch carefully," Caraway whispers.

"Did you do this?" I ask him. "When you became a Toad?"

Caraway is silent for a moment. When he does answer, his voice sounds somehow younger. "I was only five when I was initiated."

"Five?" I whisper. "Is that allowed?"

"Not usually. I was a special case."

"Why so special?" I ask. "Is it because you're rich?"

Caraway doesn't answer, which I take to be a yes. I'm distracted from Teddy for a moment. "Do you remember any of it?"

There's a long pause before Caraway responds. I am suddenly very aware of his body, mere inches from mine. I can feel the warmth of him. His scent fills my senses and drowns out the musty fabric and mothballs.

"All I remember is that it hurt."

My chest clenches. *"Hurt?"* I turn back to the crack and feel a sudden wildness in me, like I could tear down the wall that separates us and carry Teddy off to safety.

"Don't worry, Morgan," Caraway says, and the dry, superior tone is back in his voice. "Your boyfriend is a big boy. He'll be fine."

"He's not my—" But I cut myself off, because something is happening.

The masked Toad is drawing on a pair of white gloves. He opens a plain wooden box and withdraws a hook.

It looks a bit like the baling hooks that farmhands use during haying season—a black iron hook about a foot long, attached to a horizontal wooden handle. It's free of ornamentation, but the handle is worn so smooth that I know it must be very old. The masked Toad holds the hook up.

"Thou hast taken the Toad's Boon into thine own body. Now thou must give of thine own self."

I reach out and grab Caraway by the front of his Toad robe. "What are they going to do to him?" I ask.

Caraway puts his hand over mine, a strangely comforting gesture. "Just watch," he says.

I swallow and watch as Teddy stands up. He stands a good head taller than the robed figure, but that somehow doesn't make the masked Toad any less intimidating.

"Dost thou make this sacrifice willingly?"

Teddy hesitates, and for a moment I think that maybe, *just maybe,* he'll come to his senses. But then he speaks.

"I do."

The masked Toad waves the hook in a scything motion, then presses it against Teddy's chest. But he isn't attacking him with it. I see no blood. I let out a breath and feel my shoulders slump in relief.

"Look witch-eyed," Caraway breathes.

A wave of shock passes through me. "How do you know I—"

"Just do it."

I'm about to push further, but Teddy lets out a low, guttural noise. The masked Toad is still holding the hook against Teddy's breast, tensed as if pulling an invisible load toward him. I look threadwise and clap a hand over my mouth to stop from crying out.

The hook is glowing white, as if it's made from pure mettle. It doesn't take a witch to know that it is a very powerful magical object.

And it's got Teddy.

One of his strings—the strands of mettle that make up the very core of his being—is snagged on the hook, and the masked Toad is hauling backward, pulling the string so it bends toward him. I can almost *feel* the tension of it as it stretches tighter and tighter.

I can see sweat running down the back of Teddy's neck, can hear his breath coming in ragged gasps.

Caraway's hand tightens on mine.

"It's going to break," I whimper. "They're going to break him."

"Just one string. And he's giving it willingly. He'll be fine."

Mettle is always stronger if it's given willingly. But surely it still *hurts*?

The masked Toad hauls, and the hook seems to pulse with energy as it draws Teddy's string away from him.

And then there is a sudden, dreadful *snap*.

The momentum of the break twirls the string around the hook as Teddy slumps to the floor, whimpering.

I have to go to him.

I turn from the crack in the wall. Teddy needs me. They broke one of his strings. One of his *strings*. His *life-force*.

I remember seeing Ma, her strings all broken, her body limp and empty. The thought of it happening to Teddy is unbearable.

Did they do this to my da?

I struggle against Caraway's grasp, still looking threadwise, and half glimpse the masked Toad unwinding the string from the hook and placing it in a palm-sized vessel made of a marbled reddish stone. Finally, I break free and go tearing out of the closet.

"Morgan, wait!" Caraway follows me, his hands grabbing at my shirt.

"Stay *away* from me, Toad!" I cry out, not bothering to keep my voice down anymore.

I can't think. I can't breathe. Dimly I hear Caraway coming after me, hissing my name. All I can think about is getting to Teddy.

I knock over music stands and plastic crates as I charge through the storage room. Caraway reaches me just as my hand closes on the door handle, and we tussle for a minute, his hand reaching for mine, trying to pull me back, to stop me from turning it.

Our eyes meet for a moment, and we're nose to nose, clutching each other in a desperate struggle.

Then he seems to come to a decision, and stops fighting.

My hand twists on the doorknob, the door swings open, and Caraway and I go spilling out in a tangle of arms and legs, right into the main hall, as the eyes of every Toadman present turn to us.

4.

FOR THE SECOND TIME IN LESS THAN FORTY-EIGHT hours, I am lying on the ground on top of Caraway Boswell, being stared at by half my town.

There's an awful, awful silence as we disentangle ourselves and clamber to our feet.

"What is the meaning of this?"

I turn to see the Toad with the bone mask, the one who cut Teddy's string. He strides forward, removing the mask, and suddenly I realize why his voice sounded familiar.

It's Dr. Gower, the head of senior assembly at Candlecott School. Dr. Gower, who delivers interminable lectures on the evils of magic, the threat of witches, the importance of restrictions. All along he's been sneaking off to do secret Toad magic.

He *cut Teddy's string.*

He leans forward, trying to see past the glamour I'm wearing.

"Merriwether Morgan," he says at last. "I might have known."

I ignore him, my eyes finding Da in the assembled Toads. His face is pale, his jaw slack with shock.

"Miss Morgan, you have broken our most sacred laws. This temple is forbidden to women and you have breached its sanctity. Your father has failed to control your behavior and will be expelled from the Toadmen."

Da looks stricken. The other Toads turn to look at him, their own expressions a mix of sympathetic and outraged.

"N-no—" I stammer. "It's not his fault. I—"

My eyes drift toward the back of the room where Teddy stands, pale and trembling, frowning at me with *such* disappointment on his face.

I've ruined everything. Again.

"It's my fault." Caraway's voice is calm and confident. "Morgan and I . . . we're lovers. I brought her into the Frater House because I couldn't bear to be without her. We were . . . in the throes of passion. In the closet."

I turn to stare at Caraway, aghast. He doesn't show an ounce of discomfort. He's as cool and relaxed as if he's chatting with close friends.

"She saw and heard nothing," Caraway assures Dr. Gower. "Trust me, her attention was *definitely* focused elsewhere."

And Caraway Boswell actually *winks* at Dr. Gower.

I am feeling all the feelings. Shame. Regret. *Outrage* at Caraway's suggestion that I would *ever* demean myself to be his . . . Ugh.

Caraway looks around the Frater House haughtily. "You know," he says to Dr. Gower, "I've noticed that this place is starting to look a little shabby. I'll speak to my father about increasing his endowment to allow for some capital works."

Dr. Gower splutters. "I—I'm sure the Candlecott Frater

House will be very grateful, Brother Caraway," he says. "But the fact remains that the girl has already seen too much. This room— our members."

I snort. Gower is the only person in this room who I didn't already know was a Toad. Gower frowns at me, like he'd forgotten I was there.

Caraway shrugs lazily. "It doesn't matter. Morgan is going to be my consort this weekend, aren't you, Morgan?"

I splutter. The "family event" he wanted me to go to is a *Toad* thing? "I—I didn't exactly—"

Dr. Gower looks utterly baffled. *"You,"* he says. "Caraway Boswell. Are going to take *Merriwether Morgan* to the Trothal of the King Toad."

The *Trothal of the King Toad*? Is it . . . some kind of Toad wedding?

Caraway slings a seemingly affectionate arm over my shoulder, and it takes every fiber of my being not to fight him off. "What can I say?" He shrugs. "The heart wants what it wants."

"Are you *sure*?"

Despite everything that's going on, I'm frankly a bit offended by Gower's tone.

"Do you question my choice, Brother?" Caraway asks, and there's an edge to his voice that is as cold and sharp as steel. "Morgan is intelligent—joint dux with me in our year. Her spirit is strong—I'm not interested in women who are simpering syco-phants. I am looking for a true partner, and I have found one in her. I challenge you to find me a worthier consort."

My cheeks burn as I take all this in. I know he's bluffing, but . . . well, Caraway is a *very* good actor.

"Does your father know?" Dr. Gower asks. "I was under the impression your consort was Esmerelda Huntington-Smythe."

Caraway tilts his head to the side. "I'm not sure the conversations I have with my father are any of your business."

Dr. Gower's face has turned the color of a ripe plum. "Brother Caraway," he says between clenched teeth. "I appreciate your . . . ardor. But our sacred law states—"

Caraway's chin comes up slightly. His tone remains calm and casual, but his eyes glitter coldly. "You probably don't want to lecture me about our sacred law . . . *Brother Callum.*"

A long moment passes between them. I have absolutely no idea what is going on, but I can tell that Gower is hugely intimidated by Caraway. And Caraway doesn't bat an eyelash. The arrogance that emanates from him is astounding. I guess that's what happens when your father is super rich and has some posh job at Ilium. You get everything you want, and nobody is brave enough to try to stop you.

Gower takes a half step back and inclines his head slightly in defeat.

"Get her out of here," he says. *"Now."*

Caraway smiles easily. "My pleasure."

His hand reaches the small of my back, and he steers me toward the large wooden doors. Over my shoulder I catch a glimpse of Da, looking horrified and relieved, and behind him, Teddy. Our eyes meet. Teddy knows this is all a lie. He knows I would *never* do anything as revolting as make out in a cupboard with Caraway Boswell. He shakes his head slightly, his brow crinkled in disapproval.

Once we're out of the main hall, I wriggle free from Caraway's hand and spin to face him.

"What in Bella Fawr's name was all that?" I hiss.

He gazes at me, expressionless. "You want me to go back in there and tell them the truth?"

"The whole town is going to think we're an item!"

"A fact that can only increase your social standing, I'm sure."

I stomp down the hallway and pause before the main front door.

"Did you plan this whole thing?" I ask him. "Is this all some weird scheme of yours to get me to go on a date with you?"

"Not exactly," he says. "My plan was to show you Evans's initiation, then advise you to come with me this weekend to keep an eye on him. I think the Trothal is going to be . . . intense."

"Teddy is going?"

"It seems the senior Toads are very impressed by his abilities."

That doesn't sound good. "What's in all this for you? Why do *you* want me to go with you?"

His eyes slide from mine, and he almost looks awkward, in spite of the glamour. "I need a favor," he says. "Something only you can do."

I swallow. I know exactly what he's talking about, and the thought fills me with horror.

"How did you know?" I ask. "That I can see threadwise?"

"You mean witch-eyed?" he says.

I scowl. "I'm no witch."

Caraway shrugs. "Whatever."

"But how did you know?"

"Just a hunch."

"Liar," I say. "Do *they* know?" I jerk my head back at the hall full of Toadmen.

Caraway purses his lips. "We can't talk about it here," he says. "Tomorrow, in the car."

The idea that the Toadmen might know my secret fills me with dread. People in my town. My neighbors. *Da.* I can't have them knowing about the curse. They'd never look at me the same again.

"I hate this," I say. "All of it."

"Join the club," Caraway responds. "Pack Wellingtons and a raincoat—we'll be gone four days."

I splutter. "Four days!"

One of his perfect eyebrows arches. "I didn't realize it would inconvenience you so, Morgan. I'll call the King Toad himself and tell him to postpone the sacred ritual that hasn't happened for fifty years."

I let out a frustrated growl. Everything is going wrong. My perfect summer.

"Fifty *years*? What exactly *is* this event? Will the Toadmen be dancing naked under the goose moon?"

Caraway's sardonic smile slides from his face. "If only. I'll tell you all about it in the car tomorrow."

He opens the door, and a gust of cool evening air washes over me.

"Caraway," I say, but then trail off, unsure how to frame the question.

Irritatingly, he seems to understand. "Evans is going to have a headache in the morning, but otherwise, no adverse side effects."

"Do they do that to everyone?" I ask. "Did they do it to my da?"

He nods, shortly, and I see a flash of vulnerability behind the cool detachment.

"They did it to you too," I say.

He doesn't reply, but I see his Adam's apple bob.

"And you were only five."

He inhales slowly, facing out of the Frater House and gazing into the night. Then he looks back at me. "I'll pick you up at eight sharp tomorrow morning. Be ready."

And he gently pushes me out the door. I descend two steps, then turn to look over my shoulder.

Framed by the simple wooden door and lit by lamplight, Caraway looks like a marble statue. For the first time, I wonder if he's lonely, beneath all that haughty superiority. I don't think he has any friends at school. I can't quite imagine Caraway Boswell having a friend.

"Is there anything else, Morgan?" he says.

I stare at him for a moment longer, unable to look away. "Where is it?" I ask at last. "This Festival of Toads?"

Caraway speaks softly, as if he's concerned that someone might be listening.

"Deeping Fen."

The name is familiar to me, but it sounds like something from a fairy tale. "The swamp?"

Caraway nods. "See you tomorrow, Morgan."

I KNOCK SOFTLY ON Sol's front door, hoping he'll hear me. There's no answer. I knock a little louder. Nothing. Sighing and mentally apologizing to Sol's aunt, I make a fist and thump as hard as I can.

After a moment, I hear shuffling footsteps inside, and then the door opens.

Not Sol.

"What time do you call this?" Sol's aunt regards me from behind her reading glasses. Her hair is braided under a net, and she's wearing a lavender nightgown with fluffy slippers.

"I'm so sorry, Aunt Jamila," I say. "I need to see Sol. It's important."

She hesitates for a moment, then stands back and lets me inside.

Sol is wearing pink-and-blue striped pajamas, lying on his bed with headphones on. I can hear the faint strains of violins emerging from them. He slides the headphones off when I tap him on the shoulder.

"What's up?" he asks.

I sink onto his bed, and he takes my hand. I feel like I'm going to cry.

"Merry?" he says. "What's happened?"

I take a deep breath, and I tell him everything. About Caraway Boswell at the Whitsuntide fair, and the weird ritual in Mwsogl Hollow. Sol squeezes my hand—he knows how much I fear the place where my mother was cursed. Then I tell him about sneaking into the Frater House and seeing Teddy's initiation.

"They cut his *string*, Sol," I say, my voice shaking. "A bit of his life-force. They *took* it."

Sol doesn't say anything. I tell him about getting caught, and Caraway pretending that we were lovers.

Sol chuckles. "That was decent of him," he says.

"Decent!" I say, my voice rising sharply.

Sol puts a finger over his lips and glances toward his bedroom door.

"It wasn't *decent*," I hiss. "It was calculating and horrid and weaselly, because Caraway Boswell is a calculating horrid weasel."

"It sounds to me like he's on your side. He helped you sneak in. He showed you what's really going on. And he lied to protect you and your da."

I shake my head. Sol has it all wrong. "Caraway Boswell never does anything out of the goodness of his heart," I insist. "He still hasn't told me why he is so desperate for me to go with him to this weekend thing."

Sol smiles gently. "Not everyone is out to get you, Merry."

"I *know* that. This isn't about me. It's about Teddy. So what are we going to do?"

"Nothing."

I stare at him. "You can't be serious. We have to stop him from going to the Trothal. From being a Toadman."

"It's what he wants, Merry. He's been talking about it for months."

Not to me. I feel the sting of hurt and shame and anger, all mixed together.

"Sol, the Toads are *bad*. They are taking people's strings."

"You said he gave it willingly."

"That's not the point!"

"It is, though." He hesitates. "Before I came to Anglyon, my family wanted me to be a very particular sort of child. And . . . I couldn't. It just wasn't in me. They did everything they could. But nothing worked. In the end they sent me here to live with Aunt Jamila, because it was easier for everyone." He sighs. "Merry, Teddy knows who he is. What he wants to be. I won't stand in the way of that. And neither should you."

Sol has always been the peacemaker. Teddy and I are too similar—both hotheaded and impulsive. Sol is the one who patches up every fight, every disagreement. He's always thoughtful and honest, but he never, *ever* takes sides.

Which is how I know he's right.

But I just can't let it go.

"What about the magic?" I say. "The Toadmen are using dangerous magic. Illegal magic."

Sol waves a hand. "It's all just energy, Merry. The rules and regulations are meaningless. How is the energy produced from weaving mettle different from a song produced by weaving together different notes, different instruments? The world is all energy. All life-force. We should celebrate it, not fear it."

I grind my teeth. "It's *not* the same thing. Songs aren't dangerous."

"They can be. Songs can inspire people to do great things. Or terrible things. Magic is the same. It can be dangerous. Or it can be something simple that keeps your bowstrings taut."

He gestures at his bedside table, where there's a little pot of bow rosin. PERFECT TONE! the label reads, and underneath, AN ILIUM PRODUCT.

"I know all that, I do," I tell him. "I just . . . can't shake the feeling that Teddy is in danger."

"Teddy has a great and rare talent," Sol replies. "If he doesn't learn to use it properly, he'll get himself into more trouble."

"So you won't help me," I say, standing up.

"Don't put it like that," he says, reaching out to me. "I love you. Can't you let Teddy be Teddy?"

He doesn't seem to understand that I *want* Teddy to be Teddy. I just don't want him to be a Toad.

DA COMES HOME LATE, after eleven. He looks weary as he hangs his coat on the hook and shucks his boots off.

I'm sitting at the kitchen table, nursing a mug of balsam tea. I've been waiting for him for an hour, rehearsing what I want to say.

"Are you hungry?" I ask. "There's beef growler in the fridge."

He shakes his head and glances at the stairs, as if he'd like to bypass this whole conversation and go straight to bed. But he sits opposite me at the kitchen table.

"Merry—" he starts, but I interrupt him.

"Da, I saw what they did to him. They cut one of Teddy's strings. They did it to you too, didn't they? Da, that's *magic*. Not covenant magic. *Real* magic."

Da shakes his head. "Don't be silly, love. There's no magic in the Toadmen. It's just a gentlemen's club."

My fingers tighten around my mug. "But I *saw*—"

"You didn't see anything," Da interrupts me. "You've always had an active imagination."

I swallow uneasily. Da has this gentle smile on his face, like he's explaining something to a very young child. He doesn't seem . . . quite like himself. I look at him threadwise and see the brownish shadows that I expected. And his mettle seems . . . out of focus, somehow. Cloudy. Uneasiness creeps back into my gut.

"Do I really have to go to this Trothal thing?" I ask.

He nods. "It's a great honor, love. You're a lucky girl."

I don't feel lucky. "Is Deeping Fen far?" I ask.

"I'm not sure, love. I've never been."

"It's a swamp, isn't it? I feel like I read a fairy story set there once."

Da runs his fingers over the wood grain of our kitchen table. "It's an important place for Toadmen."

"Important how?"

"I can't say." Da shrugs.

I swallow down the lump in my throat. "I don't like it when you keep secrets from me."

Da's eyes sharpen for a moment. "We all keep secrets, don't we?"

"What do you mean?" I ask.

He shakes his head, but I have a feeling he's talking about the Spitalwick Hag's curse. My thread sight.

Does everyone know?

"It's late, duckling," Da says with a vague smile. "Off to bed with you. You have a big day tomorrow."

And that's it. He rises from his chair and heads up the creaking oak staircase without looking back.

I stare down at my tea. It's one of those enchanted tea bags that keeps the brew hot and perfectly steeped. AN ILIUM PRODUCT, the little paper tab says.

I WAKE AT DAWN to the usual chorus of roosters and pull on a T-shirt and shorts. Dragging out my rucksack, I toss things into it without really thinking—whatever's in my clothes hamper, plus a sleeping bag, a firestone, a knife and a few sachets of ready meals: the enchanted kind that just need a few drops of water to prepare.

Da is in the henhouse, but I don't stop to say good morning.

I have things to do, and not much time.

My plan is simple. Kidnap Teddy and drag him off to Dryad's Saddle. We'll hide out in the woods for a week or two, swimming and doing regular summer stuff, and by the time we come back, Teddy will have lost interest in the Toadmen and the town will have forgotten about me and Caraway Boswell. I can start work on Da, then. To get him out too.

It's a great plan, if I do say so myself.

It would have been better with Sol on board, but maybe a little alone time with Teddy isn't the worst thing in the world. Maybe it's finally time to find out if we can be more than friends. The thought of it sets something aglow in my chest.

The rucksack is heavy, but my spirits are light as I march through town.

TEDDY LIVES IN THE mill house on the opposite side of Candlecott. Even at this early hour, it's pandemonium. Harry and Poppy come hurtling out of the front door as I approach, bellowing joyful curses at each other. Inside the kitchen, the triplets Daisy, Rosie and Pip are practicing a dance routine they've made up, while Milla is shouting at them to keep the noise down so she can focus on the magazine she's reading. Two-year-old Finn is sitting, fat and happy, on the floor with his fist in a jar of marmalade, and

Teddy's baby sister, Lolly, is in her high chair, covered in porridge and screaming her head off.

There's no sign of Teddy or his parents.

I manage to get Milla's attention.

"He's already gone!" she shouts over the chaos. "Left an hour ago. Took his van."

"Where?" I yell. "Where did he go?"

She shrugs, disinterested. "Shouldn't *you* know? You're his friend."

I thought I was.

MY BAG FEELS A lot heavier on the way home. The town is waking up, and I see Huw Jones on a morning run. He doesn't say *good morning* the way he usually does, and I remember he was there last night, at the Frater House.

My feet turn to lead.

Everyone thinks I've been snogging Caraway Boswell in storage cupboards all over town.

I can't bear it.

There's a car at the end of our driveway. I've never seen it before. It's a faded purple hatchback and definitely older than I am. One of its headlights is missing, and the battered fender seems to be hanging on by a thread.

I check my watch. Eight-thirty.

There is no way that this car belongs to Caraway Boswell. Caraway Boswell goes places in a sleek black beast driven by a deferential white-gloved chauffeur.

Curious, I head down the driveway and in the back door, to

find the previously unimaginable sight of Caraway Boswell sitting at my kitchen table.

"What exactly was it about *be ready at eight o'clock* that you didn't understand, Morgan?" Caraway says mildly.

I glance over at Da, who chuckles. "Merry has always operated on her own timetable," he says, his voice fond.

I stare at him. What happened to his little speech about staying away from Caraway? There's a pot of tea in the middle of the table, and Caraway is holding a chocolate digestive in one elegant hand.

What is going *on*? Chocolate biscuits at *eight-thirty in the morning*? I remember how strange Da seemed last night. The slight fuzziness to his mettle.

Did the Toadmen *do* something to my da? Some kind of magic?

"At least you're all packed," Caraway observes, eyeing my rucksack.

"Are you sure you'll be all right, Da?" I ask.

"Course I will," Da responds indignantly. "What do you think I'll do next year, when you're off at the university?"

I open my mouth to respond, but I don't want Caraway to know that I'm not going.

"Can't wait for us to continue our furious academic rivalry next year, Morgan," Caraway drawls. "And of course, our furious . . . *extracurricular* activities."

"*Don't,*" I warn him through gritted teeth.

Da clears his throat. "Well, you two should probably be getting on the road," he says.

Caraway stands in a single lithe, graceful movement. He's

wearing jeans that fit him perfectly and a cream-colored knit pull-over. He looks like a model from a glamour ad. I feel like a child in my shorts and T-shirt.

Da heads around behind Caraway and I see him slip something into the side pocket of my rucksack. Then he opens his arms and embraces me.

"Be good, love," he tells me.

"Don't worry, Mr. Morgan," Caraway says, and despite everything, I'm shocked at how polite he is to my da. I thought he would be more aloof to us poor country folk. "I won't let any harm come to Merry. I swear it."

I don't think I've ever heard him use my first name before. I'm not sure I like it.

"Why aren't you going?" I ask Da. "You're a Toadman too."

Da shakes his head. "Only the high-ups go to Deeping Fen."

"But Teddy is going."

"He's lucky," Da says. "You should be proud of him."

Da's gentle smile doesn't comfort me the way it should. A part of me wants to stay, to make sure he's all right. But I know I have to go with Caraway. I need to make sure Teddy is safe.

"Okay," I say. "Let's go."

5.

THE CAR IS EVEN MORE DECREPIT ON THE INSIDE THAN it is on the outside. The upholstery is fraying, and the vinyl on the steering wheel is flaking off. Caraway leaves me to wrestle my rucksack into the back and begins a lengthy and colorful diatribe as he attempts to start the engine.

"Is that really necessary?" I ask as I slide into the passenger seat. A loose spring digs into my thigh, and I shift uncomfortably. The car smells like something might have died in it.

"It needs some encouragement to get started," he explains. "It'll be fine once it gets going."

The car coughs and splutters, and even worse smells start to emerge from behind the dashboard. I glance over my shoulder and see a black cloud of exhaust billowing out behind us.

"Useless, thrice-cursed rustbucket," Caraway declares. "You are as useful as a fart in a jam jar. Six horseloads of dung upon you, lousy excuse for a motor vehicle. I hope twelve devils take you to Annwn, where you will be melted into pellets and fed to Arawn's wild hunt."

"Have you tried a gentler touch?" I ask. "A bit of a pep talk? Some sincere flattery?"

He glances over at me with a flat look. "Don't mock me."

I snort. "Of course not. I'm so sorry. Please go back to swearing at your car."

Eventually the engine shudders and rattles into life, with all the enthusiasm of an asthmatic donkey.

The car unsurprisingly has no suspension, and by the time we get to the end of the lane and join the main road, I feel like my teeth are about to fall out of my head.

"How is *this* your car?" I ask.

"What do you mean?" Caraway says. "What's wrong with it?"

"Literally everything. You are super posh and rich. Why this heap of junk?"

The car splutters in protest, and Caraway puts a soothing hand on the dashboard and shoots me a warning look.

"It's a passion project," he says. "I'm going to fix it up."

"You're . . . passionate about cars?" I would *not* have guessed this about Caraway.

"Not particularly. But I like learning about how things work, and I want a car of my own while I'm at Staunton."

"But what about the shiny black beast you get driven around in?"

"I don't know if you've noticed, Morgan, but people who get chauffeured around in their fathers' fancy cars don't tend to come across as being particularly approachable."

I blink. "You *aren't* very approachable."

"Well, maybe I want to change that."

I stare at him. Is Caraway Boswell saying . . . that he wants to make friends at university? That he cares what people think of him? The thought is unfathomable to me. Caraway Boswell doesn't need people. He's the coldest of cold fish. The iciest of ice queens. Is it possible he's *lonely*?

To distract myself from the very confusing and unwelcome feelings that this question brings up, I lean forward to switch on the radio.

"Don't—" Caraway starts, but I've already done it.

It's an Ilium radio—one of those ones that magically interprets your mood and plays a corresponding song. But from the look of this one, it's about ten years out of date. Music streams muddily through the speakers, and I let out a little shriek of recognition.

"'Little Lights'!"

Caraway's ears have turned bright pink, even through the ice-coolness of his glamour. "It's broken," he mutters. "It only plays that one song, over and over again."

"I *love* this song."

I roll down the window and sing along into the wind.

The banners fade away, we're both alone among the crowd
Bleeding hearts side by side
In the dark you find my hand, we make a little spark
Two particles collide

Big love
Little lights combine
You and I ignite

"By all that's sacred, Morgan," Caraway begs. "Please stop."

But I can see his finger tapping on the steering wheel. I laugh and for a moment I forget that a probably evil Toad cult has ensorcelled my best friend and my father. But then the song finishes, and I remember where we're going, and suddenly I'm full of questions.

"What can you tell me about ToadCon?" I ask Caraway, switching off the radio before the song starts again. "Does it happen every fifty years?"

He shakes his head. "The Trothal is a ceremony, honoring the fabled union between the King Toad and the Fox Bride."

"So it's a wedding."

"Not a real one. More of a ritual. You know about the King Toad, right?"

I remember the knock at the door on Whitsun Eve. "He's one of the three Toads—along with the Ghost Toad and the Howling Toad. So who is the Fox Bride?"

"She's one of the characters from the story. You know, the Green Knight, the Fox Bride, the Beast."

I shake my head.

"Haven't you seen the pantomime?"

"No," I say. "I've always found a reason not to attend. I thought the Toadmen had a strict no-women policy?"

Caraway clucks his tongue, as if chastising me for my absence. "The Fox Bride is the exception. She's part of our lore— you'd know if you went to the pantomime."

"But she's not played by a real woman, right?" I ask, ignoring his dig.

"In the panto they usually get a young Toadman to play her."

I mull this over for a moment. His explanation makes sense, but still—something in me wants to press harder. "But women attend this wedding ceremony," I say. "You all bring a date?"

"Sort of. It's the only time non-Toads are permitted inside the Deeping Court. Consorts don't actually attend the Trothal ceremony, though. Just the party the night before."

"Aren't they afraid we'll find out all their Toad secrets?"

"No, Morgan. They aren't."

The way he says it makes a chill run down my spine.

"So do the top-brass Toads meet more regularly?" I ask, shifting the subject.

"There are other things," Caraway replies. "Rituals and ceremonies. But your average Toadman—like your father—would never interact with them. Even individual branches tend not to mix."

Well, that's one silver lining.

"Which is why Da hasn't been to the swamp."

"That's right. The exact location of the Deeping Court is . . . well, it's a secret. But we're heading to Deepdene now, on the edge of Deeping Fen. We'll stay there tonight."

"And what happens when we do get there? To ToadCon, I mean?"

"Remember I've never been to one before," Caraway reminds me. "But my guess is a whole lot of pomp, circumstance and skullduggery. I know there's a ball on the first night, which is why we each bring a consort."

"Ah. Less like a ToadCon, and more like a Toad *Prom*."

Caraway lets out a little snort, and it's so startlingly undignified that I begin to reassess everything I know about him.

"There'll be a bunch of secret meetings and things during the day, and then the Trothal concludes on Sunday night with the wedding ceremony."

"Between the King Toad and the Fox Queen?"

"Fox Bride, yeah."

"So you finish with a panto?"

Caraway sighs. "Not exactly. The ceremony involves more gifts to the King Toad."

"Is he, like, the president of the Toads? Who are the three Toads really?"

Caraway shrugs. "You ask a lot of questions, don't you? The Toadmen are supposed to believe that they're the real deal— magical incarnations of the actual Toads of Deeping Fen. But really everyone knows they're just people."

"Do you know who they are?"

"Their identities are secret."

I notice that he didn't answer the question. "And these gifts— are we talking fruit baskets, or more strings?"

Caraway's grim expression is all the answer I need. "If Evans pledges there, then it's over," he says. "You'll never get him out."

"So what do I do? How do I get him not to give another string?"

"I don't know, Morgan. He's your friend. Convince him."

I narrow my eyes. "How come you're telling me all this? Isn't it all supposed to be a big secret?"

"Let's just say I have a healthy disrespect for authority."

"I guess you can afford to be a bad boy when Daddy can just throw money at any trespasses you make."

It's like watching the clouds cover the sun. The relaxed expression on Caraway's face vanishes, replaced by the usual cold, haughty disdain. He turns his head to regard the fields rushing past us, and I see his knuckles tighten on the steering wheel.

"So why me?" I ask. "Why am I here?"

Caraway's jaw tightens. "There's something there, in the Deeping Court. It belongs to me. I need you to help me find it. With your witch sight."

"Thread sight."

His eyes dart over to mine, then he looks back at the road. "Sure."

"How did you know—" I break off. "*They* know, don't they? The Toadmen?"

The thought of it sours my stomach.

Caraway doesn't look at me. "Not all of them."

"My da?"

He shakes his head. "I don't think so."

"How do *you* know? Who told you?"

He readjusts his grip on the steering wheel. "I heard a rumor, that's all."

I have so many more questions, but somehow the least important one comes out first. "Who is Esmerelda Huntington-Smythe?"

Caraway blinks. "Who?"

"Dr. Gower said you were taking her to Toad Prom."

"Oh." He shrugs. "Someone my father organized. Daughter of So-and-so, you know."

I do not know. "But you're taking me instead."

"Yep." The word could not possibly be more clipped.

"Your father must be disappointed."

Again, that slightly-too-long pause. "Being disappointed in me is my father's natural state of being."

"What did you say? About why you're taking me?"

Caraway bites his lip, as if he's considering how to reply. The sight of his perfect white teeth sinking into the soft flesh of his bottom lip does something quite unexpected to my insides.

"I told him that you were equal dux with me at Candlecott, and that I . . . liked you." It seems to take him a fair amount of effort to get these last words out.

I feel my cheeks warm and suddenly it's my turn to look out the window. "So you lied," I say, trying to sound breezy.

"Sure did."

"And now you're stuck spending the weekend with someone you hate."

He looks startled. "I don't hate you, Morgan."

Liar.

"And even if I did," he continues, "I hate the Toadmen more. We have that in common."

"So why not just quit?"

"Unfortunately it isn't that simple," Caraway says, staring straight ahead at the road.

Despite the heat of the day, I shiver.

"I have to get Teddy out," I tell him. "He doesn't belong there."

Caraway glances at me. "You have feelings for him."

I don't respond to this, because it's none of Caraway's business.

"Have you told him how you feel?"

My cheeks turn warm as I remember Teddy's strong arms around me. The softness of his lips on mine.

"Careful, Morgan," Caraway warns. "Nothing like a love affair to ruin a friend group."

I snort. "How would you know? You don't have any friends."

He shrugs. "I'm just saying. You three are very close, and who knows what will happen when you and Evans finally hook up?"

Sol would be *delighted* if Teddy and I started dating. I know it. He loves us both, and maybe if we were dating, we'd do less bickering. And it's not like Sol hasn't had plenty of boyfriends and girlfriends. Of the three of us, he is definitely the most experienced in affairs of the heart. I've had a few flings—Annie Thistle in seventh grade, Thomas Goh in eighth, and Finn Anise in ninth. Then Teddy and I kissed and I didn't want to be with anyone else.

Teddy doesn't date at all. He's always too busy at the forge, or hanging out with me and Sol. Once, I made him and Sol do some magazine quiz about finding their perfect match.

I've already found my perfect match, Teddy said with a grin. *I'm just waiting until the time is right.*

I shiver at the memory of it. Caraway raises his eyebrows.

Time to change the subject. "Did you bring any snacks?" I ask hopefully.

"I did not."

I sigh. "This is the worst road trip I've ever been on."

"I'm having a wonderful time too."

"Are we there yet?"

Caraway shoots me a warning glare. "Don't start. It's a long drive."

"At least tell me we're going to stop for lunch."

"I hadn't planned on it, no."

"You're telling me you expect me to sit in this rusty tin can of a car, with you, for the entire day, with no snacks, only 'Little

Lights' to listen to on the radio, and we're not even going to stop for lunch?"

"I thought you *loved* 'Little Lights.'"

"I do, but I'm hungry."

Caraway shrugs. "It is what it is."

"I *will* kill and eat you, if I get desperate enough."

A ghost of a smile passes over his lips. "You can try."

I let another few minutes go by, then try again. "I need to pee."

Caraway nods in a businesslike sort of way. "Shall I pull over?"

"*Here?*" I splutter. "On the side of a country road?"

"I wouldn't recommend doing it in the *middle* of the road," Caraway says. "But you do you, Morgan."

"I hate you."

"I promise I won't look."

I glare at him. "We're stopping at the next food vendor we pass, or else I pee on your upholstery."

Caraway holds up one hand in mock defeat. "If you insist, my lady."

THE TEAHOUSE IS . . . FRILLY.

Standing alone on the country road, surrounded by fields and hedgerows, it is fussy, floral and (to me, anyway) extremely welcome. Caraway looks dubious but pulls over anyway, the car's engine sputtering out with a somewhat desperate wheeze. I clamber out of the passenger seat, grateful for an opportunity to stretch my legs.

The building is red brick, with window boxes spilling over with petunias and nasturtiums. Frilled curtains fill every window, and an ornately calligraphic sign over the front door reads MISS PRINNY'S TEAROOMS.

"It looks delightful," I declare.

"It looks like the kind of place one gets murdered," Caraway mutters. "Those window boxes look *very* well fertilized."

I roll my eyes. "Come on," I say, starting toward the door.

"Aren't you just going to pop in, buy a sandwich, use the facilities and then we get back on the road?" Caraway says hopefully.

I shake my head. "We're eating in. I need a break from the Purple Menace."

INSIDE, MISS PRINNY'S TEA Rooms are even frillier than I could have imagined. Eyelet lace tablecloths spill over every table, and every other available surface is blanketed in lace doilies. Potted plants and flowers in vases crowd among little porcelain statues of shepherdesses and big-headed cats, and the walls are hung with framed cross-stitch samplers, which all say things like BLESS THIS MESS and LIFE IS BEAUTIFUL. The place smells like sweet peas and lilac and hot buttered scones.

We're the only people there, and a woman who I can only assume is Miss Prinny herself bustles out from the kitchen and seats us at what we are assured is the best table in the place.

"What brings you to Miss Prinny's today?" she asks, peering down at us through wire-framed glasses. She looks old enough to be my grandmother, but her wiry gray hair still has strands of copper escaping from under her frilled bonnet.

"Just passing through," Caraway says, radiating superiority and aloofness.

Miss Prinny looks at him and does a strange double take, her eyebrows drawing together in a confused and flustered frown.

She's a redhead, so Caraway's glamour doesn't work on her. She can see him as he truly is. I desperately want to ask her what he looks like, and wonder why I never bothered to find a redhead at school and ask them. *Are* there any redheads at Candlecott? I can't think of any, off the top of my head. The Cartwrights were a family of redheads, but they moved away from Candlecott a few years ago, before Caraway arrived.

"What can I get for you, then?" Miss Prinny asks, swallowing nervously.

"Just a water," Caraway says shortly, keeping his head turned away from her.

I scowl at him and turn to Miss Prinny. "Do I smell scones?" I ask her.

She seems to relax when she looks at me. "You certainly do. Served with blackberry jam and clotted cream. I also have a treacle tart fresh out of the oven, and some roast chicken that's *so* good in a sandwich with a little seeded mustard, chopped tarragon and watercress."

"That all sounds *amazing*," I say. "I'll have a bit of everything. And a pot of tea."

Any doubts I might have had that Caraway was lying before when he said he didn't hate me evaporate. His chiseled jaw twitches with frustration, and his hands clench fistfuls of frilly tablecloth as Miss Prinny returns to the kitchen and I smile angelically at him.

"Wish you were bringing Daughter of So-and-So to Toad Prom after all?" I ask.

Caraway sighs theatrically and snatches up a newspaper, opening it wide and holding it up so he doesn't have to look at me.

The front page is facing me now, and I see the headline: WITCH TRAITOR ESCAPES.

Suddenly I'm not hungry anymore. "Is that about her?" I ask. "The Spitalwick Hag?"

I snatch the paper and read.

The witch and terrorist known as the Spitalwick Hag has escaped from a high-security facility in Scouller. An auditor spokesperson stated today that every effort is currently being made to find and recapture the Hag, and recommends that Anglyon citizens be vigilant, use fresh household protection charms purchased from reputable vendors, and report any suspicious behavior to the auditors immediately.

The spokesperson went on to state that auditors have arrested six other witches in Fishgate and Laugharne. These witches will be sent to thaumaturgical recovery center Ruddock Farm. A spokesperson for Ilium, parent company of Ruddock Farm, stated today, "We are proud to have the opportunity to rehabilitate these dangerous terrorists. We hope that under our guidance, they will find a way back to being productive members of Anglyon society."

The Spitalwick Hag.

"You really don't like witches, do you?" Caraway asks.

"The Hag killed my mother," I say shortly.

"I'm sorry," Caraway responds. "I didn't know."

"Why would anyone *choose* to be a rebel witch?" I say. "Do they hate Anglyon so much?"

Caraway shrugs. "I mean, Anglyon *is* a semifascist state entirely controlled by three giant corporations, where anyone who dares speak out gets whisked away to Ruddock Farm and drained of their life-force."

"They don't *drain mettle* at recovery centers," I tell Caraway. "They help the witches. Cure them."

"Cure them of being alive. Have you ever met a witch that's survived a detention center without becoming a husk?"

I lift my chin. "We don't have witches in Candlecott. But I'm sure there are reformed witches somewhere. They're allowed to keep doing magic when they get out, as long as they have a license and stick to covenant spells."

"One hundred measly magic tricks," Caraway scoffs. "Did you know it's illegal to make up a new spell in Anglyon? A new potion or poppet or witch bottle?"

I do know. And I also know that Teddy has made new charms in the forge. I warned him, told him he'd get in trouble, but of course he didn't listen. Teddy never listens. And now look where we are.

"Magic restrictions keep us safe," I say.

Caraway scoffs. "Magic restrictions ensure that people have to *buy* their magic, because they're not allowed to make them. Think of the money the big magic corporations would lose if people could just whip up their own glamours and potions and enchanted cleaning products."

"You sound like Teddy," I mutter resentfully.

Caraway frowns. "You don't like that he's a witch."

"He *isn't* a witch," I protest. "He's a good person. And he's a man. Witches are women."

Caraway rolls his eyes. "It's not a binary, Morgan. Strong magic ability is rare in men, but it exists. That's why the Toads are so keen to have Evans on board."

The thought of this makes me want to throw up.

Caraway is still frowning at me. Like he's *disappointed.* "You really do believe all the antimagic propaganda they feed us at school, don't you?"

I squirm inside; then my discomfort blossoms into anger. "You're a hypocrite," I reply hotly. "You complain about magic restrictions and the big magic companies, but isn't your father a director at Ilium? Doesn't a big magic corporation pay for your tuition at Candlecott, and your fancy driver and all those expensive glamours? Aren't you *literally at this moment* escorting me to some kind of networking event for an exclusive men's club that you are a member of?"

Caraway's jaw tightens, and he shoots me a look of pure hatred. But he doesn't say anything.

I lean back in my chair, feeling satisfied.

Another car has pulled up outside, a sleek gray thing containing a sleek gray man. He strides toward Miss Prinny's without looking back, while from the passenger seat emerges a much, much younger woman, blond with significant cleavage on display.

"That had better be his daughter," I mutter darkly.

Caraway doesn't answer. He is staring at the man, his face looking even more glowery than usual.

The bell over the door tinkles and the gray man enters. Gray hair, gray suit, the color of steel. Gray eyes surveying the place, lingering for a moment on Caraway and me, then gliding away.

Miss Prinny emerges from the kitchen, staggering under the weight of a tray carrying a giant china teapot, painted with violets and ladybirds, a milk jug and two matching cups. She deposits this tray on our table with a sidelong, furtive glance at Caraway.

What does she see when she looks at him?

She hurries over to Mr. Gray and his Pubescent Lady Friend.

I pour out two cups of tea and put one in front of Caraway. He stares at it, unseeing.

"Are you okay?" I ask.

After a beat, he looks up at me. "Why wouldn't I be?"

"You're acting weird. Weirder than usual."

"I just want to get going. It's a long drive."

But that's not all. His eyes keep darting over to the table where Mr. Gray is sitting, smiling indulgently while his friend prattles on in a rather grating voice.

"Do you know them?" I ask.

"No."

He's lying.

Miss Prinny emerges again with another tray, bearing a giant chicken sandwich, a slab of treacle tart and a veritable mountain of scones.

"Miss Prinny," I tell her. "You are an exceptional human."

She smiles and bobs a curtsy, but her eyes dart uneasily from Caraway to Mr. Gray. She scurries back to the kitchen.

Caraway looks distastefully at the mountain of food. "I hope you don't expect me to eat any of this," he says.

"Nope," I say cheerfully with my mouth already full of crumbly, buttery scone. "All for me. Wouldn't dream of making you eat peasant food."

Caraway's lips become even thinner, and he shifts uncomfortably in his chair as the blond woman lets out a piercing shriek of laughter.

"Oh," I say, suddenly realizing. "He's a Toad, isn't he? That's why you recognize him. He's on his way to Toad Prom too, and that girl disgracefully isn't his daughter, she's his *date.*"

Caraway swallows. "Keep your voice down," he murmurs. "Just eat and let's leave."

I glance back over at Mr. Gray just in time to see him looking directly at me. His left eye has turned milky white. His tongue darts over his lips.

My own mouth turns dry, and bile burns at the back of my throat. I can't look away. Can't even blink.

What's going *on?*

I shudder and manage to tear my gaze away. When I look back, the man's eye is normal once more, and he's leaning over to whisper something in the girl's ear, his hand sliding possessively up her thigh.

Did I imagine it? I glance over at Caraway, who is staring stonily out the window. What does it mean? A milk-white eye? Was it some kind of spell? A curse?

Suddenly, the scones don't taste so good. My stomach churns and I feel light-headed.

"I'm just going to find the loo," I tell Caraway, and get to my feet. I follow calligraphic signs to a little outhouse. The fresh air on my cheeks makes me feel normal again, and I breathe deeply.

Maybe I imagined it.

But I remember the low chanting of the Toads in the Frater House, and the *snap* as one of Teddy's strings broke. The Toads are much more dangerous than a fusty gentlemen's club.

I use the toilet and wash my hands, splashing water on my cheeks. My face in the vanity mirror is pale, freckles standing out bold against my skin. I have a sudden urge to flee—to race off through Miss Prinny's backyard and into the wheat fields. To skulk along hedgerows, out of sight of the road, until I finally arrive back in Candlecott, where I'll be safe.

I open the door to the outhouse and clap a hand over my mouth in fright.

Mr. Gray is standing before me, waiting right outside the door. His left eye is milky white again, his expression blank. Up close, I realize he's glamoured too, like Caraway. It's the glamour that makes him seem so sleek, so . . . gray.

"Excuse me," I say, and hate how wobbly my voice sounds. "A little personal space?"

Mr. Gray doesn't respond, except to run his tongue around his lips, so fast I barely see it.

I try to sidle around him, but he's a good foot taller than me, and he puts out an arm to hold me in place. His other hand touches my cheek. He touches my hair and slides his hand around to cup the back of my neck, his cold fingers on my spine.

I try to cry out, to scream for Caraway, but I can't move. Can't speak. My scalp crawls as the clammy fingers press against the base of my skull. My lungs feel like they're filling with water, and I taste silt and pondweed.

My brain is telling my body to react—to kick Mr. Gray in the balls and run. But I don't move. My stomach churns and I gasp for breath.

"Let her go," Caraway says calmly.

He's standing by the door back into the tearoom, his glamour radiating cold authority. He raises his hands and makes a complicated gesture.

I look threadwise, and I'm startled to see that Caraway has witch hands—two silvery, spectral hands that are furiously weaving a loose net made of ghostly brown threads.

Caraway is a witch?

I've only ever seen one real witch, on a school trip to Scouller. I looked threadwise to see her using her witch hands to weave mettle into a poppet, just like Caraway is doing now, except that the witch was using regular silvery-thin mettle, not the brown threads that Caraway is weaving.

Mr. Gray's life-force is thick with brownish shadows. It pulses with energy, more like tree roots than the usual gossamer threads. Like I saw in Mwsogl Hollow, wrapped around the toad bone and heading for Teddy. It's not at all like the usual familial threads— the way that I carry threads from Da, and from Teddy and Sol. This mettle is *active*. Dominant. It is almost strangling Mr. Gray, the strands reaching out to me too, like hungry tentacles. As I focus more on it, I see spidery veins branching out and away, like a kind of network. I start to follow them, using my mettle-tracking ability to travel along the threads. They disappear off behind the horizon, and I'm afraid if I follow them too far, I won't be able to get back again.

I let my consciousness sink back into my own body, just in time to see Caraway throw his net at me, snagging me with it, tugging me away from Mr. Gray, whose face twists into a snarl. My skin burns hot where the brownish net touches it, and I try to cry out in pain, but all that emerges is a wet gurgle.

Mr. Gray speaks in a voice that is not his own. It sounds water-logged, like it's coming from a long way away. *"This is unnecessary, Caraway."*

Caraway hauls on the net. "I *said*, let her go."

The silty, brackish water is still filling my lungs, and I'm finding it hard to draw a full breath. The net is searingly hot. I feel tears slip from my eyes, and I'm genuinely not sure if they're tears of pain, or of frustration from not being able to move, to fight back.

"I'm not going to hurt her," Mr. Gray says. *"I'm just . . . curious."*

I splutter as my mouth fills with foul-tasting pond water, and turn desperate eyes to Caraway.

"Leave her alone," Caraway says from between clenched teeth. "I told you I'd handle it."

The net strains, and I see bits of brown mettle fragmenting and dissolving where they touch it. Mr. Gray's lip curls in a strange smile.

"She's strong," he says in his waterlogged voice. *"But she has no power of her own."* Then his milky eye turns clear, right in front of me, returning to steely gray. He straightens his shoulders a little and releases his hold on me.

"See you tomorrow, Brother Caraway," Mr. Gray says, sounding like an ordinary human again.

The water seems to drain from my lungs, and I take a huge gulp of air.

"Come on," says Caraway, grabbing my elbow and yanking me around the side of the building and back to the carpark.

My limbs move automatically; I can't quite take in what just happened, or what Caraway did and said. My mouth still tastes like pond water. Caraway bundles me into the Purple Menace, which miraculously starts on the first try. Gravel skids under the tires as we pull out of the carpark and onto the road. I don't turn to look back at Miss Prinny's to see if Mr. Gray is watching us go.

Caraway's hands are tight on the wheel, and I get the feeling it's to stop them from trembling.

We drive for several miles before I work up the courage to speak.

"Who was that man?"

Caraway's knuckles whiten on the wheel for a moment. "Just a garden-variety Toad."

The milky eye. The darting tongue. The voice that felt like it was being summoned from far away. Suddenly all the cautionary tales we got told as kids about witches like Jenny Greenteeth feel a bit more real.

"I'm sorry you didn't get to finish your lunch," Caraway says.

I have so many questions, but I don't ask any of them. Because Caraway Boswell is a witch, and if I know one thing, it's that you can't trust a witch.

I can't believe I didn't notice it before, in his mettle. But mettle doesn't show everything, especially something you want to keep a secret.

"When did you first learn to do it?" he asks at last.

"Do what?"

His eyes flick away from the road for a moment, to meet mine. "You can follow the mettle threads."

I swallow. "Don't you know?" I ask. "You already seem to know so much about me."

"All I know is that you can do it," he asks. "No details."

But *how* does he know? Who told him?

"I was thirteen," I say cautiously.

"How far can you go?"

I shrug. "I don't know," I say. "I—I don't do it often. Only when hunting rabbits."

"You've never tried to go farther?"

I shake my head. Why would I?

"I've never met anyone who could do that before." The way he says it, I know that Caraway has met a lot of people who could do other things. Magical things.

"I'm not a witch," I say quickly, because I'm not.

"You can turn witch-eyed."

"Threadwise," I say. "It's . . . not the same thing. Witches manipulate mettle."

"And I can only work with Toad mettle," he says. "I'm not a proper witch."

"What is it?" I ask him, my voice barely more than a whisper. "The Toad mettle? I see it on my da, sometimes. Is it some kind of curse?"

"Not exactly. But it's nothing good."

I want to press him further, but a little part of me whispers a warning as I remember what he said to Mr. Gray. *I told you I'd handle it.* Handle what? Handle *me?*

I can't trust Caraway. Can't trust any Toad.

We lapse into silence.

AS WE DRIVE ON into the afternoon, the countryside grows bleak and colorless. The neat fields and hedgerows are replaced by gray moors and rocky outcrops. There are fewer and fewer signs of human habitation, and even inside the car, the air feels chilly and damp.

Caraway is as pale as the sky above us, his eyes fixed on the road.

"Why Deeping Fen?" I say at last. "Is there something special about it, or does it just have a really cheap conference center?"

Caraway glances at me. "You really don't know the story of the three toads?" he asks. "The one they perform at the harvest pantomime?"

"I have spent the last five years trying very hard not to learn anything about toads."

"Well, buckle up, Morgan, because this weekend you are going to learn far more than you ever wanted to know."

"How utterly marvelous."

We've lapsed back into banter, which is a thousand times preferable to the awkward exchange of magical secrets.

"Are you sitting comfortably?" he asks.

"No."

Caraway ignores this and begins his story. "Long ago, a Beast threatened the town of Deepdene, on the edge of Deeping Fen."

"What kind of a beast?" I ask.

"Not important. Some kind of monster."

"It *seems* important."

"Stop interrupting. The Beast captured a beautiful maiden from the town and hid her away in the depths of Deeping Fen, a gloomy and dangerous bog."

I make a disapproving noise. "Always capturing maidens. Let me guess, a knight arrived to rescue her?"

"The Green Knight."

"Does the girl get a name? I bet she doesn't. They never get a name in these stories."

Caraway glances at me. "She's known as the Fox Bride."

"She's the one getting married this weekend."

"Indeed."

"Is she a fox? Why doesn't she get her own name?"

"No idea. That's just what she's called."

"Maybe the Beast was a fox."

"Seriously, Morgan. Do you want to hear the story or not?"

"I'm fifty-fifty each way, to be honest."

I see a twitch at the corner of Caraway's mouth, and feel absurdly pleased to have made him *almost* smile.

"The Green Knight came to slay the Beast and claim the hand of the Fox Bride—*yes*, Morgan, I understand how much this disgusts you, but just wait. It's not like other stories. The Green Knight failed. The magic of the fen turned him all muddled; he became utterly lost."

"You know what I like about this story?" I ask.

"What?"

"Literally nothing. Please continue."

"After days of wandering aimlessly in the fen, the Green Knight grew very weak. He received a bite from a marsh fly that soured his blood, and found himself dying, alone and without hope or solace. A toad came along and the Green Knight told him his sorry tale, and with his last breath asked the toad to defeat the Beast and rescue the Fox Bride, as he had failed to do it himself."

"Wait," I say. "His last breath? The Green Knight dies?"

"Yes."

"From a *marsh fly bite?*"

"Yes."

"That's . . . kind of pathetic."

Caraway shrugs. "There are some pretty nasty insects in Deeping Fen."

I shake my head. "A *marsh fly.*"

"So the toad took the Green Knight's sword, gathered his two brothers, and found the Beast in his lair, preparing to eat the Fox Bride."

"Gross. Did the Beast eat the toads?"

Caraway shakes his head. "Nobody wants to eat a toad."

"Tell that to a barn owl."

"Well, *this* beast didn't want toads. All toads are toxic, did you know? They have glands that secrete poison when they get stressed."

I make a face. "Just when I thought I couldn't hate this any more."

"Anyway, the toad told the Beast that if it could answer a riddle, the toad would give it his toadstone."

"His what?"

"Toadstone. A magical jewel that lets you see through the eyes of any toad."

"Sounds very useful. What was the riddle?"

"The king's is blue, the farmer's red. Mine is cold, and yours will be shed."

I blink. "That sounds less like a riddle and more like a threat."

"While the Beast was thinking it over, one of the toad's brothers was sneaking around, looking closely at its thick hide, searching for a weak spot. This brother was known as the Ghost Toad, because he could move unseen by the keenest eyes. He found the weak point at the base of the Beast's neck, and showed it to our hero toad—"

"No hero of mine."

"—through the use of the toadstone."

"The jewel that lets you see through the eyes of any toad."

"Exactly. But at that moment, the Beast solved the riddle. The answer, in case you haven't guessed already, Morgan, is *blood*."

"I'm *shocked*. So did the toad give in and hand over the toadstone?"

"Of course not. The Beast decided it would just kill the toad and take the stone. But a horrible noise sounded at that moment, behind the Beast. A howling scream, enough to make fear creep into the heart of the very bravest soul."

"The Howling Toad, right?" I say.

"You have been paying attention after all, Morgan. Well done."

I poke my tongue out at him. "So the Howling Toad made a scary noise . . ."

"And the Beast turned its head, to see what terrible monster had made it."

"Ah. I see where this is going."

"The vulnerable spot exposed, the toad drove the Green Knight's sword into the Beast's neck, killing it instantly. It then returned to Deepdene with the Fox Bride, and the Beast's head. The people were overjoyed, and bestowed riches and honors upon the toad, making him their king. He married the Fox Bride and ruled the land with a firm, just hand until the end of his days."

Caraway leans back in his seat.

"Is that it?" I ask.

He nods. "That's it."

"It's kind of a terrible story."

"It is what it is."

"But none of it's real. It's just a story—the toad, the magical jewel. It's just pantomime stuff."

Caraway shrugs. "There's power in stories."

Unconsciously, his fingers drift to his left bicep and trace the edges of the glamour patch under his T-shirt, as if reassuring himself it's still there.

"Why do you wear it?" I ask him.

"Wear what?" he responds, as if he doesn't already know exactly what I'm talking about.

"The glamour. Rumor is you never take it off, not even to sleep."

"Don't believe every rumor you hear."

"I believe this one. Come on, tell me. Are you horribly disfigured?"

"Yes."

For a moment I can't tell if he's joking or not. "Really?"

"Car accident. I was just a little kid. I'm lucky to be alive. My parents took me to every skin specialist in Anglyon, even to a Thulian bonesetter. But there was only so much they could do."

He says it all so matter-of-factly, and I feel like a total pillock. "I'm sorry," I say.

He shrugs. "When I was little, people used to stare at me all the time. Other kids would ask their parents why I was so ugly, only to get *shhh*'d and hurried away. I get noticed enough being . . . a Boswell. The glamour . . . well, people don't stare anymore."

Of course. The haughtiness, the ice-cold beauty. It makes you look away. Makes you afraid of him.

I glance around at the faded upholstery and brittle plastic of the Purple Menace and think that maybe I understand Caraway a little better now.

It starts to rain.

The land on either side of the car has sunk, or the road has risen up, I'm not sure. But it feels like we're flying over a sea of wet, peaty marshland that stretches out in all directions, gray and brown and flat. It feels so empty. I see no birds. No animals. No trees. Nothing except waterlogged grasses and heather.

"Is this the fen?" I ask.

"Not yet," Caraway replies. "But we're getting close."

The sky darkens as evening approaches, and Caraway switches the headlights on. All I can see now is the rushing road disappearing beneath us, illuminated in yellow light. Everything else is dark gray and wet.

Caraway turns off the main road, onto something bumpy

and squelching. My stomach churns in anticipation. I'm not sure what I'm getting myself into, but I've felt relatively safe inside this ridiculous purple car. I clear my throat and taste muddy water.

"I think this was a bad idea," I say.

"No shit," Caraway responds.

"Let's go, then," I say, turning to look at the outline of his face in the dark. "Turn the car around and let's go home."

He sighs heavily. "If only."

"Then let me out here," I say, seized with a sudden urgency. "I'll hitchhike home. You can blame everything on me, I don't care."

"And what about Evans?" Caraway asks softly.

I let out a long, shaking breath. I feel like I'm about to cry. "I don't know if I can help him," I say. "So far I've just made everything worse."

Caraway watches the road for a long while. "The string he gave at that first initiation," he says at last. "It gets turned into a stone. A toadstone. The stone will be placed in a sacred chamber at that final ceremony—the wedding with the Fox Bride. If you can find the stone before that happens, then there's a chance you can get him out."

I feel a sudden flare of hope. "Where is it?" I ask. "This stone?"

"I don't know for sure," Caraway says. "But I can make an educated guess. I'll help you."

I gaze out at the blackness beyond the car. "Why do I get the feeling that we're about to do something really foolish?" I ask.

"Because we are," Caraway replies.

6.

IT'S PROPERLY DARK BY THE TIME WE PULL INTO A gravel parking lot. It's hard to find a spot for the Purple Menace, so I guess we must be some of the last ones to arrive. We crawl past a long line of sleek, expensive-looking cars, and one battered white van with a little cardboard blacksmith's hammer hanging from the rear-vision mirror.

Teddy's van.

We pull up next to the sleek car that belongs to Mr. Gray, and I suddenly taste pond water again.

I climb out of the car and my sneakers sink into several inches of water lying on top of the gravel. I shudder as cold water seeps into my socks. Moisture hangs heavy in the cold air. Everything smells damp and rotten, overlaid with the thick greasy scent of burning fat.

"Welcome to Deepdene," Caraway says flatly. "It's pretty awful."

An insect buzzes past my ear and I bat at it, unsuccessfully.

The village before us is dimly lit by yellow light spilling from windows, and from torches that spit and gutter in the gentle rain. The torches let off a foul-smelling greasy smoke that stains the timber around each one.

"It's on stilts," I observe as I take in wooden boardwalks and squat raised buildings, each with low, overhanging eaves to keep the rain from the windows.

"The only way to stop the whole place from sinking into the fen," Caraway says, and starts off toward the lights.

"Don't we need to get our bags?" I say.

Caraway waves an airy hand. "Someone will deal with them."

Of course they will. In Caraway Boswell's life, someone always deals with the bags. I remember the same haughty tone in his voice on the steps of school, that first day we met, and I remember that I hate him. Somehow this weird, creepy day made me forget. But I'm back now. Caraway Boswell, arrogant git.

He leads me up a few slimy wooden steps and along a boardwalk. The whole town seems to be built this way, branching boardwalks with dwellings leading off each one, all raised about six feet or so above the marshy ground. The houses are small and shabby. In one grimy window, I see two pale-faced children staring out at me, their dark eyes sharp with curiosity.

It's like we've stepped back in time, or into the scary part of a fairy tale, long before the happily ever afters.

"I can't believe this place exists," I comment. "It's like the worst theme park I've ever been to. Do people ever come here? Tourists?"

"Of course not," Caraway replies. "Why would anyone volunteer to come here?"

It's a fair point.

We approach a larger building—two stories, and spreading out on either side. I can hear raucous voices coming from within, and the whine of a badly played fiddle.

"Pub?" I guess.

Caraway nods and pushes the door open.

The pub smells like sour ale and stale pipe smoke. Fenlanders cluster in groups around grimy tables, clutching tankards and talking with raised voices to be heard over the fiddle player, a sallow-faced woman who approaches her craft with little joy.

The Fenlanders are pale and rather fishy-looking. They all have large, dark eyes and thin stringy hair that hangs limply around their shoulders. Their clothes are made from rough-spun cloth—the women in long skirts and aprons, the men in rough trousers and open-collared shirts. Everything looks old and grimy and spotted with mildew.

I look around for Teddy, but he isn't here.

Caraway doesn't even seem to notice the Fenlanders. Of course he doesn't—his world has no room for people like this. He approaches the bar like he owns the place, and instantly gets the attention of an older man with a grizzled beard, who I assume to be the innkeeper.

"I believe there are rooms booked for me," Caraway says.

The man pulls out a ledger. "Name," he says shortly.

"Caraway Boswell."

The change in the innkeeper is instantaneous. He swallows heavily and puts down his pen. His shoulders curl inward over his chest, like he's trying to make himself look smaller. He doesn't look up at us; instead he blinks furiously down at his ledger.

"O' course, young master. Got the best rooms prepared. Right this way."

He even *bows* at Caraway before leading us out of the tap-room and down a long, narrow corridor, then up a flight of stairs and out into what passes for fresh air in this place. We follow him across a rather slippery boardwalk and up another flight of stairs to a building with two doors facing us.

"Someone'll be up with yer bags," the innkeeper says. "An' some vittles for ye both."

He bows again and disappears into the night.

"What now?" I ask as we pause outside the doors. I feel bone-weary, like I've been walking all day, instead of sitting on my bum in an admittedly fairly rubbish car. "Is there some kind of Toad-Con mixer we have to attend?"

"Not tonight," says Caraway. "No socializing until we get there tomorrow."

"Get *where*, exactly?" I ask, looking out into the darkness. "Is there . . . a conference center or something nearby? Or are we going to be dancing in our knickers under a full moon, up to our knees in bog water?"

"Something in between," Caraway says enigmatically, and opens his door. "Just eat your dinner and get a good night's sleep. Tomorrow is another long day."

I open my own door and hesitate on the threshold. "Are we safe here?" I ask.

Caraway nods. "Sure. Just don't leave your room until I come and get you in the morning. Okay?"

"Okay."

Everything in the room is in muddy shades of brown and

green. A reed mat covers the floor. Electric lights flicker weakly in sconces on the walls, and everything smells musty and damp.

A simple single bed sits against one wall, and a small desk against the other. I can see a bathroom with a shower and toilet behind a mossy curtain.

If these are the *best* rooms in Deepdene, I'd hate to see their budget offerings.

I perch on the edge of the bed. I can hear chirping insects outside, and the drip and slap of water. Muffled voices coming from the pub.

I wonder if Teddy's nearby.

There's a knock at my door—a Fenlander with my rucksack, followed by a slight girl carrying a heavy tray, which she places on the desk.

"D'you come alonga we?" she asks, and I blink.

"I'm sorry?" I say.

"Far?" The girl tries again. "D'you come from far?"

"Oh!" I reply, understanding. "Um, yes, I suppose so."

Candlecott feels like it's on the other side of the world. I suddenly miss home, miss Da. I wish he were here, but I'm glad he isn't.

Teddy is, though. My heart jogs when I think of him. Maybe I could slip out and find him.

The girl points to something pale and floppy in a bowl. "Chitterlins," she says, then points to the other dishes. "Bread. Tur'le soup, an biled puddens f'afters."

I try to smile, but the smell rising from the meal makes it hard to feign enthusiasm. "Thank you," I tell the girl, who bobs a curtsy and hurries out.

My stomach growls. All I've eaten today are those few bites of Miss Prinny's scones, before Mr. Gray came and ruined my appetite. I'm starving.

The turtle soup smells like hot pond water—muddy and a little salty. The lumps of dark gray meat floating in it do not look enticing. Even the boiled pudding looks unappetizing—pale and sweating with semicongealed fat.

I sigh and tear off a chunk of bread. It's chalky and flavorless. I should have asked Miss Prinny to wrap up my scones for the road.

I jump suddenly as another knock sounds on my door. Scrambling to my feet, I hesitate, my hand outstretched to the handle.

It could be Teddy.

Or it could be Mr. Gray.

"Morgan, it's me."

Caraway. Could be better. Could be worse.

I let him in, and he enters awkwardly, his eyes skirting around the room like he's expecting to find someone hiding in here with me. He's holding a supermarket carry-bag in one hand.

"Can I help you?" I ask.

"I came to see if your dinner looks as terrible as mine."

I gesture toward the desk.

Caraway inspects the first bowl, picking up a fork and poking the pale floppy substance with a mix of fascination and horror. "What even is this?"

"Chitterlings," I tell him. "My gran used to make them."

"Do I want to know?"

"Pig intestines boiled in vinegar."

He shudders. "Nope."

"The rest of it isn't much better." I wave the chalky bread at him. "And there isn't enough of this to share."

He grins at me and heads over to my bed. "Well, lucky for you, *I'm* very good at sharing." He empties the bag out onto the bed, and I gasp.

If I have one weakness, it's junk food. Give me your starry rock, your aniseed spogs, your pink sugar mice. I want it all. And Caraway has outdone himself. Packets of sour apple pips and Summer Lane bars and apple stripe licorice. I don't know where to start.

"Caraway Boswell, I take back everything mean I ever said about you," I breathe, gazing reverently at the pile of sugary treats like a dragon surveying their hoard.

"You're welcome."

I tear the cellophane off a box of dew drops. "You said you didn't have any snacks!"

He shrugs. "If you'd eaten all this in the car, then we wouldn't have any left for dinner."

Of course he knew the food here would be terrible. This isn't his first visit.

"How many times have you been here before?" I ask, my mouth full of sweet gum.

"This will be my third," he says, sitting down on the far side of my bed and helping himself to one of the few savory items— a packet of shrimp-flavored crisps. "When I was five, and then again a couple of years ago."

"Why did you go?" I ask. "You said there hasn't been a Trothal for fifty years."

Caraway sits down on my bed. "Other Toad stuff," he says evasively.

"And the people of Deepdene are cool with a bunch of Toad-men randomly descending upon them every few years?"

"I believe they are handsomely compensated."

"They are . . . kind of strange."

"Deeping Fen is a strange place."

He's barefoot, in jeans and a plain white T-shirt that hugs a nicely proportioned torso. Not *Teddy* nice, of course. But not terrible. He looks . . . relaxed. It's deeply incongruous against the coldness of his glamour, but I think I'm learning to see past the haughty facade to the real Caraway underneath. And . . . it's not in the slightest what I expected.

"Is it all like this?" I ask. "Stilts and greasy lamps?"

"The Deeping Court is . . . well, it's old. And rather ornate. No stilts."

"How old?"

Caraway shrugs. "As old as the King Toad himself."

I shake another handful of dew drops into my hand. "But you said they were just people. Ceremonial positions. Do you really think the story is true? About the toad, and the Beast, and the Fox Bride?"

"Every story tells a truth," Caraway says. "And every story tells a lie. I don't know which is which."

I remember the sharp *snap* of Teddy's string. "Should I be worried?" I ask. "Is it going to be dangerous?"

"Not if you do as I say, and don't get into any trouble."

"Reassuring."

Caraway tilts his head as if to say *That's the best I can do.* Then he nods at the colored sweets in my hand. "That stuff'll rot your teeth."

"Well, you brought them in here, so I guess whatever happens to my teeth is your fault?"

Caraway shakes his head, but he's smiling.

I look at the box. AN ILIUM PRODUCT.

"Do you get a discount?" I ask. "Because your father is a director?"

The smile fades from Caraway's face, and he shakes his head. "No discount."

I pop another dew drop into my mouth and let the little explosion of blackcurrant melt on my tongue.

"These were my ma's favorites," I say, without really knowing why.

Caraway glances sideways at me. "You said the Spitalwick Hag killed her," he says. "You must have been a baby."

"She died four years ago."

Caraway raises an eyebrow. "But the Hag has been in prison for seventeen years."

"The Hag cursed my ma," I explain. "When she was pregnant with me."

I tell him about the waters at Mwsogl Hollow, and the fight that happened that night.

A slight frown crinkles his forehead. "But your ma didn't die until thirteen years later."

"She knew it was the curse, though."

"Oh." The way he says it, I get the sense that he doesn't believe me.

"I think that's why I can . . ." I wave a vague hand. "I think I got cursed too."

The frown deepens. "Morgan, your ability isn't a curse. It's a *gift.* A witch couldn't have given you that. It doesn't work that way. Your gift is your own."

I know about gifts. Everyone has one. Da's is chickens. Sol's is music. Teddy's is smithing. I don't have one. Ma always said the Spitalwick Hag stole my gift and replaced it with a curse.

"What's yours?" I ask Caraway. "Your gift?"

He looks away, suddenly uncomfortable.

"Is it something embarrassing?" I say hopefully. "Are you an incredible clog dancer? Or can you make babies cry just by looking at them?"

He toys with a packet of laver crackers. "Sure," he says. "Take your pick."

He isn't going to tell me. Fine. "What about your mother?" I ask. "I know your dad has a fancy job, but I don't know anything about the rest of your family."

"My mother is . . . very devoted to my father. She spends her whole life organizing charity dinners and benefits."

"No siblings?" I ask.

He shakes his head.

"They must be proud of you," I say. "Joint dux. The Staunton scholarship."

Caraway looks down at his hands. His shoulders are tight. "I'm not sure my father sees it that way. I'm pretty sure I'm a disappointment to him. To both of them."

I remember the look on Da's face when he saw me in the Frater House. The way his disappointment made my heart ache. It's not something I experience very often. I can't imagine feeling like that all the time.

"I bet they *are* proud, though. Both of them," I say, trying to sound reassuring.

(Why am I trying to reassure Caraway Boswell?)

His mouth twists, as if he's eaten something sour. "I'll try to remember that next time my father tells me it's my fault that my mother is crying."

I pull the crinkly wrapper from a bonfire toffee, trying to imagine the giant fancy house that Caraway lives in. I bet it's huge, and full of old expensive furniture that you're not allowed to sit on, or touch without washing your hands first. There'll be servants who do all the cooking and cleaning. Caraway would eat dinner with his parents at a comically long table, the three of them spaced out far enough that they don't have to talk to each other.

It must be lonely.

"Are you looking forward to Staunton?" I ask.

"I'm looking forward to a few years of freedom," he replies. "Aren't you?"

I hesitate. "I'm not going."

Caraway snorts. "Of course you're going. What possible reason would you have not to?"

I eat another bonfire toffee instead of answering.

"Evans?" Caraway frowns. "You're going to stay in Candlecott because of Teddy Evans?"

"Not just because of Teddy," I say. "My da too."

"And what, you'll become a goodwife? Get married and have a brood of children?"

I prickle with defensiveness. "What's wrong with that?" I ask.

"Not everyone is destined for greatness."

"But *you* are, Morgan!" He seems genuinely angry. "*You* are destined for greatness. You have to go to Staunton and learn all the things and meet all the right people and go out into the world and do something *incredible*. Tell me you don't want that."

I do want it.

That's the problem. I want to go to Staunton and stroll through ancient courtyards. Get lost in libraries. Learn everything there is to know and more. I want to sit under a huge oak tree, surrounded by blue stone turrets and spires crusted with ivy, with books and notes spread out before me in the afternoon sun.

Of course, I can't say any of that to Caraway. "I can't leave Da," I mumble instead.

"There's no way your father wants that for you," he states.

"You don't know my da."

"I know he wouldn't want you to give up on your dream to molder away in Candlecott."

"It isn't my dream."

But Caraway can see the lie. He tilts his head to the side.

"What are you afraid of?" he asks, in a tone that implies he already knows the answer.

"I don't want to be alone," I tell him.

"Morgan, there are thousands of other students at Staunton. People like you, smart and full of fire. You'll make new friends."

The thought of it fills me with horror. New friends? I don't want new friends. New friends would mean I'm leaving Teddy and Sol behind. Demoting them. It would be the very worst kind of betrayal.

"That's not it, though," he says. "Not the thing you're *truly* afraid of."

In the back of my mind, I hear a shrill cackle. Caraway's eyes are on me, and it's like he can hear it too. Like he knows.

"Nothing," I say. "I don't want to talk about it anymore."

Caraway watches me for a long moment. "I get it," he says. "The future is scary."

This, I can relate to. "Sometimes I wish nothing would ever change," I murmur.

I look into Caraway's eyes and see a kind of hollow dread there, and I know that Caraway wants the exact opposite. He wants everything to change.

The thought of it makes me feel ill. I look down at the toffee wrapper in my hand.

AN ILIUM PRODUCT.

I swallow the toffee all in one gulp and feel it travel down my throat like a ball sinker attached to a fishing line.

Caraway has obviously arrived at a similarly uncomfortable place, because he climbs off my bed abruptly.

"It's late," he says. "I'd better go."

"Thanks for the snacks," I reply, getting up and following him to the door. "You didn't have to share them with me. That was nice."

Caraway hesitates on the threshold, a frown crinkling his brow.

"Morgan," he says, then breaks off.

His eyes don't look like glaciers in this moment—instead they're the softest pale blue velvet. He puts a hand out and tucks a loose strand of hair behind my ear, and without thinking I raise my own hand to rest on his bicep, keeping him there, close enough to feel the tremble in his breath.

My heart is beating faster than it should be. I'm not sure what's about to happen, but I get the feeling it's something momentous.

I can feel the glamour patch under Caraway's T-shirt, and I have a sudden desire to tear it off. I want to see the real Caraway. No glamour. No fake chill. I want to know who he really is, with all his defensive barriers stripped away. My fingers trace the edges of the patch, and suddenly I feel him stiffen and turn his face away from mine.

His face. Of course he feels self-conscious about it. I want to tell him that I don't care how he looks. That . . . I think maybe I want to know him properly, without any masks between us. But the words get stuck in my throat.

"Good night," Caraway says shortly over his shoulder, still keeping his face hidden from me.

He can't get away fast enough.

I close the door, feeling deeply confused. There was a moment there, where I thought that Caraway and I . . . I shake my head. Ridiculous. I don't want that, and neither does he.

I sweep the junk-food wrappers into the bin and lie down on my bed, still fully clothed.

But I can't stop thinking about it.

About him.

About his hand on my hair. His eyes. His bare feet tucked under him as he relaxed on my bed.

This is very, very bad.

I am *not* here to explore weird feelings for Caraway.

Go and see him, a terrible voice inside me says. *Just to be sure.*

I'm halfway across the room before I stop myself. This is nonsense. It's just . . . been a long day. I don't *like* Caraway. I hate him. Caraway is a stiff-necked, priggish, arrogant doorknob of a human being. He's the coldest of cold fish, and the only feeling I have in regard to him is contempt.

Prove it, says the voice.

I slip my still-wet sneakers back on and step outside. As I raise my fist to knock on Caraway's door, I stop. There are voices coming from inside. Caraway's and . . . someone else. It's a voice I recognize. It's the same voice I heard coming from Mr. Gray's mouth at Miss Prinny's.

"*—forced to explore other options,*" the waterlogged voice is saying.

"But . . . *her?*" Caraway asks. "Surely she isn't good enough for us."

Is he talking about *me?*

"*I have assessed her,*" the voice says, wet and slimy as pond scum. "*She is ideal. Are you getting sentimental?*"

"Of course not," Caraway responds. "She is nothing to me."

"*Then you will bring her to our king.*"

There's a pause, then Caraway asks, "Why was Edward Evans invited? He's nobody."

"*He is strong,*" the voice says. "*The strongest initiate I have seen in a long time. I have plans for him.*"

I back away from the door. I can taste pond water in the back of my throat, and my hands feel clammy and ice-cold.

Caraway still hasn't explained why he was so keen for me to accompany him to Deeping Fen. He said something about using my thread sight, but what if it's more than that? What if there is another plan? A plan that involves me *and* Teddy? It can't be anything good.

We have to get out of here.

I head down the steps and slip through the back door to the pub, in the long corridor the innkeeper led us down. Then I look threadwise. I know Teddy has been here. I can find him.

Mettle-tracking is hard. People don't leave their mettle behind unless it's in a place of significance. Mettle collects in places that are important—where there are keepsakes and mementos. It can be generated when people sing familiar songs, or dance, or even perform daily rituals like making tea or brushing their teeth. It lingers in dead things that once lived—rock and bone and twig. But it's strongest in the living.

I don't care what Caraway says, I'm no witch. I cannot manipulate mettle. But I know that what I can do is unusual. I can see echoes of mettle in the air, where a person has recently been. Identify who it belongs to, and, if I try very hard, use it to track them down.

I don't know if it's a gift or a curse. But I know it's how I'll find Teddy.

The air in the pub is as thick with mettle as it is with smoke. A few eyes turn to me when I enter, but the Fenlanders clearly want nothing to do with me. The bartender studiously ignores me, like he's hoping I won't do anything as foolish as trying to order a drink.

I take a deep breath, my lungs filling with the acrid scent of muskweed smoke. The Fenlander mettle is easy to dismiss: it's all thickly braided together, connecting them to each other and to this place.

There are other threads, though, solitary silver echoes, each one shadowed with spidery brown Toad mettle. I breathe deeply and fix Teddy in my mind, just Teddy, and let all the other threads fade away. And I see it, the faintest wisp of silver, leading out of the pub and down a boardwalk. I stand very still and follow the echo with my mind, letting it carry my consciousness along with it. It takes a great deal of concentration, and sweat breaks out on my brow despite the clammy chill of the evening. The trick to it is tuning out all the other echoes, and the real live mettle that is so bright and loud it would drown out all else. I have to work very hard.

Teddy's echo leads to a series of cabin-like structures leading off a central boardwalk. I let my sight return to normal and follow the path with my feet, until I am standing before a door.

I know what I have to do. What I *want* to do. Teddy needs to know that he can trust me. That I'm the person, more than anyone else, who has his best interests at heart. It's time for us to choose each other. Not Toads. Not Caraway or any other nonsense. Me and him. It feels *right*, and I know he feels it too.

I open the door and step in.

Teddy turns his head. He's shirtless, jeans sitting low on his hips. The fireplace lights him up as if he's made of gold, and it's nothing to cross the room to go to him. Shock registers on his face, but before he can say anything, I put my hands on his chest, rise up onto tiptoes, and press my mouth to his.

It's perfect.

I melt against him, letting my fingers splay across the comforting solidity of his chest, allowing myself a moment to admire the smooth curves of his muscles.

Teddy.

My Teddy.

At last.

He puts his hands on my shoulders and gently draws away. His cheeks are flushed, his eyes wide.

"Merry?" he says.

I can barely form words. "I'm here to rescue you," I tell him.

His brow furrows. "I don't need *rescuing*."

And he lets his hands fall from my shoulders, turning to pull a T-shirt from his overnight bag.

"Are you *mad* at me?" I ask, confused.

"Yes!" Teddy explodes. "You keep *spying* on me, Merry! You nearly ruined everything, back at the Frater House. Your da was nearly *expelled*. And now you've somehow invited yourself here!"

"I didn't *invite myself*," I tell him, defensive. "You saw what happened. I had to come."

"You could have gotten out of it," he says. "You can always find a way. But no. You had to come here, so you could continue to poke your nose into *my* business."

This stings. Teddy's business *is* my business. It always has been. That's the way it is with best friends.

"Teddy," I say. "The Toads are dangerous. Really dangerous. They're messing with all kinds of illegal magics."

Teddy shakes his head. "I know what I'm doing, Merry. I don't need you to look after me."

I feel tears rising behind my eyes, but clamp down. I will *not* cry in front of Teddy. I have to make him *see*.

"Well, maybe *I* need you to look after *me*," I say. "They know about me, Teddy. About the witch's curse. They know I can see threadwise. And I think they told Da."

Teddy hesitates, and for a moment I think I'm finally getting through to him. But then he brushes it aside like it's nothing.

"And what was *that* all about?" he says instead, waving a hand at me. "You barge in here and *kiss* me? Why?"

My cheeks flame red. "I—I thought that's what you wanted."

He shakes his head. "You made me *swear* not to fall in love with you," he says at last. "You *expressly* forbade it."

"When we were *seven*," I say. "Things are different now."

"Yeah," he says, shaking his head. "Yeah, they are."

I hope that this horrible place sinks right into the fen, this very instant, taking me and Teddy with it. I can't bear to stand here for another moment. I turn to flee, but the door behind me opens, and Sol is standing there, wearing his pajamas.

Questions fly into my mind. Is Sol joining the Toadmen too? Or is he here as Teddy's date?

Like, *date*, date?

Surely not.

"Hi, Merry," Sol says, his eyes darting to Teddy.

At least he has the good grace to look slightly ashamed.

"You were coming all along," I say, astonished. "I came to you for *help*, and you lied to me!"

Pink stains Sol's brown cheeks. "I didn't lie," he says quietly.

"As good as."

My brain catches up to what's going on, and my panic abates somewhat. Of course that's who Teddy would bring as his consort. There's no rule stating you have to bring someone you're romantically interested in. Caraway brought me, after all. Teddy invited Sol, one of his very best friends.

A tiny candle of hope flickers in my heart. I shouldn't have sprung this all on Teddy. Our feelings for each other have gotten all mixed up in this silly fight. I can fix it.

"Merry was just leaving," Teddy says shortly, and I wince at his tone.

Sol looks between us, his expression torn. "Teddy," he says. "Why don't we all just sit down? We've got a lot to talk about."

Teddy frowns at him, shaking his head in a sharp, decisive jerk. "She's not ready to listen."

He's talking about me like I'm not even here.

"We could just play cards or something," Sol suggests. "The three of us?"

But Teddy turns away from us both. "I'm tired," he says.

Sol puts a hand on his shoulder and murmurs something in his ear that I can't hear. Teddy just glowers down at the fire.

"It's okay," I say. "I'll go."

Sol gives me a hug. "He'll come round," he says softly. "We'll talk again tomorrow."

Something about the tone of his voice makes me want to weep. But I can't break down in front of them, so I flee.

IT STARTS RAINING PROPERLY as I make my way back up the steps to my room. My limbs feel like they don't belong to me anymore, my movements automatic and jerky. My face is hot and my eyes burn with tears that I don't dare let free.

I grit my teeth and try to swallow away the lump in my throat, then realize that I'm standing outside Caraway's door, not mine. I can't hear any voices from inside this time.

I should go back to my own room. Go to bed.

Maybe in the morning, Teddy will have calmed down. He'll apologize. Tell me I'm right. Sol will back me up, I know he will.

The three of us will leave this awful place, and our perfect summer can really begin.

I'm still standing outside Caraway's door. My hand makes a fist and rises up to knock.

What am I *doing?*

My skin is tight on my face. Everything feels slow and surreal.

I force my arm down to my side and start to turn away. But as I do so, Caraway's door opens.

He looks surprised to see me standing there, and I can only imagine how I look—clammy and wet, hair hanging in strings like a Fenlander, fists clenched.

We stare at each other for a long moment. I can't read Caraway's expression, but whatever it is, it isn't his usual cold haughtiness. And it's not the relaxed ease he had before when we ate junk food in my room. He looks . . . haunted.

I open my mouth to tell him . . . what? What possible reason can I give for standing outside his door in the middle of the night?

But whatever I'm going to say, I don't get the chance to say it. Caraway reaches out and scoops me inside, his fingers lacing into my hair and gently easing me toward him. Every rational thought I've ever had evaporates into mist, because suddenly I am kissing Caraway Boswell, and he is kissing me back.

What starts out as tentative and soft quickly escalates. Our bodies crush together, his arms tightening around me, pulling me even closer. His fingers slide under the hem of my shirt, skimming across my lower back. It feels like fire on my skin, and I dimly remember the tugging pull of the Toad-mettle net when he hauled me away from Mr. Gray. My face is slick with rain but it doesn't matter. Nothing matters except Caraway's mouth, and

Caraway's hands, and the little catch in his breath as I graze his bottom lip with my teeth.

"Afanc's scales, Morgan," he curses softly, and spreads both of his hands flat against my back, as if he wants to touch as much of my skin as he can without breaking our embrace.

Someone who is as cold and aloof as Caraway has *absolutely* no right to be as good as he is at this, and even if he *is* good at it, it shouldn't matter, because it's Teddy I want. I should be doing this with Teddy. This is all wrong, even though every single inch of me is screaming that it is, in fact, very bloody right.

Then he pulls away.

His hair is tousled where my fingers were moments ago, his cheeks flushed beneath his glamour. I can sort of see through the iciness of it, can spot the subtle changes that give me a glimpse of the real Caraway underneath.

"Bringing you here was a mistake," he says hoarsely.

I remember what I overheard him saying earlier.

She is nothing to me.

But that kiss didn't feel like nothing.

"I think you should go home," Caraway continues. "Before you get into any more trouble."

This stings, more than it should. How can Caraway kiss me like that, then tell me he doesn't want me anymore? Was the kiss *that* bad?

No. The kiss was good. *Very* good. And the slightly wild expression around Caraway's eyes, the flush on his cheeks, the color on his lips—I know it was good for him too.

So why does he want me to leave?

I shake my head. "I—I can't go home," I say. "I need to be

here. Teddy—I shouldn't have kissed him, but I know I can make him understand . . ."

"You . . . ," Caraway says, holding up a hand. His voice is hoarse. "You kissed Evans? Tonight?"

I nod. "But I—"

The open, searching expression on Caraway's face drains away, and all that's left is the coldness of his glamour. It feels ten times as strong now as it ever has before, and instinctively my eyes slide away. I shiver, repelled by the haughty condescension emanating from him.

I back out the door into the rain. Caraway says nothing. I say nothing.

I slip back into my own room and climb into bed, still in my wet clothes.

My lips are tingling from where they were crushed against Caraway's moments ago. My skin is still hot where his fingers were splayed.

I slide my own fingers beneath my waistband and try to imagine Teddy. Teddy, kissing me back. Staring into my eyes. Whispering words of devotion. But Caraway's face keeps creeping in, his dark sweep of hair replacing Teddy's golden curls. Caraway's glacial eyes. Caraway's hands on my skin.

Outside, I can hear the steady fall of rain, the buzzing of insects, and the far-off cry of some forlorn marsh bird.

Everything is wrong.

7.

I'M WOKEN THE NEXT MORNING BY THE SALLOW-FACED fen girl, bringing me a tray bearing something for breakfast that she calls "milk mess," which seems to be dry bread soaked in rather watery-looking milk. There's also a pot of muddy tea.

There's a chill in the air, so I pull on jeans and a flannel shirt, pack up my bag and head out the door just as Caraway steps in front of it to knock. We collide awkwardly, and the physical proximity of him brings back all sorts of feelings and sensations that I'd rather forget.

He looks slightly surprised to see me, as if he had expected I'd take up his suggestion and flee Deepdene in the middle of the night.

He obviously doesn't know me that well.

What happened last night was a mistake. All of it. I got all mixed up and carried away, but no more. I'm here to protect Teddy, and nothing is going to distract me.

"I'm ready," I tell Caraway, carefully stepping away from him. "Let's go to Toad Prom."

Caraway hesitates for a moment. "You don't need your bag," he says curtly, nodding at my rucksack. "Someone will bring it."

I drop the bag and follow him down the steps away from our rooms.

Good. We're not going to talk about it.

DEEPDENE IS COLORLESS IN the early-morning light, but I get a better sense of it now than I did in the dark. Rickety stilts and stairs stagger over the marshy wetness below—pools of muddy water and gray tufts of heather and spike rush. The buildings are constructed from various kinds of timber, as well as gray slate and sheets of rusting corrugated iron. Ramshackle doesn't even begin to describe it.

Fenlanders peer at us suspiciously from doorways and grimy windows.

"Shouldn't they be worshipping at your feet?" I murmur to Caraway. "I thought they made the toad from your story their king?"

"That was a long time ago." Caraway shrugs. "Even kings fall out of favor. Especially kings."

"But none of it ever happened," I say. "It's just a story."

"The Toadmen believe it's true."

"Do you?"

He doesn't respond.

There's a dock at one end of the village. Brown water spreads out before us in a still lake that smells strongly of peat and sulfur. On the other side, I see where the fen begins. Twisted trees sprout from spongy-looking hillocks, dripping with vines and frothy gray lichen. I can't make out much from here, just watery channels winding between patches of unstable ground.

"So that's Deeping Fen," I say. "Looks like an awesome place for a fancy party."

Caraway's mouth quirks in response to my sarcasm, but I can tell that he's on edge. Is it because of what happened last night? Or is it just being in this wet, ugly place that stinks of damp and rot?

I remember his hands on me, his mouth on mine, and my insides flutter and thrill.

She is nothing to me.

I turn away from him. I have to be careful. I'm here to stop Teddy from pledging himself to the Toadmen, and nothing more. Caraway can't be trusted. He needs something from me—there's a reason why he was so desperate for me to be his consort. Does it have something to do with the waterlogged voice?

What does he *really* want from me?

A line of suited gentlemen and their consorts are boarding a flat barge floating by the dock. They are all of the same category as Mr. Gray—oldish, immaculate, glamoured. There is a little more variety in the consorts, but on the whole they are younger and prettier.

"Is that it?" I ask. "I thought Toad Prom would be bigger."

"People arrive over several days," Caraway says. "There'll be a few hundred Toadmen, I think."

I shudder. "Too many Toads."

Caraway doesn't disagree.

I spot Teddy and Sol and feel an unfamiliar pang of jealousy. They look so comfortable as a pair, like they don't even care we're not all together. Hopefully I'll get a chance to talk to them on the way to Deeping Fen. But Caraway doesn't lead me down to the barge. Instead we head down a flight of slippery steps to another dock, where a much smaller flat-bottomed boat is waiting for us. Just big enough for two.

I sigh. "Of course you get a private boat. I bet Daddy paid for it, right?"

"In a manner of speaking." Caraway's voice sounds tight and cold.

He puts out a stiff hand to help me board, and I have a sudden flashback to that hand on my back, fingers splayed against my skin, Caraway's mouth hot and urgent against mine. There's nothing of that hunger in his face or behavior today. Perhaps we were both drunk on enchanted snack food.

I ignore his outstretched hand and step onto the boat, which wobbles alarmingly in the brown water. Gingerly, I sit down on one of the padded seats, looking longingly over my shoulder at Teddy and Sol.

The three of us should be heading off camping today. Hiking up Dryad's Saddle and pitching a tent by the Mira. Not crouching in a creepy boat in the middle of a bug-infested swamp. The voice I heard last night said they had *plans* for Teddy. What kind of plans? Whatever they are, they can't be good.

"Here," Caraway says, holding out a scrap of black cloth. "Put this on."

It's a blindfold. "No way," I tell him.

But the people on the barge are all being blindfolded too.

"The location of the Deeping Court is a secret," Caraway tells me. "You have to be blindfolded."

"Even Toadmen?" I ask, watching Sol tie Teddy's blindfold.

"Even Toadmen."

"Even *you?*"

Caraway holds up his own black slip. I look around.

"But how do the boats . . . go? Are they motorized?"

Instead of answering, Caraway just ties the cloth over his own eyes. I look over and see that everyone on the barge is blindfolded and waiting.

"Come along, Morgan," Caraway says, his voice weary. "You're holding up the whole procession."

Reluctantly, I tie the blindfold over my eyes.

"No peeking," Caraway instructs. "I mean it. There will be consequences."

The blindfold smells like lavender and sage. I breathe it in and immediately feel calm, even sleepy. Enchanted, then, because there's no other way I'd be feeling calm right now.

The boat starts to move. I can hear the rippling of water around us. How is it moving? I can't hear a motor.

"You must be silent in the fen," Caraway warns, his voice low. "There are dangerous creatures here."

"Great," I say, but I can't quite bring myself to feel angry or anxious or even irritated. I hear a faint splash, like an oar or a pole being lowered into the water, and something else, like the scurrying of small animals.

"Caraway?" I say in a low voice. "How long will it take?"

"Shh."

The calming scent from the blindfold dissolves any other questions I might have, and I relax into the padded seat, which is unexpectedly comfortable.

We leave behind the greasy scent of smoke. The inhabited sounds of Deepdene—footfalls on wooden paths, Fenlander voices—are replaced by strange birdcalls and the buzzing of insects. The faint splashing coming from the boat is rhythmic and soothing, and I sink into a kind of doze, and it's some time before I come back to myself.

It's the scent of bog water that does it, cutting through the calming aroma of lavender and sage. Suddenly I'm at Miss Prinny's again, Mr. Gray with his hand around the back of my neck; his milky eye is staring at me, and that waterlogged voice hissing from his mouth.

I can't breathe. My lungs are full of pond water and I'm drowning and behind it all, I hear the harsh cackle of witches.

I struggle with my own drowsiness for a moment, like I'm trying to escape from a heavy blanket, and then it's gone, and I can breathe again. I'm awake.

It was magic. Something in the blindfold that turned me sleepy. I feel uneasy, violated. They used magic on me, took away my free will.

This is why magic was once banned in Anglyon. Magic users had so much power over ordinary folk. It created an imbalance. Then the witches revolted at the Battle of Goose Spring, and the government came up with a compromise—the hundred covenant spells, licenses for practicing witches. Regulation for corporations, so magic became something safe and predictable. Available at supermarkets and malls. For everyone, not just those who happened to be born with the ability.

But what the Toadmen are doing isn't covenant magic.

How do they get away with it? Why is this place not swarming with auditors, hauling Mr. Gray and his friends off to recovery centers along with all the witches?

I know the answer, of course.

There are three big magic corporations in Anglyon—Ilium, Moracle and Welch. Ilium is the biggest—it makes most of the glamour patches and enchanted food products you find at the supermarket. Like the junk food I can still taste at the back of my throat. The people of Candlecott may not *do* magic, but we all use Ilium products. You can't live in Anglyon and *not* use them. And Ilium's magic isn't dangerous, like witch magic. It's made in laboratories and factories and, yes, Caraway, recovery centers. Half the witch recovery centers in Anglyon are owned by Ilium. They give the rebel witches an opportunity to give back to society. To be useful.

And Caraway's dad works for Ilium. Director of thaumaturgy, whatever that means. Who knows how many other Toads work there?

I guess magic restrictions don't apply to them.

All that power, that money, that magic. All in the hands of a bunch of rich men who don't have to play the same game as everyone else.

I hear an echo of Caraway's voice in my head. *Think of the money the big magic corporations would lose if people could just whip up their own glamours and potions and enchanted cleaning products.*

It's all just energy, is what Sol said.

I feel suddenly outraged that I'm here at all. That I'm following ridiculous Toad rules like a good little girl.

I'm going to take the blindfold off.

Or at least shift it a bit so I can peek out from underneath.

I'm going to do it.

Right now.

Now.

Now.

My hands aren't obeying my brain. My body feels relaxed and comfortable, but I can't move it. A frisson of panic ripples through me, but is quickly dulled by the enchantment in the blindfold.

Of course, I don't *entirely* need my regular eyes to see.

I look threadwise, and silvery mettle threads appear all around me. I still can't see the fen, or the boat, or Caraway. But I can see Caraway's mettle. The swirls and braids and knots that make up his life-force, all coalesced into the vague shape of a sitting human. Some of those threads are reaching out to me, and some of mine are reaching back out to him, entwining together at the tips. Probably left over from the huge mistake we made last night.

Caraway's mettle is still shot through with shadowy brown Toad mettle, and I remember the taste of pond water, and the wetness in my lungs.

I widen my awareness, and the thrumming of unease grows stronger.

There's someone else in the boat with us.

Or some*thing.*

It's another swirling knot of mettle in the vague shape of a human, standing at the prow of the boat.

I've never seen anything like this mettle before. It's intricate and dense and busy, in the same way that a swarm of bees is. But it's *all* Toad mettle. It's . . . organic, somehow. Rootlike and slimy and pulsing with power.

Somehow there is actually pond water *in my mouth* now, and the cold grit of it overpowers the lavender-scented enchantment of the blindfold. Suddenly my hands are my own again, and I rip the blindfold from my face as I spit out the water.

The figure in the boat wears a long black hooded robe. It's shaped like a man, but I've seen its mettle and I know it isn't human. It's facing away from me, looking out over the water. It holds a long pole that it's using to propel the boat forward. I glance around. We are in a narrow channel of water. There's no sign of the barge. No sign of the Deepdene dock. Around us are just brown muddy water and floating clumps of peaty vegetation. Straggling, hunched trees grow straight out of the water, reaching twiggy branches up to the sky, dripping with pale lichens. Vines and epiphytic plants cling to every surface, and the air smells strongly of mud and decomposing plant matter and sulfur.

Suddenly it doesn't seem entirely out of the question that Caraway has brought me here to kill me. Am I going to be sacrificed to some kind of arcane Toad god?

He didn't kiss like someone who was planning to kill me, though.

But perhaps it was all an act. Designed to put me at ease.

I glance back at the hooded figure, at the hands holding the pole, and my heart judders in my chest. They aren't human hands. The skin is greenish brown and lumpen, covered in warts.

My breath hitches as I gulp in fear, and slowly, the figure's head turns toward me. I can't make out its face beneath the hood, but I see the glinting of eyes.

Hundreds of eyes.

Without thinking, I let out a scream.

The sound reverberates around the twisted marsh willows and spongy mounds of sedge and cattails.

The robed figure *shudders.*

Then it collapses in on itself, the dark cloak falling heavily to the bottom of the boat with a thump, as the robed figure disintegrates into hundreds of small, scuttling creatures.

Toads.

Everywhere. All over the boat, scrambling over the sides and plopping into the water. Brown and warty with slitted, staring yellow eyes.

They're on my lap, on my hands. One gets tangled in my hair and I shudder and fling it away.

Caraway tears off his own blindfold and glances around, sweeping toads from his own lap before turning to me in horror.

"What did you *do?*" he demands.

"What did *I* do?" I retort, hurling another toad from my leg into the fen. "What did *I* do?"

"I told you there'd be consequences for taking off the blindfold. How did you even do it?"

I stare at him, dumbfounded. How I got the blindfold off is *hardly* the most pressing topic of conversation right now.

"Someone was steering the boat," I tell him. "Someone who just *exploded into a thousand toads.*"

"Yeah," Caraway retorts. "And now they're not steering the boat anymore. Now *nobody* is steering the boat, and I am stuck in this cursed bog with *you,* of all people."

I want to smack the sneer right off his face, but I'm afraid if I tried, I'd just start kissing him again. My heart is going a million miles per hour, my breath coming fast. I want to grab ahold of him and drive this terrible place out of my mind.

"Get me *out* of here," I say from between clenched teeth. "*Now.*"

Caraway folds his arms over his chest. "And how do you expect me to do that?"

Something in my gut starts to sink. "Tell me you know where we are."

"Morgan. Deeping Fen stretches for hundreds of miles. I have been here precisely twice before, and both times I was a good boy and kept my *thrice-cursed* blindfold on like I was told. I have *absolutely* no idea where we are, or how to get out of here."

I'm about to reply, when something bumps the bottom of the boat.

Caraway and I immediately go still and silent.

"Did we hit a rock?" I whisper.

Caraway shakes his head, a barely perceptible movement.

All the toads have vanished, slipped away into the fen.

The water beside the boat ripples, and something long and thin breaks the surface, like an eel's fin.

A really, really big eel.

My eyes meet Caraway's and he raises a finger to his lips. He warned me about dangerous creatures before we left Deepdene. I assumed he was being dramatic.

Everything goes silent. Even the birds have stopped their strange, wailing calls. I hold my breath. The water is as smooth and still as glass. Caraway's eyes bore into mine, his body as tense as a bowstring.

The creature bursts from beneath us in an eruption of mud

and fen water, which splatters everywhere as it rises into the air. Its body is as thick as a hundred-year-old tree trunk, skin like shining wet leather, the color of dried blood. A single fin, as sharp as a razor, runs the length of its body. It rears up and crashes back down again, before rising once more.

The boat rocks alarmingly in the water, and I see loops and coils of rubbery skin rising around us. For a moment I think there are more of the creatures—a lot more—but then I realize it's only the one. One very, *very* long, very thick nightmare eel worm. Its enormous body curves round, and I see where its head should be, but there's just a blunt featureless stump. Somehow this—the lack of any eyes or ears or mouth—fills me with even more horror. Its body smashes against the boat, and I am upended into the water.

It's colder than I expected, and deeper. My jeans and sneakers drag me under for a moment, and I taste brackish, muddy water. I'm back at Miss Prinny's again, Mr. Gray holding me pinned in place, his left eye milky and pale.

I kick out and manage to break the surface, taking in a great lungful of air. I strike out for the nearest floating hillock, while the monster thrashes and roils around me. I can't see Caraway anywhere.

Scrambling onto semi-solid ground, I slide and drag my way up to the top of the hillock, where a scraggly gray alder sprouts inelegantly. I grip it with one hand to keep myself upright and search the water for the monster, trying to catch my breath.

Nothing.

All I see is swamp, stretching in every direction. Marshy, sodden earth. Brown water. Twisted ancient trees looped with choking vines and other epiphytes. I let out an involuntary sob.

How am I going to get out of here?

The water boils for a moment, and then I see Caraway's head break the surface. He takes a great gasp and then is dragged back under again. I dither on the edge of my peat hill for a moment, then spot the pole that the toad-boatman held, floating maybe five feet away. The worm-eel thing has disappeared under the surface once more, so I take a deep breath and charge back into the water up to my hips. I reach out and snag the pole, trying not to think about what else might be hiding beneath the water. Then I scramble back to solidish ground and lean out, holding the pole at one end.

I wait. For longer than any person should be able to hold their breath. But just when I'm sure that Caraway will not be coming up, ever again, his face bursts free from the water and he takes a gasping sob of a breath.

"Grab hold!" I yell, and thrust the pole toward him.

I'm not fast enough, though. A rust-colored coil encircles him and pulls him under. I shove the pole at the worm, trying to make it let him go, but I can't see beneath the surface of the water and am afraid I'll inadvertently hurt Caraway.

The water grows calm again, but I keep the pole dangling in the water, like the Garreg-nuu fishermen do, wrapping catgut around the end of a stick and flipping eels out of the water.

I can hear sobbing, and am surprised to discover that it's coming from me. I don't want Caraway to die. He may be the most annoying human on the planet, but he doesn't deserve to die.

Finally, a hand emerges, pale fingers wrapping around the pole. I haul. The water turns white and foamy as Caraway struggles against the creature. I plant my heels into the peaty mud and pull. Inch by inch, Caraway moves closer, until he's within my reach.

I drop the pole and grab him by the arm, hauling him onto the bank. I slip and we end up tangled together and covered in mud.

"Thanks," he pants, his voice thick and strained.

But it isn't over yet.

The creature rears up out of the water before us, towering over our little hillock, then thrusting down toward us. The tip of its blunt head spirals open to reveal a gaping mouth surrounded by row upon row of sharp yellow teeth.

It is without a doubt the most terrifying and disgusting thing I have ever seen.

Caraway's hands are spread out before him, a look of intense concentration on his face. Instinctively, I flick threadwise for a moment, and see him weaving another of his Toad-mettle nets, trying to snag the creature and stop it from plunging its gaping, toothed head toward us. The flesh-petals contract and expand, making the teeth ripple. Caraway has slowed its dive to us, but it's descending closer and closer. It's only a matter of time.

Viscous slime drops from the creature's maw and lands, burning, on my arms. I can smell rotting flesh and sludge. Caraway grunts with effort.

"I can't hold it much longer," he says between gritted teeth. "Do something."

Do something. But what can I do? I'm no witch. And I'm hardly a fighter. All I have is a wooden pole.

Ah.

I bend and snatch up the pole, then brace myself. "Let go," I tell Caraway.

"What?"

"Do it. Now."

With a last gasp of effort, Caraway lets his mettle net disintegrate. The force holding the monster away from us is gone, and it plunges toward us blindly, at lightning speed. I grip the pole in my hands and squeeze my eyes shut as the creature drives straight down onto it, impaling itself on the smooth wood, the fleshy toothed petals of its mouth just inches away from my face. With a raw, animal scream, it rears back again, the pole still embedded in its throat. It whips in the air, still screaming, its body crashing into trees, which splinter under its bulk. It thwacks onto the surface of the water, bucking and writhing, then burrows down headfirst into the muck, slipping deeper and deeper until the thin barbed whip of its tail is swallowed and vanishes.

We stand there, shoulder to shoulder, filthy with mud and soaking wet. But the creature doesn't return.

"Is it gone?" I ask in a whisper.

Caraway nods. "For now," he says, then takes a few staggering steps away from me and vomits into a watery channel, sending the fen water back where it came from.

It must be a really expensive glamour, because he manages to look handsome and elegant even when vomiting. And maybe it's just the glamour, but all smeared with muck, his hair caked with it, he looks . . . almost *heroic*. Something squirms inside me, which I put down to lingering adrenaline from our near-death experience.

Caraway wipes his mouth with a wet sleeve, then turns to me.

"I told you to stay quiet."

And just like that, I'm back to wanting to kill him again.

"What now?" I say, looking around at the fen and shivering. There are no landmarks. No indications of where we could go. What I can see of the sky overhead is heavy with cloud, so I have no idea where the sun is, or even what time it might be.

"We should find some solid ground," Caraway replies, looking around. "Somewhere we can wait."

"Wait for what?"

But of course he doesn't respond, just wades into the narrowest channel between us and the next bit of solidish ground. I want to tell him I think he's a conceited prat, but I guess we did just save each other's lives, so I'll save it for later. I bite back a shudder when I think of what could still be lurking beneath the water, and step after him.

I HATE EVERY SECOND of our journey through the fen. The water is cold, but the air above it is humid—not warm, but wet. I cannot get dry. Cannot warm up. I'm sodden and filthy and clammy, my clothes chafing against my skin. Midges buzz in my ears and sink their tiny mouthparts into my flesh, feasting on my blood, leaving behind itchy swollen welts.

Caraway and I do not talk. I've learned my lesson and don't want to draw attention to any other horrific monsters that might be lurking beneath the surface of the water. At one point, a shellycoat wraps clammy fingers around my ankle and I manage to swallow my scream, kicking and scrambling out of the water, my whole body shaking with fear. The shellycoat doesn't attempt to follow, just watches me with lamplike yellow eyes, its scaled forehead peeking just above the water.

I've seen shellycoats before, in the Mira back home. They're harmless, remnants of a time when monsters roamed Anglyon. They use those glowing eyes to try to lure fishermen into their depths, and on an ash moon they might succeed, if the fisherman has had a few too many nips from his hip flask.

This one looks different. Hungrier. Cleverer. Its fingernail-like scales are grayish brown and spotted with mildew, eyes burning with an intensity it's hard to look away from. Caraway looks over his shoulder at me and at the shellycoat, making a twisting gesture with his left hand. The shellycoat opens a gaping, fishlike mouth to bare tiny black teeth at him, before sinking silently back into the swamp. I'm exhausted, my empty stomach churning with fear and hunger. Every clump of vegetation we pass is spongy and insubstantial, some of them floating between channels of brown water. There are plenty of trees, but they seem to be rooted in the mucky soil at the bottom of each channel, protruding upward through the water like skeleton fingers.

It's getting harder to see, so I assume we must be approaching nightfall. Finally, Caraway pauses and looks over his shoulder at me.

"Up there," he says in a low voice, pointing.

There's a larger hillock than usual in front of us, with gray stones clustered on the top.

Stones.

Stones mean solid ground.

With a little sob of relief, I scramble up the hill after Caraway, to what looks like a ruined building. Little remains of it other than crumbling stone walls that reach no higher than my waist.

Everything is overgrown and thick with moss. A broken pillar stands on one side of what must once have been the doorway, and another is lying horizontal, crumbled and half buried in trumpet creeper and supplejack. Although they're worn, I can see that the pillars were once intricately carved.

"What is this place?" I ask.

Caraway shrugs. "Deeping Fen has been a sacred place for thousands of years," he says. "Long before the Toadmen."

I run my fingers over one of the carvings, wondering who made these marks, and when. Who would want to live here, in this stinky, sunless bog?

I suppose, through the right eyes, it *could* be considered beautiful. The starkness of the trees. The lacy foam of lichens and mistletoe. The looping coils of greenbrier and bittersweet. The mournful cries of birds.

But it's not a patch on Candlecott. On swimming in the Mira and drying off on its grassy bank in the sun.

I feel a sudden pang of homesickness, which is ridiculous. I've barely been gone a day. Clearly I'd never survive at Staunton.

Of course Staunton University has many things to offer that Deeping Fen doesn't.

Dry land, for one. Showers. Food.

"What now?" I ask.

Caraway settles himself with his back against a mossy stone wall. "Now we wait."

I look around at the eerie fen and shiver. "For what?"

Caraway's tone is brusque. "My father will realize we're missing, and send someone."

He says this with such confidence. "Your father must be a very important Toad," I remark. "Head of Toad Relations? Master of Toad Ceremonies?"

"Something like that."

"How will they know where to find us?"

"The toads from the boat."

Caraway looks away from me, across the fen, and it's clear that we're not going to talk anymore.

My teeth are chattering. We need to dry our clothes somehow. A fire, perhaps, if I can find any dry wood. I prowl around the ruin, gathering twigs and bundles of oakmoss. None of it is what I would call *dry*, but maybe I can get something going.

I wish I had my rucksack. It had all been packed for camping. Firestones. My knife. Self-heating Ilium meals.

Guess I'd better do it the old-fashioned way.

I arrange my twigs and oakmoss and set up a hand drill and fireboard. It's hard without a knife, but I manage to use a flat bit of old rock to smooth off the rough spots and dig out the holes in the fireboard. I glance over at Caraway to see if he's watching, but he has his eyes closed, his head back against the stone wall.

I hold the fireboard steady with my knee and start to spin the drill stick back and forth between my palms. I know it's going to take a while to generate enough dust and friction to make a coal, so I focus on breathing deeply and not letting the drill slip out of the notch I've made in the board.

After a fruitless twenty minutes or so, I stop to rest my aching arms and shoulders. There's been not so much as a wisp of smoke. Perhaps everything is too wet and I'm wasting my time. Although the exertion has warmed me up a little, so it wasn't entirely wasted.

"What on earth are you *doing*, Morgan?" Caraway asks, his eyes open a crack.

"Trying to raise a demon to devour you whole," I respond cheerfully.

"Well, you're not doing a very good job."

"Perhaps you'd like to have a go?"

Caraway climbs to his feet and rubs his upper arms with his hands to warm up, before coming over to crouch next to me. I can feel his presence, inches away, and I'm suddenly very aware of my wet shirt clinging to my skin, my jeans damp and tight around my thighs.

"You hold it like this." I demonstrate with the hand drill. "And twirl it back and forth to create friction."

Caraway watches, his expression unreadable. "Would you be open to a different technique?" he asks when I'm finished.

As if Caraway Boswell knows how to light a fire without a match. I bet he can't even light one *with* a match. He usually has servants to do it for him.

"Be my guest," I say, rising to my feet and taking a step back.

I watch as Caraway's brow knits in concentration; then he makes a strange gesture with one hand, and a little curl of flame rises from the oakmoss pile. He leans forward and breathes on it gently. The oakmoss catches properly, then the twigs. Caraway straightens up, a smug grin on his face.

"You *cheated*," I say accusingly.

"I can put it out again," he offers. "And you can go back to twirling sticks."

I want to push him back into the swamp. "Why didn't you tell me you could light it with magic?"

"You looked like you were having fun."

Caraway is poking sticks into the fire like it's somehow offended him.

"You'll smother it," I inform him, and elbow him aside.

I get the fire going properly, grudgingly admitting to myself that Caraway's magic flame is doing a much better job of dealing with the damp wood than any one I could have coaxed. The warmth of it soaks into me and my muscles start to unclench.

"Are there other witches in your family?" I ask Caraway. "Besides you?"

Caraway feeds a twig to the fire. "We don't call ourselves witches," he says. "It doesn't go with the Boswell brand. We're *thaumaturges.*"

"But it's the same thing."

"Not quite. My magic isn't innate. It's borrowed."

"The Toad mettle," I say, remembering. "Is that how the Toads can do magic? They can't do it themselves because they're all men."

"It's a bit more complicated than that," Caraway says. "Magical ability is *usually* stronger when paired with female energy. But female energy doesn't just exist in people who were born female. And magic doesn't only exist with female energy. Take Evans. He's bursting with magical potential, and he's *quite* the masculine specimen. I assume you've seen his abs."

I shift uncomfortably. "You said it's borrowed magic," I say, because I don't want to think about Teddy's abs right now. "Where is it borrowed from?"

"I genuinely don't know," Caraway replies. "I think . . . from the fen itself? I'm not sure. It's definitely strongest at the Deeping Court."

"So that's why you're going to Staunton," I say. "And not a thaumaturgical college. Because you're not a real witch."

Caraway nods. "I—I made a deal with my father. Four years of normal life, at a normal university. After that I'll join the family business."

He looks away from me as he says this, like he's ashamed. Poor thing. It must be so hard for him to know that he'll be super rich and powerful one day.

"Aren't you afraid I'll out you to an auditor?" I ask, purposefully baiting him. "Pretty sure that wasn't covenant magic you were doing back there."

Caraway's lip curls. "I'm not afraid of auditors."

Of course he isn't.

It's rare the auditors come to Candlecott. When I was six, they came for Goody Henderson, after a rumor started she was brewing illegal witch drams. And three years ago they came for Beca Mendis, a girl a few years above me at Candlecott. She was caught attempting to bring her pet cat back from the dead after it got hit by a car. Neither of them ever returned to Candlecott, and people don't really talk about them. There's a general understanding that they didn't *belong* in Candlecott. I had always assumed they'd done their time in a recovery center and then moved on somewhere else to start new, better lives, unburdened by magic.

But what if they didn't? I didn't really know Goody Henderson or Beca, but I don't think they were evil people. They weren't *terrorists.* But they still got taken away from their homes. And here are Caraway and his Toad friends, getting away with whatever they want, just because Caraway's dad is powerful.

"It must be so easy to be you," I say, and I can't hide the bitterness in my voice.

There's a long silence before Caraway answers. "You have no idea what my life is like."

"I can guess. Money. Servants. No consequences. Even the auditors can't touch you. You can go anywhere you want. Do anything."

Caraway makes a bleak huffing noise. "You think *this* is what I want? Crouching in the dirt with you in this awful place?"

Even though I completely agree with him, I still feel a little stung by his words.

"Well, hopefully it'll all be over soon," I tell him. "And you can party with your Toad friends."

Caraway's face twists. "As shitty as today has been," he says, "the one good part of it is that it's delayed our arrival at the Deeping Court."

I shake my head. "I don't get why you're a Toad," I say. "You seem to hate it so much."

"I don't have a choice."

"Why not walk away?" I ask. "Is it the money? Are you afraid you'll have to get a proper job and earn an honest living?"

Caraway's brows draw together in a frown. "No," he says, offended. "Of course not. I don't care about money."

"That's something only people with money say. Is it your father? He won't let you leave?"

He turns to me, his expression serious. "If there were a way

I could walk away and never see another Toad again—including my father—then I would. In a heartbeat. I'd give up every penny I have."

"So why don't you?"

Caraway stares at the hissing fire and is silent for a long time. I don't push him.

At last, he speaks. "It isn't that easy. You can't just walk away."

"Why?" I say. "What's the *deal* with all of this? The Toads, the creepy brown mettle, the *magic.*"

Caraway hesitates.

"You can trust me," I say. "I hate you, but I hate the Toads more."

His shoulders tense, and I suddenly regret telling him that I hate him.

Because I don't. Not anymore.

I don't *like* him.

(Although my traitorous body is reminding me that there were things we did together that I liked *very* much.)

I just don't hate him anymore.

"Tell me *something,*" I say. "Anything."

I feel the ache in him. The despair. I think of my own future stretching out before me—Teddy, Candlecott, lazy summers by the Mira. What if my future were like Caraway's—set in stone and just as heavy, with the weight of expectation? What would I do to escape it?

Caraway lets out a long breath. "Remember the story?" he asks. "The three toads?"

I nod. "The Howling Toad, the Ghost Toad and the King Toad."

Caraway leans forward and stares into the fire. "They're ceremonial positions, within the Toadmen. The identity of the three men who hold each position is a closely guarded secret. They only ever appear masked."

"So they're the ones in charge?"

He nods. "The Howling Toad is the enforcer. The stories say that he is utterly brutal, that he loves causing people pain. Takes a sick kind of pleasure from it."

I shudder. "And the Ghost Toad?"

"Intelligence. He has spies everywhere. He knows everything."

"What about the King Toad?" I ask. "What do the stories say about him?"

Caraway spreads his hands. "Nothing. Only the story I told you about the monster in Deeping Fen."

"You don't know *anything* about him?"

"The identity of the King Toad is the most closely kept secret of the Toadmen. But I believe he'll make an appearance at the ball tomorrow night."

I consider this for a moment. "We could unmask him."

"Right," says Caraway with a snort. "There's no way that could go badly."

"Do garden-variety Toads know all this?" I ask.

"Someone like your father would know the story of the three toads, and the general power structure modeled after them," Caraway responds. "But he would have no idea who they truly are."

"Do you know?"

Caraway hesitates for a moment before answering. "Of course not."

"What about the Fox Bride? Is that a ceremonial position too?"

"She's not part of the power structure of Toadmen. She just attends the Trothal."

"So she'll be there this weekend?"

Caraway shifts uncomfortably. "Someone will be chosen to represent her."

"Who?"

For a long moment, he says nothing. Then he sighs. "I don't know."

"Tell me what your gift is."

The question takes him by surprise. He hesitates for a moment before answering. "Fear," he says at last. "I know what people fear the most."

Of course Caraway Boswell has a creepy gift. I should have known.

"Must be useful," I say. "For getting your minions to do your bidding."

"Sure."

"So what's my greatest fear?" I ask, keeping my tone light.

"Magic."

I'm silenced by this. He's not wrong. Caraway stands up and brushes dirt from his jeans, as if by doing so he could make them magically not encrusted in mud.

"Going somewhere?" I ask, looking out into the gloom.

"Call of nature."

He disappears into the darkness, and over the crackle of the fire, and the insect buzz of the fen, I hear the low sound of his voice.

Is he talking to himself? Is there someone out there? Or is it the same person he was talking to last night? I shiver as I remember the waterlogged voice. The disdain in Caraway's.

She is nothing to me.

When he comes back, he positions himself on my left side, instead of my right. This puzzles me, until I realize that his glamour must have gotten soaked through in the ordeal with the fenworm. It probably won't be working as well. Even the really good-quality ones only last a couple of days, less if they get damaged. Caraway is leaning away from the firelight, twisting his head to the side so his face is obscured by shadows.

"I don't care how you look," I tell him.

His voice floats out of the darkness. "I don't care how you look either."

"Your face," I explain. "I don't care how you look without the glamour."

There's a blank pause, like he doesn't know what I'm talking about. "You don't know that."

There's a vulnerability in his voice that makes me want to throw my arms around him and tell him that everything is going to be okay. That someone will love him for who he truly is. That he doesn't have to hide anymore. There is something enormous behind this impulse that I can't bear to face.

"I mean, I hate you anyway," I babble, trying to recover my composure. "So what does it matter? In fact, part of me hates you more because you're so handsome."

"You think I'm handsome?" The vulnerability has gone and I can hear the smirk in his voice.

"It's just the glamour."

"Sure."

"Shut up."

He laughs, and the sound is so surprising to me that I swing my head around to stare at him. His face emerges briefly from the darkness. It looks peculiar, like his failing glamour isn't sure how to handle a genuine laugh. His eyes crinkle at the edges, and his mouth spreads open into a wide grin.

"What?" he asks, seeing my expression.

"I've never seen you laugh before," I admit. "I wasn't sure you *could*."

He draws back indignantly. "I laugh all the time."

I give him a flat look.

"Well, maybe not *all the time*," he admits. "But I can laugh. I have fun sometimes."

"Really?" I ask. "And what does Caraway Boswell do for fun?"

He hesitates. "I read," he says. "And I go for runs along the river. And I work on my car."

I imagine him bent over the open bonnet of the Purple Menace, the strains of "Little Lights" drifting out from the radio, and it occurs to me that all of the things he just mentioned are solo activities.

"Do you—do you have any friends?" I ask.

"No," he says, and I'm taken aback by how quickly he answers, and how honest he sounds.

I don't really know how to respond. It must be really hard, going to school every day—to *boarding school*—and having no friends. No one to share your victories with, or to whinge to when things go wrong. Eating lunch alone, day after day.

My friends are everything to me.

"I'm sorry," I say.

Caraway's gaze darts away into the blackness. "You don't need to feel sorry for me," he says shortly. "I'm fine. Anyway, it's time to go."

And he stands abruptly, passing a quick hand through the flames, which snuff out without so much as a curl of smoke.

"That's a handy trick," I say as we are plunged into darkness.

Not quite darkness. I can see it now, a pinprick of light moving toward us through the hunched trees and dangling vines.

It's a boat. Identical to the one we came here on, gliding silently across the water, which has turned black in the gloaming. A tall figure in a robe wields a pole, illuminated by a golden spill of light from a lantern that hangs from the prow.

"Is this one also going to explode into toads if I look at it?" I whisper to Caraway.

He shrugs. "It will if you look at it too much, talk to it or try to interfere with it in any way."

The boat bumps gently against the edge of the hill, and Caraway holds out his hand to help me aboard. This time, I'm too exhausted to refuse, and I sink gratefully onto the padded seat. Caraway sits next to me, and I am thankful for the warmth of his body against my side. He ties my blindfold on himself, his fingers gently pushing the hair from my face. I let the scent of lavender and sage wash over me. I don't resist it this time.

We don't speak—I don't want to attract the attention of any more fenworms. My head grows heavy, and the world seems close and small and soft.

I don't realize I've fallen asleep until I feel a gentle nudge in my ribs.

"Morgan. We're here."

My head is on Caraway's shoulder. Wild hounds of Annwn, have I been *drooling* on him?

I pull the blindfold off and look around.

The boat has pulled up against a stone dock. We're somehow *inside*, and I can smell damp stone and brass. Lanterns burn orange against a thick stone wall, and the light they throw illuminates a domed ceiling above us. Everything feels old and clammy.

The robed figure stands motionless in the boat. I glimpse the brown, warty skin that holds the wooden pole, and my own skin crawls.

Given that we got a private boat and everything, I'm expecting there'll be someone to meet us. A phalanx of Toadmen, or at the very least Caraway's father. Surely he's worried about his son, lost in the fen?

But we see nobody as we cross the chilly stone floor, and Caraway leads me through an arched doorway and down a wide corridor built of the same gray stone.

We don't encounter a single person as we hurry down corridor after corridor, each lit with glass lanterns that spill yellow light onto the stone walls and floor.

There are doors, sometimes, or other archways. Caraway seems to know where he's going—although didn't he say he hasn't been here for years?

We pass a larger archway, and as we hurry by I glimpse a grand hall, lined with suits of armor, the silver visors styled like toad heads.

We turn another corner and Caraway leads me up a flight of stone steps, each one worn in the middle where feet have trod for possibly centuries.

I'm so tired I can barely see.

"This place is a rabbit warren," I mutter. "Or a toad burrow, I guess."

"Nearly there," says Caraway. We go up another flight of steps, and Caraway opens an ornately carved wooden door and stands back to let me through.

It couldn't be more different than the poky, damp rooms in Deepdene. The walls are paneled with a dark, warm wood—mahogany, I think, or teak. A cheery fire burns in an ornately detailed stone hearth. There are expensive-looking armchairs and a cherry-velvet chaise lounge, and a dining table set for dinner, with silver-clochéd platters set out along the center, and twinkling crystal goblets.

"Oh," I say softly. "This is . . . really nice?"

I head through an ornately carved archway and see an enormous four-poster bed—each mahogany post intricately carved with leaves and berries and flowers . . . and toads.

Through a smaller archway I see white marble and brass taps—the bathroom.

I let out a little moan of longing and flop onto the bed, face-first. I am so, so tired.

The bed is as soft as it looked. It's like lying on a cloud. I am never leaving this bed. Never ever.

"You don't want to eat something?" Caraway asks. "Shower?"

There's no way I could move, not even if I wanted to. I try to tell Caraway this, but all I can manage is a muffled grunt.

I hear him chuckle softly, and the last waking part of me thinks that it is a truly extraordinary thing, to hear Caraway Boswell laugh twice in one day.

8.

WHEN I WAKE, WEAK DAYLIGHT IS STRUGGLING through an intricately paned window. I blearily check my wristwatch and am shocked to see that it's after eleven in the morning. I guess there isn't much light here in this weird Toad castle.

The bed is absurdly comfortable, and it is a struggle to leave it. However, the growling in my stomach wins, and I crawl out in search of food.

"Hello?" I say as I enter the sitting room. "Caraway?"

But the room is empty. There's a rumpled blanket on the chaise lounge, along with a neatly folded white T-shirt and plaid pajama pants. I guess Caraway slept out here. That was . . . nice of him. I guess.

I prowl around the apartment, opening drawers and cupboards, but nothing seems out of place. In fact, the room is kind of perfect. Every piece of furniture seems beautiful but also comfortable. Everything fits, in an elegant but not ostentatious way.

Well, maybe a *bit* ostentatious.

There's something not right, though. A muddy scent of pond-weed and rancid sweat. It takes a moment for me to realize that the smell is *me*, and I recoil in horror and flee to the bathroom.

The shower is enormous—the size of our entire bathroom at home. I let the jets pummel my back, washing away the stench of the fen, before turning my attention to the veritable apothecary of soaps, salts and lotions lined up on a little stone shelf. Every single one labeled with AN ILIUM PRODUCT.

I try a bit of everything and step out of the shower silky smooth and smelling like a florist's.

After drying myself on the thickest, fluffiest towel I have ever encountered, I venture back out into the bedroom and find my rucksack at the foot of the bed. I pull on jeans and a T-shirt, roll-ing my filthy clothes into a ball and kicking them into a corner of the room. Hopefully Toad Castle has a laundry service I can make use of.

Back in the sitting room, a meal has been laid out on the din-ing table. I lift a cloche and let out a little moan of pleasure as I see eggs, bacon, grilled tomato, black pudding and a mountain of toast.

I haven't eaten anything apart from Caraway's junk food two nights ago, and the half a scone I had at Miss Prinny's before that. I'm starving. But I've read enough fairy stories to know that the food here could be dangerous. Regretfully, I replace the cloche, my stomach growling in protest, and fish a packet of chips out of my rucksack. They're crushed almost to dust, but they'll have to do for now.

"Not hungry?" Caraway says, and I jump, scattering chip crumbs all over my lap.

"Where have you been?" I ask.

Caraway doesn't answer. Gone is the muddy, fen-soaked Caraway of last night. He's back to his perfect crisp jeans (seriously, who wears *ironed jeans?*) and a white linen button-down shirt. His hair is perfect (of course), and he must have applied a fresh glamour patch because he is simply *radiating* cold indifference.

"You really should eat," he says. "We've got a big night ahead."

He wants me to eat. Is Caraway trying to drug me?

I glance back at the cloche. "After you," I say.

"I already ate. Breakfast with my father."

This does nothing to ease my suspicions.

"I'm more of a sweet tooth," I tell him with a shrug. "Shame there's no griddle cakes. Do you have any junk food left?"

"You ate it all in Deepdene."

"*We* ate it all in Deepdene."

There's an awkward pause. It feels weird to be here, together in this fancy apartment. *Our* fancy apartment. Without the drama of fighting Mr. Gray or the fenworm, or the squalor of Deepdene. It feels more and more like I'm Caraway's *date*. Which I am, I guess.

"Will you need any help getting dressed tonight?" Caraway asks abruptly. "I can call someone to do your hair."

I stare at him. "I am dressed," I say, gesturing down to my shirt and jeans.

"Dressed for the ball," Caraway says.

"The ball," I repeat. "The Toad ball. Toad Prom."

Caraway nods. "The very same."

"Don't we have better things to do? You promised me you'd

help me find Teddy's missing string. And you still haven't told me what favor you need me to do."

"We'll do it all tonight," he says. "But we have to make an appearance at the ball first. Once we've arrived and everyone's seen us, it'll be easy to slip away."

I realize that I really haven't thought this whole business through at all. "I . . . don't think I can go," I tell Caraway. "Maybe I can just stay here in the room? You could tell everyone I've got a headache, and I can go looking for the string."

"You're coming."

"Actually," I say, "tell them I've got my period. There's no way all those old men will ask questions about that."

"I'm not telling them you have your period."

"Coward."

"Why the sudden reticence?" Caraway asks with a frown.

"The thing is . . ." I chew on my bottom lip. "I . . . didn't bring anything to wear."

"That's a pretty terrible excuse."

"I'm serious, Caraway. Look."

I lead him into the bedroom and empty my rucksack out onto the bed.

Caraway's eyes narrow ever so slightly as he surveys my camping equipment. "You were going to run away," he guesses. "That's where you were when I came to pick you up. Why didn't you?"

I don't answer. Why do I feel so embarrassed? Of *course* I tried to run away.

"Evans." Caraway nods, understanding. "You went to find him and convince him to go with you. But he'd already left."

I lift my chin slightly in acknowledgment.

Caraway's glacier eyes bore into mine for a long moment. "You should have run away without him," he says at last. "You would have been better off alone in the woods than here."

"I wish I had," I reply, and I'm satisfied to see a little flicker of emotion in those cold eyes.

There is a sudden tension between us, so much that I'm surprised the air isn't crackling with it. I could close the distance between us in two steps. Caraway's eyes dart to my lips, and I feel heat spread throughout my body. Is that what Caraway wants? Is it what *I* want?

But Caraway turns to leave. "There's a gown for you in the wardrobe," he says over his shoulder.

"A *gown*?" I hear myself say. "Like . . . a ball gown?"

Caraway shrugs. "Not sure."

No no no no. "I am not a *gown* kind of girl."

His eyes slide over me, and I suppress a shiver. "No," he says. "You're not."

My mouth suddenly feels dry.

Caraway nods at me. "I'll be back at seven to pick you up. Try to stay out of trouble."

"Where are you going?" I ask.

"Toad business."

"And I'm just supposed to stay here by myself?"

"Yes."

Then he's gone.

I head back into the bedroom, opening the heavy wardrobe door to inspect the contents.

It sure is a gown. A cascading waterfall of wheat-colored tulle and lace, embroidered with a thousand delicate blue silk corn-flowers. I slam the wardrobe shut again.

I am *not* wearing that.

I'll ruin it.

I'll look ridiculous.

I bet it won't even fit.

In fact, I'll put it on and *prove* that it won't even fit.

The dress is as soft as butter against my fingers as I pull it out of the wardrobe. I'd expected that so much fabric would be heavy, but it's as light as air. With one eye on the apartment door, I yank off my jeans and T-shirt and slide the dress on over my head, letting the fabric ripple over my body. My skin breaks into gooseflesh, and my cheeks grow warm. There aren't any compli-cated buttons or laces or zippers. It's going to look like a potato sack. I hitch up the long skirts and head on over to a large gilt-framed mirror that sits against one wall.

A princess stares back at me.

The dress clings and drapes in all the right places. The satin bodice, richly embroidered with golden vines and flowers, fits me like a glove, creating just the right amount of cleavage—modest, but not *too* modest.

Uffren's cauldron, I'm not even wearing a *bra*.

Below the embroidered bodice, the lace-and-tulle skirt falls elegantly to the floor, embellished with flowers almost the exact same color as my eyes.

It's a masterpiece. The most beautiful thing I've ever seen. And I am *not* a gown kind of girl.

It's enchanted, of course. But this kind of enchantment is *ex-pensive*. This dress must cost a fortune.

I *definitely* should not be trusted with this dress. I will trip over it, or spill something on it, or get the long train trapped in a door.

There's a pair of shoes in the wardrobe too, delicate satin things embroidered with cornflower-blue thread. I have *never* worn a heel this high. I've never worn a heel at all. I hate heels— fashion designed to hobble women and make it harder for them to run away.

But I slip these on and of course they fit perfectly too. And are as comfortable as sneakers. Instead of tottering around like a giraffe on stilts, I glide serenely around the room.

I wish Ma could see me like this. She always wanted me to wear pretty things.

I wonder who chose this dress for me. Who knew that the color of the silk cornflowers would match my eyes?

It couldn't have been Caraway. Could it? I feel a tingle of anticipation as I imagine him seeing me in this dress. Caraway, who has only ever seen me in a school uniform, or sloppy jeans or shorts. Will his eyes widen? Will he take a step toward me? Reach out and hook me toward him, like he did in Deepdene?

Not that I want him to, of course.

Caraway won't be back for hours. I have plenty of time to find Teddy and Sol and see if I can repair some of the damage I did last night. See if I can get Teddy to leave this place before he binds himself even further to the Toads.

I change back into my regular clothes and slip out the door into a long stone corridor.

Looking threadwise, I'm shocked to see the spidery brown veins of Toad mettle so thick in the air that I can barely make out anything else. I suppose it makes sense. This is Toad HQ, after all. But there's so *much* of it, like a spidery vein reaching from every Toad in Anglyon to this one place. I shudder as I realize this is exactly what it is. The Toads are a brotherhood, after all. It makes sense that they're all connected. I wonder how they do it. Not by covenant magic, that's for sure.

The spidery Toad veins are leading downward, to a chamber that must be deep underground. I dread to think what's down there. A million actual toads, probably, hopping around in the mucky fen and being generally warty and disgusting.

I take a few deep breaths and start to pace the corridors, trying to find an echo of Teddy. But the Toad mettle is so thick, it seems impossible. I go up and down staircases when I find them, trying to let my instincts guide me.

At the foot of one staircase, I find a robed and masked Toadman standing sentry. He stares at me impassively, not reacting at all. One of his eyes under his mask is milky white, just like Mr. Gray's was in the tea shop.

"I guess I'll just . . . go back up," I tell him.

He doesn't respond.

I return up the stairs and slip down another corridor, feeling unsettled. I take a moment to try to relax, a few more deep breaths to tune out all the Toad mettle. While I'm standing there, I hear footsteps approaching from around a corner.

I don't want another encounter with a Toadman, so I open the first door I come across, slipping inside and pressing my ear to the door.

The footsteps approach, and my heart thumps so loudly I'm surprised the whole castle isn't vibrating along with it.

But whoever it is passes by my hiding place, the sound of their footfalls receding into the distance.

I breathe a sigh of relief and turn to look at the room I'm in.

It's a library. The kind of library that I have dreamed of my whole life.

In Candlecott, our library is a dusty little room at the back of the town hall. People donate books once they've read them, but there's no real organization. My school has a decent reference library, but barely any fiction outside the moldy old classics we are forced to read. Sometimes Da takes me into Foxford to use the bigger library there. But the Foxford library is barely a cupboard compared to this.

Every wall is a bookshelf, from floor to ceiling, dark, warm wood crammed with leather-bound volumes with gold-embossed spines. The *scent* of it is exhilarating. I want to live here. To read every single book in the place. Maybe if I try hard I can get through all of them before I die of old age.

A fire burns in the ornately carved stone hearth, crackling gold with violet sparks. The air is thick with the scent of rich leather and something floral that reminds me of exploring the riverbanks of the Mira in late summer, searching for mitten crabs. Wild lotus, I think. And the honey-sweetness of chokeberry.

I walk over a richly colored carpet to the nearest bookshelf, running a light finger over the spines, before pulling out an exquisitely bound copy of *The White Book of Rhydderch*. I let it fall open in my hand, admiring the marbled endpapers and breathing in the earthy scent of aging paper.

"You must be Merriwether Morgan."

I jump, startled to realize I'm not alone in the room. A man is seated in one of the leather armchairs, a book resting on his knee. He's about the same age as my father, silver-haired and elegant, dressed in an immaculate dark gray suit with a wine-dark brocade waistcoat. He gazes calmly at me through silver-rimmed spectacles.

"I—I'm sorry—" I stammer. "I didn't mean to interrupt."

"You're not interrupting anything. I've been looking forward to meeting you."

I open my mouth to ask him how he knows who I am, but the man looks around and asks, "Do you like our library?"

I nod. "It's lovely."

He smiles at me, and his pale blue eyes twinkle. "I agree. It's a safe haven for me. When things get too rowdy downstairs, I know I can always come here for some peace and quiet."

"I really am sorry to disturb you," I say, backing toward the door.

"Fine choice," the man says, nodding his head at the book in my hand. "That volume contains one of my very favorite poems, 'Gwahodd Llywarch i Lanfawr.' Have you read it?"

I nod. I know the poem well. It's one of my favorites too. In it, King Llywarch grieves for the sons he sent off to die in battle, lamenting how lonely he feels, ruling without them.

"Of course you know it," the man says, looking almost apologetic. "Caraway has told me how gifted a student you are."

I look up at the man sharply. Who is he?

"But where are my manners?" The man rises from his chair gracefully and steps toward me, holding out his hand. "I haven't introduced myself. Thurmond Boswell."

I stare at him for a moment, thunderstruck. "You're . . . Caraway's father."

The man's smile turns rueful. "I suppose he's told you what a tyrant I am."

He's still holding out his hand, and flustered, I step forward to shake it. His hand is warm, his grip firm, but not bone-crushingly so. "He—You're not what I expected."

Thurmond Boswell chuckles. "Caraway always had a flair for the dramatic. When he was seven years old, he decided he wanted to be a circus clown when he grew up. Colored in his nose with a red marker every morning before lessons."

I can't imagine Caraway as a circus clown. I can't really imagine him as a child at all, to be honest. Thurmond Boswell is . . . nothing like I thought he'd be. He is one of the richest men in Anglyon, with his fancy job at Ilium as well. I thought he'd be tall and stern and forbidding. Not this mild, avuncular man sinking back into his leather armchair and gesturing at the one opposite him.

"Please, join me."

He leans over to the side table with the tea service, pouring a second cup before I can decline. I perch on the chair, confused but powerfully curious.

"Milk? Sugar? Lemon?"

I shake my head, and he passes me the cup and saucer. I inhale the fragrant steam but do not drink. Mr. Boswell's eyes flick from the teacup to my lips, and I see the faintest ghost of a smile on his lips.

"You know," he says conversationally, "Caraway has always struggled to make friends. Until he met you, of course."

"Me?" I blink. Caraway and I aren't friends. Are we?

"Oh, I've heard all about you, Merriwether Morgan. From the moment Caraway arrived at Candlecott, you treated him like any other student. That was new for him. He's so used to being toadied to, if you'll pardon the expression. Being spoiled. Being a *Boswell*. It's hard for a child. That's why we sent him to school in the country, away from all the other wealthy children. He was horribly bullied before he went to Candlecott, has he told you?"

Caraway, bullied? I can't imagine it.

"I suppose the accident made it worse," I murmur.

"What accident?" Mr. Boswell asks with a puzzled frown.

"The car accident," I say. "Caraway's face. The reason he wears a glamour all the time."

Mr. Boswell blinks, tilting his head slightly as he considers my words. "Is that what he told you? Interesting."

He stands abruptly and walks over to lean on the mantelpiece, gazing into the fire, which leaps and crackles under his gaze. "Ms. Morgan, do you have my son's best interests at heart?"

The scent of lotus and chokeberry seems stronger than before. I take a sip of my tea, without even thinking about it. It's perfect, steeped exactly how I like it, at precisely the right temperature.

"Of course I do," I reply, and wonder as the words escape my lips if I really mean it.

Mr. Boswell smiles. "I know you do. I'm an excellent judge of character, it's something I pride myself on. Caraway has a bright future ahead of him, if he can just stay on the right path. More tea?"

I look down at my tea and realize I've drunk it all, but I don't remember anything after that first sip. Strange.

"Mr. Boswell, can I ask you something?" I say.

He gestures for me to continue. "Of course."

"Why is Teddy here? I thought that Toad Pr—the Trothal was just for the most senior Toadmen?"

Mr. Boswell steeples his fingers thoughtfully. "Your friend is talented," he says. "Very talented. I haven't seen someone with his gift for charms in . . . decades. I believe he could be the greatest smith of his generation."

He says this with such certainty that I realize he must somehow have *seen* Teddy before. Assessed his talent. Has he been to Candlecott?

I blink. "Really?" I ask. "I mean, I know he's very good. But I didn't realize . . ."

Mr. Boswell tilts his head to one side. "He has had a fine apprenticeship in Candlecott, but he needs further instruction. We can help him. Introduce him to the best charmsmiths in Anglyon and beyond. There's a silversmith in Oenotria who can make unbreakable chains, as fine and delicate as spiderwebs. Or I know of a damascener in Tianxia who can capture a dream in a pendant. Being a Toadman opens doors that would otherwise remain closed to him. Gives him access to tools that he never dreamed could even exist."

The casual way in which Mr. Boswell talks about illegal magic is genuinely shocking to me. Like he knows that there's no accountability for him. No auditors will knock on his door and drag him off to a recovery center. It's Ilium that owns half the recovery centers.

I wonder if he knows about me. What I can do. Did Caraway tell him? Or can the Toadmen sense it somehow? *Smell* the witch's curse on me?

"But . . ." I swallow as I recall the violent snap when the hooded Toad took one of Teddy's strings.

It's like he knows what I'm thinking. "It seems barbaric, doesn't it? But it's a commitment, something that each of us understands and agrees to. The sacrifice binds us together. We are a brotherhood."

I think about the spidery brown mettle veins. Is that what he's talking about? Does giving up a string bind them to all the other Toads? A Toad network?

"The pain lasts only a moment," Mr. Boswell continues. "And I think you can see"—he gestures around at the opulent library—"that the benefits are well worth a brief moment of discomfort."

When he puts it like this, it sounds so sensible.

"I know you want what's best for your friend," Mr. Boswell says. "Trust me when I assure you that we want that too. That's why Edward Evans is here. He is our honored guest. I am going to personally introduce him to some of the most powerful men in Anglyon this weekend."

So reasonable. Kind, even. But I can't trust him. Can I?

"These connections do not just benefit Edward," Mr. Boswell adds. "My son informs me that you are a highly intelligent young woman. You may not have any magic ability of your own"—he smiles sympathetically—"but you have talent nonetheless. Having a friend as gifted as Edward Evans will open doors for you too. Not to mention your association with my son."

His eyes are searching mine, still kind, but with a hypnotic intensity. The scent of lotus and chokeberry is suddenly stifling, and I struggle to keep my eyes open.

"You and I want the same thing. We are on the same side. Will you help me, Ms. Morgan?"

"Yes," I say, and something chimes inside me, like I've sworn a real oath. "I'll help you."

"I knew I could count on you."

He puts down his own teacup and rises to his feet, straightening his cuffs with precise, elegant movements.

"Now I suppose you'll want to see your friends," he says. "Why don't I show you to Edward's room? This old place is so large, it's easy to get turned around."

"Thank you," I say, standing and moving to put *The White Book of Rhydderch* back on the shelf.

"Keep it, if you like," says Mr. Boswell.

"Oh, I—I couldn't." I look down at the book. It's beautiful.

"Consider it a gift from an old Toad."

"Thank you," I say again. I've never owned a book this beautiful before, and I feel a sudden rush of fondness for this eccentric man who just wants to look after his son.

Outside the library, away from the scented smoke, my head begins to clear. I remember the taste of pond water. Thurmond Boswell may look like a harmless old man, but I'm sure he's dangerous.

He leads me down a series of corridors and stops outside a plain wooden door.

"I'll leave you here," Mr. Boswell says, his eyes twinkling. "I don't want to intrude on your reunion."

"Thank you," I tell him.

Why has he brought me here? Why is he acting so kind to me?

Mr. Boswell ducks his head in a little bow, then wanders off down the corridor.

I look at the door threadwise, and my unease lessens somewhat. This is Teddy's room. He's inside. And Sol. I just really need to see my best friends. To be with people I trust completely.

I take a breath and knock on the door.

Nobody answers, but when I press my ear against the door, I can hear the low murmur of voices inside. I knock again, but nobody comes.

After a moment's hesitation, I put my hand to the doorknob and turn. The door isn't locked, and swings silently open.

Teddy and Sol's apartment is like a smaller, less-fancy version of the one I'm sharing with Caraway. The door opens into a sitting room, with comfortable-looking chairs facing a hearth with a cheerful fire. I see Teddy's bag open on the chaise, his clothes strewn about the room, and I smile to myself. He's such a mess.

The doorway to the bedroom is open, and in a moment, my entire world shifts on its axis, and everything is different.

The bedclothes are rumpled. Bathrobes and towels on the floor. A silver tray with a bottle of amber-colored clurichaun wine, half drunk, and two crystal goblets.

I stare at the smooth curves of Teddy's arms, his back, his thighs. His sun-kissed skin and golden hair, contrasted against the dark angular limbs of Sol.

In the two heartbeats before they notice me, I see it all, the messy tangle of them, gleaming with sweat. I see Teddy's head thrown back, his lips parted with pleasure, his expression delirious. And I see Sol, gazing at Teddy through thick lashes, his mouth curling in a smile so breathless and sweet that I know this isn't the first time they've ended up in bed together.

The White Book of Rhydderch slips from my fingers and falls to the carpeted floor with a *whump*. Sol's head snaps up, then Teddy's. There is a moment of shocked eye contact, which is absolutely more than I can bear right now. I leave the book on the carpet and flee, stumbling through the apartment and back out the door. I get halfway down the corridor before I hear him.

"Merry, wait." It's Sol, standing in the corridor behind me, hurriedly tying the belt of a fluffy white bathrobe.

I turn, and we stare at each other for a moment.

"Come back in," he says. "Let us explain."

I shake my head. "I—I can't."

"I'm sorry we didn't tell you. I wanted to, but Teddy said you'd get upset. You wanted this summer to be perfect, and . . . well, we wanted to give you that."

For a moment I picture the three of us, lounging by the Mira, our fingers stained purple from damson plum juice. And something wrenches inside me, because now I really know that whatever happens this summer, it isn't going to be that.

"How long?" I ask.

Sol bites his lip. "A year," he confesses, his gaze sliding from mine.

A year. Teddy and Sol have been seeing each other for a year. Sneaking around behind my back. Hooking up.

No wonder Sol refused to help me with Teddy. He knew it all, long before I did.

And here was me thinking *I* was the one Teddy loved.

A part of me expects him to come to the door too. To try to talk me round. But he doesn't, and that hurts more than anything.

Humiliation burns through me as I remember pressing myself up against Teddy in Deepdene.

"Please," Sol says. "Nothing needs to change with us. We both still love you. Just come in and you'll see."

But I know that Teddy doesn't want me to come back in. Teddy doesn't want anything to do with me. He's made that very clear.

"I—I have to go and get dressed for the ball," I stammer, and run away.

This time Sol doesn't follow.

IN STORIES, THE BOY gets his first glimpse of the girl in her ball gown as she comes down a flight of stairs. She pauses demurely so he can take in her beauty. His eyes widen and his breath catches. He tells her she looks beautiful, and she blushes and tries to hide a smile.

I hope Caraway isn't expecting a moment like that.

He arrives at seven, as promised, to find me sitting on the floor in the bedroom, surrounded by tulle, my face puffy and streaked with tears.

At least I managed to put on the ball gown.

"Morgan? What happened?"

I look up to see Caraway, holding a white cardboard box, a wrinkle of concern between his brows. I'm momentarily distracted from my abject misery by his outfit. He's wearing a black velvet frock coat with silver-embroidered cuffs, over fitted black trousers and a silk damask waistcoat. A neckcloth spills from his collar in some kind of elaborate knot. Everything is perfectly tailored to show off the angles and contours of his body.

He looks unfathomably good. A perfect ice prince.

"Morgan?" Caraway asks again, his voice gentler this time. He puts down the white box and sinks to his knees about three feet away, which is as close as he can get without navigating the tulle.

"I saw Teddy and Sol."

Caraway tilts his head to the side. "Did you have another spat with Evans?"

"No. I—They were in bed. Together."

My voice wobbles on the last word, and I start to cry again. Caraway's eyebrows rise as understanding dawns.

"I thought it was the three of us," I sob. "I thought that no matter what happens, no matter where we go, we'd always have each other."

"And has that changed?"

"Of course it has! Everything has changed. I had this idea in my head of what our friendship was, and . . . and it was all a lie. I thought we shared everything, but then it turns out that Teddy is a Toad, and Sol is his *boyfriend*."

"They still care about you, though."

I shake my head. "They must think I'm such a fool. I bet they've been laughing behind my back this whole time."

"You know that's not true."

"I don't know anything, not anymore," I say, dissolving into a fresh flood of tears.

I want my ma.

"I get it," Caraway says. "It hurts when the person you love wants somebody else."

There's a rawness to his voice that jerks me out of my self-pity for a moment, and I look over at him. Through the ice of his glamour, I can see the concern on his face. The sympathy. The understanding. It makes me feel a tiny bit less alone.

"I brought you some cake," he says, and proffers me the white box. "You said you wanted something sweet."

Enchanted food be damned. If ever there was a time when I needed cake, it's now. I tear open the box and sigh a little as I see the perfectly sculpted creation inside.

"White fudge and apple, with an ambrosia and greengage filling," Caraway says. "Shall I get you a fork?"

No time for forks. I sink my fingers into the soft, pillowy layers and scoop out a handful, shoving it into my mouth. It tastes as good as it looks, sweetness spreading through my mouth and diluting the poisonous misery I feel inside.

I am *so hungry.*

I attack the cake, not caring how I look, or what Caraway must currently be thinking of me. Judging by his expression, he's slightly alarmed.

"Can I ask you something?" he says when I've finished and am licking icing from my fingers.

I nod, and Caraway hands me a napkin before he speaks. "I've seen plenty of people hanging around the forge, all moon-eyed for Evans. He's a good-looking fellow. Would you feel better if he were having a secret relationship with one of them?"

"*No.*" I'm startled by the vehemence of my voice. "Of course not. Teddy deserves better than them. He deserves . . ."

Me. I thought he deserved me. But if it isn't going to be me, then Sol is the next-best thing. And if I'm being entirely honest with myself, Sol is probably the *first*-best thing.

"They're kind of perfect for each other," I admit.

I take a deep breath and try to see through my hurt feelings to the other side. They *work* together as a couple. Sol's quiet strength, and Teddy's brash confidence. I think about all the little affectionate glances they shoot each other. The little touches and grins. I see it all differently now, and I'm suddenly not sad that Teddy isn't my boyfriend. I'm sad that he and Sol fell in love and I *missed it.*

I didn't get to go through it all with them—the anticipation, the tension, the dizzying release and joy when it finally happened.

Caraway is watching me carefully as I go through these mental revelations.

"Getting your heart broken really sucks," he says. "I'm sorry, Morgan."

My feelings are hurt, because my best friends didn't think they could trust me with their secret. I feel . . . left out.

But my heart isn't broken.

I realize, with an overwhelming sense of relief, that I don't love Teddy. I mean, I love him. Of course I do. But I'm not *in love* with him.

Maybe I never was. I was in love with the *idea* of it, of him. Of us being together forever, never changing. There was a comfort in that. But . . . maybe I want more than *comfort.*

And just like that, the whole future I had imagined for myself is gone, wiped clean like a school blackboard. It's . . . terrifying, to have absolutely no idea what might come next. But also kind of exhilarating.

"Come on," says Caraway, reaching out a hand to me. "Let's get you cleaned up."

I take his cool hand in my rather sticky one and let him pull me to my feet. The tulle and lace settle around me, and Caraway guides me gently into the bathroom and runs the tap, passing me a hand towel after I splash my face with cold water. I look up at myself in the mirror, blotchy and puffy, and see Caraway hovering over my shoulder.

"I look terrible," I say.

"Like one of the boiled puddings back in Deepdene," Caraway agrees.

"Thanks," I say to him, and I'm surprised to find that I mean it.

"You're welcome," he replies, and I know he means it too.

I look at us, side by side in the bathroom mirror. Even though my face and hair are still a mess, we look good together, in our party finery. I have a tingling flashback to the intensity of our kiss in Deepdene. I'd shut a mental door on that night, because I was so sure it was Teddy I was supposed to be with.

But now I know that Teddy and I will never be a thing.

Another possible future unspools before me. I'm at Staunton University, sitting under an old oak tree, books and notes spread out before me. Someone crosses the lawn toward me. Caraway. He brings me a coffee and we split a rhubarb muffin. He sits with his back against the tree, and I lean into him, breathing in his familiar scent of bergamot and old leather.

It's just one possible future. There are so many now. Countless strands, like silvery mettle floating on a summer breeze.

But it's not a *terrible* future.

Caraway smiles at me through the mirror, and I smile back.

"I think . . . despite all my best intentions, you and I seem to be friends now?" I say.

Caraway hesitates for a fraction of a second before nodding. "Sure," he says. "Friends."

I suddenly remember the strange conversation I had with Mr. Boswell. How kind he was, how different from what I had expected. Was it all lies? Or was he right, and Caraway is just an overly dramatic angsty teen?

"Where were you today?" I ask him. "What did you do?"

He shrugs. "Toad stuff," he says evasively.

A long moment passes between us, and I'm suddenly confused all over again. Who do I trust?

"Why aren't you wearing Toad robes?" I press. "Where's your frilly bonnet?"

"They're for tomorrow," Caraway responds, screwing up his nose in distaste.

"What happens tomorrow?"

"The wedding."

I swallow. "I need to get Teddy's stone before then, right?"

He nods.

"And do whatever it is you want me to do."

Another nod.

"And you're still not going to tell me what it is."

"Correct."

I get the impression he won't be drawn into any further discussion on the matter.

"I guess we should go?" I say. "I hope you won't get in trouble if we're late."

"It's okay," says Caraway. "The cool kids are always late. We don't have to rush."

"Give me five minutes and I'll try to do something with my hair," I tell him.

He nods and steps out of the bathroom.

I look at myself in the mirror and wonder how to proceed. I have no makeup. No jewelry. Not even a hairbrush. I twist my hair into a messy bun, but it doesn't look messy in a deliberate and elegant way. Just straight-up messy.

I yank open the drawer under the vanity, hoping for *something*, and see . . .

Glamours.

Lots and lots and lots of glamour patches, each one in its neat plastic sleeve.

And not the three-for-ten-quid cheap ones you get from the supermarket either. *Fancy* glamours.

AN ILIUM PRODUCT.

Teddy, Sol and I used to wear glamours when we played make-believe as children. Teddy always went for the hero-knight patches, ending up square-jawed and excessively muscled. Sol wore handsome prince patches, even before he told us he was a boy, and as soon as he put one on, he'd seem more relaxed, more *himself.*

I always wanted to be a warrior, or an assassin, but the only patches available for girls were insipid princesses or glittery fairies. I tried wearing the boys' patches, but the stubble looked weird on my chin and I didn't *not* want to be a girl, I just didn't want to be the kind of girl who always needed rescuing. So instead I chose animal patches, sprouting red fox ears and a long fluffy tail, or shimmering with fish scales.

My fingers brush over the little plastic packets, and I read the names. *Wanderlust. Serenissima. Euphoria. Cottage Dreams. That Girl.* I pause over one called *Golden Hour,* then glance back up at my reflection.

I really can't go to the ball like this. Without hair or makeup, I look like a kid playing dress-ups. I need . . . something. And this is what I have.

I tear open the *Golden Hour* packet, peel off the plastic backing and press the patch to my upper arm.

The transformation is immediate. The messy bun is fuller, the wisps of hair escaping from it twirling into delicate tendrils. My lips stain the color of damson plum juice, and something happens around my eyes that makes the blue of them pop beneath long, dark lashes. Suddenly the silk cornflowers of the gown seem more vibrant, almost glowing against the golden wheat-colored dress. The freckles that spray across the bridge of my nose become more symmetrical and distinct, and a healthy rose flush spreads across my cheeks. I look like a harvest goddess, a cornflower fairy, a May Queen.

"Morgan?" Caraway calls from the sitting room. "Are you all right in there?"

"I'm coming," I say, and even my voice sounds different. Sweeter and more musical.

This is a *very* expensive glamour.

I nearly trip over my rucksack as I head through the bedroom, and as my slippered toe collides with it, something falls out of the front pocket.

The thing that Da slipped me, just as I left with Caraway. It's an Ilium-branded ampoule, a single dose of Sebrium, a potion that strips all intoxication from a person—magical and otherwise. Da always makes me take one with me whenever I go to a party. *There's boys that'll take advantage of a nice girl like you,* he says. *You must keep your wits about you.*

I wish he'd taken his own advice. Then he'd never have joined the Toads.

I slip the ampoule into my bodice and step over my rucksack.

I'm expecting a big reaction from Caraway, but I'm disappointed. He glances up at me from where he's examining the contents of a velvet-lined box with a frown.

"Nice," he says, then slides a mask from the box onto his face.

It's a toad, because of course it is. But stylized black and simple, the hooded eyes looking almost elegant against Caraway's pale skin. It's only a half mask, leaving his mouth and chin bare.

"Where's mine?" I ask.

He draws another mask from the box. It's beautiful—delicate and ornate, crafted from cherry-red leather. A fox, although it has tiny, perfect feathers instead of fur, ginger and white, and a pointed black nose. The feathers elongate at the top to form the ears—partridge feathers, from the looks of it. Caraway doesn't look exactly pleased to see it.

"I hope this doesn't mean I'm the Fox Bride," I joke.

Caraway stares at the mask for a moment longer. "So do I," he says, and I don't think he's joking.

"She's played by a Toad, right?" I say. "That's what you said.

A younger Toadman always plays her in the panto. So it's the same here?"

"I've never seen this ceremony before, remember?" he says. "I—I really don't know what will happen."

He seems genuinely thrown by the mask.

"Come on," I say, spinning so my back faces him. "Put it on and let's get this over with."

Caraway ties the mask onto my face with the golden ribbons that trail from each side. He gently turns me back to face him, and we stare at each other for a moment, toad to fox. "Be careful tonight," he says. "The ball can be . . . a lot."

A shiver of fear washes over me. But I dismiss it. I'm not afraid of a bunch of old toads having a party.

9.

IT'S LIKE A FAIRY TALE.

Caraway and I pause at the top of a grand, curving staircase and take it all in.

The room is huge. Glittering chandeliers hang from an ornate gilded ceiling. The walls are hung with velvet drapes, which conceal cozy cushioned alcoves. Below us are maybe five hundred people dressed in the most beautiful clothes I have ever seen. Feathers, lace, silk and leather. Every face masked—a menagerie of mice, birds, rabbits and of course toads. I don't see another fox.

The floor is an ocean of gray marble, polished so much that it looks like the guests are dancing on water.

A string quartet plays on a stage on one side of the room. On another I see delicately leaping fountains, towers of champagne glasses and tables laden with delicacies.

Some people are dancing, gowns elegantly dipping and sweeping the floor. Others mingle and chat, dainty glasses held in perfectly manicured hands. I'm glad I put the glamour patch on—otherwise I'd be the only person in this room without one.

"I feel like a herald should introduce us or something," I murmur to Caraway.

What I can see of Caraway's face is tight. "Probably not a good idea."

As we descend the stairs, I make out bodies moving inside the alcoves that line the walls—private spaces for talk and probably other things. I search the crowd for Teddy and Sol, but there are too many people. It's all so *much*.

"Wow," I say. "You're right. This is a lot."

Caraway sighs heavily. "We won't stay long. Don't drink *anything*. Try to keep a level head."

I look around at the swirling riot of color. The golden light spilling from the chandeliers. The glittering of jewels and sequins on masks. And I think about Thurmond Boswell's words in the library.

Caraway always had a flair for the dramatic.

He does seem like the kind of person who would hate a party.

At one end of the hall is an enormous toad statue—it must be nearly as tall as the cottage where Da and I live. It appears to be made of gold, but it can't be—it's too big. Its hulking presence absolutely dominates the space, and I notice that there is a golden throne set in front of it, on a dais.

A man appears, wearing a perfectly tailored gray suit. His silver toad mask covers his entire face, but as soon as he speaks, I recognize him as Mr. Gray, from Miss Prinny's.

"I see you finally made it," he says to Caraway, his voice odiously polite.

"All in one piece," Caraway responds, significantly less polite.

Mr. Gray turns to me. "Lovely to see you again, Miss Morgan."

"Ms.," I respond shortly.

Mr. Gray chuckles, the sound hollow under his mask. "Brother Caraway, your father would like a word." His eyes flick to me. "Alone."

Caraway opens his mouth to protest, but I get there first. "It's fine," I tell him. "I want to find Teddy and Sol."

He hesitates, then nods. "I'll be back soon," he says, touching a hand to my elbow. "Try not to get into any trouble."

And he follows Mr. Gray back up the grand staircase. I guess Thurmond Boswell isn't at the party yet. He doesn't seem like the social type either.

As I move onto the main floor, heads turn to look at me, and I hear a low hum of conversation as Toad murmurs to Toad, eyes glittering behind masks. I put my hand up to my fox mask, grateful that nobody can see my face.

I skirt the edge of the dancers, marveling at how graceful they all seem, skirts swirling and feet stepping in complex patterns. Robed figures wearing full-face bronze toad masks move smoothly through the groups of people, holding trays of drinks or perfectly sculptured canapés.

The dresses are *extraordinary.* One has a bodice made entirely of book spines, all worn leather and gilt lettering. Another looks like glittering silver frost, the wearer in a mask seemingly made of icicles. I brush past a woman in a close-fitting gown of butterfly wings, with a cloud of real butterflies flitting around her head.

When I spot Teddy and Sol, it's like the butterflies have taken up residence inside my chest.

Of *course* they're a couple. I don't know how I didn't see earlier. I hang back in the crowd for a moment, watching them.

Sol's mask is a fish, glittering gold, bright against his brown skin. He's wearing a tuxedo jacket that's covered in sequins, overlapping like scales as they fade from bright gold at his shoulders to a rich burnished orange at the hem. He glitters and sparkles as he moves, his eyes burning bright and golden behind his mask. Even his skin shimmers with gold—he's wearing a glamour too.

Teddy has taken a more traditional approach. His toad mask looks like it's made from hammered black iron, and I wonder if he made it himself. He's in a black tuxedo jacket that hugs the curves of his chest and biceps perfectly, and a black-and-gray tartan kilt falling to his knees. The outline of his jaw is a little stronger than usual, his skin free from blemishes. I guess everyone is glamoured tonight.

They sip their champagne and gaze adoringly at each other. Teddy whispers something to Sol, who laughs. They look so *happy*, and I am so happy for them. My devastation from before has gone, dissolved on my tongue like a snowflake. All I feel now is warmth. I cross the floor to them, and they move apart awkwardly, like they don't want me to see their closeness.

Sol opens his mouth to speak, but I hold up a hand. "Please," I say. "Let me go first."

He nods. Teddy is watching me warily from beneath his mask, his shoulders tense.

"I'm sorry about before," I say. "I— It was a shock. But I'm more sorry that you didn't think you could tell me. I'm not blaming you—it's my fault. You were right." I address this to Teddy. "I *would* have freaked out. I *did* freak out. I know you were just trying to protect me. But I'm okay now. I—I'm better than okay. I'm really, really happy for you both."

A flush stains what I can see of Teddy's cheeks. Sol's hand sneaks into Teddy's.

"And Teddy, I'm sorry I threw myself at you, back in Deepdene," I add. "This . . . thing had just happened with Caraway and I was confused. I'm so embarrassed about it now."

Teddy nods, and I see his shoulders loosen. "How about we never mention it again?" His voice is playful, and I know everything is going to be all right.

"Great idea."

"I love your dress," Sol says, touching a finger to the embroidery at my waist. "Do a spin."

I oblige, and Sol makes approving noises.

"Why are you wearing a fox mask?" Teddy asks.

"I don't know. It's just what I was given."

"Right." Teddy's tone is a little flat, and I wonder if he's still mad at me.

"Why do you ask?" I say. "Is it because of the Fox Bride?"

"They haven't—they haven't asked you to *do* anything, have they?" Teddy bends his head down to mine and lowers his voice.

I shake my head. "No, nothing."

He nods. "Okay. That's okay."

We spend a few more moments admiring each other's clothes and talking about how fancy the party is. None of us have *ever* been to anything like this before. In Candlecott, parties are held in fields or barns. Just my dress alone must cost more money than my house is worth.

I can't spot Caraway in the crowd, but I don't mind. I'm with my friends now. Everything's going to be okay. The three of us are reunited. I feel a lightness in my heart that's been missing for days. As soon as Caraway gets back, we'll sneak out to find Teddy's string. But right now . . . Well, it's not every day you find yourself at a fairy-tale ball. Why not enjoy it?

Sol, Teddy and I dance under the sparkling chandeliers. We look at all the fancy gowns and suits and masks and whisper to each other, giggling. Sol and Teddy drink glass after glass of sparkling champagne, and I politely refuse the masked waitstaff, until suddenly I look down and see a half-empty glass in my hand. Did I drink it? I don't remember doing it, but I can taste sparkles and starlight on my tongue. Nothing terrible happens. After all, I already drank some of Thurmond Boswell's tea and ate the cake that Caraway brought me. Nothing terrible happened then either.

Where is Caraway?

I can't believe he dragged me to Toad Prom and then ditched me.

I snag another glass of champagne from a masked and robed Toad bearing a tray. Then a tiny little cake from an ornate table by a marble toad fountain. It melts on my tongue, layer after layer of perfect flavor—violet, honey and evening summer breezes.

Sol finds me again. Teddy is off talking to some important Toads, and I remember what Mr. Boswell said—that he would introduce Teddy to some powerful people this weekend. People who could change Teddy's life. I'm happy for him. I'm happy for us all.

Sol and I dance until we can barely breathe, then collapse into one of the velvety alcoves, breathless and glistening with sweat. The alcove is all plush plum-colored couches and cushions, little gilt tables bearing thimbles of bitter orange brandy and powdery sugared madeleines. The low ceiling is studded with tiny lights like stars, and an ornate lantern hangs in the middle like a goose moon.

"How did it happen?" I ask. "You and Teddy."

Sol sits up and looks at me, his gaze penetrating. His pupils are so large, his eyes seem almost entirely black.

"It's okay," I assure him. "I'm on board. I'm team Sol/Teddy."

Sol laces his fingers into mine fondly and sinks back onto the couch so his head rests on my shoulder. He smells of sugar and oranges and Teddy.

"Remember when you did that chemistry intensive?" he asks. "You went away for our spring half-term break."

"Sure," I say. I'd beaten Caraway to be the one student that Candlecott sent and had felt *so* smug about it. But I hated the actual intensive. Hated being away from my friends and family. Hated the city where witches and magic junkies just casually walked the streets. Candlecott was safe. But in the city—or even at Staunton University—you never know what kind of trouble you might find yourself in.

"We went camping without you," Sol continues. "Down to Hazel Vale. We were exploring the forest down there and came across an old well. And . . . well, you know what they say about abandoned wells."

I nod. "If you give up a secret, then the well will grant you good fortune."

"Precisely. So I went first," Sol says. "I told it that I was afraid my family wouldn't accept me. For who I am now, you know."

I squeeze his hand. When Sol had first left Habasah when he was five years old to come and live with his aunt in Anglyon, his family believed that he was a girl.

"What secret did Teddy give up?"

Sol smiles softly. "He told the well that he was in love with me. That he had been since we were little kids."

I feel the tension of the moment as if I'd been there. Can picture the ruddy glow on Teddy's cheeks. The wide-eyed shock on Sol's face.

"But he never *said* anything," I say. "All that time?"

Sol shrugs. "He didn't think I felt the same way, and, well, he knew that if he did anything to mess up the three of us, you'd kill him."

I concede the truth of this with a nod.

"And you felt the same way?" I ask Sol.

He tilts his head from side to side. "I didn't, until that moment. I'd honestly never considered it before. I didn't even think he liked boys. I just never thought . . ."

The silly smile on his face makes my insides squirm with delight for both of them.

"The camping trip got *a lot* more fun after that," Sol says with a grin, and we both start to giggle.

"I really am just *so* happy for you both," I tell Sol, trying to be serious for a moment. "You know that, right? And I'm sorry I was such a maggot about it."

Sol hugs me. "I'm so glad you know everything now. I hated keeping secrets from you."

I rest my head against his shoulder for a moment.

"So tell me about Boswell," Sol says. "What's he like, away from school?"

"Caraway?" I ask. "He's . . . not what I expected."

I tell him about the Purple Menace. About how Caraway

saved me from Mr. Gray. About eating junk food in Deepdene and fighting the fenworm together.

"You sure have been having an adventure," Sol says. "It's like something from a story."

"Yeah," I agree. "I just hope it's one with a happy ending." In all the whirl and glitz of the evening, I've forgotten why I'm really here. "Sol, I still think it's a bad idea for Teddy to do this."

Sol takes my hand. "This is what he wants," he says gently. "He's been promised all sorts of opportunities. This is his dream, and I think as the people who love him best, we have to respect that."

He's right, isn't he? Have I been making this into more than it ever needed to be?

"But aren't you worried about the magic?" I say. "The stuff they're doing here is incredibly powerful. It's dangerous."

Sol shrugs. "Energy is energy," he says. "Some people nurture a rose by giving it water and sunlight. It's all life-force. All energy."

I fall quiet. Sol didn't grow up on cautionary tales of Jenny Greenteeth. He didn't live in Candlecott when the witches came. When my mother was cursed. He doesn't understand.

But . . . maybe he's right. Maybe with the right teacher, Teddy can learn to control his magic. Can use it to make beautiful things. I'd love to believe that.

If only I could stop hearing the cackling of witches in my dreams.

"It sounds like you and Caraway make a pretty good team," Sol says, clearly trying to change the subject.

I take another sip of brandy and let my worries melt away for a moment. I remember the patient way Caraway held my hand as I sobbed my heart out over Teddy and Sol. That was only a few hours ago. It feels like another lifetime.

"Most of the time he's a posh, snobby prat," I say. "But . . . I don't know. He has depths. And he's a pretty good kisser."

Sol clutches my wrist dramatically. "You *kissed* him?"

I grin and shrug.

"I can't believe you've been telling me about his crappy old car and giant nightmare worms but not mentioning that you *kissed* him. Tell me everything."

I grin. "A girl has to have some secrets."

"Are you going to do it again? Kiss him, I mean?"

I pause for a moment. I feel so safe here, with Sol in our little velvety alcove. The glittering whirl of the ball just a few feet away, there when we want it. But for now, a moment of quiet.

"Maybe," I admit, and Sol squeals.

"You should invite him camping with us," he says.

I snort. "Can you imagine Caraway camping? Cooking his own food?"

"He'd probably bring a butler."

We dissolve into giggles, and I can't ever remember feeling so happy.

We stay curled up together for ages, sipping bitter orange brandy and trading secrets. And for once, I'm not afraid to dream about the future.

"How will you and Teddy make it work?" I ask. "When you leave?"

Sol nibbles on a madeleine. "We've talked about it, of course. He's saving some money to come and visit me in Habasah. Meet

my family. And . . . well, he's heard about a possible apprenticeship in Oenotria, so we could meet there for a while. We'll figure
it out."

"I know you will."

A head pokes around the velvet curtain. "There you two are,"
says Teddy. "I've been looking for you everywhere."

Sol and I giggle again, and Teddy flops down on the couch.
"This party is amazing," he says giddily.

"Right?" I agree, before remembering that I'm supposed to
be getting Teddy out of here. "But maybe it's time to go?"

Teddy laughs. "Go?" he says. "Why?"

My mind is full of glitter. "Because—" I shake my head. "I
don't know. None of it's real, is it?"

"Does that matter?"

It did matter. It mattered a lot. But I'm finding it hard to hold
on to a single thought.

"Merry," Teddy says, his tone suddenly serious. "I know you
don't like Toad stuff. But . . . let's just have tonight before we start
fighting about it again. Please?"

He takes my hand, and I squeeze it.

It's so good to have him back. I hate fighting.

"We'll talk properly tomorrow," Teddy says. "About everything. We'll work it all out."

Tomorrow. Something's happening tomorrow.

But I don't remember what it is.

"Okay," I tell him. "Tomorrow."

"Great."

Sol grins and pats us both on the knee. "Well done, kids."

"D'you want to know what I'm wishing for?" Teddy asks me.

I blink at him, confused.

"Didn't Caraway tell you?" Teddy says, shaking his head. "At the end of the ball, there's a ceremony. The Toads offer gifts to the King Toad. If your gift is accepted, the king will grant you a wish."

It sounds like something from a fairy tale.

"What gift did you bring?" I ask Teddy, looking around for a wrapped package.

"Oh, it's not a real gift," Teddy says with an airy wave of his hand. "It's symbolic. I'm going to give him the sound of my hammer striking the anvil."

"And what will you wish for?"

"The Toads have Gofannon's Hammer."

I blink. Gofannon was a son of Dôn in the stories from long ago. A great metalsmith who could forge many magical weapons and artifacts. His hammer was itself a powerful weapon, as well as being his main smithing tool.

"That's just a story," I tell Teddy.

He shakes his head, his eyes lit up like two candles. "No, Merry. It's real. And they have it here in the Deeping Court, kept with many other treasures. I'm going to wish to forge something with it. Imagine what I could do with something that powerful!"

I suddenly remember Mr. Boswell's words to me, back in the library. *Being a Toadman . . . gives him access to tools that he never dreamed could even exist.*

"I might never get another chance to come here," Teddy says, with a sigh of longing. "Most Toadmen don't."

Sol touches him affectionately on the waist, then looks over at me. "We don't get to make wishes," he says. "Toads only."

"What would you wish for, if you could?" Teddy asks, leaning into Sol's hand.

"I'd ask for smooth passage to Habasah."

Teddy stiffens, just a little, and I know he's worried about Sol leaving.

"And a safe return home again," Sol adds, his lips curling in a smile. Teddy relaxes once more.

"What about you, Merry?" he asks.

Sol winks. "Maybe you'd wish for another kiss from Caraway?"

I swat his arm as Teddy turns to me, eyebrows raised. "*Another* kiss from Caraway?" he says. "What did I miss?"

Sol fills him in gleefully as my cheeks burn red.

"Well, well, well," Teddy says smugly. "Turns out all that fiery hatred was fiery passion all along."

"Shut up," I say, punching him in the arm.

We giggle and sip our brandy, and talk nonsense, the way we always do. And even though everything is still fairy-tale shimmer and glitter, I feel like things are finally back to normal.

Our conversation lapses, and I turn to see Teddy's hand on Sol's thigh, their heads bent close together. I hide a smile, and suddenly I want to see Caraway. I want to admire him in his fancy suit and touch his cheek and tell him what a nice time I've been having.

"I'm going to go and find some more food," I say, extracting myself from the plush velvet.

"You want us to come with you?" says Sol, but his heart isn't in it.

I shake my head. "You two stay here."

I leave them to it and plunge back into the ball. Things have grown more raucous. The music is faster. The dancers spin wildly. The laughter in the air is like the ringing of a thousand bells. I push through it all, on a mission.

"It's her!" I hear a drunken voice cry, and turn to see a Toadman pointing at me. "The Fox Bride!"

He bows theatrically before me, and, confused, I bob a curtsy back. The Toadman takes my hand and kisses it.

"An honor, my lady."

There's a sort of terrace, halfway up a staircase. The Toads there wear sober gray suits. Their masks are gold or silver, covering their whole faces, the way Mr. Gray's did. I guess that's the VIP section. They don't seem to have consorts with them, and they don't hold drinks. They watch the crowd, occasionally murmuring to each other. They look so *boring*, like they're not having a good time at all. What more could they ask for? I guess fancy balls are wasted on old people.

My eyes scan the room, and I spot Caraway, standing on his own by a leaping fountain. He looks aloof and cold as always, but the sight of him stirs something inside me. He's an ice prince, but he's a handsome ice prince. I push through the crowd and grab his arm. He turns to look at me in surprise.

"Where have you been?" he hisses.

"Enjoying the party."

He's distracted, his eyes roving the crowd. His gaze flicks up to the terrace where Mr. Boswell and the other Toads watch; then he leans in, his lips against my ear.

"There's going to be a ceremony," he murmurs. I can feel his breath against my skin, and it sends a delicious shiver down my spine. "In about half an hour. If we slip out now, we can get there and back before anyone notices."

"Get *where* and back?" I ask. Dimly I recall that there was somewhere we were going to go. "Is this the favor you need from me?"

"Yes."

I feel a fizz of excitement. In all the dazzle and spectacle of the ball, I'd forgotten that Caraway and I were on a mission. Secret agents! It's thrilling.

He grabs my hand, and that's thrilling too, the cool of his palm against my warm one. I lace my fingers into his like it's the most natural thing in the world. We weave through the crowd past dancers and towering platters of cured sculpin, oysters and gooseneck barnacles garnished with gold flakes and Gaguni caviar.

I tug Caraway to a halt, staring at a woman clad in a gown made entirely of blue feathers. A real bluebird perches on her crooked finger, watching her with a beady eye. She whistles gently to it, and it sings back. Caraway looks over his shoulder at the woman, and his lip curls in distaste. How can he not be impressed? The woman is so beautiful, full red lips beneath her feathered blue mask. Caraway pulls at my hand, and we continue to wend our way through the crowd. People glance at us as we pass, then look away, disinterested. To them we're just another couple, stealing away to a velvety alcove for some private canoodling.

I remember Sol's delighted squeal when I told him that Caraway and I had kissed.

Are you going to do it again? Kiss him, I mean?

Caraway slips behind a velvet curtain, and I follow, expecting to find another cozy alcove. Instead there is a narrow flight of stone stairs.

"Come on," he mutters over his shoulder. "We don't have much time."

"Are we going to break into someone's room?" I hiss after him. "Are we looking for Teddy's string?"

Caraway doesn't answer, just charges up the stairs. I grab a fistful of tulle and lace in one hand to raise my skirts so I don't trip, and follow him up the stairs. We pass a small wooden door after two flights, but Caraway doesn't pause. After four flights, my heart is pounding.

"Wait," I gasp. "I need a break."

Caraway doesn't even slow down. He just keeps climbing, so I follow, even though my chest aches and my throat rasps from trying to draw deeper breaths. I don't mind, though. It's all part of the adventure.

Eight flights, and we run out of stairs. The wooden door at the top is unpainted and without ornamentation. Caraway listens at it for a moment before turning the handle and stepping through. My head spins, but I follow, breathless and a little dizzy.

Another corridor with doors leading off. It could be the one that our apartment is on. They all look the same. But Caraway seems to know where he is going. He passes one door, then another. Then he stops outside the third door, putting his ear to it once more.

He tries the handle, but it's locked. He keeps his palm on it, though, and frowns in concentration. I look threadwise and see him doing something complex to the lock, strands of Toad mettle weaving in among tumblers and shanks. There's a click, and the door swings open.

The apartment inside is palatial. I'm in an entrance hall that is bigger than our entire house, white marble floor and wood-paneled walls. Doors lead off to the right and left, and the other end of the hall opens up into what looks like an enormous living room, the marble floor softened with richly colored rugs and clustered with leather armchairs before a huge fireplace. Floor-to-ceiling windows line the wall at the other end of the living area, but I can only see inky blackness outside.

"Whose apartment is this?" I ask.

Caraway doesn't answer.

Whoever the apartment belongs to, they have good taste. It's luxurious, but in an old-fashioned, elegant way. Golden light spills from brass sconces on the walls. I can smell leather and sage and sandalwood. A dark polished wooden cabinet lines one wall, displaying what I'm sure are priceless vases and small sculptures.

I pad after Caraway, who is in what looks like an office, the room dominated by a large mahogany desk, inlaid with maroon leather and mother-of-pearl.

"I need you to turn witch-eyed," he says.

"Threadwise," I correct.

"Whatever." Caraway looks nervous, even beneath the radiance of his glamour. "Evans's stone is in here somewhere. A round brownish gemstone. Can you find it?"

My heart leaps. We're here to find Teddy's stone. His missing string. Eagerly, I look threadwise around the room. It's more difficult than usual—there's so much Toad mettle everywhere, and the champagne makes everything blurry. I prowl through the apartment, searching for an echo of Teddy's mettle, but I keep getting distracted by how *nice* everything is. How luxurious and expensive, but never ostentatious. I trail my fingers along the back of a leather chair and marvel at how soft it is. I inhale the scent from an exquisite arrangement of spidery orchids. I stare dreamily at the spines of books on a bookshelf, and imagine spending time here, reading in perfect comfort.

"Anything?" Caraway's voice drifts from the study.

I can't concentrate. Maybe fresh air will help. I slip out through the glass door into the night and breathe in the fen below—rich peat, stagnant water and something dark and fungal.

The terrace is astonishing. Sculpted marble, with the crenellated exterior of a Gothic castle. I see the dark, still water of a swimming pool, glittering with stars reflected from overhead.

The *stars*.

They're breathtaking, a dazzling spill of diamonds scattered across the velvet sky. I stand like a statue, my face tilted up to the heavenly glory of it all.

I don't know how long I stand there, but it must be a while, because Caraway comes looking for me.

"Are you okay?" he asks.

"Look," I breathe, and reach out for him, putting my fingers to his chin and tilting his head up to look at the sky. His hand settles in the small of my back, and my skin ripples into gooseflesh. I remember the closeness of the robe storage cupboard at the Candlecott Frater House, Caraway's body pressed against my back, his hand over my mouth. The scent of mothballs, bergamot and old leather.

So much has happened since then.

I turn to face him and see the whole galaxy reflected in his eyes. In some ways it's easier to look at him with his toad mask on. I don't get so misled by the coldness of his glamour. Mask upon mask upon mask. We stare at each other for a long moment, so close and silent. Fox and Toad. Then I lean forward a little, so our bodies touch. His hands are still on my waist, and I feel them tighten, pulling me closer. His breath hitches, eyes sliding to my lips. An electric thrill flutters deep in my stomach.

I reach up and push my fingers into his hair, and he tilts his head back a little, lips parting. Around us, the world is inky black, speckled with stars. I forget we're supposed to be secret agents. Nothing exists but me and Caraway in the beautiful darkness of the night.

The kiss is butterfly-light, the most delicate brushing of lips, but I feel it in every part of my body. My hands are still wound into Caraway's hair, and I gently pull his head down toward mine. The kiss deepens, and I don't just feel it in my body anymore. The feeling spreads until it floods the terrace, the whole of Deeping Fen, the whole world. It is everything and everywhere. I imagine people waking up on the other side of the world and putting their fingers to their lips, feeling them tingle. Sailors at sea, gripping the rails of their ships a little tighter as the ocean shudders beneath them. Birds getting caught in the rising current of air generated by our kiss, letting it carry them up toward the stars.

This means *something*. It means *everything*. I feel it in the way we hold each other, like we are each a treasure so rare and perfect that we're afraid to let it go, lest it be destroyed forever.

I know Caraway feels it too.

My fox mask presses against his toad one, and I wonder if the story got it wrong. Perhaps the toad *was* noble and brave. He did rescue the Fox Bride, after all. Perhaps they fell in love.

Or perhaps tonight we write a new story, witnessed by the stars.

The kiss breaks, and Caraway's eyes search mine.

"We have to find the stone," he whispers. "We don't have much time."

I nod. The kiss has sharpened my focus, and I let my awareness drift outward until it snags on the familiar silvery trail of Teddy's mettle, wrapped in thick ropes of Toad magic like parasitic vines. I take Caraway's hand and lead him back into the apartment, back into the study, running my fingers over leatherbound book spines until I find the one that isn't a book at all. I pull it out, opening the box to reveal a single stone nestled within, a shiny brown marble.

"Here," I say, plucking it out.

"Are you sure?"

I smile at Caraway. "Of course I'm sure."

We found it. Now that we have Teddy's stone, we can go, and he will be safe from Toadmen.

My attention is caught by a framed photo on the bookshelf. Thurmond Boswell, a little younger perhaps, shaking hands with an angular woman wearing an expensive-looking linen shift.

"This is your father's office," I say, as realization dawns. "Is that your mother?"

Caraway glances at the photo. "That's Ophelia Welch," he says. "CEO of Welch Wellness."

"She can't be a Toad, though. She's a woman."

"Not all powerful people are Toads."

I blink. "So why is your father—"

"Come on," Caraway interrupts, taking the toadstone from me and slipping it into his pocket. "We have to go."

He leads me out of the apartment and along the corridor to another flight of stairs. Down, this time. Down and down and down.

"Are we going back to the party?" I ask.

"Not yet."

The air changes as we descend, growing stale and frigid. I feel a tingle of fear at the base of my spine, and I kind of love it. It's all part of the adventure. I can feel the kiss still buzzing on my lips, can still taste starlight and champagne.

Eventually we find ourselves in a dark stone passage. Caraway lifts a hand and coaxes a flame to his palm.

"Pretty," I whisper. The stone walls seem to suck up my voice.

I follow him down the passage, letting my fingers trail along the rough, damp stone of the walls and enjoying the sensation of it on my skin.

The passage ends at another door, and Caraway stops, putting his ear to it. Then we step through to find ourselves in a cavernous hall.

It's a little bit like the Frater House, but on a much, much bigger scale. Benches fill most of the space, with a wide aisle running down the middle. At one end of the room is a pair of huge oaken doors, intricately carved, and at the other is a dais with a golden throne in front of a weirdly glittery wall.

"What now?" I ask.

Caraway takes my hand and leads me down the aisle toward the dais. I look over my shoulder at the huge carved doors, recognizing the characters from the story he told me about the toads. I spot the Green Knight, looking foppish and confused, surrounded by the twisted vines of the fen. The Fox Bride, a cunning smile on her face. The Howling Toad, its mouth open wide. The Ghost Toad, almost indistinguishable from the foliage. And the King Toad, crowned and noble (or as noble as a toad can be, anyway).

"Why isn't there a Beast?" I ask. "Isn't the whole point of the story that the toad saves the people of Deepdene from a Beast?"

But Caraway doesn't answer. He's stopped, frozen, head cocked.

I hear it too. Footsteps outside the doors.

Someone is coming.

I hitch up my skirts, and we dash down the aisle and up onto the dais. The wall behind the throne has an odd texture. As I approach I see that it's a kind of grid, with each square containing a stone, just like Teddy's one, nestled in Caraway's pocket, brownish yellow, but highly polished, gleaming in the dim light.

We duck behind a heavy velvet curtain, just as the huge carved doors swing open.

"Do come in," says a silky, masculine voice from the other end of the room.

I hear two sets of footsteps approaching and peek out from behind the curtain, careful to make sure I can't be seen.

The grand hall is dimly lit by the same glass-covered lamps as the rest of the Deeping Court, so at first all I can see is two shapes, slowly approaching the throne. Both masked. I feel Caraway tense beside me as they draw closer and I can make them out more clearly.

The first man is wearing a full-face mask, not the half-face kind that the guests at the ball wore. The mask is white, a blank outline in the shape of a toad's skull.

I suppress a shudder when I see it.

The Ghost Toad.

"The thing is, Brother Alec," he says over his shoulder at the second figure hovering just behind him, "when you joined us you made certain promises. And while I'm very sympathetic to your position, I fear you have forgotten those promises, and thought that maybe this would be the right place to remind you."

His voice is familiar, but I can't quite place it through the champagne fog.

I can sense the fear radiating off the second figure. "My lord," he says, his voice trembling. "Please . . ."

He's clearly come straight from the ball. He wears a tuxedo and a black glittering half mask.

The Ghost Toad wanders up onto the dais with all the calm in the world. He circles behind the throne and looks up at the wall of stones.

"What do you see, Brother Alec?" he asks, gesturing to the wall.

"Stones, my lord," says the other Toadman, who has crept up behind the Ghost Toad like a dog expecting a beating.

"Do you know what they are?"

The Toadman shakes his head.

"They are toadstones, formed from the strings of Toadmen.

One of them is yours, you know. You gifted it to the king when you were initiated, do you remember?"

The Toadman nods, gazing up at the wall.

"You have gifted him strings since then, of course. You wouldn't be here otherwise. With every string you have given him, he has given you back power tenfold. Riches. Power. Everything your heart has ever desired. Has he not?"

"Y-yes, my lord."

"Of course only one of your stones is here on the wall. That very first one you gave, when you swore an oath to keep the secrets of the Toadmen."

My gaze travels up the wall as I take in the Ghost Toad's words. One stone for every member of the Toadmen. There must be hundreds of thousands of stones on this wall. Maybe a million. I had no idea there were that many Toadmen. I suppose not all of them are still alive, but still. That's a lot of Toads. A lot of mettle, just to decorate a wall.

I'm suddenly filled with gratitude for Caraway, who helped me steal Teddy's stone before it made it onto the wall.

"We are a brotherhood," the Ghost Toad explains. "Each stone is connected to the others through the power of kinship, of fraternity. It is not a connection that can be broken."

I remember asking Caraway why he couldn't just walk away from the Toads.

It isn't that easy.

"I hear you have a new paramour, do you not, Brother Alec?" the Ghost Toad asks.

The Toadman nods.

"What is her name?"

"B-Bessie."

"And Bessie doesn't like that you are a Toadman, does she?"

The Toadman shakes his head.

"She is jealous of your brotherhood," the Ghost Toad says. "She wishes to have you all to herself. She whispers poison into your ears, and weakness seeps into your heart."

He wheels away from the wall abruptly and stalks over to the throne, laying his hand on one ornate golden armrest.

"Have a seat, my brother."

The Toadman takes a step back and shakes his head.

"My lord," he says. "I couldn't . . ."

"Go on," urges the Ghost Toad. "I won't tell anyone. See how it feels."

Slowly, the Toadman approaches the throne. I see the tremble in his hands as he gingerly lowers himself to the golden seat.

"What do you think?" the Ghost Toad asks.

"V-v-very nice, my lord."

The Ghost Toad makes a disapproving sound. "Not very comfortable, though, is it? Leadership never is. For all the gold and riches bestowed upon him, a leader must bear a heavy burden. So it is for our king. And so it is for me. I do not wish to be down here with you, Brother Alec. I would love to be up there, enjoying the revels. But I must do my duty, just as you must do yours."

He reaches into the inner pocket of his jacket and pulls out what looks like a very sharp silver knitting needle, with a mother-of-pearl handle. He stands behind the trembling Toad, caressing his cheeks softly with the point of the needle.

"What is it she likes best about you?" the Ghost Toad asks,

moving the needle down until it is over the Toad's chest. "Your tender heart?"

He moves the needle lower, and the man whimpers.

"Your impressive manhood?" the Ghost Toad chuckles softly. "No, I don't think so."

"P-p-please," the Toad gasps. "I'm sorry."

"I know you are. But you haven't answered my question. What is it that this girl likes about you, more than anything else?" He taps the needle gently against the man's temple. "Certainly not your capable mind or quick wit, I think we both know that. Come, now. Tell me."

"M-m-my s-smile," says the Toad, his voice turned all squeaky and hoarse. "Sh-she says she likes my smile."

"Ahhh. A smile can be an incredible thing."

The needle glides up to the top of the Toad's skull.

"Your smile starts up here, you know. In your brain. The seventh cranial nerve, here"—the needle taps on one side of his skull and then the other—"and here."

With a flick of the needle, the Ghost Toad slices through the string attaching the mask to the Toadman's head. It falls to the ground with a clatter, revealing a pale face shining with sweat.

"Then your smile travels along the hearing nerve," the Ghost Toad continues, as the needle dips down and circles the Toadman's ear, "and through the parotid gland before branching out to connect with the facial muscles. But if we stop just before that branching happens . . ." The needle pauses, just above the hinge of the Toad's jaw. "Imagine, that beautiful smile of yours controlled by such a tiny little bit of nerve."

I realize I'm holding my breath.

"One tiny bit of nerve. One tiny little pinch . . ."

I barely see the needle dip into the man's flesh. It's in and out within the space of a heartbeat. The Toad doesn't cry out. There's no blood. Just a flash of silver, then one side of the Toad's face is collapsing like it's a melting candle. His left eye grows heavy-lidded and starts to water. The left corner of his mouth droops downward in a gaping frown. My fingers dig into the palms of my hand.

"Oh dear," says the Ghost Toad. "I wonder what Bessie will say about your smile now?"

The Toad takes a shuddering breath, but says nothing.

"I think we'll leave the other side," says the Ghost Toad, slipping the needle back into his inside pocket. "For now, anyway. Remember, Brother Alec. We are a family. You can't give up on your family." He gestures at the wall of stones. "I'm afraid you are one of us forever."

The Toadman hesitates for just a fraction of a second, as if not quite believing what has just happened. But then he bows his head.

"Yes, my lord."

"You may go."

The Toadman scurries away back up the aisle and through the huge carved doors.

The Ghost Toad stands still for a long moment, one hand resting gently on the throne. Then he straightens his cuffs, and I suddenly realize where I've heard his voice before. I squint and look at him threadwise to confirm it, and see the ropes of mettle, toadish and silver, stretching between him and Caraway.

Thurmond Boswell.

The Ghost Toad is Caraway's father.

The world slows down for a moment. Mild-mannered, tea-sipping Thurmond Boswell. I knew he was powerful—with his job at Ilium and everything. But this is something else. He stole that man's *smile*. I remember what Caraway told me about the Ghost Toad.

He has spies everywhere. He knows everything.

The huge doors swing closed with an ominous *boom*, and I swing to face Caraway.

"You knew," I accuse him. "Your father is . . . You *knew*."

He doesn't deny it.

"He's a . . . a *monster*."

He seemed so mild, earlier today in the library. So kind. He said he'd look after Teddy, and I believed him. "I can't believe I had tea with him" is all I manage to say.

Caraway's brow darkens in a frown. "You had tea with him? With my *father*?"

"I ran into him in the library. He . . . he was so nice. He gave me a book."

"And you took it? Did he make you promise anything?"

"N-no," I stammer. "Nothing."

Will you help me, Ms. Morgan?

"I can't believe you didn't tell me sooner."

I let out an indelicate snort. "I can't believe *you* didn't tell *me* your father is the *Ghost Toad*."

"It never came up in conversation."

Suddenly, I remember that I hate Caraway Boswell. "You lied to me. You told me all about the three toads, but you didn't mention that one of them was your *father*."

"No, I didn't."

"You've done nothing but lie to me. Everyone in this place is a liar."

He blows air out of his cheeks. "Good. Finally, you're getting it."

We glare at each other for a moment, the heat of our words simmering between us. Then his hands are on me and we're kissing again, our masks mashed together. This kiss is not a perfect one. It's heated and furious, teeth grazing skin, fingers pressing hard. I push him back against the wall of stones and he growls, deep in his throat, as I press myself against him.

I yank off his mask and my own and let them fall to the ground, and he cups my face in his hands, his fingers hot against my skin.

"You'll be the death of me, Morgan," he mutters into my mouth.

He's not wrong, because I am absolutely going to kill him, as soon as I get this kissing out of my system.

"Shut up," I retort.

The searing crush of the kiss is almost too much to bear. I'm on fire, lit up and glowing like a Hollantide lantern.

Then he pulls away. I see his chest rise and fall. Pink splotches color his cheeks. I want more.

"You've been drinking," he says, his face falling.

I shrug. "So?"

"I thought you really . . ." He shakes his head. "Never mind. Come over here."

He walks to the wall of toadstones, and I follow him, my lips still burning and my head full of stars.

"Tell me which one is mine."

I want to tell him to eat a bag of toads, but I hear the slight tremble in his voice, and it undoes me. I look threadwise at the wall.

"That one," I say, pointing.

"Here?" Caraway places his fingers on the stone, and I nod.

"Are you going to take it?" I ask.

Caraway hesitates. "No," he says at last. "Not yet. They'll notice if there's one missing. That's why we needed to get Evans's before it went up here."

I put my hand on Caraway's shoulder. "Thank you," I say.

"It's nothing," he responds.

But I'm beginning to think that it isn't nothing. That maybe Caraway is starting to matter, to me. Or has all the champagne and enchantment turned my head? I can't tell anymore.

The last vestiges of my anger burn away and I'm left with something unexpected.

"Oh dear," I murmur.

"Are you okay?" Caraway responds.

"I don't think so," I say. My face flushes hot as words start to tumble uncontrollably from my mouth. "I—I was talking to Sol about you, and I realized that when you bring me a coffee and a rhubarb muffin at Staunton, I'm actually really *happy* to see you. And—well, I wasn't expecting that. You weren't part of my *plan*, and now it turns out you're evil Toad royalty, which makes everything all the more complicated, because I don't want that for you. Or for me."

Caraway reaches down and picks up his mask, staring at it,

his expression hollow. "I never should have listened to him," he says. "Never should have involved you in any of this."

Listened to who? His father? The Ghost Toad?

"I involved myself," I remind him.

"No, you didn't."

I've had too much champagne. Tears are slipping down my cheeks, and I know that this time I don't look like a boiled pudding, because the glamour patch will turn each tear into a sparkling drop of fairy dew. I'll cry the way dainty maidens in books cry—delicately and beautifully.

Caraway wipes my tears with his thumb and presses his lips to my forehead. I close my eyes and breathe him in.

His father is the Ghost Toad.

This cannot end well.

He gently ties the fox mask back over my eyes, and replaces his own.

"We have to get back," he tells me, and gives me a gentle push down the stairs to the aisle, before turning for a moment toward the wall of toadstones. With his back to me, I see him put his hand to his own stone for a moment, bowing his head.

I wish we could steal his stone too. That he could escape from this awful place with me and Sol and Teddy.

Caraway turns and together we hurry down the aisle and through the doors.

THE PARTY IS STILL in full swing. But there's something new in the air, a breath of expectation. Space has been cleared around the toad statue and the golden throne. The King Toad's throne.

Caraway hustles me into an empty alcove. "Stay here," he orders. "Talk to no one. I'll come and collect you once it's all over."

I'm going to object, but he kisses me, swift and hard. Then he's gone.

I put a trembling hand to my mouth.

This is all wrong. Suddenly the glitz and glamour of the evening feel overwhelming. I don't want to be here anymore. I don't belong here, among these beautiful people with their beautiful gowns and their rich food. I had a nice time playing in fairyland, but now I desperately want to go home.

I sink down to the velvet couch, and the alcove spins around me.

Caraway was right. I shouldn't have drunk anything.

Tinkling music sounds from outside, and for a moment I wonder what will happen if I go back out there. Give myself over to the giddy whirl of the night. Lose myself in dance and drink and revels. The party whispers sweet promises to me, but all I can think about is Caraway's lips on mine, sweet and hot and shimmering with starlight.

My vision blurs double and I can't hold a thought for more than a few seconds before it drifts away.

Come back, the party calls. *You're missing out.*

But I can't. I need to focus. There are more important things at stake here than glitter and champagne bubbles.

I have to sober up, and fast. Thank goodness for Da's paranoia.

I pull the little ampoule from my bodice and snap the top off, swallowing the contents in a single gulp. It tastes of plastic and milk thistle.

It doesn't take long to work. The downside of Sebrium is that it doesn't strip you of the hangover. It hits me harder than Teddy's hammer hits the anvil. My head pounds and I break out in a cold sweat. My stomach churns and I lean over and vomit into an ice bucket, careful not to get any on my dress.

What I wouldn't give for a swig of Ken Lanagan's hangover dram right now.

The alcove seems different, now that the enchanted food and drink are out of my system. The rich plush velvet now seems moth-eaten and threadbare. Spiderwebs cling to damp stone walls, and I can hear a noise like the clicking of insects.

I push aside the curtain and step out into the hall, and bile rises in my throat once more.

I'm in a nightmare.

10.

THE MUSIC HAS STOPPED, ALTHOUGH GUESTS STILL
dance and spin as if it hasn't. I can still hear laughter and
screams of delight, but behind that is silence. The ballroom
no longer sparkles with golden light. I glance up and see no glittering crystal. Instead a sickly pale light emanates from chandeliers made of yellowing bone, dripping with black wax.

Before me, a masked woman in an elaborately embroidered gown licks acidic-looking slime from her fingers as if it is
the most delectable syrup she has ever tasted. The stench of it
is overwhelming—sour rot and putrescence. Behind her, a man
shoves a handful of what appears to be raw animal entrails into
his mouth, and my stomach churns as I see maggots squirm between his fingers. All the food is rotten. Mountains of festering
raw meat and decomposing slime.

My stomach heaves again, but there's nothing left in it to
come out.

The hall is clammy and damp. The velvet drapes on the
walls now appear as burial shrouds—tattered and stained. The

walls themselves are spattered with mold and dripping with condensation.

The string quartet is gone, and the swish and swirl of the dancers seem eerie without them, laughter ringing in damp echoes throughout the hall.

The older Toads watch from their balcony VIP section, their full-face masks impassive as always. None of them are holding drinks. There are no robed Toads bearing trays up there. They're not eating or drinking. Which means they can see this nightmare as it really is. Is it all of the Toads? Could Teddy see through the glitter to this horror beneath?

No. There are plenty of garden-variety Toads down here. Younger ones, shoveling maggoty rotting meat into their mouths and drinking glasses of what looks like bog water. One of the older men on the balcony points down into the crowd, and I follow his gaze to see a much younger Toad, his consort on all fours like a dog, a leash attached to a studded collar around her neck. On-lookers watch and laugh, their voices edged with malice. I push through the crowd and see the woman in the blue feathered dress, the one who had a bluebird perched on her finger. Except it isn't a bluebird anymore. I watch her coo at the muddy toad in her palm, and shudder as she places a delicate kiss on its warty head.

I think about the cake that Caraway gave me. He's done nothing but lie to me this whole time.

I can't believe I almost fell for it.

I need to find Teddy and Sol.

My memory of before is hazy, and I can't quite remember which alcove they're in. I poke my head into one and see the writhing of naked limbs—more than I can count. The next is only two people, and I see the flash of a chain and hear the snap of a leather whip.

I hear a sob escape my throat as I yank aside each damp filthy curtain. I see three women licking blood from each other's fingers. A man lying naked on a velvet couch, moaning in ecstasy, his skin crawling with black shiny beetles.

I find them at last, and my heart calms a little.

They're asleep, curled up together on the filthy cushions. They look so peaceful. Teddy's arms are wrapped protectively around Sol, who sleeps with a faint smile on his face.

An earwig wriggles from Teddy's nostril, and I bite back a scream.

We have to get out of here.

I sink to my knees beside them, my gown billowing out around me, and start to shake them.

"Wake up," I mutter. "Come *on.*"

But they do not wake, no matter how hard I shake. I dig my nails into Sol's palm. Yank on Teddy's hair. But they don't so much as stir.

"Leave them," a voice says in my ear. "They'll be fine."

I scramble to my feet and whirl to face Caraway.

"I told you to stay where you were," he says, his eyes as cold as the marble floor of his father's apartment.

I shove him against the wall, but this time I don't want to kiss him. "What is all this?"

"The King Toad's Ball. I didn't want you to see it how it really is."

"You should have *told* me."

I wouldn't have drunk the champagne. I wouldn't have

danced with Teddy and Sol. I would have made sure they didn't eat or drink either.

I look around wildly. "Why?" I ask him. "Why is it like this?"

Caraway glances outside the curtain, up to where the VIP Toads gather. "Entertainment," he says shortly.

I never should have trusted a Toad. I was right about Caraway all along. Of course he finds all this entertaining. I can't bear to look at him.

"You *drugged* me," I say.

He manages to look horrified. "I *told* you not to drink anything," he said. "The food just makes you see the illusion. It's the drink that changes the way you feel."

I push past him, back out to the ball. I'm going to scream. Or throw up again. Or . . . *something.*

People are starting to gather around the King Toad's throne, which is different too, no longer gold and red velvet. Now it is made from yellowing bone and black basalt, a pair of enormous rusty swords crossed over the back.

Robed Toad attendants are ushering everyone into a semi-circle around the throne, with a wide clear area before it. I glance around at the attendees, and all I see is eyes shining eagerly from behind their masks. They can't wait for what comes next.

A Toad in a red robe and mask appears on the dais and raises his hands for silence.

"Behold," he says in a booming voice that fills the space and sends shivers down my spine. "The King of Toads."

Everyone sinks into bows or curtsies, and even I bob down a little and duck my head, because I don't want them to know that I've sobered up. But I glance up to see the giant gold toad statue seem to melt a little, its jaw sinking down, down, down, creating a great open cavernous maw. It is from this new darkness that the King Toad emerges.

He's tall. Taller than any man I've ever seen. His body is obscured beneath thick black robes, and his face is covered by a toad mask made of highly polished gold, with two red rubies winking out where there should be eyeholes. An ornate crown sits atop the masked head, twisted branches made of hammered gold and glittering with jewels.

Who is under that robe? Another powerful man, like Thurmond Boswell? Perhaps it's the CEO of Ilium, or someone from one of the other big magic companies. Or perhaps it's someone from high up in the government. Whoever it is, they must be on stilts, because nobody can be that tall.

The crowd starts to cheer and whoop when they see him, like he's the headline act at some kind of music festival. He makes his way slowly, gracefully, across the dais, gliding in a distinctly nonhuman fashion. Then he sinks down onto the throne, raising a gloved hand in acknowledgment of the crowd.

The red-robed Toad steps forward once more. "Welcome, my brothers and your consorts, to the Deeping Court, and to the King Toad's Ball. You are fortunate indeed to attend—it is an honor bestowed on only a select few. Many have wished to meet the King of Toads, but few have. You have drunk his wine, eaten his food and worn his riches on your fingers and around your throats. But this is not the limit of His Majesty's generosity. You now have the opportunity to offer him a gift, and in return he will grant you your heart's desire." The red-robed Toad looks around the room, his eyes glinting through the dark holes of his mask. "Who will be first to present their gift to our mighty and munificent king?"

There's a moment of silence; then a masked Toad steps forward. He's wearing tight leather trousers and has a dark wine stain on his white shirt. I see his hands trembling as he sinks to one knee.

"I will," he says, his voice cracking. "I am a mere farmer's son, and I'm . . . humbled before your magnificence, my lord. I gift the first apple of summer to you."

Two more robed Toads step forward. One holds a bowl, the other a black iron hook. It's identical to the one I saw in the Frater House back home. The one that was used to cut one of Teddy's strings.

My blood runs cold.

"Do you give this gift of yourself willingly?" The Toadman intones.

"I do."

One robed Toadman holds out a bowl. Another sweeps the scythe, and I look at it threadwise, but there is such a whirling riot of the brownish, swampy mettle that I let out a little involuntary gasp. The mettle writhes and surges through the room, wrapping every single guest in a choking hold, spreading pulsing veins of magic down the walls and strung through the air like vines. It's nothing like the usual delicate, silvery mettle I'm used to. This magic is powerful and ugly. I'm expecting it to coalesce on the enormous robed figure of the King Toad, but it doesn't. It all goes down into the floor, traveling down. I travel with it, my consciousness sinking into the stones beneath my feet and falling down, down, deep into the bowels of the Deeping Court.

There's something down there.

Something huge and powerful.

Mettle. The Toadmen are harvesting mettle from members. They must be storing it down there. For what? To power their illusions, the strange, twisted magic I've witnessed since coming here? Or perhaps for Thurmond Boswell to sell to Ilium?

As I sink farther down, the mettle threads around me constrict, like I've been *noticed*. Panicking, I rise back up and into my own body again, just in time to see the black iron hook snag on one of the farmer's strings. The robed Toad pulls, but it's not like it was with Teddy in the Frater House. This time there is almost no resistance at all. There's a faint *pop* and the string breaks easily, spiraling in on itself from the force of impact, until it forms a ball, not unlike an owl pellet. The ball drops into the outstretched copper bowl with a *tink*, and everyone applauds. I blink and disable my thread sight.

Do these other Toads know what just happened? They can't see the thread break, but they can see the hook. They've had it done to them, at their own initiations.

How can they be clapping and cheering?

I'm literally shaking after brushing up against whatever is beneath the Deeping Court. That great reservoir of mettle. And the fact that it *sensed* me, somehow. That's never happened before when I've used my mettle-tracking gift. Is it some kind of magical security system?

My head aches suddenly from the intensity of it all, and I think I might be sick again.

"Your offer has been accepted," says the red-robed Toad solemnly. "What is your wish?"

The farmer Toad doesn't seem to have noticed his missing string, but I see him wobble a little on his knees, hear the slur in his voice. Whatever enchantment is on the guests at the ball must dull the impact of it.

"I wish for coin," he says. "Enough to pay my family's debts."

Everyone looks at the King Toad, who remains impassive for a moment. Then his great head lowers in a nod. It doesn't look quite right. The movement is jerky. Unnatural.

Could the King Toad be some kind of puppet?

"Your wish will be granted," the red-robed Toad declares.

There's more applause, and people start to jostle toward the front of the crowd. Everyone wants to give the King Toad a gift and make their wish.

I watch as more Toads make their pledges. A happy childhood memory. The crusty heel from a fresh loaf. The first song played on a new lute.

String after string is cut. I've heard it doesn't hurt so much if it's given willingly. And it's more powerful too. But it's still *lifeforce*. Those strings won't grow back.

Out of the corner of my eye, I spot Teddy, moving toward the front of the crowd, Sol at his elbow. They are sleep-mussed and beautiful, but I see the eagerness on Teddy's face.

Gofannon's Hammer—the actual tool wielded by the legendary smith. Of course Teddy wants to see it. To use it at a forge. I think of the little cardboard one he has hanging from his rearvision mirror. It's all he's ever wanted. His desire to join the Toadmen makes sense now. Of the three of us, Teddy has always been the most ambitious, and the most talented.

But even if it's true—even if Gofannon's Hammer is real, and the Toadmen have it . . . surely it's not worth losing a string over?

I remember the sundering feeling as the hook snapped Teddy's string in the Frater House, while I watched helplessly.

I'm not going to let it happen again. Every string that Teddy gives will bind him closer to the Toadmen. And now that I've seen what they really are—cruel, powerful, dangerous—I can't let it happen. Teddy's *life* is at stake.

The King Toad still sits motionless on his throne.

I elbow my way through the crowd, stepping on feet and pulling on capes and jackets. A few people murmur in surprise, but nobody tries to stop me. They're all drugged senseless.

"Who is next?" booms the red-robed Toadman.

Teddy takes a step forward, but I'm faster. I stumble out into the open space at the front of the crowd.

"Me," I say. "I'm next."

A murmur of surprise ripples through the crowd.

"Merry," Teddy says. "I told you that consorts don't present gifts."

"First time for everything," I reply, and swallow down the sting when I see disappointment on his face.

"Merry." Teddy's voice is low. *"Please."*

I'm suddenly aware I'm at a crossroads. If I go through with this, then I'm not sure Teddy will ever forgive me. But if I do nothing, then he'll become a Toadman. And after what I saw the Ghost Toad do, I just can't let that happen. I bite my cheek to keep my expression neutral.

Whatever happens next, I'm going to lose my best friend.

"My gift is a kiss." The words coming from my mouth sound a lot more confident than I feel.

The red-robed Toad regards me for a long moment; then I see his eyes flick up to the balcony where the VIP toads are watching, and I follow his gaze to see the Ghost Toad himself. Thurmond Boswell—masked and unrecognized, but *him* all the same. Caraway is there too, at his father's elbow, staring at me. His fists are clenched, his jaw tight.

The Ghost Toad's head lowers in a nod, and I get the feeling that he's somehow *pleased* I've broken this sacred Toad law.

"The King Toad welcomes the Fox Bride," the red-robed Toad announces. "And bids her to present her wedding gift."

I touch my fingers to the fox mask as uneasiness spreads through me.

I'm not the Fox Bride.

Am I?

I'm afraid I might be doing something unforgivably foolish. But I make my way up onto the dais.

Up close, the King Toad is even larger, a broad-shouldered figure, bigger than any man has the right to be. My heart is hammering so hard that I can't hear anything else. I'm breaking the rules again. But now I know what's at stake. I could lose everything.

But I have to do *something.*

Even though the King Toad is seated on his throne, I still have to rise up on tiptoes to reach the mask. My skin crawls as I lean closer to the smooth golden surface. He doesn't react. Doesn't move at all.

And I just *know.*

There is no King Toad. All of it is just an illusion, like the champagne and glitter. And I'm done pretending.

As my lips brush the cold metal of the mask, I reach out and grab a fistful of black robe. It's clammy and damp.

And I yank.

11.

IT'S JUST LIKE IT WAS ON THE BOAT. THE BLACK ROBES fall to the ground with a damp *whump*, and toads scatter everywhere, hundreds of them, hopping and scurrying away into dark corners, until all that is left is the huge golden mask, resting on the empty throne.

The assembled crowd is totally silent for a moment. My heartbeat grows sluggish as I wait for . . . what? To be clapped in irons and dragged away?

My eyes dart to Caraway, but I can't make out his expression beneath his mask. His father lays an affectionate hand on his shoulder, and my stomach roils.

Then the silence is broken by applause. Cheers and laughter. The crowd thinks it was all part of the show. Sol whoops and shouts my name, delighted, but Teddy is still glowering.

The red-robed Toad steps forward. "The King of Toads thanks you for your gifts," he says. "Please continue to enjoy the ball."

The crowd immediately disperses, returning to the festering platters of food, or whirling around to music that isn't really there.

I step back off the dais but am suddenly surrounded by black robes and copper-colored toad masks. The red-robed Toad appears before me, so close that I have to bite my tongue to stop from flinching.

They wouldn't hurt me here, in front of everyone. Would they?

"Please come with us, Miss Morgan," the red-robed Toad says, his tone as smooth as butter.

I'm the only sober girl in an ocean of Toads. I can't fight them. There's nowhere to run. The futility of it all lights a kind of recklessness in me, and I lift my chin.

"I don't think we've been introduced," I say boldly. "Who are you? Master of ceremonies? Or perhaps Master of Toads."

"You will come with us."

"No thank you," I reply. "I'd rather get back to the party."

"I insist."

I don't seem to have a choice. I think I might have made a terrible mistake. Or several terrible mistakes.

"Teddy," I call. "I'm sorry—I had to do it. The Ghost Toad . . . he's—"

The red-robed Toad digs his fingers into my arm. "That's quite enough, Miss Morgan."

Teddy doesn't even look at me.

We go back up the main staircase, past the VIP terrace, where full-face toad masks turn to watch me. The Ghost Toad has gone, and so has Caraway. I feel like I'm being dragged to the principal's office in front of the whole school, except the principal is probably going to kill me.

The Master of Toads leads me down corridor after corridor. They all look the same—how does anyone find their way around this place?

My body is shaking with fear, my limbs moving robotically. But nobody seems to have told my mouth, which continues to taunt the Master of Toads in a prattling diatribe.

"So what's the plan?" I say to his back. "Toad jail? Some kind of amphibian torture chamber? Or is it just straight-up Toad detention? Will I have to write lines? *I must not disrupt Toad ceremonies.*"

The red-robed Master of Toads doesn't respond. We go up another flight of stairs, then another, then down another endless corridor, finally halting in front of a door like all the other doors. The robed and masked Toads surround us, silent as ever.

The Master of Toads nods to the door.

I hesitate for a moment and then reach out and turn the handle, stepping inside to meet my fate.

Except it isn't a torture chamber, or an interrogation, or even a detention room.

It's *my* room. The apartment I've been sharing with Caraway. I turn, confused, ready for an explanation from the Master of Toads, but the door has already swung closed. I reach for the handle, but the door is locked.

I unmask the King Toad as a fraud, and my only punishment is being sent to my room without any supper?

I don't think so.

But nobody comes. After half an hour or so, some of the tension drains from my body, leaving me with sore muscles and a pounding headache—lingering aftereffects of the Sebrium. I eye a crystal water pitcher on the table longingly, but I've learned my lesson. No food or drink. Instead I find my old canteen in my rucksack and take a swig from it. The water in there is room temperature and stale, but it helps with the headache. I fish out an Ilium-branded ready-to-eat meal and scowl at the packaging.

Hot and tasty in one minute! Just add three drops of water to activate.

No wonder Thurmond Boswell works for Ilium. Ilium is all about making promises that sound great at the time but ultimately leave you disappointed. This enchanted meal will be hot, and it will have a taste. But that's about as much as I can hope for.

Magic is all illusions. It's never as good as the real thing.

I rip the wrapping off and stare at the plastic bowl filled with little brown cubes. Then I sigh and shake the three drops of water from my canteen. The synthetic mettle activates, the cubes swelling and spreading as steam begins to rise from the bowl.

One minute later, I'm holding . . . well, it doesn't look much like the beef stew on the wrapper. But it is, as promised, hot. I dig in using the plastic spoon provided. It is as bland and fake as they always are.

Some of the stew drips down the front of the intricate lace gown, leaving a spreading brown stain. I feel a spike of panic, followed by a surge of satisfaction.

Good. I hope all the Ilium cleaning potions in the world can't get the stain out.

I peel the glamour patch from my arm and roll it into a ball, then stick it to the underside of the dining table like it's chewing gum. Then I pull off the ball gown and leave it on the floor in a puddle, making sure I step on it multiple times as I head back to my rucksack for my real clothes.

Being petty is a good distraction from thinking too hard about what's happened, but I can't hide from it forever.

Caraway lied to me about everything. I knew I couldn't trust him. And then I kissed him, and it was amazing.

But that was just enchantment. Caraway is like everything else here—his beauty is an illusion, and underneath he's rotten to the core.

Maybe the kiss was actually terrible, and it was just enchanted champagne that made it amazing?

Except it was pretty amazing back in Deepdene too.

Unless he drugged me there too. The junk food.

The food just makes you see the illusion. It's the drink that changes the way you feel.

I don't know what to believe.

My eyes flick over to his bag, sitting neatly at the foot of the chaise where he slept last night.

Information is power.

Keeping an eye on the door, I sneak over to the bag and gingerly unzip it. It's obviously very expensive, all brown suede and satin lining. I see neatly folded clothes—shirts, jeans, a woolen jumper. Socks. Underwear. A novel—*The Burnished Mirror*—I wouldn't have thought Caraway read that kind of thing. I hear plastic crinkle in a side pocket as I replace the novel, and unzip it carefully.

Caraway's glamour patches. They aren't Ilium-branded ones. There's no fancy packaging or suggestive name. The plastic wrapper is plain, and there's a printed sticker on each one with CARAWAY BOSWELL written in neat black pen. These glamours are bespoke. Made specifically for Caraway. I wonder what would happen if I put one on.

Or maybe I should flush them all down the toilet.

There's a light knock on the door and I shove the patches back into the bag.

"You've locked me in!" I yell at the door. "Knocking seems a bit pointless."

After a moment, the door opens to reveal Thurmond Boswell, maskless but wearing the same dark gray suit as at the ball. He's carrying the leather-bound copy of *The White Book of Rhydderch* in one hand. He looks so *friendly*, but I remember the cold way he drove his needle into that Toadman's face, cutting away his smile. He's a monster.

"I believe you dropped this," he says mildly, placing the book on a side table.

"I don't want it," I retort. "I want nothing to do with this place."

Thurmond Boswell smiles gently. "I'll just leave it here in case you change your mind."

He walks over to the window, pretending not to notice the crushed gown on the floor.

"So?" I say, clenching my fists into balls to stop my hands from shaking. "Am I expelled from Toad Camp? Will I be sent home in disgrace?"

He doesn't reply, just gazes out the window at the darkness beyond. Then he turns abruptly and crosses the room to pick up the fox mask from where I discarded it on the dining table.

"Did Caraway tell you the story of the three toads of Deeping Fen?" Thurmond Boswell asks.

I can't think of a clever reply, so I just nod.

Thurmond Boswell turns the mask over in his hands. "Did he tell you why the Fox Bride is named the Fox Bride?"

"He said he didn't know."

A tiny hint of a smile twitches at Thurmond Boswell's lip. "Did he, now?"

More lies.

"I assume you're going to tell me," I say. "About the Fox Bride."

Thurmond Boswell runs a light finger over the tiny ginger-and-white feathers on the mask. "If you insist. The Fox Bride was a village girl who was beautiful and clever. A little *too* clever for her own good. Cunning, one might say."

I scowl. "Cunning as a fox?"

"Indeed. She was promised to the Green Knight, but she didn't wish to marry him. So she ran away, into the fen."

"I thought the Beast stole her."

Thurmond Boswell shakes his head. "It makes a nicer story if it is all the Beast's fault. But the truth is not so pretty. The Fox Bride was a witch, sly and scheming. She lured the Green Knight after her, and set him upon treacherous paths."

I've spent my whole life believing that witches are the most dangerous thing in the world. But now I'm starting to think it might be toads after all.

"She led him to the Beast?"

"She did. Right to his doom."

I *knew* the Green Knight didn't die of a marsh fly bite.

"But the toad saw everything. He and his brothers tricked the Beast and killed it. The Fox Bride saw how clever the toad was—

244

even more cunning than herself. She agreed to return to Deep-dene with him as his bride."

I make an unimpressed noise, and Thurmond Boswell chuckles. "It is no coincidence that you were given this mask, Ms. Morgan. You are being offered an opportunity."

"I'm no witch, and I have no desire to become a Toadwife."

"Perhaps not, but you want your father to be safe, don't you? You want success for your young smith friend and his paramour."

"Is that a threat?"

"It doesn't have to be."

His expression is still mild, but there's a hint of steel in his tone. I know he's more than capable of carrying out any threat he might make.

"The Fox Bride was smart and beautiful—like you. She was cunning, more than capable of defeating the Green Knight. He wasn't worthy of her talents."

"And the toad was?"

Thurmond Boswell smiles. "She saw in him an opportunity for power, and she took it."

"Power," I say flatly. "From marrying a frog. Did he turn into a prince when she kissed him?"

"Goodness, no. What use would that be? Handsome princes are commonplace. She recognized the power of the toadstone. Think about it, Ms. Morgan. The ability to see through any toad's eyes. Think of the secrets you could learn."

"I've had enough of secrets."

"The Fox Bride gathered the toad's most loyal human followers and made them pledge undying loyalty to the King Toad. As a symbol of their fealty, each of them carved out one of their own eyes and replaced it with the eye of a toad, allowing the king to use their sight."

I suddenly remember Mr. Gray, his left eye turned milky. The strange voice coming from his mouth.

Thurmond Boswell's voice. The Ghost Toad.

"It was you," I say. "At the tea shop. You spoke to me through Mr. Gray."

Thurmond Boswell says nothing, and I'm suddenly *furious* at him. At Teddy for getting into it all. At Caraway for being such a lying weasel *and* such a good kisser.

"I know who you are," I tell Thurmond Boswell. "What you do."

He smiles gently. "Of course you do," he says. "You saw what happened in the Great Hall. Hiding with my son behind the curtains, quite the pair of little foxes."

Hot anger suddenly dissolves into fizzing fear. Thurmond Boswell notices this, and his smile deepens.

"You listened to the conversation I had with a young and disobedient Toadman," he says. "You saw what happened."

I lift my chin. "I saw enough to know that you're evil."

He chuckles. "Such a dramatic word. I'm afraid the truth is far more mundane. The Toadmen are not evil. We're *powerful*. Those who ally with us can expect great fortune and success. Those who betray us . . ." He spreads his hands in a rueful shrug.

"So is that what's going to happen to me?" I say. "You're here to make me . . . disappear?"

"Not exactly." Thurmond Boswell steeples his fingers together and observes me over the top of them. "I'm in a difficult

cult position, you see. If you were anybody else, you'd be dead. Plain and simple. Your father would be dealt with too. A terrible accident, perhaps a lost fishing boat or a poorly timed falling branch."

My blood runs cold, and I swallow heavily.

"Luckily for you, I'm here to make a deal."

He hands me the fox mask, and my fingers close around it without thinking.

"What deal?" I ask.

Thurmond Boswell smiles his mild smile, like we're negotiating what to have for breakfast. "There is a ceremony tomorrow afternoon."

"The wedding," I say, remembering what Caraway told me about the Trothal. I look down at the mask. "You want me to be the Fox Bride at some Toad ceremony."

"Indeed. It's a very formal affair. An ancient tradition."

My stomach sours. "What would I have to do?"

Thurmond Boswell hesitates for a moment. "Wear your mask. Follow instructions. Nothing more."

I don't believe him.

"Why me?" I ask. "You know I'm trouble. Why not use someone more . . . docile?"

Thurmond Boswell sighs. "I'm not doing it for you. I'm doing it for Caraway. For his escort to be chosen as the Fox Bride is a great honor."

"I don't know if he'll see it that way."

"Ms. Morgan, Caraway is my legacy. He is a colt, headstrong and full of bravado. But his wild streak will be broken over time.

He will come to value what we offer. The doors it opens. He will realize that it is better to be inside than out. He can achieve great things as a Toadman. Better than that, he can achieve *good* things. Make the world a little less ugly."

He makes it all sound so reasonable. But I saw him, in the Great Hall. He took that Toadman's smile away with one twist of his silver needle.

Thurmond Boswell tilts his head to the side. "Has Caraway told you anything about his mother?"

"Not much."

"She is a fine woman. A great woman. She presides over charities. She spends her days caring for those less fortunate than she. She has a warm and gentle heart, but she understands that compassion is not enough. To do real good in the world, you must have resources. You must have power. And there is great power in being a Toad consort."

I hate this. I hate all of it. I hate it because Thurmond Boswell is evil and cruel. And I hate it because he's also not wrong. I'm sure Mrs. Boswell *does* do real good in the world. But at what cost?

"I'm just Caraway's date," I tell him. "We're not getting married or anything."

"You have great potential," he replies. "The Toadmen could help you realize it."

"Hard pass."

"Be smart," Thurmond Boswell says. "Be *cunning*. See the opportunity I am giving you for what it is, and take it. The Toadmen can make all your wishes come true. See what we've done for your father."

Unease settles in my gut. "What do you mean?"

"To win the poultry competition ten years in a row." Thurmond Boswell smiles indulgently. "Quite the achievement."

I don't believe it. I can't. Da's gift is chickens. He puts so much love and time into them. How *dare* Thurmond Boswell take credit for that.

"Ms. Morgan, to be a Toad consort is to walk an easy path. All other roads will lead to your ruin."

"And what if I refuse?"

"I'm so glad you asked."

Thurmond Boswell clicks his fingers, and the door to the apartment opens. A robed Toad enters, carrying a leash. Behind him is a man, the leash attached to a collar around his neck.

I let out a little involuntary sob and stumble forward.

"Da."

I throw my arms around him, breathing in his scent of lavender and freshly split firewood. There's something else, though. Hemlock and aniseed and the wet-wool smell of magic. I pull back and look directly into his face.

"Da?" I say. "Are you okay? Did they hurt you?"

He doesn't focus on me. There's a befuddled look on his face. A foolish grin that doesn't reach his eyes. Bile burns at the back of my throat. They've enchanted him.

"Da," I say again. "Can you hear me?"

Nothing. The Toadman tugs on the leash, and Da moves away from me without complaint.

"What did you do to him?" I say, rounding on Thurmond Boswell. I can hear the tremble in my voice.

Thurmond Boswell takes the leash from the robed Toad, who bows and exits the room.

"Insurance," he replies. "I know you, Merriwether Morgan. You're just as hotheaded and coltish as my son. It's why he likes you. I've asked your father to join us, to ensure your good behavior."

Da giggles. He doesn't seem to know where he is. I can't bear it—the expression on his face or the stink of magic coming off him in waves.

"If you've hurt him . . . ," I say to Thurmond Boswell between gritted teeth.

"He is not hurt," he replies coolly. "He's perfectly happy, as you can see."

I can't bear to see Da like this. Practical, sensible Da. Da, who makes me take a vial of Sebrium whenever I go out. I wish I hadn't taken it last night. Maybe it could have snapped him out of whatever magic-addled trance he's in.

"Your father will remain in this state until the wedding is over," Thurmond Boswell explains. "If you behave yourself, then you and he will be sent back to Candlecott. You will both have your memories magically altered so you have no memory of this weekend. Everything can go back to how it was, and you can have your perfect summer."

My heart judders in my chest. How does he know me so well?

"Let me be clear, Ms. Morgan." Thurmond Boswell's tone remains mild. "I know you think you're cute and clever, but if you step out of line, your father will pay. You will pay. Evans will pay, and so will his consort. I will find everyone who has ever cared about you, and I will make them suffer. This is not a game that you can win. I suggest you start thinking about what it is that you *truly* want."

Late nights in libraries. Furious academic debates. The grassy courtyard at Staunton. Notes spread under the oak tree.

I clench my fists at my sides. "This seems like an awful lot of blackmail, just for one little wedding ceremony."

Thurmond Boswell ignores this. "Someone will deliver a gown for you to wear this afternoon."

Da makes a soft gurgling sound, like a baby, and reaches out a hand to touch something that isn't there. I notice he's wearing a golden ring on his left hand. I've never seen it before. He lost his own wedding ring ten years ago, on a fishing trip to Thistle Cove—Ma gave him no end of trouble about it.

"Come along, Brother Alain," Thurmond Boswell says to Da, and gently tugs on the leash. "One more thing," he says as if he's just remembered. "Has Caraway told you the real reason why he wears a glamour?"

I open my mouth to reply, but Thurmond Boswell doesn't wait for an answer. With a smile that's just on the charming side of smug, he leads Da from the apartment, and I hear the lock click behind him.

I sink to the floor, my breath coming in fast gulps and wheezes. Sobs tear at my chest and my whole body shakes.

Da.

They have Da.

I know what Thurmond Boswell is capable of. He will hurt Da. He'll hurt everyone. I believe his threats.

I lost Ma. I can't lose Da too.

I just can't.

I try to take deep breaths, but they don't come. My heart hammers and I can't focus on anything. Can't *think*. Whenever

I close my eyes, all I see is the loose, addled smile on Da's face. The deadness in his eyes. I have to get him back. No matter what.

WHEN CARAWAY FINALLY COMES in, he is alone, still wearing his finery from the ball. He puts an enormous white box on the sofa and crouches down next to me, touching me gently on the arm.

"Are you okay?" he says, his voice urgent. "Did they hurt you?"

"They have Da." The trembling has left my body, and I feel empty and hollow.

Caraway hesitates. "I know."

Of course he knows.

"How did he do it?" I ask. "Your father? What did he do to my da, and how do I undo it?"

"I—I'm not sure," Caraway says.

I hold out my hand. "Give me Teddy's stone."

Caraway looks away. "I—I can't."

Did he return it? Give it back to his father?

"Why did you bother with it all?" I ask, shaking my head. "Letting me think we were saving him?"

Caraway says nothing, then reaches into the pocket of his jacket, unfurling his hand to show me a dull brown gemstone, round and smooth, about the size of a hazelnut.

I reach out for it, but his fingers close around it in a fist. "It's mine," he says. "I swapped it with Teddy's. I needed you to tell me which one was mine so I could remove it."

A cold heaviness expands in my core. The favor he

mentioned—this must have been it. The truth of what he wanted all along.

He was never going to let Teddy go. The only person Caraway wanted to help was himself.

"Is—is that why you brought me here?"

He nods, not meeting my eyes.

"Everything was fake," I say. "All of it."

His eyes dart up to meet mine. "No," he says, his voice rough. "Not all of it."

I don't believe him. "Why?" I ask. "Why do you want your stone so much?"

Caraway pauses for a moment. His knuckles are white where he's clutching the stone. "I gifted it to the King Toad when I was five. The stones bind us all together. As long as my stone exists, the Ghost Toad—my father—knows where I am."

The shadowy brown mettle. A network of magic that links all the Toadmen.

"You stole your stone because you want to leave?"

A sharp, fervent nod.

"Your father said that only that first stone is on the wall. What happens to the other strings you gift?"

"I don't know," Caraway says. "But I do know that the more strings you give, the stronger you become."

"But your strings are your life-force. They don't grow back. If you give too many, you die."

"The King Toad gives power in exchange for the stones," Caraway explains. "The stronger the connection is between a Toadman and the king, the more powerful the Toad becomes. More wealth. More luck. More power. Until you're completely dependent on him. So few strings that you wouldn't be able to survive without the Toad mettle."

I think about the Toadman sitting on the throne in the Great Hall, hands trembling as the Ghost Toad took his smile.

"So it isn't too late for you?" I look at the fist that clutches Caraway's toadstone.

"Maybe," he says. "But I have to try."

"You've got it now," I say. "Can't you smash it?"

He shakes his head. "Not by any conventional means," he says. "It's almost unbreakable."

"Almost?"

"I—I know a resistance witch in Scouller who thinks she might be able to do it. But I have to get my stone to her."

Witches, again.

I stand up and make for the door. Caraway grabs my arm, his fingers tight on my flesh. "What are you doing?"

"Going back to the Great Hall," I say. "I'm going to find Da's stone. And Teddy's. And we're going to take them to your witch."

"You can't," he says. "The wedding begins soon. The hall will be crawling with Toadmen."

I wrench my arm away. "I wasn't inviting you to come along."

"Morgan, have some sense. There are easier ways to get your da back."

"Like what?"

"Give them what they want," Caraway says. "Go to the wedding. Be the Fox Bride."

"What do I actually have to *do*, though?"

"It's just a ceremony. Go along with it. Play nice and they'll let you go."

I snort. "I'm not a fool, Caraway. There's no way your father is going to let me go home. Not with everything I know."

"He'll alter your memory. It's what they do to all the escorts. So they can't take any Toad secrets home."

I look Caraway in the eye, but all I see is glamour. Lies upon lies. Has he ever told me the truth?

"Morgan, I've talked to my father about this," he says. "He swore to me that you and your father would be sent home unharmed."

I don't believe that Thurmond Boswell will let me go so easily.

"What about Teddy?" I ask.

Caraway shrugs. "You don't have to worry about him," he says. "He *wants* to be here, and he's in no danger. The Toadmen will help him. Bring him all the success he desires."

"In exchange for his *life-force*."

"It's his choice."

I narrow my eyes. "But not yours."

"I didn't get to make a choice," he says simply. "Look, Morgan. I'm sorry I lied to you. I'm sorry I brought you here. I didn't know we'd get into so much trouble—the swamp monster, and that stunt you pulled with the King Toad. I thought it'd be simple. We'd go to the party, you'd have a great time, you'd help me find my stone and then your memory would be altered and you'd go home. I never meant for it to get this *complicated*."

But it did. It did get this complicated and now my da is lost in himself.

"Just play nice, for once," Caraway continues. "They'll let you both go home. It'll all be over. Come on. The wedding starts in an hour."

The way he says *the wedding* makes me uneasy.

"It's not a real wedding, though," I say. Just to be sure.

"Of course not. It's just a ceremony."

Suddenly I remember Thurmond Boswell's parting words.

Has Caraway told you the real reason why he wears a glamour?

I swallow. "Okay," I say. "I'll play nice. Why don't you have a shower while I get dressed?"

"Are you sure?" he says. "There's nothing else you need from me?"

"I'm fine. And you have been wearing those clothes for quite some time."

Caraway hesitates, then nods and vanishes into the bathroom. I hear running water. I open the white box and see layer upon layer of white tulle and lace.

It's a wedding gown.

I wait until I hear the water stop running, then I go into the bathroom.

Caraway is standing in front of the mirror, brushing his teeth. A towel is wrapped around his waist, and it takes a great deal of effort not to be distracted by his bare chest and shoulders.

He looks up at me, startled. "You're not dressed yet."

I say nothing. Just step forward and dig my nails under the edge of the glamour patch on his upper bicep.

Caraway's eyes widen in shock.

"Merry, no!"

But I'm too fast. I rip the patch off in one swift jerk.

12.

CARAWAY SPINS AWAY FROM ME TO FACE THE WALL, HIS hands over his face.

"Don't look," he says. *"Please."*

But it's too late for that. "No more secrets," I tell him.

I reach out to prize his right hand from his face. After a moment of resistance, he lets me, but keeps his left hand cupped over the other side.

I stare at him, baffled.

Without the glamour, Caraway looks . . .

The same.

Sure, the waves of cold haughtiness aren't there. But his features are unaltered. Perfect cheekbones. Full lips. He's still beautiful, in his strange, elfin way. Same Caraway.

"I don't understand," I say.

Caraway's bare shoulders slump in defeat, and he turns to face me, letting his left hand fall to his side, as we gaze at each other.

Caraway's right eye is as it always was, glacier blue.

But his left eye is the same dull yellowy brown of a toadstone, a horizontal black slit across the middle.

A toad's eye.

I stare at him, my mouth slack with horror as I recall the story Thurmond Boswell told me, not an hour ago.

As a symbol of their fealty, each of them carved out one of their own eyes and replaced it with the eye of a toad, allowing the king to use their sight.

Caraway blinks, and a thin transparent membrane slides up from his lower lid, over the toad eye, as his upper lid descends normally. I shudder, and he recoils from the expression on my face.

"You should never have come here." His voice is bleak.

"Only the King Toad's most trusted advisers get the toad eye," I say. "Is that right?"

Caraway hesitates, then nods. "I was five. My father promised me I could have a new bike if I went through with it."

I want to ask him if it hurt. If he was scared. But I say nothing.

"I'm his heir, Morgan," Caraway continues. "The Three Toads aren't elected. The positions are hereditary. One day *I* will be the Ghost Toad." His voice cracks on the last words, and tears well in his eyes. "I told you I know everyone's fears. Well, so does he. Did you know that gifts can be inherited too? Imagine, for a moment, what it's like. As a child, I knew everyone's fears. I *felt* them. I knew what it was to fear the dark. To fear fire, or water. To fear being alone. To fear all the monsters under the bed. And I met so many people whose greatest fear was my own father."

I swallow. "What's your fear?" I ask him, but I already know the answer.

"Becoming him."

He pushes past me into the living room, yanking on jeans and a shirt.

"That's why I took my stone back," he says. "I'm sorry I lied to you. I'm sorry about what's happened to your father. I truly am. But I can't be the Ghost Toad. I won't."

"Does he know about any of this? Your father?"

"He knows my fear, of course," Caraway says. "But that's it."

"How do you know he's not watching this through your eye? Right now?"

My mouth turns sour as I think of the kisses we shared. He was there for it all. The Ghost Toad. Watching. *Feeling.*

Caraway shakes his head. "I can feel him. And"—he points at his toad eye—"it changes."

It goes cloudy. Like Mr. Gray's did, outside the bathroom at Miss Prinny's. I knew Mr. Gray was wearing a glamour. To hide his own toad eye. All the senior Toadmen must have one. I remember Caraway suddenly drawing away from me in Deeping Fen, as we sat side by side by the fire in the ruins. Withdrawing his face into shadow.

"That's how they knew where to send the boat, when we were lost in the fen. He looked through you."

Caraway nods. Without the glamour, I see every feeling written clear on his face. His brows curl together plaintively.

"I don't have a choice," he says. "I can't control it. It's all him."

He looks miserable. It tugs at my heart, and I am disgusted with myself. Letting hormones get in the way of my own good sense. But I'm not here for Caraway, and I never was.

I just need to get Da out of here.

"I've been such a fool," I mutter. "I can't believe I almost let myself fall for you."

His unglamoured cheeks flush. "You—you fell for me?"

I scowl at him. "I said *almost.*"

He lets out a sigh that seems to carry all the weariness of the world. "Morgan," he says, his voice strained. "I—I should have just told you everything. I thought if you knew"—he gestures to his gleaming toad eye—"I thought you'd hate me."

I take a moment to look at him. His true face, unglamoured and open to me.

"You were right," I say, because everything would be easier if it were true. "I do hate you. I always did. Nothing's changed."

I see how much this hurts him, and I'm glad, even though it hurts me too.

"You lied to me about all of it," I say to him. "About your glamour. About your father." I pick up the fox mask from where I dropped it on a side table. "You even lied to me about this. About her. You made me think she was a maiden in peril, when all along she was . . ."

A witch. I am so sick of this world of lies and deception. I just want to go home.

"I'm going to attend this ceremony," I say. "And then me and Da will go home, after which point I hope I never see you again."

Caraway nods, then picks up his bag and leaves, shutting the door gently behind him. And I don't know what's wrong with me, because this is definitely the right thing to do. And there are more important things to be thinking about right now, like Da and how we get out of here alive. And only a few days ago I thought

Caraway Boswell was the most insufferable priggish stuffed shirt I'd ever met.

But my heart still feels like it's breaking.

THE GREAT HALL IS as solemn and ostentatious as it was last night—more so, even, with torches burning in sconces on the walls, throwing light around to create leaping, sinister shadows and causing the wall of toadstones to glitter, like hundreds of thousands of watching eyes. Toadmen fill the wooden benches, robed and masked. Most of the hall is filled with garden-variety Toads—their masks brown and simple under frilly white bonnets, with more frills on the white sleeves under their black broadcloth vestments.

At the front sit two rows of Toads with silver masks, like the one Mr. Gray and the other VIP Toads were wearing at the ball last night. Their robes are simple—somber and black, with no frills or bonnets or bows. Now that I know what I'm looking for, I can see that each of them has one toad eye, yellowy brown with a horizontal slit and that unnerving double lid. No glamours today. Caraway sits there with them. I recognize him instantly. He tries to meet my eyes, but I look away.

On the dais, the King Toad sits once more on his throne, huge and imposing under his golden mask. Or at least he would be imposing, if I didn't know he was just a big old pile of toads. I wonder how many of the men in this room know the truth. That Thurmond Boswell pulls all the strings of this puppet king.

Thurmond Boswell, masked and robed, standing at the shoulder of the king. The sight of him makes my hands curl into fists.

On the other side of the king is the Howling Toad. He isn't as tall as I expected, but his mask is terrifying enough. It's the color of dried blood, the mouth open wide in a silent black scream. Is there a real man under there? Or is he another puppet?

The Master of Toads stands at the front of the dais in his red robe, and then there's me, off to the side at the very front of the stage, looking like a giant meringue.

The bridal gown is enormous and weighs a ton. And it's enchanted, so I know that the weight of it is deliberate. A millstone around my neck. Layer upon layer of white tulle and satin and lace, binding me up like a trussed chicken. Every part of the dress is heavily embroidered with pearls and dainty beads, from the enormously wide skirt to the shoulder-crushing puffed sleeves. I have a new fox mask, full-faced this time and glittering with ornamentation. The fox fur is made from finely hammered sheets of bright copper and white gold, overlapping in scales. Rubies stud the edges of it and surround the eyeholes. And topping it all off is an enormous white headdress dripping with lace and jewels and strings of pearls. I can barely turn my head under the weight of it. I'm afraid my neck will snap.

Stand still and be silent. Those were my instructions. I can see my father sitting off to the side of the hall, right in my eyeline. He is the only person in the room who isn't masked. He stares into space with a vacant grin, quiet and unheeding of all that is going on around him. I want to gather him into my arms and protect him, and then tear down every pillar of this hideous Toad shrine.

The ceremony begins, and of course it's more mettle for the King Toad.

I watch threadwise as one by one, the garden-variety Toads

step forward and kneel before the king. The Master of Toads swings the black iron hook and snags a mettle string. Some are more resistant than others. The first few snap with very little pressure, giving way as if they are no stronger than spiderwebs or strands of hair. But then there is one as tough as catgut. The Master of Toads has to haul on it for several minutes before it snaps with an audible *twang.*

Each string curls in on itself, forming a ball, which is shaken from the end of the hook into a large copper bowl, held by another robed Toad. Soon the bowl is nearly overflowing with strings.

I wonder how they turn the strings into toadstones. And what do they use them for, if only the first one goes onto the wall?

I remember the power I sensed underneath the Deeping Court. I guess the stones are a convenient way to store mettle.

I prickle again at the thought of them getting away with all this. Magic restrictions were created for a reason. Auditors take hedgewitches off to recovery centers all the time for selling non-covenant healing potions or charmed poppets. That's nothing compared to this.

I guess when you're powerful enough, you can get away with anything.

When each Toad has gifted his string, he files back along the central aisle and retakes his seat. The shock of strings snapping dulls after the first fifty, and I enter a kind of daze. My body is going numb under the crushing weight of the bridal gown, but there's something in the delicate white satin slippers—enchanted, of course—that keeps me upright.

Every now and then, my eyes turn to the hulking mass of the King Toad, and I imagine I see the fabric moving a little as the toads inside crawl over each other. Thurmond Boswell is the real power here, collecting all the mettle and . . . what? Selling it to Ilium? Where it's used to make glamour patches and enchanted energy drinks?

I glance over at the Howling Toad, trying to glimpse any signs of humanity beneath that mask.

A familiar set of shoulders catches my eye, and I watch as Teddy approaches the dais and sinks down on one knee. He doesn't even glance at me.

What would have happened if I hadn't snuck into the Candlecott Frater House? I wouldn't be here, for one. Nor would Da. Caraway Boswell would still be someone I view with uncomplicated loathing, instead of the tumultuous storm that currently rages in my heart.

It seems like such a long time ago. I can't believe it was only a few days. All I could think about then was my one perfect summer. Now I'll take any kind of summer. I just want to get out of here with Da.

The Master of Toads swings the hook, slicing through one of Teddy's strings like it's butter. I feel it as sharply as if it were one of my own.

I thought I could help him. But I made everything worse. I ran roughshod over all of Teddy's hopes and dreams, and the only thing I achieved was turning him against me.

The string coils in on itself and drops into the bowl. Teddy rises to his feet and retreats down the aisle. Hopefully the next time I see him, all this will be over, and I won't remember any of it.

I'm not counting my chickens.

Eventually, every garden-variety Toad has gifted a string.

"And now we welcome our newest brother into the Inner Council of Toadmen," the Master of Toads declares.

A black-robed Toad stands and kneels before the King Toad. One of his eyes beneath his silver mask is swollen and red. A brand-new toad eye. I wonder how he got chosen. What he had to sacrifice.

Just as he did with the others, the Master of Toads swings his hook and takes a string from the kneeling Toad. Then, one by one, the remaining two rows come up and pledge themselves to the king.

As Caraway kneels before the King Toad, I half expect him to do something reckless. But he just bows his head. His string breaks with barely any resistance, like a loose thread of hair being tugged free by a comb.

And it's done. Every Toad has gifted a string.

I guess it's time for the wedding part of the proceedings.

Thurmond Boswell turns to me as the Master of Toads speaks. "The wedding gifts have been presented. Now the Fox Bride shall pledge herself to her king."

I wish someone had let me see a script before we started this. The Ghost Toad didn't mention anything about a pledge when he came to my room, but then again, I knew he wasn't telling me everything. He gestures for me to approach the throne, and I see his eyes flick toward Da, who is staring vacantly into space.

I swallow and shuffle forward, the dress making it almost impossible to move.

The Master of Toads gestures toward me. "You are the Fox Bride, are you not?"

I swallow. "I guess so."

He opens a small lacquered box. Inside is a golden ring, nestled in silk.

"Make your bridal vow. Do you pledge yourself to the King of Toads? Give yourself whole and unblemished to him? Pledge your undying allegiance, and the allegiance of any children you bear henceforth, to him? Swear to spend your days in fealty to the mightiest authority, to serve and honor him with your words, your deeds and your body."

I feel the weight of his words.

Feel them in my bones.

Of course this is no pantomime ceremony. I should have known.

I remember the promise I made to Thurmond Boswell in the library, the feeling of it binding me. If I make this pledge, I will be bound to it.

Forever.

I will be a Toadwife. Bearing little Toad children to . . . whoever they decree. To Caraway? Or to Thurmond Boswell himself? I will lose my free will. My family. I'll lose everything.

Caraway's head snaps to the red mask of the Master of Toads, then to his father. Did he know this was going to happen?

"I—I can't," I stammer.

There is a long moment of silence. Then Thurmond Boswell speaks. "I think our blushing young bride might prefer a more . . . intimate ceremony."

The Master of Toads nods, and gestures toward the rows and rows of seated Toads. They stand and shuffle out of the room.

Nobody speaks. The only sounds are the scuff of shoes on the stone floor and the swishing of robes.

I watch Teddy leave and feel more alone than ever.

The Howling Toad descends the steps from the dais and goes to stand over by my father.

Caraway stands to leave, but his father shakes his head. "No," he says. "You can stay."

I look at Caraway and silently implore him with my eyes.

Do something. Help me.

But Caraway doesn't do anything. I guess now that he has his stone, he doesn't need me anymore. He just wants out, and can I really blame him?

I look back at Da, the Howling Toad looming over him. I see that he is wearing heavy leather gloves, plated in black iron.

"N-no—" I stammer. "Wait—"

But the Howling Toad makes a fist and smashes it right into Da's face. Da isn't expecting it, so his head snaps back in his seat. Blood pours from his nose and over his lips into his mouth. He licks his lips and blows a sticky red raspberry, then giggles once more. His right eye is starting to swell shut already. The Howling Toad pulls his fist back again.

"No!" I cry out. "Please."

The Master of Toads gestures toward the King Toad. "Make your vow."

Swear to spend your days in fealty to the mightiest authority, to serve and honor him with your words, your deeds and your body.

"I c-c-an't."

Crunch. Another blow to Da's face. His nose is a bloody pulp now, completely shattered under the force of the Howling Toad's iron-gloved fist.

It's as if they are tearing my own heart from my chest. How can I choose? My beautiful da, the kindest, gentlest man I've ever met. Or my whole life. My children. My future.

"If I may, Brother." It's the Ghost Toad, stepping forward and putting a hand on the Howling Toad's shoulder. "This may take a little more . . . finesse."

The Howling Toad moves away from Da, but I feel no sense of relief as I watch the Ghost Toad pull the silver needle from inside his robes.

"He has a beautiful smile, your father," the Ghost Toad says in that infuriatingly calm voice.

I remember the quick flash of the needle, the sudden slackness of the Toad's face.

He's going to take Da's smile.

Ma always said that Da's smile was the first thing she noticed about him. They'd met at a market in Fyansford where Da was selling eggs. Ma was there with her friends, shopping for ribbons and good-luck charms for their upcoming exams. Da said she was the prettiest girl in the market. He abandoned his egg stall and followed her like a lost puppy to a big marquee where people were dancing. But some other fellow asked Ma to dance before Da could get there first. Dejected, he had returned to his egg stall only to discover that it had been knocked over by an escaped ram. Smashed eggs everywhere. He crouched down on the grass, trying to clean up the mess before the eggs started to smell. Then he looked up and Ma was there. She'd noticed him too, and followed him after her dance ended.

Surrounded by eggshells and broken yolks, he was, Ma would say. *But when our eyes met he smiled, and it was like the sun coming out from behind a cloud.*

I think of the proud smile on Da's face when I told him I was joint dux of Candlecott School. Of the triumphant smile when he unfurled Bran the Blessed's extraordinary golden tail, winning the Candlecott Poultry Prize for the tenth year running. Of the fond, gentle smile he'd give me when I said good night. The surprised smile when I made him laugh.

Da is smiling right now, but it's not his true smile. This dazed, vacant smile doesn't reach his eyes. It doesn't warm my heart. The idea that I might never see the sparkle of his true smile again is almost too much to bear.

"Will you let him go?" I ask Thurmond Boswell. "Will you make him whole again?"

The silver needle glints as the Ghost Toad rests the tip on the hinge of Da's jaw. "I swear it."

"Okay," I say, my voice low. "I'll make the pledge."

The Ghost Toad doesn't withdraw the needle, but he doesn't press any harder either. He's not going to back off until I've done it.

The Master of Toads proffers the box to me. The golden ring glints in the torchlight.

How did it come to this? Four days ago the most important thing in my life was avoiding conversations about going to Staunton. I was afraid to leave Candlecott. To leave Da and Teddy and step into a terrifying world of magic and witches. I just wanted everything to stay the same. I thought that was what I was going to get here. Thurmond Boswell promised that if I participate in the Trothal, then Da and I could go home. We could go back to normal, without any memory of this awful place.

But he lied to me.

Of course he did.

And now everything will change. I'm about to pledge myself to the King Toad. To give up everything I love in order to serve this horrific brotherhood of selfish, cruel old men.

The Ghost Toad might still be lying. Maybe he's going to hurt Da no matter what I do.

But I have to do everything I can to save him, and this is all I have.

I reach out to take the ring.

"Stop." The voice rings out as clear as a bell, and my knees tremble with relief.

The Ghost Toad turns to Caraway. "She is the Fox Bride. She must swear."

"She is unworthy. She is no witch."

"She is far better than a witch," the Ghost Toad replies. "Her mettle is as strong as a witch's, but she has no power of her own. She will make a fine wife for our king, and cause no trouble."

Any doubt I might have had that my mettle-tracking ability is a result of the witch's curse evaporates.

"There's more," Caraway says. "She—she's not unblemished. Her virtue is ruptured."

A murmur passes through the silver-masked Toads.

"Do you have evidence?" the Master of Toads asks.

Caraway reaches up and slowly removes his mask, his hands lingering over his chin. Then he saunters casually up onto the dais. He takes my chin in his hand and inspects me for a moment. I see no warmth in his expression. No compassion. His mouth is twisted in a sardonic smile, his one toad eye narrowed with haughty disdain, even without his glamour on. He leans forward and kisses me roughly on the mouth, like he's claiming me as his own. I stiffen in shock. This kiss is nothing like the ones we shared before. I feel something press against my lips, and he pushes something cold into my mouth with his tongue. Then he pulls away.

"I took it," he says with a smirk. "Her virtue. Her maidenhead. You can inspect the sheets in our apartment."

I feel fire spread to my cheeks. Caraway and I . . . we didn't . . . He's lying, but why? And what did he just put in my mouth?

A toadstone. The one from his pocket. *His* stone. He slipped it into his mouth when he took his mask off.

But why?

The Ghost Toad spreads his hands. "I believe we can make an exception to the rule of chastity."

A murmur of surprise goes through the remaining Toads.

"My lord," the Master of Toads responds. "The girl is not virtuous. She cannot wed our king."

"You could give her to me." It's the first time the Howling Toad has spoken. His voice is reedy, with a singsong quality to it.

He advances on me, slow and predatory. I lift up my hands, as if to protect myself from him, taking a step backward as the bridal gown rustles around me.

Da tilts his head to one side, blood still streaming from the crushed mess of his face. His left eye is swollen completely shut now.

"No," the Ghost Toad says with a sigh. "We don't have a backup. She'll have to—"

He breaks off suddenly. His eyes through the mask turn milk white. The room goes completely silent, everyone watching him.

The Ghost Toad's lips curl in a smile, and the cloudy white fades from his eyes. "Auditors have found the Hag," he says. "They have taken her to Ruddock Farm."

A noise comes from under the Howling Toad's mask, like he's smacking his lips.

"So we don't need this one after all," the Master of Toads says, glancing at me. "We should kill her."

The Ghost Toad shakes his head. "I still think this one is better. Less dangerous." He sighs. "I'll have to consider it further."

"Send her to Ruddock Farm too," Caraway says suddenly. "She won't be able to get into any more trouble there. You can send for her when you're ready."

I want to protest, but the toadstone is cold and hard in my mouth.

Ruddock Farm. Caraway wants to send me to a recovery center. A place where witches and traitors go. The government claims they are just work camps, designed to rehabilitate dissidents. I've never believed the other rumors about them. That the camps drain mettle. That nobody returns, unless it's dead in a box or as a vacant husk. But now . . . I don't know what to believe.

The Howling Toad giggles, high and sharp.

There's a long moment as the Ghost Toad considers Caraway. Then he nods.

"Let it be so," he says, and my mask and headdress are abruptly yanked away.

I can't speak. The toadstone is like ice in my mouth, my lips and tongue frozen solid. I point with a shaking hand to Da.

The Ghost Toad chuckles. "Oh, Little Fox," he says. "You should know better than to trust the word of a Toad."

The silver needle flashes. I try to leap forward, but two Toads grab me by the arms, holding me back.

Da's face doesn't crumple. He's still smiling.

But there's fresh blood gushing from his throat, mingling with the darkening flow from his broken nose.

I can't scream.

Blood spills from my father's body, the floor growing slick with it.

He doesn't struggle. Doesn't appear to feel any pain.

I watch as the light goes out of his eyes and the flow of blood begins to lessen.

I can't look away.

I can't tell him I love him.

He doesn't look at me. He'll never look at anything again.

"Take her away," the Ghost Toad commands, and a black hood scented with hartshorn and eucalyptus is pulled over my head.

Then all is darkness.

13.

BLACKNESS. THE RUMBLE OF AN ENGINE. THE SICKEN-ing scent of hartshorn and diesel fuel.

My thoughts are fleeting and ragged at the edges. My stomach churns from airlessness and the sensation of motion without sight. I'm in a van or a truck.

Da.

Caraway's toadstone is still in my mouth. Still cold. I don't know what to do—whether to spit it out or to swallow it. Neither of those ideas seems good, so I just keep it there, tucked against my cheek like a squirrel's acorn. I don't understand why Caraway gave it to me—I thought his whole plan was to steal it for himself, to get him out of the Toads forever.

Perhaps he knew it would silence me.

I'm never going to see my father again. Never see his smile. Never see his weathered hands cradle a newly hatched chick.

I don't know how much time passes. It could be hours. Could be days. Perhaps I've just fallen out of time altogether.

When I try to move my hands, I realize they are bound tightly with iron manacles. Iron blocks the flow of mettle—prevents magical connections. I couldn't look threadwise even if I wanted to.

Occasionally I think I hear voices—the drivers of the van, perhaps, or other passengers. Perhaps it's just my mind playing tricks on me. I don't care either way. I don't want to see anyone, or speak to anyone.

Da is dead, and nothing else matters.

I DON'T REALIZE THAT the vehicle has stopped until I hear the squeal and scrape of a door opening and mild voices speaking quietly. I'm ushered out of the van with cool, polite hands. My knees buckle, but I manage to stay upright. My head spins.

The hood is lifted, and the sudden light causes a stabbing pain in my head. I screw my eyes shut, trying to shield them with my manacled hands. At the same time I gulp in lungfuls of air, fresh and cold. I blink my watering eyes and see steep hills in the distance, a white van, and two figures standing on either side of me.

Auditors, their hands clasped politely in front of them.

We don't get many auditors in Candlecott, but I've seen them before, of course. Always in pairs. Always in neat gray suits. Always one redhead, to see through any charms or glamours. Perhaps a few days ago I would have been relieved to see them. But now I just don't care.

"It's lovely to meet you, Miss Morgan," one of them says mildly, as if we've just shared a taxi together.

I say nothing. There's no point.

"You have excellent timing," the redheaded auditor says.

"The director of thaumaturgical recovery is visiting today. He's going to personally assess you."

They usher me up a paved garden path. On either side are neat garden beds surrounded by little hedges. Brightly colored spears of snapdragon rise above pansies and billy buttons like something out of a storybook cottage garden, and behind them are a row of rosebushes, each with evenly spaced, fat blooms. It all looks so perfect, it doesn't seem real.

At the end of the garden path sits a perfectly charming building. Large enough to officially be a mansion, it's all pale gray and pink stone, fringed with pink rambling roses. Windows with white shutters thrown wide open. Gables and turrets and a redbrick chimney emitting perfect puffs of white smoke.

"Welcome to Ruddock Farm," one of the auditors murmurs.

INSIDE, IT'S JUST AS charming. Warm wood paneling contrasts with crisp white ceilings and intricately patterned wallpaper. Framed paintings on the walls feature pastoral scenes of ducks and sunsets. The floorboards creak reassuringly under my feet, and the air smells of lavender and freshly baked shortbread.

The auditors show me into an office—high-ceilinged and lined with bookshelves and ornate cabinetry. A fire crackles in the grate, and I'm suddenly reminded of Thurmond Boswell's library. My stomach turns sour. I must be careful. This place may look charming, but it's full of witches, and who knows what else.

The auditors duck their heads deferentially, then back out of the room, leaving me alone.

I run my tongue over the stone in my mouth. It's still ice-cold, after all this time.

I don't know when I'll next get to be alone.

I spit the stone into my hand and stare at it. It's a piece of Caraway's life-force.

Why did he give it to me?

Footsteps are approaching. I make a fist around the stone, just as the door opens.

"Well, hello there," says a thin, reedy male voice.

At first I mistake him for another auditor. He has the same mild affect, the same polite tilt of the head. The same bland, forgettable face. But he's not an auditor. He's alone, for one. Auditors always travel in pairs. And this man isn't wearing a suit, he's in a white coat, like a doctor.

And he has an eye patch, a simple white circle over his left eye, almost unnoticeable behind his silver-rimmed spectacles. His mouth is puckered and weak, his blotchy skin deeply lined although he doesn't seem to be that old.

"Goodness, let's get these hideous things off you," he says, and steps forward to unlock my manacles, gently removing them and placing them on his desk. "That's a very pretty dress you're wearing," he adds with a smile.

I look down and realize I'm still wearing the Fox Bride's wedding gown.

"Are you all right, my dear?" the man says. "You look quite unwell."

It feels like I haven't spoken for days. "They killed my father," I say, my voice hoarse.

Saying it out loud makes it true, and my knees go out from under me. The man helps me into a chair.

"Don't worry," he says. "Everything is going to be fine."

But it isn't. It will never be fine again.

No Ma. No Da.

Nothing.

My fingers start to uncurl from around Caraway's toadstone.

None of it matters anymore.

"I am Dr. Veil," the man continues. "Director of thaumaturgical recovery for all of Ilium's recovery centers."

Ilium.

Ruddock Farm is owned by Ilium. It was Thurmond Boswell who sent me here, after all. I grip the toadstone tightly again.

Is this man a Toad too?

"Believe me, Ms. Morgan," Dr. Veil says with a smile. "I am no spy. I have nothing to gain from your suffering. I work quite separately from the other arms of Ilium, and I am not interested in politics or power. My only goal here is to rehabilitate the poor unfortunate souls who have lost themselves in dangerous magics."

"I'm not a witch," I say.

"I know," he replies. "And I will not force you to stay here. It will take a few days to process your paperwork, and then you will be free to go."

I swallow uneasily.

"We'll make you comfortable," Dr. Veil promises. "Get you some clean clothes, and something to eat."

He indicates the door.

"You might have noticed when you came in," he said, "there

is no wall around Ruddock Farm. No guards. Not even any auditors—the ones who dropped you off have left. This is no prison. Our clients are all here because they choose to be."

I remember what the Ghost Toad said, the milky white still draining from his eye.

"Even the Spitalwick Hag?" I ask.

Dr. Veil nods. "So you've heard about our newest resident. A most sorry case indeed. So far, she has been unwilling to participate in my recovery therapy. But it's early days. At the moment she is being kept apart from our other clients until she is ready to participate."

I swallow. The witch who killed my mother is here, somewhere in this very building.

Everywhere I go there is death.

"Don't worry, Ms. Morgan," Dr. Veil assures me. "You will not come into contact with her."

I glance toward the door, uncertain.

"I oversee a number of recovery centers," Dr. Veil says. "I'll be returning to the city this afternoon, and I'll start the process to get you safely released. I'll be back the day after tomorrow with good news, I'm sure of it."

I don't trust Dr. Veil, but I don't have a choice. So I nod, and he smiles. "Someone will show you to your room."

He rings a bell on his desk, and a few moments later the door opens to admit a little girl wearing a blue gingham dress, trimmed with white lace. She can't be older than eleven. She looks . . . familiar, somehow.

"This is Sweetpea," he says. "Our youngest resident here at

Ruddock Farm. She came to us a few days ago. Begged us to take her in. She'd been kidnapped by witches, you see. Barely managed to escape. You two have a lot in common."

"Everyone has been so kind," Sweetpea says with a childlike lisp. "I love it here."

Dr. Veil smiles indulgently at her before turning back to me. "Here at Ruddock Farm, we preserve the anonymity of our clients by encouraging them to take on a pseudonym. If it's all right with you, while you're here, you'll be known as Delphinium."

"Okay."

"Sweetpea, would you be so kind as to show Delphinium to her room?"

"Yes, Dr. Veil." There's a hardness to the little girl's eyes. A glint of steel.

"Thank you. Delphinium, I'll see you in a few days with what I hope will be welcome news."

I FOLLOW SWEETPEA UP a grand staircase and down a long corridor lined with more tranquil paintings and credenzas cluttered with doilies and porcelain vases. There are fresh flowers everywhere, but somehow the floral scent of rose and jonquil in the air doesn't quite feel fresh, but more like a bottled perfume.

"Do you find it scary?" I ask Sweetpea. "Being around all the witches?"

The girl glances at me scornfully. "What makes you think I'm not one of them?"

I notice her lisp has vanished.

She stops in front of a wooden door. "Here," she says.

I put my hand on the brass handle and turn. "Um," I say to Sweetpea. "Thank you."

A little frown creases her forehead. "What's your deal?" she asks abruptly. "You're wearing a wedding dress, but you don't have a ring."

I don't know how to answer this, so I just shake my head.

Sweetpea's eyes narrow, like she doesn't trust me. "You should clean yourself up," she says. "You stink of toad."

Suddenly I remember where I've seen her before. "You were at the fair," I say. "Asking questions about the Hag."

She doesn't respond, just marches off down the corridor.

MY ROOM IS SMALL and cozy, with bright white walls and a window overlooking the garden. A vase of fresh flowers sits on a nightstand next to a bed draped in a cheerful embroidered quilt. Through a smaller door I see a small bathroom with a white porcelain toilet, a vanity and a claw-footed bath, steam rising from it enticingly.

There is no lock on my bedroom door, which makes me uneasy. I don't want a witch just randomly wandering in while I'm in the bath, so I take a wickerwork chair from beside the window and wedge it under the door handle, just to be sure.

I slip Caraway's toadstone underneath the pillow. Then, with no small amount of relief, I peel off the Fox Bride dress. I never want to see a ball gown ever again.

I sink into a lavender-scented bath with a sigh, and as I finally allow myself to unclench, tears start to leak from the corners of my eyes.

I keep seeing the flash of the silver needle. The sudden gush of crimson. The crunching sound as the Ghost Toad's fist connected with Da's face.

I hear again the total lack of emotion in Caraway's voice as he told his father to send me here. I know how he feels about these places, that witches are lucky to leave alive. So why did he do it? In the moment, it felt like a betrayal, but then why slip me his toadstone? Was he trying to save me? Is it some kind of tool, some kind of message? I don't understand.

As a symbol of their fealty, each of them carved out one of their own eyes and replaced it with the eye of a toad, allowing the king to use their sight.

Is that what it is? Is Caraway using the toadstone to spy on me? Is it so the Ghost Toad can keep watching?

I must fall asleep at some point, because when I open my eyes again, the light is quite different and my fingertips are pruned. The bathwater is still warm, though, and I spy an Ilium bath sachet dangling from the tap, the kind that keeps the water at just the right temperature and releases just enough perfume into the steamy air.

I climb out of the bath and wrap myself in a fluffy white towel—another Ilium product, I'm sure, as it seems to be extremely absorbent and yet remains featherlight.

The Fox Bride gown has gone from the bedroom. In its place, a dress is laid out on the bed. The chair is still under the doorknob, so I have no idea how it got there.

I don't like that.

I pull on clean underwear, soft wool stockings (Ilium again—no runs), a white linen underdress, and a forest-green pinafore with a full skirt that falls to my shins. Everything is exactly my size, even the brown leather ankle boots. There's a white lace cap as well, but I leave that on the bed. I already look like one of those settlement institute girls who get pulled out of high school and taught how to be a good homemaker on an Ilium-sponsored farm somewhere.

My stomach rumbles, and as if in reply, I hear the gentle chime of a bell somewhere in the building. Cautiously, I remove the chair and open my door. I don't see anyone.

I take a deep breath and look threadwise, trying to identify any potential danger.

What I see makes my knees go out from underneath me, and I sink to the floor.

Mettle.

So much mettle.

It looks like a tornado made of thousands of silver threads, each one streaming up and tangling with the others, as if it's being sucked toward the sky. My consciousness gets sucked in, and I feel myself being whisked up with it, away from Ruddock Farm, so fast it all happens in the blink of an eye. I've never traveled so far from myself before. I didn't know I *could* go this far. I'm high up in the cold air, a mountain spread below me, rocky and remote, with only a single dirt road winding down away from Ruddock Farm. I see the grand house, and the shockingly bright color of the gardens, intense against the gray-and-brown sparseness of the rocky peaks.

Tracking mettle has never felt like this before. I've lost control, pulled away from my body by this swirling tide of energy. What if I can't find my way back?

I force myself to fight it, to push against the tide, inching my way back down to myself. If I were a witch, then maybe I could use the mettle itself, haul myself back like I'm on a rope. But I'm powerless. Perhaps this is what the Spitalwick Hag intended when she cursed me inside my mother's belly. I grit my teeth and keep moving back. It seems to take hours, although I'm sure it's just a few moments.

Finally, my consciousness reenters my body, and I screw my eyes shut, allowing the world to return to normal.

My lower lip is bleeding where I've bitten it. Dark half-moons stand out on my palms where my nails have dug in. I run a shaking hand through my hair.

I don't know what that was, but I am definitely not doing it again.

I get to my feet, my legs weak underneath me. I feel hollow and dizzy. I need food.

Slowly, I make my way along the corridor and down the stairs, and then follow the sounds of scraping chairs and the clinking of cutlery until I find myself in a large dining room.

My heart starts beating fast as I enter—there are maybe a hundred women in here, all dressed similarly. Long tables are set with white lace tablecloths and floral-patterned china, with large covered tureens running down the center of each table. A fire burns cheerily in an ornate fireplace, and little porcelain statues and vases crowd the carved mantelpiece. There are more pastoral landscapes framed on the walls, and there are enough doilies to make Miss Prinny feel right at home.

The women don't *look* like witches. I see no gnarled fingers or black nails. No stringy hair or warts. They're not cackling over cauldrons or hissing curses the way Jenny Greenteeth does in stories. They're not really doing anything, just sitting quietly, hands folded in their laps, heads bowed. Waiting.

It's eerie.

I hesitate on the threshold, unsure as to what I should do. I don't really want to eat with them. Perhaps there's a kitchen I could go to, or organize to have something back in my room. I spot the little girl—Sweetpea—with an empty seat next to her at the end of the row. I don't *think* she's a witch, and maybe if I sit next to her she can explain what the deal is with this place.

She doesn't look up as I slide into place next to her, but her head turns just *ever* so slightly, so I know she's seen me.

The woman opposite me smiles. She's wearing a white blouse with a scalloped collar, her hair pulled back in a neat braid underneath a white lace cap.

"Hello," she says to me. "It's lovely to see you."

I don't reply.

The bell chimes again, and witches reach forward to remove the tureen covers, revealing hot rolls, baked potatoes, a rich-looking stew and green beans. I sigh with longing. I know I shouldn't eat it. I should have learned my lesson. But honestly I could use a little enchantment right now. Anything to take me away from the horror of what happened in Deeping Fen.

I copy the other women, helping myself to food until my plate is full. The food looks *incredible*, straight out of a catalogue or magazine. Too perfect, I realize as I take my first bite.

Bloody Ilium food again. It is as tasteless and disappointing as the instant stew I had back in Deeping Fen—in fact, I'd swear it's the same stuff.

Once again, magic makes promises it cannot deliver on.

The witches eat like dainty feminine robots. Nobody talks or makes eye contact. Gold flashes on each left hand—every single one of the women wears an identical wedding ring.

"Creepy, isn't it?" Sweetpea says to me.

I'm startled to hear a voice in among the gentle clinking of cutlery on china. None of the other women seem to have noticed.

"Are they . . . okay?" I ask.

She shrugs. "Depends on what you mean by okay."

I take another mouthful of tasteless potato. The woman opposite me dabs at her mouth with a lace-edged napkin and takes a sip of water from her glass.

"Can they hear us?" I ask Sweetpea.

"Oh, sure," she responds, then raises her voice. "Hey, Iris, how's your lunch?"

The woman looks up and smiles. "It's delicious, thank you for asking, Sweetpea."

Then she looks back down at her plate. Somehow this makes everything even creepier.

"Are they all witches?" I ask Sweetpea.

"Yep. The most dangerous women in Anglyon, if you believe everything you read in the newspapers."

"What's made them like this?"

Sweetpea points to her own bare finger. "You gotta honor and obey, once you get a ring."

"Dr. Veil said they are all here voluntarily."

Sweetpea snorts. "Not exactly."

"You don't have a ring, though. Is that why you're not like . . . them?"

She nods.

The bell chimes again, and the witches neatly place their napkins by their plates and stand.

"What now?" I ask Sweetpea.

"Half an hour taking the air in the gardens," she says. "Then back to work."

I follow her out another door and into the neatest, prettiest cottage garden I've ever seen. Tidy garden beds overflowing with peonies and hollyhocks, each one perfectly formed. At the bottom of the garden I can see tomato cages and trellises of beans and peas, and straight rows of carrots and radishes.

All at once? Peas are a winter crop, and tomatoes shouldn't be fruiting for at least a few more weeks.

I bend my head to smell a particularly plump rose, but it has no scent. Looking closer, I see no bees. No crawling insects. Not a single weed or a blade of grass out of place.

"Disgusting, isn't it?" Sweetpea says. "Might as well be plastic."

"It's all fake," I say. "Like the food."

Sweetpea nods. "Everything here is fake," she says darkly.

The other witches are walking in pairs, often linked at the elbow. If you weren't paying attention, you'd see friends strolling through lush gardens. But the women don't speak to each other. They don't look around at the flowers. They smile contentedly but don't seem to be very interested in anything.

"So are you going to tell me why you didn't get a ring?" Sweetpea asks.

"I'm not a witch," I explain.

Sweetpea raises her eyebrows. "Uh-huh."

I don't want to talk about it, but there's something about the set of Sweetpea's jaw that makes me think she won't let it go.

"You know the Toadmen?" I ask, and Sweetpea's expression goes dark.

"Sure," she responds.

"I—I went to their big Toad Prom event as a guest of one of the high-up Toadmen's sons, Caraway. And . . . well, it all went very wrong. They took my father, and made him . . . different. I made so many mistakes. In the end, they wanted me to pledge myself to their King Toad—who I'm pretty sure doesn't actually exist—to be his bride."

Sweetpea frowns. "The Fox Bride?"

"How do you know about the Fox Bride?"

"Everyone knows that story," Sweetpea says, but something in her tone is off. "The three toads and the Fox Bride. I'm assuming you refused."

I nod. "Caraway convinced them to send me here instead of killing me, and then he gave me a—" I break off.

"A what?" Sweetpea's eyes are sharp.

I shake my head. "Nothing. He gave me a kiss, that's all."

I'm not sure if she believes me or not. I snap the head off a poppy and examine its perfect crinkled petals.

"Then they killed my da in front of me."

"Bummer."

I swallow heavily. She doesn't care. Why would she? But it hurts so much to say the words out loud.

"What about you?" I ask, to change the subject. "Why are you really here? Dr. Veil said you were kidnapped by witches, but I saw you last week at the Candlecott fair."

Sweetpea's face remains neutral. "No you didn't," she says. "It must have been someone else."

But I know it's her. I remember that hard glint in her eyes.

"You're not a witch," I say. "You don't have a ring, and only witches get rings, right?"

She nods. "Right."

My shoulders sag with relief. "Good."

"I'm not completely powerless, though," she adds. "And neither are you."

I don't want power. I just want to go home.

We keep walking, past a witch sitting alone on a wrought iron garden bench. Her cheeks are sunken, her eyes vacant. She doesn't ever seem to blink.

"What happened to her?" I ask Sweetpea under my breath.

"She's a husk," Sweetpea replies at normal volume. "Lost too much mettle."

I swallow, thinking of the mettle tide, the terror of being unmoored from myself. "Do they . . . cut strings here?" I ask.

"Only if you're naughty."

"And that's legal?"

"Nobody in here cares about what's *legal*. And nobody outside cares about us."

Her face is hardened against the cold, her lips a thin line.

"So why did you come here?"

Sweetpea stares up at the bright blue sky. "There are worse places to be imprisoned," she says.

"Do any of them ever . . ." I wave a hand suggestively.

"Do magic?" Sweetpea responds. "No. The rings prevent that."

"Even the Spitalwick Hag? She escaped from prison, surely she could escape from here."

"She can't do magic," Sweetpea says. "They made sure of that."

"Where is she now?"

"Basement," Sweetpea replies. "Chained up in irons."

"Good," I say. It's what she deserves.

"Friend of yours, is she?"

"She killed my mother."

"Huh." Sweetpea glances at me speculatively. "So I guess you don't like witches."

"There's a reason why they're all here."

Sweetpea says nothing.

"It's safer for everyone if they are locked away," I add.

Sweetpea pulls a trumpet-shaped blossom from a spike of hollyhock. "Imagine if someone were to let them all go free. A whole army of angry witches."

There's a glint in her eye that I find unsettling.

The bell rings again, and the women all turn immediately and head toward a large barn without hesitating.

"Back to work, I guess," Sweetpea says.

I'M NOT ENTIRELY SURE whether I should go into the workshop—after all, I'm not a witch. But Sweetpea is going, and she's the only other normal person here, so I follow her.

The building looks like a storybook barn—rough timber with a bright white trim. Inside there are workstations, each with a simple task laid out on it. The witches file in and stand in front of a workstation.

"Are they going to do magic?" I ask Sweetpea, who shakes her head.

"Just grunt work."

The work is tedious and repetitive. I see one woman sprinkling Ilium-branded sachets on tray after tray of seedlings. Another pulls the petals off daisies and lines them up on a sheet of wax paper to dry. Yet another uses a tiny syringe to extract the nectar from honeysuckle flowers, filling a row of little glass vials.

"Here," Sweetpea says, passing me a broom. "Make yourself useful."

I spend the next few hours sweeping up discarded stems and leaves and placing them in plastic garbage bags. I guess magical gardens don't need compost heaps.

The women work methodically, without speaking. It's like being in a room full of robots. Sweetpea slips away at some point and doesn't return.

Who would have thought I would end up here, surrounded by witches?

I glance down at the flagstones beneath my feet. Is that where she is? The Spitalwick Hag?

I shudder, and hope that Dr. Veil's rings are as effective as Sweetpea says they are.

By the time of the first bell, my hands are blistered and my feet ache from standing. I follow the other witches back into the dining hall and eat my tasteless magic food along with the rest of them. Sweetpea is still nowhere to be seen, but I'm too tired to wonder what happened to her.

The final bell rings, and I follow the other women back

upstairs and fall into my bed, sliding my hand under the pillow to make sure Caraway's toadstone is still there. I close my fist around it and feel weirdly comforted by its presence. I don't know why. I should definitely hate Caraway more than I do.

I'm bone-weary, but sleep is elusive.

I try to think of anything but Da, but the alternatives are not particularly calming either. Perfect, scentless flowers. Vacant robot-witches. The Spitalwick Hag down in the basement.

Eventually I drift off into a restless sleep, haunted by dreams of a woman with stringy dark hair and a cruel, shrill laugh.

14.

I **WAKE EARLY TO FIND GRAY LIGHT SEEPING IN THROUGH** lace curtains. For a few brief moments, I don't remember that both my parents are dead.

Then everything rushes back, and the world ends all over again.

I'm tempted to stay in bed all day and hide from the world, but I need to get out of my head, so I drag myself down to breakfast and face another room full of strange, placid witches. We eat, then head off to work, where I polish the windows in the barn with some fancy enchanted no-streak spray, then sweep up the scraps again and dust the windowsills.

After lunch, Sweetpea joins me at a deep sink and we wash little vials and jars until they are sparkling clean.

"There aren't any guards," I remark.

"Nope."

"So what's to stop all the witches from just leaving?"

Sweetpea looks at me like I'm a fool. "The *rings?*" she says.

"You don't have a ring," I say. "Why don't you leave?"

Sweetpea scowls. *"You* don't have one either," she says. "But I don't see you strolling out the door."

I have nowhere else to go.

Suddenly, one of the women nearby lets out a hoarse cry. I look up to see her clutching her hand, blood pouring down her wrist. A bloody pair of garden shears lies discarded on the floor next to her.

I try to close my eyes against the bright red of it, but memories project themselves on the back of my eyelids. It's unbearable.

"Lobelia, no," mutters Sweetpea, grabbing a cleaning rag and rushing to stanch the flow of blood.

I see a flash of gold under the blood and realize that the wound is on her ring finger.

Did she try to cut it off?

A few of the witches near her have stopped working and are staring blankly down at their stations. I see a few trembling hands. One witch has tears rolling down her cheeks.

"Get it *off* me!" Lobelia cries, her voice ragged and strained. "Get it *off!*"

"This isn't the way," Sweetpea whispers urgently to her.

Lobelia lashes out, and Sweetpea goes crashing into a table, scattering scissors and rose petals.

With a muffled sob, Lobelia starts to rush toward the door, but the other witches close ranks to block the way. She wheels around, shaking her head like she's trying to clear it of something. I'm suddenly reminded of taking the Sebrium at the Toad Ball, the jarring stench and horror of it all. Lobelia staggers toward me and grabs me by the collar. I smell the sweetness of her breath, mixed with the hot tang of blood.

"Get out," she snarls between clenched teeth. "Get out while you can."

Two witches appear behind her, their expressions mild. They don't say anything as they snap iron cuffs around her wrists and place a snaffle bit in her mouth, working the awkward spikes in between her teeth. She tries to fight them off, but they are implacable, buckling the strap tight. Lobelia's cries turn to incoherent grunts and gasps. The witches take an arm each and drag her from the workshop.

There's a long pause, the remaining witches still and silent. Then, one by one, they resume working. None of them speak, although I see eyes drifting toward the smears of blood on the table, and the discarded gardening shears.

Sweetpea picks herself up off the floor and dusts petals from her dress. She looks devastated.

"Is she going to be okay?" I ask.

"No," Sweetpea replies, her voice low and dark. "She isn't."

That night, my bloodstained clothes vanish while I'm in the bath, replaced by soft new linens, laid out neatly on my bed.

LOBELIA REAPPEARS THE NEXT day, and I can't help but gasp when I see her. Her cheeks are hollow, like she hasn't eaten in weeks. Her eyes are sunken, her skin pallid and stretched thin over her bones. There is a vacancy in her eyes. The other witches may be docile, but they're still alert and responsive. I don't need to turn threadwise to see that she's alive, but not really *living.*

"They took her strings," I murmur.

"Another husk," Sweetpea says, her voice bitter.

"We have to get out of here," I tell her. "Let's just leave."

Sweetpea snorts. "You think you can just walk away?" she says. "He won't let you."

"There are no guards," I say. "No fences."

"You're deluded," she hisses, grabbing me by the elbow and yanking me away from the other women. "This place looks like something out of a catalogue, but it's still a prison."

"Dr. Veil said—"

"Dr. Veil is a *monster*. He takes their strings. He takes their mettle. He takes these women—these intelligent, powerful women full of fire—and he *breaks* them." Her fists clench.

"Why were you looking for the Hag?" I ask her. "Why come here? Are you trying to *help* the witches?"

"Of *course* I am," Sweetpea responds. "They don't deserve this. No one does."

"They're witches," I tell her. *"Criminals."*

Sweetpea's mouth twists. "They're *heroes*," she replies. "They're all that stands between us and the enemy."

"You're just a little kid," I say. "The world is complicated. It's not all about heroes and enemies."

"Oh, wake *up*," Sweetpea says. "You think the Toadmen are bad? They're just a cog in a much larger machine. Ilium. Moracle. Welch. All the big magic corporations. Auditors. They all serve one master."

"You've been listening to too many fairy stories."

"And you haven't listened to enough."

"I wish there were no magic," I say bitterly. "Magic ruins everything."

"Magic is the only thing that's going to get us out of here," Sweetpea says. "I need you to help me."

I stare at her. "You want me to help you break a hundred witches out of a recovery center?"

She nods once, sharp and fierce. "There must be something you can *do*. What's your gift?"

I shudder as I remember the inexorable pull of the mettle tide, whisking me out of my own body and into the cold mountain air.

"I don't have a gift."

"Then something you *have*. Some way in."

The toadstone, tucked under my pillow. Could it help Sweetpea? Her eyes narrow as she watches me.

"What is it?" she says. "Tell me."

More witches in the world isn't going to help anyone.

"Nothing," I say. "It's nothing."

She growls with frustration. "Fine. Then help me break into Veil's office. There must be something in there—some device or potion that can get the rings off."

I shake my head. "I'm going to leave," I tell her. "You can come with me if you want, but I won't stay here another day."

The glint goes out of Sweetpea's eyes, her mouth narrowing to a thin, pale line. "Fine," she said. "Be it on your head."

ON MY WAY TO the workshop after breakfast, I pause outside Dr. Veil's office. I want to make sure he isn't here before I try to escape. His door is locked.

All traces of Lobelia's breakdown have been cleared away. No bloodstains. Once again, Sweetpea is nowhere to be seen.

"Where did you go?" I ask her when she reappears at lunch.

"None of your business," she says shortly.

She has a cagey look and only toys with her food.

"You're going to get yourself into trouble," I warn.

"Good," she replies. "That's what I'm here for."

I have no time to respond to this, because Dr. Veil is walking into the dining room. Every head turns to look at him. One hundred witches smile placidly and dab their napkins at the corners of their mouths.

"Ladies," he says, his tone fond and fatherly. "It's lovely to see you all, as always. I'm delighted by the progress you're all making. You should all be very proud."

The women break out into light, pattering applause, which stops after precisely five seconds.

"On a more serious note," Dr. Veil continues, his brows creasing in a frown, "it seems that a theft has taken place. Someone has broken into my office and stolen something very dear to me. I'm afraid it will need to be returned at once."

I don't dare look at Sweetpea. There's a long silence while the women look curiously around. Then a witch raises her hand.

"Yes, Clematis?" Dr. Veil says, smiling indulgently. "Do you have something to share?"

"Dr. Veil, I saw Delphinium trying to open your office door just this morning."

It takes a moment for me to remember that *I* am Delphinium. Dr. Veil's eyes turn to me, his forehead creased in surprise and disappointment.

"I—I was just checking if you were in," I stammer to Dr. Veil. "I didn't—"

"Please stand up, Delphinium."

I stand, still trying to explain. "As soon as I found the door locked, I—"

Dr. Veil holds up a hand, and I fall silent. "I'm sure this is all a misunderstanding," he says. "But perhaps you could turn out your pockets, just so we can be sure?"

I shrug. Caraway's toadstone is tucked safely under my pillow. I slip my hands into my pockets and instantly recoil as I feel something brush my right hand. Something *alive.*

"Show us, please, Delphinium."

Gingerly, I withdraw the thing in my pocket and hold it out to him, my blood running cold.

It's a toad.

It's tiny, not much larger than my thumb, dark brown with a red splash on its back. Its throat bulges and it lets out a high-pitched croaking sound.

It takes all my self-control not to drop it and scream.

Dr. Veil gently removes it from my palm, cradling it in his own hand. Then he looks up at me. "I'm very disappointed in you, Delphinium."

"I didn't—" I say. "I don't know how it got there."

But I do. I look over at Sweetpea, who is staring back at me, her eyes wide and innocent. She shakes her head.

"Stealing is *wrong*," she says with a childlike lisp.

"Delphinium, please follow me to my office," Dr. Veil says. "We have matters to discuss."

My insides turn watery and I taste bland Ilium stew in

the back of my throat as Dr. Veil turns and heads back to the corridor.

Sweetpea watches me, totally unashamed.

"Traitor," I mutter.

She shrugs. "We could have been on the same side. It's not too late."

Out of the corner of my eye, I see Lobelia, her hands fluttering gently in front of her, her eyes vacant. The other witches have turned back to their meals. The glazed, placid expressions on their faces remind me of . . .

Da.

Da, who had a wedding ring on his finger that I'd never seen before.

"Wait," I say to Sweetpea. "Help me."

"Help yourself."

She walks away, and I have no choice but to follow Dr. Veil.

"I THOUGHT WE HAD an understanding, Delphinium," Dr. Veil says as he sinks into the chair behind his desk. "But you lied to me."

He's still holding the tiny toad cupped in one hand and is stroking its back gently with his thumb.

"You lied to me too," I reply. "You're a Toad. The wedding rings that all the women here wear—my da had one too, back in Deeping Fen." I swallow down the tears that threaten to rise at the mention of Da. "That's why you don't need guards, right? The rings make the witches docile."

A corner of his thin mouth lifts in a smile, and he leans forward. "I can take away your witch sight," he says. "I know you don't want it. Let me help you."

"Like you helped Lobelia?"

His eyes turn down with exaggerated regret. "I can't save everyone," he says. "Some of them won't accept the therapy. But you will, Delphinium. I have a good feeling about you."

He places the toad carefully on his desk, then reaches into a drawer, pulling out a large black hook. I stiffen. I know what it's for.

"I won't give it willingly," I warn him.

Dr. Veil sticks his bottom lip out in a disappointed pout. "That's a real shame," he says. "It hurts more if you're not willing, did you know?"

Before I can answer, he swings the hook at me, and I feel it snag on one of my strings. Dr. Veil's eyes gleam as he pulls, my string growing taut.

A cry of pain slips from my mouth, and his mouth curves in a smile. "Does it hurt so *very* much?" he asks, his cheeks flushing an ugly, mottled red.

I long to turn threadwise and let the mettle tide drag me away from my body, from this pain. But I can't. I know I might never come back if I give in to it.

My string gives way with a *snap* that I feel in every single part of me. A bit of my life, gone. I know it won't grow back. Whatever I am from this day forth, I will be less than I was.

The grief of it is almost unbearable. How can the Toads give it so freely? How could Teddy? I've seen him gift two strings now, and he would have given a third on the night of the ball if I hadn't stopped him. How many have those senior Toads given? How many has Caraway?

My string curls in on itself to form a ball, which Dr. Veil catches in a little silver dish.

"Just relax," he says. "This next part takes a few minutes."

He picks up the tiny toad again, gentle as Da with a newborn chick.

"It's a painted natterjack," Dr. Veil informs me conversationally. "Terribly poisonous, you know. Tetrodotoxin. Can kill you in five minutes, and let me tell you, it's not an easy death. But they are useful creatures. Quite extraordinary, really."

He picks up my string with his free hand. I watch, horrified, as he pokes the coiled string into the toad's mouth. The string is nearly as large as the toad, but within seconds it is gone. I feel a kind of woozy sickness envelop me, and a foul-tasting belch erupts from my throat.

"Manners," Dr. Veil says mildly.

My skin breaks out into a clammy sweat.

Dr. Veil raises the toad to his lips. "Thank you for your service," he whispers to it. Then he pulls a sharp scalpel from a container I assumed held pens. With one smooth stroke, he slits the toad's belly open. Bright blood spills onto the silver dish as the toad jerks once, twice. Dr. Veil peels back the flesh of it, and there is a *clunk* as a bloody lump falls from the toad's belly into the silver dish.

Dr. Veil discards the corpse of the toad and wipes the blood from the lump with a soft cloth.

It's a toadstone. So that's how they're made.

Dr. Veil produces a golden ring from a little drawer.

"We're making a pact, you and I," Dr. Veil says. "You have gifted me this stone, and in exchange I give you this ring. It's a pledge. A promise. That I'll help you. Heal you from the damage magic has wrought on your soul. I'll make you pure again, my dear."

I stand so fast that I knock the chair over. But before I can even turn to run, cool hands are on me. Witches, their eyes vacant and their smiles mild.

Dr. Veil holds out the ring, and I'm back in the Deeping Court again.

No matter what I do, I can't escape it.

"I won't be the Fox Bride," I say through clenched teeth.

Dr. Veil smiles. "Don't worry, Delphinium," he says. "You're no bride. Just a bridesmaid."

He catches up my hand in his and slips the ring onto my finger.

It's like the opposite of Sebrium. My world seems to shrink, and I'm overcome by a rosy, comfortable glow. Thoughts start to evaporate from my mind. I'm sinking into a soft and fluffy cloud. I start to relax, grief and tension flowing from my body, leaving nothing but lightness and contentment.

Then Dr. Veil holds up the stone, and I flinch away from it, revulsion rising in me. I taste pond water, and my skin turns clammy. I can't bear to look at it and turn my head, whimpering.

"Yes," Dr. Veil whispers. "Turn away from it. From your magic. It has poisoned you. Do you see now?"

"T-take it away," I stammer. "Please."

"Of course."

Dr. Veil opens a simple metal box on his desk. It's full of toadstones, a hundred or more.

The sight of them all makes me cry out with horror. They are oily and foul. The air is wretched with the stench of them.

Dr. Veil drops my stone in and snaps the lid closed.

Instantly, the rosy glow returns, and it's like the stones were never there. I want to forget about them, about how they made me feel.

So I do.

"Turn witch-eyed," Dr. Veil commands.

I shake my head. "I—I don't want to."

No more magic for me. Not ever.

"Just try," he says. "Just for a moment."

I refocus my eyes to look threadwise, but nothing happens. I try again.

"I can't do it," I say.

Dr. Veil smiles. "Good."

I feel a wave of relief. The witch's curse is gone.

I'm free.

I touch the ring, simple shining gold and so beautiful. I try to tug it off so I can admire it better, but it won't budge from my finger.

"You can't take it off," Dr. Veil tells me. "You're going to stay here, with me."

"Thank you, Dr. Veil," I say.

He smiles at me. "I bet you feel better already."

"I do."

So much better. Better than I have in months.

I'm not sure what I was so sad about before. I don't remember. I just feel . . . content.

15.

GO BACK TO WORK AND PULL PETALS FROM FLOWERS.
I don't get tired.

I eat my dinner, and it's delicious.

I go to bed and close my eyes, expecting to sink further into the soft rosy clouds.

But there's something in the bed with me.

I can smell it. Slimy algae and ancient peat. Throbbing. Calling to me.

The poison of magic.

I want to be free of it. I've never wanted anything so badly.

I sit up, lighting the lamp on my bedside table, and pull back my pillow.

Another stone.

Revulsion overcomes me, and I dry-heave, scrambling back away from it. I need it to be gone. Away.

But I know I can't touch it. This knowledge sits in me like lead. If I touch it, it will take me back. Poison me once more. I wrap my hand in layer upon layer of linen and, flinchingly, bat it from my bed.

I'd love to flush it down the toilet or hurl it from the window, but I daren't pick it up. So instead I roll it into the bathroom and pile towels and linens on top of it. Once it's out of sight, the pulsing, fetid call of it lessens. I close the bathroom door and crawl back into bed.

Sweat has broken out on my forehead.

Tomorrow, I'll tell Dr. Veil.

But for now, I want to forget about the stone.

So I do.

The rosy clouds rise around me once more, and I sink into a dreamless sleep.

Everything is fine.

SWEETPEA SEEKS ME OUT in the garden the next morning after breakfast. "We need to talk," she mutters, dragging me off behind the foxgloves.

"Good morning, Sweetpea," I say. "It's so nice to see you."

"Shut up."

"You seem upset," I observe. "You should go and talk to Dr. Veil. He made me feel *so* much better."

"What did he do to you?" she asks. "When he gave you the ring? Do you remember anything?"

I shake my head and smile.

Sweetpea slaps me across the face, hard. The bright pain cuts through my rosy contentment for a moment, and I put my hand over my burning cheek, my mouth falling open in indignation.

"Why did you—"

But before I can continue, Sweetpea crams a handful of peppery herbs into my mouth. I taste the sharp mintiness of pennyroyal, and suddenly I feel exhausted and shivery, like I have the flu. Fen water rises in my throat, and the ghost of a drowned memory rises along with it.

"He took something from you," Sweetpea says. "What was it?"

I look at her, my sight clouded with silt. "There's something in my room," I murmur, and every word feels like a boulder in my mouth. "Something dangerous. I have to tell Dr. Veil."

I shudder and spit out the pennyroyal, turning to head inside, but Sweetpea grabs my arm.

"Let me help you," she says, her voice suddenly gentle. "I'll get it from your room and take it to Dr. Veil. No need for you to get any more upset."

I smile at her, calm once more. "Thank you, Sweetpea," I say. She's a good girl.

I WORK. I EAT. I admire the flowers.

When I return to my room at the end of the day, everything seems fine. I hesitate in the doorway to the little bathroom, a hint of uncertainty clouding my rosy glow.

But I don't see anything. Just the bath, the toilet and the vanity. Neatly folded towels on a brass rail.

It must have been a bad dream.

* * *

SWEETPEA FINDS ME AGAIN in the garden the next morning.

"Good morning, my friend," I say in greeting.

Sweetpea makes a disgusted sound in the back of her throat and pulls something from her pocket. A small, round stone, the size of a marble.

I freeze, suddenly rooted to the spot. Foul water rises in my throat, and I shrink away from her. From it.

"T-take it away," I stammer. "Please."

"What is it?" Sweetpea asks. "What does it do?"

The revolting, throbbing call of it fills my head. I have to get away.

Sweetpea grabs me by the waistband of my skirt and yanks me back into place. For someone so small, she certainly is strong.

Tears slip down my cheeks. "Please," I beg her. "I can't."

"What *is* it?"

I shake my head.

Cold sweat breaks out on my brow. Sweetpea holds the wretched thing out to me, and my knees begin to tremble.

"Don't let it touch me."

She narrows her eyes and grabs my hand. I gibber incoherently as she forces my fingers open, one by one.

Dizziness engulfs me and black spots dance before my eyes.

Then she forces the stone into my palm, and suddenly, Da is dead and I'm drowning.

The rosy clouds turn to liquid, deep and impossibly sweet. I can't breathe. I kick and struggle against it, but it's thick as honey, and every movement takes so much effort.

Everything *hurts* so much. My lungs. My heart. Every memory comes rushing back and it's all pain and suffering and grief.

"Help me," I gasp to Sweetpea, and then it pulls me under again.

Dimly I can hear her shouting, but I can't make out any of the words. Can't see anything except the sickly-sweet pull of my impending death.

The rosy ocean is full of nightmares. The horror of the nightmare ball in Deeping Fen. Caraway, his toad eye staring at me. The light draining from Da's eyes.

I thrash out again, kicking with all my strength, breaking the surface and taking in a gasping lungful of air.

"Ring," I manage to say to Sweetpea, and thrust my hand toward her.

She tugs at it, but it won't budge. "What's going *on?*" she says, exasperated.

I get it now. But I don't have the breath to explain it all. "Not . . . my . . . stone," I gasp.

Sweetpea is smart. Her eyes narrow as she looks at the stone in my hand. "It's a string. He makes their strings into these stones." She speaks slowly, like she has all the time in the world and I'm not drowning right in front of her. "You need your own stone to take the ring off. But someone else's stone does . . . something interesting. You can think again, right?"

It's taking all my effort to stay above the deep pull of the rosy tide. "Can't think. Can't breathe."

"Great," she says, and snatches the stone back from my hand.

The sweet liquid evaporates into clouds, and I almost sob

with relief as I stop fighting and all the misery of the real world drains away.

Sweetpea is muttering to herself, but I don't listen. I'm just enjoying floating around again in rosy contentment.

I feel so *good.*

"We've got to get in there," Sweetpea says. "You're no use to me like this, except maybe as bait."

She eyes me thoughtfully.

I don't say anything, because she hasn't asked me a question. I gaze around at the flowers. They're so beautiful. Soon we will go in to work. I love to be productive.

A sharp spike of pain rakes me across the face, and I cry out as the softness of the clouds hardens momentarily.

Sweetpea is holding a thorned rose cane in her hand. I put a hand to my cheek, and when I pull it away again there is blood on my fingers.

"Why would you do that?" I ask her.

"Accident," she replies shortly. "Let's go see if the good doctor will fix you up."

"Thank you," I say. "You're a good friend, looking after me like this."

Sweetpea makes a frustrated noise. "I can't tell what is the ring's control, and what's just you being a pain in my ass."

DR. VEIL LOOKS GENUINELY pleased to see us. "What has happened to you, Delphinium?" he asks, eyeing my bloody cheek with interest.

"She had an accident," Sweetpea explains.

I don't remember the accident. But Sweetpea says I had one, so that's what must have happened.

"Does it hurt?" he asks.

I nod, and he pats a chair. "Come and sit over here."

He opens a cabinet and pulls out a bottle of ointment and a cloth. The ointment makes the scratch on my cheek smart, and I let out a whimper.

"It stings, doesn't it?" he says. His voice sounds different, like he's a little out of breath.

"*So* much," I tell him.

His breath gets faster. I'm glad he's here to help me.

"Can I hold her hand?" Sweetpea asks, her voice high and childlike. "For comfort?"

"Of course you can, my dear," Dr. Veil replies, turning away to remove the plastic cover from an Ilium bandage patch.

I feel Sweetpea's fingers brush mine, and then I'm drowning again, the rosy liquid dragging me under before I realize what's happening.

Every time it happens, it's like Da has died again. The grief of it is just as sharp. Just as fresh.

I kick and struggle against the pull of it, breaking the surface just in time to see Sweetpea shove the metal box on Dr. Veil's desk, knocking it to the ground so the toadstones inside go tumbling out, skittering and bouncing on the floor.

Dr. Veil's face clouds over.

"Sweetpea," he says. "What a naughty little girl you are. I should have given you a ring after all."

I can barely focus on them through the thick, sweet liquid, but I manage to slide off my chair and onto the floor, where I paw at the stones, desperately trying to find my own.

"On behalf of the resistance witches of Anglyon," Sweetpea says, "I'd like to welcome you to your death. Any last words?"

I hear Dr. Veil chuckle. "The resistance witches of Anglyon must be pretty desperate, to send a little girl to do their dirty work."

How will I tell which one is mine? Do I have to pick up every single one and try to take the ring off? The rosy liquid seems to be growing thicker, or perhaps I'm just running out of strength to fight it.

"What's next?" Dr. Veil is asking. "What's the next step in this clever plan? Do you think you're just going to saunter on out of here?"

My hand lands on another stone, and I just *know*. It's like Sol plucking the perfect harmony on his crwth, or the bright ringing of Teddy's hammer on the anvil. I snatch the stone up, and it feels like coming home.

I slip the wedding ring from my finger.

It slides off as smooth as butter, and it's like taking ten doses of Sebrium all at once.

"Next?" Sweetpea says, squaring her shoulders. "Let me tell you what's next. First of all, I'm going to break every single one of your fingers, so you can't touch us anymore. Then I'll pull out your intestines and feed them to you, because that seems like a fun way to pass the time. After that I plan to pluck out your eyelashes, one by one, and use them to stitch your mouth shut, so you can't speak to us ever again. Finally, I will rip your entire head off, and spit down your throat, because that is what you deserve. Then, and only then, will I *saunter on out of here.*"

My head pounds and my mouth turns dry and foul. It's all I can do to not vomit. But at least I can breathe again. My ring drops to the carpet with a soft *thump.*

Dr. Veil is laughing, a high giggle laced with mania. "Go on, then," he says to Sweetpea, holding his arms wide. "Take your best shot."

Sweetpea cracks her knuckles, then tilts her head from side to side to loosen her joints. She's an eleven-year-old girl, and he is a full-grown man.

"Let's do this," she says, but before she can do anything, Dr. Veil kicks her in the chest.

She grunts as the air goes rushing from her lungs, her legs buckling beneath her.

I don't have much time.

I take a breath and look threadwise.

For a moment I'm afraid I've lost the ability—that even though I've taken the ring off, it's still managing to block me. But then the silvery threads spring to life before me.

It's a relief to have my gift back, and now I truly believe that it *is* a gift. It's not a curse, and it never was. It's a part of me.

This time, I don't fight the mettle tide. I let it lift me up into the cold mountain air. Then I slide sideways to drop out of the stream, and examine it carefully.

Witch mettle, drained from every prisoner here. Better than cutting strings. Strings don't grow back, they're a finite resource. But these rings drain a witch's *energy*—energy that is refilled each day with sleep and food and exercise. No wonder I feel like I've been ill.

The rumors were right. These recovery centers really are mettle farms. Recovering mettle from witches powerless to resist.

The braid of witch mettle streams off into the distance. I can't say for sure where it's going.

But I can guess. That vast power store beneath the Deeping Court.

I sink back down into my body—easy, now that I understand the mettle tide a little better.

Dr. Veil is lifting Sweetpea by the front of her dress so that her outraged face is pressed right up against his.

He's almost entirely Toad mettle. Thick with it. It pulses through him, thick ropes of it. I don't see any regular human mettle at all. I remember what Caraway told me, back in Deeping Fen.

The stronger the connection is between a Toadman and the king, the more powerful the Toad becomes. More wealth. More luck. More power. Until you're completely dependent on him.

"You defied me," he hisses at Sweetpea, saliva and blood spraying from his mouth. "You will regret it."

He shoves her away from him, and she goes flying across the room to smash against the wall.

I look down at the toadstones that litter the floor, searching them threadwise, seeing each strand of mettle that binds the stone to the ring, stretching out to the hand of every witch here.

There's one in particular that I'm looking for.

Sweetpea tries to stand again, but Dr. Veil is there before she can, swiping at her face with one closed fist.

I close my eyes and see a fist smashing into Da's face. See his head snap back and blood pour from his nose and into his mouth.

A kind of frenzy descends upon Dr. Veil, and he hits out at Sweetpea over and over again.

The fingers of my right hand close over the one toadstone in this room that might be able to save us.

"Give up?" Dr. Veil hisses.

With slow and deliberate effort, Sweetpea pushes herself into a crouch and spits bloody saliva to the floor. "Nope."

He hits her again, and again, and I don't think I can bear it.

"Stop." I don't realize I've spoken until Dr. Veil whirls to stare at me.

Witch hands form before him, created from the twisted ropes of Toad mettle. They shine wetly, like they have just been plunged into the mud of Deeping Fen. And then they reach for me, wrapping around my throat. I can't breathe, and it's like I'm drowning all over again, except this time it isn't rosy sweetness, it's the thick, muddy water of Deeping Fen.

Dr. Veil hauls me up off the floor and onto his desk. "Well," he says, his voice sickly-sweet as he leans over me. "Look who's awake."

I flinch away from his fingertips. "Leave her alone," I gasp. "She's just a kid."

"Speak for yourself," Sweetpea says from behind Dr. Veil, her voice ragged with pain.

He turns and shoves her back to the floor, stomping on her crumpled form with a heavy boot, letting out a little grunt of satisfaction as she falls silent.

He turns back to me. "He should have let me kill you," Dr. Veil whispers, and his face is so close to mine, I can smell the sourness of his breath.

He pries my left fist open, jostling my hand to dislodge my toadstone. It goes tumbling onto the floor to join the others.

"So *naughty,*" Dr. Veil whispers, and I feel flecks of his saliva on my skin. "So *sneaky.*"

His breath grows shallow.

I reach out, slowly, to the container on his desk, and wrap my fingers around what I hope is a scalpel and not a pen.

"I knew you'd try to do something wicked like this, *Little Fox,*" he whispers, and it's all I can do to not crawl off the table.

And now I know for sure. Dr. Veil is the Howling Toad.

He grins, blood and saliva gleaming on yellowed teeth. "I'm afraid this might hurt a little."

I move faster than I've ever moved before. One hand reaches up and snatches the eye patch from Dr. Veil's face. I have just a moment to see his brown, amphibian toad eye, widening in surprise. Then my other hand whips up, driving the scalpel right into the center of it. Except it isn't a scalpel at all, it's a fountain pen. But the sharp tip is enough. The eyeball resists for a moment, then gives way. Blood spurts out, covering my hands and my face. Dr. Veil recoils with a grunt, pressing a hand to his eye.

Then he laughs again, a wet, gurgling sound that fills me with dread. He leans forward once more, pressing the full weight of his body into mine as I struggle beneath him. His blood drips onto my face, into my mouth, the hot metallic tang of it mingling with the bile that rises in my throat.

"So clever," he hisses. "Cunning, some would say. I see why my brother wanted you to be the Fox Bride."

I can feel the tremble in him. The pent-up energy, and I remember Caraway telling me about the Howling Toad.

The stories say that he is utterly brutal, that he loves causing people pain. Takes a sick kind of pleasure from it.

I glance down at Sweetpea. She's not moving. I don't think she's even breathing. I struggle against Dr. Veil, wishing I could go to her, see if she's still alive. Tell her how brave she was.

"You have no idea what I could do to you," Veil says, taking visible pleasure in every word. "How I could make you suffer."

I want to laugh in his face. He can't make me suffer any more than I already have. "You'll die eventually," I tell him. "And then everything will change."

Dr. Veil runs a finger down my cheek. I can smell the blood on him.

"Nothing will change, Little Fox. Men may come and go, but the Toadmen remain. Always."

"Except for the King Toad," I say. "He's not real. It's just toads under a cape."

Dr. Veil grimaces, his mouth full of blood. "It is true that no man hides under the King Toad's mask. But there is power deep beneath the halls of Deeping Fen. A power that you cannot begin to imagine."

He hauls me up off the desk and drags me over to where Sweetpea is lying, crumpled and still.

Dr. Veil stares at her, trembling with excitement. He lifts his fingers to his throat and caresses his own skin gently, his eyes glassy.

"You did this," he says softly to me. "It's all your fault. Your father is dead. Next will be your friends. Then every single miserable soul in your pathetic little town."

Sweetpea looks so small.

He drops my toadstone back into the metal box. "Safe and sound," he says. "Now come along. I want you to meet the Fox Bride."

THE BASEMENT IS COLD and clammy, built from large bluestone blocks. Dr. Veil shoves me down a long, thin passage with a low ceiling, lit with weak fluorescent lights that ping and spit overhead.

At the end of the passage, there is a door.

I know what's in there.

"No," I whisper to him. "Please."

"Don't worry," he says. "She's as harmless as a kitten. As long as you don't get too close."

He shoves me inside, and I'm face to face with the most dangerous witch in Anglyon.

She's not at all what I expected. I'd imagined someone ugly, covered in warts, with stringy dark hair and black, curving fingernails. A witch from a storybook, like Jenny Greenteeth.

But the Spitalwick Hag is just a woman, maybe fifty years old. Her skin dark, with purple bruises over her wrists and ankles where black iron manacles keep her chained to the wall behind her. A wickedly spiked snaffle bit is inserted between her teeth, buckled behind her head to keep it tight. Her head has been roughly shaved—weeping cuts stipple her skull. Her frame is painfully thin beneath the grimy linen shift she wears.

There is a golden ring on every single one of her fingers.

I swallow. That's a lot of power, to keep one witch contained.

I take a step toward her.

Her eyes are closed, and I'm reasonably certain she's not conscious. She's alive, though. I can see her chest rise and fall with each breath.

No wonder the people of Candlecott wanted her gone.

No wonder they couldn't force her.

It's lucky anyone left that fight alive.

Of all the horrors I've faced since I left Candlecott, this is by far the worst. Face to face with the witch who killed my mother.

"You would have made an adequate Fox Bride," Dr. Veil says to me. "But she . . ." He smacks his lips. "She is magnificent. Such power. Such strength."

I don't dare to breathe. Every trembling step I take feels like a fresh betrayal of Ma. Of what she fought for. Of what she died for.

But I have no choice.

"It was always her," Dr. Veil continues, almost conversationally. "We've been planning it for sixteen years. She almost ruined everything when she escaped last month. That's why we needed you. Just in case."

I'm close enough that I can see the Hag's eyelashes trembling against her sunken cheeks.

"Of course," says Dr. Veil. "Nobody escapes the Toadmen."

I don't want to do this.

But I must.

I lean forward and kiss the Spitalwick Hag on the mouth, the iron of the snaffle bit cold against my lips. I feel her body tense suddenly.

Dr. Veil pulls the black iron hook from beneath his lab coat. "You're too clever for your own good, Little Fox," he says, reaching forward to yank me away from the Hag. I crumple at his feet. "I think it's time to put you out of your misery."

He plants a boot on my chest and loops the black hook around all of my strings at once.

I cry out in pain as he hauls.

"You can't imagine the strength of these witches," he grunts as the strings strain against him. "Didn't you wonder what powers the enchantments of Deeping Fen? Or were you too busy sneaking off to canoodle with young Caraway Boswell?" Veins stand out on Dr. Veil's neck as he pulls on the black hook. "Ruddock Farm is home to some of the most dangerous, powerful creatures who have ever lived. And has a single one of them ever escaped?" He shakes his head, droplets of sweat flying from his brow. "Why did you think *you* could? *You're* not even a witch."

The pain is unbearable. I scream as he attempts to rip every bit of life-force out of me.

"No," Veil continues. "You're just a silly little girl, playing silly little games. You cannot reckon with the power and might of Toads."

The strings are stretched so tight now, just a little more will sever them forever and end me completely, turn me into a mindless husk.

Tink.

Veil turns his head slightly at the noise.

Tink.

He relaxes, just a little, and the strain on my strings lessens.

A golden ring tumbles to the floor, then another. And another. Dr. Veil drops the black hook, and my strings are all mine again.

Tink. Tink. Tink.

The rings slip from the Spitalwick Hag's emaciated fingers, which flex, finally free from their bondage.

Dr. Veil inhales sharply.

The Hag gazes coolly at him as the iron collar falls from her neck and lands on the stone floor with a heavy *clunk*, followed by the shackles from her wrists and ankles.

"Not possible," Dr. Veil hisses.

"You were right, Dr. Veil," I say, trying to control the tremor of fear in my voice. "I'm not a witch. I never thought I could stand against you and win."

The Spitalwick Hag spits something small and round onto the floor.

"But she can," I say.

THE ROUND OBJECT BOUNCES and rolls to land at Dr. Veil's feet.

Her toadstone, slipped from my mouth to hers with a kiss.

The Hag glances at me. "I'd take a few steps back, if I were you," she says dryly.

I stagger backward, away from Dr. Veil. He makes no attempt to stop me.

The Hag snaps her fingers, and I see a bright green flame appear at her fingertips.

Just a little spark.

The corner of her mouth twitches.

And then she strikes.

I don't need to look threadwise. I can *feel* the surge of mettle as she unleashes her magic in a torrent of raw, undiluted rage.

The walls shudder around us, and I brace myself in the wooden frame of the doorway.

There's a rumble of thunder, and the entire basement splits open with a rending, creaking groan. Dust and rubble pile in behind and around us. The Hag's fingers flick briefly in my direction and the stones around me stabilize, forming a kind of protective cave.

I can feel icy drops on my cheeks and look up to see that the whole building has been torn asunder. Dark clouds hurl rain down on us.

Wind starts to howl around Dr. Veil, stones and earth lifting up and whirling around him in a torrent. Huge roots and vines erupt from the basement floor and wrap around Dr. Veil's arms and legs. Ravens appear in the air and swoop down to peck at his bleeding toad eye. Beetles and hornets rise in clouds, whirring and humming as they dive at him.

Thunder rumbles again, and the air crackles. Then a bolt of lightning arcs down from the sky as the air fills with the scent of ozone and charred flesh.

He doesn't even get the chance to scream.

Within moments it's all over, and there's nothing left of the Howling Toad but a pile of wet ashes.

Rubble skitters behind me and I turn to see Sweetpea, her face smeared with blood and dust. She's limping, but alive.

"What'd I miss?" she asks.

16.

"**T**HAT WAS A BOLD MOVE," SAYS SWEETPEA, SOME TIME later. "She could have killed you."

We're back in Veil's office, collecting the last few toadstones from the floor. She's had her cuts and bruises patched up, and a witch has administered a healing draft.

"I know," I say. "I couldn't think of anything else to do."

"You're kind of a badass, Delphinium," she says admiringly. "Who would have guessed?"

I don't *feel* like a badass. I feel scared and weak and helpless. I only wore a wedding ring for two days, but my whole body aches and I can't stop shivering.

How must the other witches be feeling? Some of them were being drained for years.

"Hey, I'm not the one that voluntarily came here to try to bust out the most dangerous witch in Anglyon."

Sweetpea grins. "I like to think big."

"Why, though?" I ask. "Why were you looking for her, back in Candlecott?"

"I heard she'd escaped," Sweetpea says. "And I thought, *That's someone I want on my side.*"

"What side is that?"

"The right side."

AFTER WE'VE REUNITED THE remaining stones with their witches, we all gather in front of the remains of Ruddock Farm for a council.

The witches look different now that they're free. Some are sharp-eyed and burning with rage. Others seem sad and pensive. Some are very weak, leaning on each other with sweat sheening on their brows.

The Spitalwick Hag looks like she could run a marathon. She and Sweetpea stand at the front of the group.

"I was sent by a chapter of resistance witches in Inglenook," Sweetpea says. "Our goal is to liberate as many witches from detention as we can, and ultimately to stage a revolution, overthrowing the tyranny of auditors and reclaiming the right to do magic."

This is met with a long moment of confused silence. "But you're just a child," one of the witches says.

"You came here on *purpose?*" another says, disbelieving.

"Someone had to."

There's a pause as everyone reassesses their opinion of Sweetpea. Not me, I already know what she's capable of.

"So what happens now?" asks a witch.

"Auditors will be on their way," Sweetpea says. "They'll know what's happened."

I think about the Ghost Toad, who has eyes everywhere. But I drove a fountain pen into Dr. Veil's toad eye. Thurmond Boswell can't *see* what's happened at Ruddock, but he sure is going to notice that his free-flowing stream of witch mettle has suddenly dried up.

"We need to make a proper plan," the Spitalwick Hag says. "We've got some time—a few hours, even a day or two if we're lucky. We should use it. Make a proper plan, so we don't end up here again."

"Some of us just want to go home," one woman says. "We have families."

The Hag scowls. "Families that will be in danger as soon as they know you've escaped," she snaps.

"Exactly!" the woman retorts. "We need to get them to safe houses."

"My people are standing by," Sweetpea says. "We have safe houses waiting."

"Safe houses aren't enough," I say, and eyes turn to me. "As long as your toadstones exist, the Ghost Toad will be able to find you. And that means auditors can find you."

"So we smash them," Sweetpea says offhandedly.

She takes a stone from a witch and places it on the ground. Then she lifts a bit of masonry rubble in one hand and brings it down hard. The toadstone goes pinging away from her like it's in a pinball machine. Several witches have to duck as it ricochets off a tumbled-down wall and goes skittering into a lavender bush.

"Fool," mutters the Hag darkly. "You can't break a magical object with brute force."

"You can't break it at all," says another witch.

"Sure you can," says yet another. "Magic breaks magic."

The Hag examines her own stone, brows furrowed. "A

lightning bolt might do it," she muses. "Or a really focused surge of mettle."

A witch shakes her head. "A surge would make it explode," she says. "It'd kill anyone nearby. You need something that can contain the sudden release of mettle."

"What about a magic sword?" asks another witch. "Naegling? Or the Bright Blade of Cosgarach Mhor?"

"You can't break a marble with a sword," another replies with an eye roll. "The blade is entirely the wrong shape. It'd just go pinging away like the girl's just did."

"A hammer, then."

"Do you *have* a magic hammer?" the second witch says, her voice dripping with sarcasm. "And do you know anyone who can wield one?"

I do.

The witches continue to bicker, and I catch Sweetpea's eye and gesture for her to follow me.

We slip around the side of the building and perch on a wrought iron bench.

"I'm guessing you're not super keen on staying to help lead the newly minted witch revolution?" Sweetpea says.

"I'm no witch," I say. "I can't help them."

Sweetpea gives me a disbelieving look. "I just watched you match magical stones to their owners."

"I have witch sight," I explain. "But there's nothing I can actually *do.*"

Sweetpea snorts. "A hundred witches are free because of what you did," she says. "That's not nothing."

I'm about to protest that it was the Hag who defeated the Howling Toad, but I stop, suddenly remembering the feeling of zipping along the brown threads of Toad mettle, feeling my consciousness leave my body and rise up and out of Ruddock Farm. Sweetpea is right. It's not nothing.

"I know where there's a magic hammer," I say instead.

"Interesting," a husky voice says from behind me.

It's the Hag, her dark eyes on me, thoughtful.

I cling to the bench beneath me to stop my hands from trembling.

"You have nothing to fear from me, child," she says. "I owe you my life."

I say nothing.

"She thinks you killed her mother," Sweetpea offers in explanation.

The Hag's brow creases in a frown. "Did I?" she says. "When?"

My voice returns to me. "Mwsogl Hollow," I say. "Seventeen years ago."

The Hag sighs. "A regretful conflict," she says. "Born from misunderstanding. But I wasn't aware that anyone perished."

"My mother fell sick," I say. "Thirteen years to the day after you cursed her."

The Hag stares at me for a moment, then takes a few steps forward, sinking to her knees before me. I flinch away from her.

"I didn't curse your mother," she says softly. "And even if I had, magic doesn't work that way. She would have died within days, not after thirteen years."

Ma talked about her curse all the time. Blamed it for every

little thing that went wrong. If the milk went sour. If she dropped a plate. If a fox got into the chicken run.

If Ma burned the dinner, it was the curse. If she snapped at Da, or forgot to pick me up from school.

My eyes fill with tears.

I guess sometimes it's easier to blame our shortcomings on magic. Then nothing is ever our fault.

"I'm deeply sorry that you lost your mother," the Hag says. "But . . . sometimes people just get sick. I know that might be hard to believe."

It isn't hard to believe at all, and that's what makes me feel sick with guilt. How eagerly I've accepted the Hag's version of things. How quick I was to betray my mother's memory.

But I know the Hag speaks the truth.

She touches a finger to my cheek. "Good people bless you, child."

Then she rises and returns to the other witches.

"You're taking on the Toads, then?" Sweetpea says.

I nod.

"You know this doesn't end with them, right? There may be plenty of Toadmen working high up at Ilium, but they're not the be-all and end-all. Ilium will survive without Toads. Not to mention Moracle and Welch and the auditors."

"They're all linked, aren't they?" I ask. "I thought it was Toads behind it all."

Sweetpea shakes her head. "There are things much worse than Toads."

I sigh. "There was a time when I thought witches were the scariest thing in the world."

"Yeah," says Sweetpea. "Well, don't believe everything they teach you at school." She stands up and brushes her hands together briskly. "Guess we'd better find you a ride."

WE HEAD OUT PAST the ornate gardens to where a pair of white vans sit in a neat gravel carpark. I swallow down a wave of nausea as I remember the suffocating closeness of the hood, the scent of diesel and hartshorn.

The mountains around us are sharp and rocky. I can imagine that in winter they are deeply coated in snow. Even now in early summer, the air has an icy bite to it. I shiver. I've felt cold since the gold ring came off.

"Which way do I go?" I ask.

"There's only one road out," Sweetpea says with a shrug. "You can drive, right?"

"Sure," I say, sounding more confident than I feel. I've driven Teddy's van a couple of times on the back roads around Candlecott. But never on my own.

Sweetpea hesitates. "You should wait," she says. "Have something to eat. Find some proper clothes. Get a good night's sleep."

"I can't," I tell her. "I have to leave now."

She nods, understanding. "Good luck," she says.

"You too."

"And . . . you know. Holler if you need anything."

I grin at her and climb into the driver's seat. The key is in the ignition and I turn it, the engine rumbling to life. I wind down the window and lean out.

"Who do I holler for?"

She hesitates. "Winnie," she says at last. "My name is Winnie. Now get out of here."

I MAY HAVE OVERESTIMATED my driving ability. The van is a manual, and I really don't know anything about gears.

The mountain road is made of tight hairpin bends and narrow stretches complete with vertiginous drops. The wheels of the van seem to skid along, gravel thrown back up onto the undercarriage, which rattles and shudders. I'm moving as fast as I dare, which is not much faster than a walking pace. I don't want to get caught by any approaching auditors, but I also don't want to drive the van off the edge of a cliff and plummet to my death.

The bonus of driving very slowly is I don't have to change gears very often.

Daylight is fading. My fingers ache from clutching the steering wheel so tightly, and my bladder is uncomfortably full. I should have gone to the loo before I left. I should have brought some terrible Ilium food as well. Or at the very least a bottle of water. I was in such a hurry to leave, I did everything wrong.

I just feel so *tired*. Drained and fragile, like I'll crumble to dust if I stop moving for even a moment.

Entirely plausible nightmare scenarios keep appearing in my mind. I drive right off the cliff to my death. I run headlong into a squad of auditors. I arrive in a town and am immediately recognized and arrested. It's difficult to think of a scenario that *doesn't* end in either my death or my imprisonment.

Eventually my bladder wins, and I put the van in neutral and pump the brake, rolling to a stop. There's no point in pulling over; if someone's coming the other way then I'm done for.

I squat by the edge of the road and let out a sigh of relief as I gaze out across valleys and peaks, softened by dusk, all silvery edges and deep inkblot shadows. It's certainly the most breathtaking toilet experience I've ever had. When I'm done, I stand and look out for a moment longer, breathing the petrichor scent of evening and feeling my heart still for a moment.

I barely register the crunch of tires on gravel. It isn't until the van has rolled several meters down the hill that I notice it and let out an incoherent curse word as I race after it, skidding across the loose gravel in my thin-soled boots.

But it's too late.

With the slow grace and dignity of a gliding swan, the van keeps rolling forward, even when the road curves to hug the mountain. It sails off the edge of the cliff, its nose dipping forward suddenly.

And then it's gone.

I hear a metallic scrape, a wrenching noise, and then, several seconds later, a distant crash. Then there's silence, save for the skittering of tiny rocks slipping down the mountain after my van.

"Well, fuck," I tell nobody in particular.

I start to walk, because there's nothing else I can do. The light slips away until I can barely make out the road in front of me. The air grows cold and thin, and I shiver in my thin linen skirt.

I've come too far—I won't make it back to Ruddock before dark if I turn back now.

Eventually I can't see in front of me at all, and I stop. I can't risk walking right off the side of the mountain and joining the van at the bottom of the ravine. I hunch down into a sitting position, wrapping my arms around my knees, tight as I can to keep warm. My muscles ache, and I'm hungry and tired. But more than anything, I just feel very, very silly.

What was it Dr. Veil said about me and Sweetpea?

Just a silly little girl, playing silly little games.

I've made nothing but mistakes, from the moment I learned that Teddy was joining the Toadmen and this whole terrible business started.

All I've done is destroy the people I love. I've been selfish, and silly, and naive.

I put a hand into my pocket and feel the two toadstones there, snuggled up against each other. Me and Caraway. It's too dark to hide from myself anymore. I did fall for him. Maybe a lot earlier than I've been willing to admit.

All that rivalry, that competition. I *liked* it. I liked him. I liked beating him, yes, but I also liked the challenge. Liked spending time with him.

I take Caraway's stone in my hand and touch it to my lips. I wish I'd told him how I feel, when I had the chance.

It's comforting, holding the stone. Like I have a little piece of him here with me. It makes me feel less alone.

And maybe I'm not alone.

Maybe . . .

I close my eyes and take a deep breath. Then I activate my witch sight. I focus on Caraway's toadstone, clutched tightly in my hand, then follow the spider-thin thread of Toad mettle that joins it to him. It floats up, high in the cold, thin mountain air. I feel other threads connect to it—all the Toadmen, and the witches back in Ruddock who I'm sure are still trying to figure out how to destroy their stones and break that connection once and for all.

The web of mettle stretches over the whole of Anglyon. I know which one is Caraway's. I can *feel* it. But something is wrong. I expect Caraway's thread to float out over the mountain and down to the lowlands, back to Deeping Fen, or to Scouller, or even home to Candlecott. But it's like my consciousness is on a leash, and as soon as I travel a certain distance, I stop and am pulled abruptly back down to the ground, back down to the side of this thrice-cursed mountain.

I guess I've reached the limit of my gift.

A faint glow illuminates the inside of my eyelids, and I open my eyes with a start. But there's nothing, only inky blackness surrounding me. I close my eyes again and try once more to follow Caraway's mettle thread, but once more I get yanked back down to the cold, dark mountainside.

Frustrated, I let my witch sight fade and put Caraway's stone back in my pocket.

There's that faint glow again, and I see it with open eyes this time. It's too early for dawn. The light fades after a few moments, and I wonder if I just imagined it. But a few seconds later it appears once more, a dim glow ahead of me, swinging from left to right and growing steadily brighter with every beat of my heart.

I hear the rumble of an engine, and a weird mix of relief and fear washes through me as twin headlights round a corner. I rise creakily to my feet, throwing my hands up to shield my eyes from the light. I can't see anything.

It must be Toads. Or auditors. Who else would be driving down this lonely freezing road in the middle of the night? If only I had a weapon.

The car rolls to a halt in front of me. I can't see anything, just blinding white light. I hear one car door open, then another. Then the sound of boots on gravel.

That's it, then. I guess I'm going back to Ruddock. Or else they'll just kill me. Do they know about the breakout? They mustn't, otherwise there'd be more of them. That's not so bad, then. We'll get there, and the witches will deal with them, then I steal another van and start over, and this time I don't forget about the parking brake. In which case, all I have to do is make sure they don't kill me.

"Please," I say, reaching my hands forward in surrender. "Don't hurt me."

The voice that returns to me through the night is the last one I was expecting. "Oh, Morgan. Don't be so dramatic."

I'm frozen in shock. I hear a gentle thump, the sound of a not-too-hard arm punch, and then a second, quieter voice speaks.

"Stop being a dick, she's terrified."

I let out a little gasp of disbelief.

"S-Sol? Caraway?"

And then Sol is here, catching me up as I slump, exhausted, into his arms.

"I've got you," he says, and I burst into tears.

They bundle me into the back of a car, Sol next to me, holding my hand. I look around blearily and realize that it's the Purple Menace. I let out a little shout of hysterical laughter, and Sol squeezes my fingers.

"It's okay," he says. "You're safe now."

"Only if I can figure out how to turn around on this cursed mountain road," Caraway mutters, and starts his usual routine of swearing at his car. The sound of it is so ridiculous and familiar that I think I might cry again.

"How did you know I escaped?" I ask.

"We didn't," Sol replies. "We were on our way to rescue you."

Caraway is wearing a patch over his toad eye, and nausea roils in my gut as I remember the resistance-then-give of Dr. Veil's toad eye as I drove the fountain pen into it.

Having successfully turned the Purple Menace to face the other way, Caraway proceeds to hurtle us down the mountain at an alarming pace. I let out a little yelp as he revs the accelerator, and dig my fingers into Sol's arm.

"I know, right?" he mutters quietly, and I giggle, delirious with exhaustion.

Caraway reaches out and flips the Ilium radio on.

Big love
Little lights combine

"That bloody song," Sol mutters. "He's been listening to it nonstop."

I close my eyes and let the words wash over me.

In the dark you find my hand, we make a little spark
Two particles collide

Big love
Little lights combine
You and I ignite

17.

CARAWAY CHECKS US INTO A RATHER SEEDY-LOOKING motel at the foot of the mountain. We pile into the one room, and for the first time I see Caraway's and Sol's faces in full light. Caraway isn't wearing his glamour, and his usually ice-cool perfect face seems drawn and anxious. The eye patch over his toad eye is definitely magical—black velvet with some kind of witch mark stitched on it in silver thread.

"It's to stop *him* seeing," Caraway explains, touching a hand to it. "He knows where we are, of course. But this way he can't see or hear us."

Sol is staring at me, horrified. "Is that . . . yours?" he says, gesturing to my face.

I put a finger to my cheek and feel the blood crusted there. "No," I reply. "It's Dr. Veil's."

"Have a shower," Sol instructs. "Then you can tell us everything."

"I'll get us some food," Caraway says, and slips out of the room.

I close the bathroom door behind me and peel off my filthy Ruddock linens, careful to place the two toadstones on the edge of the washbasin. I get a glimpse of my reflection in the mirror and understand why Sol looked so shocked. My entire face is covered in dark red blood. My eyes are watery with exhaustion, dark circles under them.

I step into the shower, the hot jets of water washing away the horrors of Ruddock. I let warm water run into my mouth, over my face, and see dark blood swirl down the drain.

Goodbye, then, Dr. Veil. Good riddance.

I wash my hair with tiny motel shampoo and conditioner, and scrub every inch of my body. The motel towel isn't nearly big enough, but I do my best, then ball up my clothes and shove them into the rubbish bin. If I could burn them without setting off a smoke alarm, I would.

Sol lends me a T-shirt and some tracksuit bottoms, and I emerge in them, pink and clean and feeling more clearheaded than I have in a long while.

Caraway returns from the vending machine bearing an armful of plastic packages. I reject the instant beef stew with a shudder and tear open a cobblestone bar, pretty much inhaling the whole thing. Sol chuckles and helps himself to a packet of hotroot sticks. Caraway looks at me disapprovingly as I lick chocolate and plum toffee from my fingertips.

"You should eat some real food before you make yourself sick on the sugary stuff," he cautions.

"None of this is real food, Caraway," I inform him, and help myself to a box of fluffy sweet ambrosia.

Sol and I sit cross-legged on the bed, and I'm reminded of

eating junk food with Caraway in Deepdene. He doesn't join us, though. He sits by the window, peering out through a thin gap in the curtains, like he's expecting intruders at any moment.

"What was your plan?" I ask, my mouth full of airy marshmallow. "How were you going to get me out of Ruddock Farm?"

Sol and Caraway exchange a look. "We hadn't quite figured that part out," Sol admits.

"We would have," Caraway says, staring out into the blackness.

"Did you walk all the way?" Sol asks. "In those thin shoes, with no water or food or anything?"

"Not exactly," I tell him. "I stole a van."

Sol frowns. "I didn't see a van."

I cram a fairy cake into my mouth so I don't have to answer straightaway. Caraway raises his eyebrows, and I feel my cheeks flush.

"I got out to pee," I admit. "And forgot to put the parking brake on."

A twitch around Caraway's lips, and he turns to look back out the window.

Sol chuckles, but I see the tightness in his smile. The gray circles under his eyes.

"Where's Teddy?" I ask him, although I suspect I already know the answer.

Sol's Adam's apple bobs as he swallows down a surge of emotion. "Still at Deeping Fen," he says. "When they took you away . . . Caraway came to us. He told us everything that had happened. About what they did to your da. He said we had to do something, to help you escape. I agreed at once, but Teddy . . ."

A tear slips down his cheek, and I reach over to squeeze his hand.

"It's not his fault," Caraway says, not looking away from the window. "They've been working on him for months now. He's given two strings—that's enough for them to get their claws into your mind."

I glance over at Caraway. How is *his* mind unclawed?

"What about you?" Sol asks me. "What *happened*, Merry?"

I tell them everything—about Dr. Veil and his golden rings, about the placid witches, and Sweetpea, and the Spitalwick Hag chained in the basement.

Sol's breath draws in sharply. "The witch who killed your mother?"

"I—I don't think she did. She says she didn't, and I believe her."

"Dr. Veil had a toad eye?" Caraway asks with a frown.

"He was the Howling Toad."

Caraway stiffens. "Are you sure?"

"Positive."

Sol leans forward. "You said he *was* the Howling Toad. Does that mean he isn't anymore?"

I tell them about Sweetpea and how brave she was, about how she took on Dr. Veil and never stopped fighting. I tell them about finding the Hag's stone and slipping it into her mouth with a kiss.

Caraway's eyes flick to mine, and I see pink flush his cheeks.

I can't stop thinking about something Dr. Veil said to me.

No man hides under the King Toad's mask.

"I don't think there *is* a King Toad," I say. "I think it's just the

Ghost Toad and the Howling Toad. And maybe that's how it's been all along."

Sol tilts his head. "He wasn't really at any of the ceremonies," he says. "You showed us he was just toads all the way down."

"It's possible," Caraway says. "I've been snooping around the Toads for my whole life, and I've never seen the King Toad. Or even heard any rumors of who he might be."

"Because he *doesn't exist*," I say. "Which means that now that the Howling Toad is dead, only your father is left."

Caraway swallows. "They'll anoint a new Howling Toad."

"You said the positions were hereditary. Did Dr. Veil have a son?"

Caraway spreads his hands. "I don't know. I didn't even know who the Howling Toad was. If I had known . . ." He breaks off, standing abruptly. "You two should get some sleep. I'll keep watch."

And he's gone, slipped out the door and into the night. The room feels somehow empty without him, and I stare down at the junk-food wrappers that litter the bed.

"He was really worried about you," Sol says quietly.

"Really?" I hug my knees and breathe in the comforting scent of Sol that's embedded in his clothes.

Caraway doesn't seem exactly relieved to have found me. He's barely spoken to me. And he hasn't touched me once. Not that I expect him to, or *want* him to.

Except maybe I do want him to.

It seems a ridiculous thing to be thinking about, given everything else that's going on.

"Let's get some sleep," Sol says, tidying away our empty

wrappers and pulling back the covers. "We'll figure out our next steps in the morning."

I climb under the blankets next to Sol and listen to his breathing become slow and even. My body aches with exhaustion, but every time I close my eyes I see Dr. Veil's fist smashing into Sweetpea's face, setting my heart racing once more.

I slip out of the bed, careful not to disturb Sol, and out of the room.

CARAWAY IS SITTING ON a wooden bench, gazing silently out into the darkness. There are no other cars at the motel. No other guests as far as I can tell. The only light I can see is the neon sign above the motel office.

Caraway glances up as I sit down next to him.

"I couldn't sleep," I say.

He nods but doesn't say anything.

I pull the pair of toadstones from my pocket and hand Caraway his. He takes it, turning it over in his fingers. He sighs heavily.

"I should never have involved you in any of this, Morgan," he says at last, and there's a brokenness in his voice that stirs something in my heart. "I didn't know—I swear to you I thought the Trothal was just a meaningless ceremony. I had no idea that they'd—" He breaks off and shakes his head. "No idea what they'd ask from you."

"We both made some pretty poor decisions," I say.

"And then during the ceremony—I thought you'd be safe at Ruddock Farm. That's why I gave you my stone. It was a message. A promise that I'd come for you. If I'd known I was sending you into the clutches of the Howling Toad . . ." He shakes his head.

"The stone saved me," I tell him. "*You* saved me."

Caraway doesn't respond, just turns the stone over and over, gazing out into the night. I want to ask him what happens next. If he's still determined to unmake his stone and run away from the Toadmen forever. But I don't say anything. For a long while we just sit there, side by side.

"Do you remember the first day we met?" Caraway asks, breaking the silence.

"Sure," I reply. "You arrived at Candlecott and were a total dick."

"It was my first time away from home without my mother or father. I was terrified. Begged Mother not to make me go, but of course it was never her decision. Father wanted me to go somewhere far away from the city, where I wouldn't be spotted by any redheads who could see . . ." He gestures at the toad eye beneath the patch.

"You didn't go to school in the city?"

He shakes his head. "Private tutors. But in Candlecott, my father could control who saw me and who didn't. Candlecott has an old and loyal Frater House, so there'd be plenty of Toads to keep an eye on me. And it was easy for my father to move the two redheaded families to another town."

"How did he do it?"

Caraway shrugs. "I'm not sure. I imagine he organized enticing job opportunities, and if that didn't work, he would have resorted to more aggressive measures."

I shudder.

"Mother was supposed to come with me that day. But Father called her away to some Toadwife duty at the last minute, and I went alone. You were the first person I saw, on your knees, scrubbing the steps. I thought . . ." He swallows.

"That I was some kind of servant?"

He shakes his head. "I thought you were terrifying. So confident in your own skin, when I was hiding under a glamour. I was instantly jealous of you. I wanted to *be* you. To be your friend. To be—" He breaks off.

This new knowledge about Caraway is a revelation to me. He hadn't seemed frightened, or nervous, or anxious. He'd seemed like an entitled snob who didn't care about anyone but himself.

"I asked you where the headmaster's office was," Caraway continues, "and you told me. And then I just stood there. Hoping that something charming or clever would come out of my mouth. Something that would make you like me. But it didn't, and you just looked at me like I was a dying fish flapping around on a riverbank."

"So you told me to carry your bags."

Caraway blinks. "What? No, I didn't."

"You said *send someone to fetch my bags.* Like I was a maid."

Caraway looks horrified. "I said it to my *driver,*" he says. "Not to *you.* Hecate's pointy *hat,* Morgan, what kind of ass do you think I am?"

I shrug. "The kind who orders his driver around without making eye contact or saying *please?*"

"That's fair," says Caraway, wincing. "Bloody hell, though. No wonder you didn't like me."

"You didn't like me either," I tell him.

"I *always* liked you."

My jaw drops. "Lies! What about the time when you beat me at the academic decathlon? Or the Lewis Quiz?"

"You were my *rival*," Caraway says. "But that was part of the attraction! You were the only one I could compete with. You never tried to suck up to me like the other boarders did, because of who my family is. I liked you from the very beginning, Merriwether Morgan. I . . . I still like you."

"So why did you—" I break off, not knowing quite how to describe the betrayal I'm feeling.

"Why did I lie to you? Use you? Force you to attend a nightmare ball in the middle of a cursed swamp that resulted in the death of the person you loved the most?"

I've been avoiding thinking about Da. It hurts too much. "Yeah," I say. "That."

Caraway sighs. "Because I'm selfish. Because I wanted to be free. Because I knew you could help me find my stone."

He knew all along. From before any of this started. Thurmond Boswell knew too, and Da.

How?

I didn't tell anyone about my ability. Except for Ma, and . . .

"Teddy," I say, and a part of me realizes I knew all along. "Teddy told the Toads that I can see threadwise."

Caraway sighs. "Yeah. I didn't want to tell you."

I wonder how long the Toadmen had been working on Teddy before I found out about it all. What they tempted him with. What threats they made.

"Oh, Teddy," I murmur.

"He told the Toads, and my father told me. It was months

ago. That was when I had the idea to get you to come with me to the Trothal and help me get my stone back."

"Was he always planning to make me the Fox Bride?"

Caraway shakes his head. "It was supposed to be the Spitalwick Hag. Then she escaped, only a few days before the Trothal. Father had to scramble, which is why he used that Toad's eye to inspect you at Miss Prinny's."

I swallow away the taste of pond water. "And clearly he liked what he saw."

"He realized you had enough strength and natural magic to be the Fox Bride but couldn't wield any of your power. He thought you'd be easy to control."

I hear Sweetpea's words again. *I'm not completely powerless.*

"Did you know?" I'm almost afraid to hear the answer.

"I knew he wanted you to be the Fox Bride. But I didn't know what that meant. I thought it was just appearing at the ceremony. He swore to me that it was ceremonial, and that you wouldn't remember anything afterward. That you'd have your memory altered like all the other consorts, and that would be that. I didn't know they were planning to use the Hag. Or any of the rest of it."

His voice is sincere, his unglamoured face open and honest. I believe him.

"What does the Fox Bride actually *do?*" I ask. "Why do they need someone who's strong?"

"I don't know. I think—I think she's the key to how the Toads use mettle, even though they're not witches themselves."

"Like you."

He nods. "I've been able to manipulate mettle since I was five, but only Toad mettle. I can't even see the real thing, let alone touch it."

I tell him about the great tide of mettle flowing out of Ruddock Farm. "It was the wedding rings," I say. "They were draining the witches and sending it away. To the Deeping Court, I think. To your father."

Caraway sighs deeply. "I thought I could protect you from him," he says. "I was wrong. You should hate me."

"I don't hate you."

"Merry, I'm so sorry about your father." There's a sudden rawness in his tone that takes me aback. My heart starts to hammer as Caraway turns to face me. His face is open and earnest, with no glamour to hide behind. All I can see is the emotion that's written so clear in his expression.

"Run away with me," he says, reaching for my hands. "We'll go to the witch in Scouller and destroy our stones, and then they won't be able to find us. We'll go somewhere safe."

The way he says it, I know he doesn't mean Candlecott. I have tried to avoid thinking about it, but I know I can't go back there. Everyone will be looking for me—Toads, auditors. I'm a felon. Escaped from a recovery center. They'll tell everyone I'm dangerous, that I'm a resistance witch.

I'll never see my home again.

Never see Bran the Blessed, or collect eggs from Gliten or Enid or Gwenhwyfach. Never stroll past Teddy at the forge, or eat griddle cakes at the Whitsuntide fair. Never hike up Dryad's Saddle or laze in the warm grass on the banks of the Mira.

I guess it wouldn't have been the same without Da anyway.

I can't go to Staunton either. No grand university experience for me. No libraries. No books spread out under the oak tree.

Every road that was once open to me is now closed.

"We'll leave Anglyon," Caraway says. "We could go with Sol to Habasah. Or anywhere."

I hear the ache in his voice. The longing for freedom. I can give him what he wants. And would it be so bad? Adventures with Caraway, and maybe Sol too. We could see the world. Find out who we really are, together.

Caraway's hands squeeze mine, our fingers braided together.

"Please," he says, and his voice breaks a little. "Come with me. I have it all planned out."

Reluctantly, I pull my hands away from his. He looks down at my fingers, and I hear his breath tremble.

"I—I have a different plan," I say slowly.

His gaze snaps to mine. "What do you mean?"

"I get it now," I tell him. "The resistance witches. I thought they were all criminals, but they aren't. They're just fighting for a better world. I—I didn't know. About the Toads. About Ilium. The auditors. None of it's fair."

"I know," Caraway says. "But what can we do?"

I think of Sweetpea, who never gave up, and hear her words echoing in my head.

A hundred witches are free because of what you did. That's not nothing.

"I'm going back to Deeping Fen," I tell him. "I'm going to take every toadstone out of that wall, smash them all to bits, and destroy the Toadmen forever."

Caraway stares at me for a long moment. "You can't just smash a toadstone," he says at last. "It's unbreakable."

I shake my head. "Not unbreakable. You just need something very powerful to hit it with. Like Gofannon's Hammer."

"*Gofannon's Hammer?*" The words slip out of Caraway's mouth in a strangled yelp.

"It's in the Deeping Court. Your father told Teddy he could use it."

It takes Caraway a few moments to process this information. Then he shakes his head. "You can't go back," he says. "They'll kill you."

I shrug. "They haven't managed yet. And I have to try. For Da. For Teddy."

"You don't even know how to find the Deeping Court. Nobody does. It's secret, remember? The blindfolds?"

I remember the sensation of floating outside my body, traveling along the spidery brown threads of Toad mettle. "I can find it," I say firmly.

Caraway takes a deep breath. I hear the catch in it and feel the sudden tension in his shoulders. Then he exhales.

"No," he says. "I'm not putting you at risk again."

"I'm putting *myself* at risk, thank you very much," I tell him pertly. "And I wasn't asking your permission. I'm not asking you to come with me."

I see the hurt on his face, a flash of it.

"But you can if you want to," I add. "I . . . I want you to."

Caraway turns to look out at the night once more, and a long moment passes before he responds.

"I can't refuse you," he says quietly. "If you want to go back, then we go back."

I feel a surge of relief. Of fear. Of . . . something else. Something bigger than all the other feelings.

There are only inches between us. The night feels very still, as if the world is holding its breath.

"Merry—" Caraway turns to face me, and I can read every emotion on his face.

The door behind us opens and Sol is there.

"Is everything okay?" he asks.

Caraway's cheeks color, and he looks away.

"Yeah," I tell him. "We're just talking about . . . about what happens next."

Sol nods and takes a deep breath. "I've been thinking a lot about that," he says. "I want to go back to Deeping Fen. I'm going to get Teddy out."

"Sol—" I say, but he holds up a hand to interrupt me.

"I know what you lost there, Merry," he says. "And I would *never* ask you to go back. I'll do this on my own. I have to try."

"I'm coming," I tell him. "We both are."

Sol looks visibly relieved. "Are you sure?"

I nod. "I want to take them down."

"Good," Sol says. "Good. Okay. I'll . . ." He glances to me, and then to Caraway. "I'll leave you two to . . . whatever this is."

He disappears back inside, and Caraway and I are alone again.

"He really loves Evans, doesn't he?" Caraway says.

"Of course," I reply.

"It's . . . nice. The way you three are. The way you care about each other."

He sounds so lonely, it almost breaks my heart.

In the dark you find my hand, we make a little spark
Two particles collide

"We'll have to be careful," Caraway says, looking suddenly businesslike. "Smart. We'll have to plan everything."

"Caraway," I say, looking at his face, at features that are so familiar, they are like my own.

"Because my father will do everything in his power to stop us, and he has a lot of power."

"Caraway," I say again.

"Don't think he'll go easy on me just because I'm his son. He won't hold back."

"For Hecate's sake, just shut *up*," I tell him.

And then I kiss him.

It isn't like the other times we've kissed. I'm not shocked at how my body responds to him. I'm not angry or defensive or astonished. This kiss is a promise, and we're making it together.

I put my hand against his cheek and slide my fingers into his dark hair. Everything is bergamot and old leather and the sweet taste of ambrosia and plum toffee.

I slide closer, and his arms go around me. I feel the tension drain from his shoulders as we hold each other, our heartbeats synchronizing.

We stop kissing to take a breath but don't pull apart. Our foreheads touch as we lean against each other.

"I'm crazy about you, Merry," Caraway admits softly. "Always have been. Since that first day."

"I'm crazy about you too," I whisper as my stomach does somersaults.

"Is it wrong to feel happy right now?" he says. "When so much could go wrong?"

I shake my head and smile. I feel happy too. Happy and grieving and anxious and angry, all at once.

We're sitting on a rickety bench outside a seedy motel. A pink neon light proclaims that there are vacancies, and all around us is just a gravel parking lot, and darkness. It's a long way from being a romantic location.

But for the first time in a very long time, I'm certain I'm exactly where I need to be.

18.

DEEPING FEN IS ABOUT AS AWFUL AS I REMEMBER. Midges buzz in my ears, and everything feels clammy and still as Caraway maneuvers the barge he bought from a Fenlander for a truly outrageous sum of money through the murky brown water.

Sol looks nervously around. "And you're sure we won't run into any giant swamp monsters?" he asks.

"Positive," I say, sliding witch-eyed and scanning the water once more.

Every now and then, Caraway puts his fingers to the black-and-silver eye patch, as if double-checking that it's there. I have no doubt that Thurmond Boswell can track our toadstones, but as long as we can stop him from seeing through Caraway's toad eye, there are some secrets we can keep.

Caraway's one good eye meets mine, and I feel a little frisson of energy at the connection between us. We haven't had much time to talk since that night outside the motel. Haven't had much time alone either, as Sol is with us. But that's okay. There'll be plenty of time to talk after all this is over. For now, it's enough to meet his eye and smile, or to feel his fingers brush mine when we're close.

Sol has clearly noticed this new energy between us, and a satisfied little smile dances around the corners of his mouth. I poke my tongue out at him, and he rolls his eyes fondly.

This is going to work. It has to.

I steer us through the swamp, following the strands of Toad mettle that all lead to the Deeping Court, and avoiding the writhing coils of energy under the surface of the water where fenworms lurk.

"We should go over the plan again," says Caraway, and Sol and I exchange an amused look. We have been over the plan approximately one million times.

"Good idea," says Sol, patient as ever.

Caraway's knee bounces up and down, his cuticles chewed to the quick. It's quite a novelty to see him so nervous, so uneasy.

"They'll be expecting us," he says. "My father may not be able to use this"—here he puts a finger to the black-and-silver eye patch—"but he'll definitely be tracking our stones. He will have heard about Ruddock Farm by now, he'll know that the Howling Toad is dead."

So much effort to break *out* of witch jail, only to turn around and break *into* Toad HQ. Am I making a terrible mistake?

"But we have a secret advantage," Caraway continues.

Sol does jazz hands. "I don't have a toadstoooone," he sings.

"Exactly. My father can't track you. I'll bring Morgan in as a prisoner. Fall on my sword, tell him I'm committing fully to the Toads, blah blah blah. Now that the Hag has escaped again, he'll need you to be the Fox Bride. It'll take a while to get the ceremony set up. My father loves a show. So I'll have plenty of time to break you out of wherever he stashes you."

The idea of being a Toad prisoner once more isn't super enticing, but I know it's the only way to get into the Deeping Court.

"Meanwhile you, Sol, will sneak off, undetected, and find Evans. You'll explain the plan, and he'll have a miraculous change of heart and come over to our side, even though he's shown no sign of wanting to do that so far."

It's true that this is the weakest part of the plan, but I just *know* that Sol can bring Teddy around.

"Evans and Sol will find the Hammer, while Morgan and I . . ." He glances at me.

"We find the current Fox Bride," I say.

I'm sure she's in there. The rings. Brides and bridesmaids. The great braid of witch mettle. I'm sure it's all going to her. They're using her as a filter, a vessel, to transform the witch mettle into Toad mettle.

Caraway continues to look uneasy. We all know that Thurmond Boswell will not stand idly by while we dismantle the source of all his power. There will inevitably be some kind of confrontation, and I just don't know how it will all shake out. I'm prepared for it to go very, very badly.

I've got nothing to lose.

Sol looks around the fen once more. Of the three of us, he's the only one who hasn't seen it before, as he remained blindfolded for his first journey like a sensible person.

"It's beautiful, isn't it?" he murmurs. "In its own way."

There's something solemn and eerie about the fen. The drooping mosses and lichens. The ancient twisting roots. The hiss and call of insects and marsh birds, and the rattle of frogs and toads. It feels like nothing has changed in here for hundreds—maybe thousands—of years. I think about the Beast that threatened the Fenlanders, and how a clever toad defeated it and became king.

"It's weird that we don't know what kind of a beast it was," I say out loud.

Caraway looks at me quizzically.

"In the story," I explain. "The Beast that the toad defeats. Was it a fenworm? Or something else? Why doesn't the story say?"

"Dunno," Caraway says, shrugging. "I guess the Toadmen didn't think it was important."

But I know that everything in old stories is important.

Sol looks around nervously, as if expecting a Beast to erupt from the water at any moment. I keep pondering it, until something much larger than a Beast looms before us, emerging from the swamp like a mountain.

The Deeping Court is built from ancient gray stone crusted with moss and lichen, rising from the brown waters of the fen like a giant squatting toad. I have actually never seen it before, not from the outside. It was dark when Caraway and I arrived the first time. It's big, so big that I'm surprised the Toadmen have managed to keep it a secret. I guess there are misdirection charms in the fen around it.

I clasp my hands tightly around my knees as Caraway maneuvers our boat between the huge roots that curl around the court, holding it in place like some kind of elaborate cat's cradle. I never wanted to come back here.

"There," I say, pointing toward a cavelike space between two roots, and our boat glides silently into the darkness, our eyes adjusting to make out the covered stone docks.

I'm expecting a squad of Toadmen to be waiting for us as Caraway steers the boat over to a place where we can disembark. Or Thurmond Boswell himself.

But there's nobody. The docks are silent, the only sound the gentle slapping of water on stone. I clamber out of the boat and exchange glances with Caraway and Sol. Maybe . . . this is going to be easier than we thought? Maybe Thurmond Boswell is so distracted by the breakout at Ruddock Farm, he hasn't even spared a thought for his wayward son.

Or maybe it's a trap.

I close my eyes and let my awareness travel along the strands of Toad mettle. Instantly I notice that there are fewer Toads around—the Trothal is over, after all. But the roiling mettle still pulses deep beneath my feet. The source of all the Toadmen's power. That'll be where we find the Fox Bride.

It doesn't take me long to locate Teddy. "He's in the same apartment you shared with him," I tell Sol, and quickly give him basic directions to get there.

"Good luck," says Caraway as I hug Sol.

He nods, smiling nervously before ducking up a stairwell and out of sight.

I reach out and grab Caraway's hand. "What now?" he asks.

"Now we find her."

"How?"

I shrug. "We head down. That's all I know."

We descend stairs and travel corridors, expecting to be accosted at every turn by robed and masked Toads. But the halls are empty. I keep my witch sight activated, in case I can sense anyone coming toward us. But there's nobody. I let my consciousness wander and check in on Sol, who has nearly made it to Teddy's apartment. As far as I can tell, they're the only other people in the Deeping Court. And although this should fill me with relief, I can't help but feel unsettled. This is all too easy.

We reach the corridor outside the Great Hall and pause. Caraway silently pulls me closer and I step into the circle of his arms, inhaling his scent of old leather and bergamot. We stand there for a while, letting our breaths sync up together. A moment of calm before . . . whatever comes next.

Then, reluctantly, we break apart, and Caraway pushes on the ancient carved doors, which swing slowly open.

Thurmond Boswell is inside, waiting for us. My witch sight didn't pick up his presence at all, but of course the Ghost Toad has ways of going undetected.

"Welcome back," he says calmly. "You two have had quite the adventure."

Caraway steps forward. "I've recaptured her," he says. "She murdered the Howling Toad. I've returned her to the Deeping Court, to be the Fox Bride."

Thurmond Boswell turns his mild gaze onto his son. Then he reaches out and tugs the black-and-silver eye patch away from Caraway's toad eye.

"Did you really think you could hide from me, Caraway?" he asks. "A scrap of cloth is never going to separate us, no matter how many witch marks it bears. I see everything. I watched you travel up the mountain like a knight in shining armor, determined to rescue your lady fair. I heard you make your little plan. I saw you outside the motel, and I felt what you felt."

My blood runs cold.

Thurmond Boswell chuckles, like an indulgent parent. "A fox and a toad, fallen in love. It's quite poetic, don't you think? Can it last, though? A fox is a predator, after all, and the toad seems so juicy and fat. Eventually the fox's true nature will prevail, and it will eat the toad."

I'm sick of riddles. "Are you going to kill us?" I ask. "Because I'm getting bored."

"Of course the toad has the last laugh," Thurmond Boswell continues. "Every toad carries toxic poison just beneath its skin. The feast will be the fox's last. Both will die." He sighs. "I've been indulgent with you for far too long, Caraway. Hoping you would come around in time. But I see that I have only made the problem worse. I should have been firmer. Taken you in hand from a young age. Sending you off to that country school was a mistake."

Caraway lifts his chin and faces his father. "I won't let you control me anymore."

"Luckily, it's not too late," Thurmond Boswell continues, ignoring his son. "The Toadmen are gifted horsemen, did you know? We can break any young stallion, no matter how headstrong. You will remain here in the Deeping Court. Perhaps after a year or two of devotion to the King Toad, you will learn patience."

"There is no King Toad," I say. "He doesn't exist. It's just you. You have all the power. You could stop all of this."

A crinkle of surprise appears between Thurmond Boswell's brows. "No King Toad," he says. "Who told you that?"

I narrow my eyes. "The Howling Toad told me, just before he was vaporized by the Spitalwick Hag."

He purses his lips. "What a troublemaker you are, Little Fox."

He still doesn't know about Sol. We have a chance. But it's like he can read my mind.

"It's true that I cannot sense the whereabouts of your little friend," he says to me. "But I know how to make him come to me."

I glance at Caraway, who looks stricken.

There has to be a way out of this.

"Ms. Morgan, did I ever tell you how the story of the Fox Bride ends?"

I don't respond. I'm not here for story time. But Thurmond Boswell doesn't seem to notice.

"She betrayed her king and husband, eventually," he says. "Fell for a silly human because she was weak. But the Toads see everything, and the Fox Bride was caught and returned to Deeping Fen to face justice."

I don't care about the King Toad, or the Fox Bride. It's all nonsense anyway.

"Do you know what the King Toad did, Merriwether Morgan?"

I ignore him.

"He *ate her up*," Thurmond Boswell continues, in a tone of great satisfaction. "And all of her cunning and cleverness became his. That's why you cannot win, Little Fox. You cannot outsmart the King Toad, because he has the strength of a knight, the cunning of a fox, and the power of a toad."

"There is no King Toad," I say again.

Thurmond Boswell cocks his head to the side as he considers me, in a gesture that I've seen Caraway mirror exactly. "I wonder if you will still be saying that," he murmurs, "while you're being eaten up."

The door to the Great Hall opens to reveal Teddy and Sol.

In an instant, I know what's happened. My two best friends, who I know and love so very well. I can read every expression on their faces. I see the hard determination on Teddy's, wavering slightly but holding strong. The wild hope on Sol's. His eyes light up as they fall on me and Caraway, but dim when his gaze journeys to Thurmond Boswell.

"Teddy?" he says. "What's going on?"

"Well done, Brother Edward," says Thurmond Boswell with an approving nod. "If only my son showed as much promise as you do. Perhaps your good influence will rub off on him."

A tear slips down Sol's cheek. "You lied to me," he says softly to Teddy.

Teddy stares straight ahead, and a vein pulses along the line of his jaw. I can see that he's hurting too. But I'm so angry at him, I don't care. How could he do this to me? To *Sol*?

"We made a deal, didn't we?" Thurmond Boswell says, looking as smug as a cat with a baby chick in its jaws. "Brother Edward here is going to fill a recently vacated position, and I'm going to give him everything his heart desires."

"What position?" Sol asks, but I already know the answer.

"The Howling Toad had no heir, you know," Thurmond Boswell explains. "Very poor form on his part, I must say. So it falls to me to find a suitable replacement for him." His eyes dart to Teddy's approvingly. "Are you ready, my brother?"

"*No.*" The word slips out of my mouth. "You can't. Teddy . . ." My voice breaks when I say his name. "Don't do this."

Sol's face is slack with shock. He looks paralyzed, unable to speak.

"Don't worry, Little Fox," Thurmond Boswell says with a genial smile. "You won't be left out. It's your big day, after all."

Teddy's jaw remains set as the Ghost Toad speaks these words, and I feel my heart break all over again.

Caraway's hands twist as he begins to weave mettle with a kind of grim determination, his eyes locked on his father's face.

But Thurmond Boswell is clearly expecting this. He snatches me around the waist with one arm, yanking me tight up against his body, my back to his chest. His other hand grips the silver needle, pointed right at my throat.

Caraway freezes.

"Oh, Caraway," Thurmond Boswell murmurs. "Always so dramatic. There's no need for any of that. Lead the way, Brother Edward."

He escorts us onto the dais. "You're very lucky, you know," he tells me and Sol. "You will be the first non-Toadmen to witness this most ancient and solemn ceremony."

There's no lever he pulls, or switch he flicks. But suddenly the floor beneath us shakes and rumbles, and we begin to move, the dais and the wall of toadstones behind us sinking slowly, inexorably downward, toward the great storm of Toad mettle that lies beneath the Deeping Court.

I reach out and grab Sol's hand. He looks at me, and in the dim underground light, I can see tears glinting in his eyes.

"I'm so sorry," I whisper to him. "I thought we could help him."

"It's not over," Sol says, in a voice loud enough to be heard by everyone on the dais. "I'm going to get him back."

Teddy stares grimly down at the floor. Thurmond Boswell chuckles softly.

We pass through an area of cold, clammy blackness, then emerge into a huge cavern, easily twice as large as the ballroom, hung with softly glowing chandeliers made from yellowed bone. As we descend, I take in piles and piles of treasure. Gold and jewels spill from chests like something out of a fairy story. Marble statues, gleaming suits of armor, piles of crumbling grimoires and other forbidden spellbooks, great glittering hunks of diamond and sapphire. There are strange objects resting on marble plinths that I'm sure are ancient magical artifacts. I see a white-hilted sword, a carved drinking horn, a squat blackened cauldron.

And in the center of it all is her.

The greatest treasure that the Toads possess.

The Fox Bride.

She is little more than a skeleton—papery skin stretched tight over bone. Her eyes are dark, sunken hollows that stare blankly. She sits on a throne made of yellowing bones, strung about with thin tubes and wires that puncture what's left of her flesh at various points—wrists, throat, heart. The tubes have been there for so long that her skin has partially grown over them, fused into one horrific kind of mettle machine. She wears an identical version of the pearl-encrusted wedding gown that I left at Ruddock Farm, but it hangs loose on her emaciated frame—even with the enchantments woven into it, it can't disguise the fact that this woman is barely alive.

I see the gold ring shining on her bony finger. One of the tubes leads to a large glass vial sitting in an ornate golden cradle. There's a toadstone set into the cradle, and I instantly know that it belongs to her.

I squeeze my own stone in my fist.

Every few seconds, a slimy brown drip lands in the vial.

Toad mettle.

Mettle stolen from witches, focused in the body of the Fox Bride and extracted for Toads to use.

That drip must be slower now. After the witches in Ruddock Farm took off their rings and cut the connection to the Fox Bride.

But it's still dripping. I wonder how many other recovery centers there are. How many imprisoned witches.

The moving platform reaches the bottom and the floor stills beneath our feet.

"Say hello to your predecessor, Little Fox," says Thurmond Boswell.

His tone is so smug, it's all I can do to stop myself from punching him in the face.

"Who was she?" I ask.

"A witch," he says. "She was known as Jenny Greenteeth."

I'd thought Jenny Greenteeth was just a story, made up to frighten children. "How long has she been here?"

"Half a century."

Fifty years. "That's why you have the Trothal," I say. "The Trothal happens when the Fox Bride is about to die and you need a new one."

Thurmond Boswell inclines his head. "It was supposed to be the Hag, of course," he says. "Until she escaped. But then you came along. You have occupied my son's thoughts for many years, but I dismissed you completely—you were obviously no witch, nor did you come from a family of money or influence. But then Brother Edward told us what you can do. Your gift. Incredible, really. You're a perfect vessel for magic, delicately attuned to mettle but utterly unable to wield it for yourself. It's like you were *made* to be the King Toad's bride."

I glance at Teddy, but he's not looking at us. Not listening. He's striding away from us, his eyes fixed on one of the stone plinths, on a simple hammer with a dark iron head, the wooden handle worn smooth over centuries of use. It's larger than a usual blacksmith's hammer but otherwise looks entirely unremarkable.

Teddy wraps his hand around the shaft and pulls. I see the muscles in his arms bulge, but the Hammer doesn't move at all.

"Not yet, my brother," Thurmond Boswell chides him gently. "Not yet."

Then he turns to me.

"Here we are, Little Fox, in the true heart of Deeping Fen. No more stories. Here you must kneel before the King of Toads."

He sinks to one knee, bowing his head. Hair stands up on my arms and my skin crawls as I hear the sound of something vast moving in the shadows behind me.

As I turn around, I hear Dr. Veil's words in my head and realize that I've been hugely, impossibly foolish.

No man hides under the King Toad's mask.

19.

T HE KING OF TOADS IS NO MAN.

He is a toad.

A huge toad.

He is probably the size of our barn at home, vast and spreading warty brown, with lamplike bulging yellow eyes and a wide, lipless mouth that splits his head right across the middle. Giant pustules on his skin leak a viscous gray fluid, which a masked, robed and gloved attendant collects in cylindrical glass jars, working slowly around the enormous bulk of the creature, careful not to get a single drop on his skin.

"Kneel before your king, Little Fox," says Thurmond Boswell. "Before your betrothed."

I don't kneel. I *won't*.

Thurmond Boswell chuckles. "You will kneel," he says. "You made me a promise, remember?"

I remember the taste of tea. The scent of lotus and chokeberry in his library. The oath I made.

I'll help you.

"I swore I'd help you with Caraway," I say. "Not this."

"If you do not submit to the King Toad," Thurmond Boswell says, "then Caraway will die. Now *kneel.*"

The oath overrides my will, and my knees buckle. I fight it as long as I can, and end up falling forward, my hands going out to catch myself. My toadstone goes flying from my fist, skittering across the marble floor of the chamber, finding rest against the thick warty skin of the King Toad.

For a moment, everything is still.

Then he stretches out a huge arm to it and picks it up in surprisingly delicate long fingers. It is barely a speck against his enormousness, but he raises it to his eye and examines it carefully. I look threadwise instinctively and see a huge, ghostly witch tongue emerge from the king's mouth and lick the stone.

"Mmmmm," he says, his voice so deep that it makes every stone of the Deeping Court vibrate. "Such *energy.* Such *cunning.*"

And before I can say anything, he pops my toadstone into his mouth and swallows it whole.

I stare at him in horror. A piece of my life-force. Gone forever, gulped down in an instant like a child with a boiled sweet.

"What a treat," the king rumbles, his wide toad mouth spreading in satisfaction. "A wedding gift from my new bride."

"You will not touch her," Caraway declares, striding forward.

The King Toad chuckles. "Or else what?"

He reaches out his witch tongue and wraps it around Caraway, once, twice, immobilizing him. When the tongue withdraws, Caraway remains pinned in place, unable to move, bound by brown Toad mettle as thick as my wrist.

"Such cheek, and from a tadpole too," the King Toad says.

"The young ones never used to be this impudent. There are changes afoot in the world, and I do not like change."

"I used to think that too," I say, trying to sound bold. "But I've come to realize that sometimes things need to change."

The King Toad's huge eyes linger on Caraway, then roll back to me. "Perhaps you are right," he says before surveying the rest of us.

"A delightful family reunion," he booms. "My Brother Ghost brings me his son, as well as a fresh Toad, straight from the fen." He regards Teddy with approval. "A hale and hearty toadlet, to be sure. And his consort, I see." He glances at Sol without much interest before turning to me again. "And you, my blushing bride."

"I will *never* be your bride," I tell him.

And I dash forward to the vial of Toad mettle at the foot of the Fox Bride. It's *her* toadstone in the cradle. I'm sure of it. I'm determined to smash it if it's the last thing I do.

The King Toad makes a lazy gesture with one toad arm, and rivers of molten gray flow from beneath the piles of treasure, whipping up around me to form a cage of stone. It wraps tight around my thighs, my waist, my wrists, holding me in place as it hardens. More stone encircles my head, pouring into my mouth like a stone bridle.

The rumble of his laughter makes gold coins skitter from their piles and spill across the floor. "You're too clever by half, Little Fox," the King Toad chuckles. "Wait there while I deal with some business."

Thurmond Boswell raises his head from where it has been bowed. "Sire," he says. "I present to you my candidate for Howling Toad. As you know, the previous holder of the office died with no heir. I believe that this young man will make us a fine brother."

Teddy kneels before the King Toad. I try to cry out, but the stone bridle swallows all my words.

"I pledge myself to you anew, my king," Teddy says, a tremble of anticipation in his voice.

"Are you sure?" the king booms to Thurmond Boswell. "He is very young."

"He is pliable, my lord. And the most powerful mettlesmith I have seen for many years. Naturally gifted with magic."

The King Toad's ghost tongue emerges from the vast cavern of his mouth, wrapping around Teddy's head and tasting deeply. Satisfied grunts emerge from his throat.

"Yes," he murmurs, withdrawing his tongue. "He *is* strong. Stronger than I have seen for many centuries. Well, toadlet? Do you wish to become the Howling Toad?"

"Teddy," Sol says in a low voice. "Please."

Teddy hesitates for a moment, then closes his eyes. "I do, my lord," he says. "I will serve you for the rest of my days."

The King Toad gestures to his attendants. "Leave us," he commands, and they melt away into the shadows. "It has been many centuries since I have performed this ritual," the King comments to no one in particular. "Many years since my Brother Ghost or Brother Howl has not produced an heir to carry on his power."

"Teddy," Sol says. "Just *listen* to me."

But Teddy's head remains bowed.

"I bestow upon you the power of the Howling Toad," the

king intones. "You will wield the might of my brother and enforce my law. You will be my hammer. My club. You will wreak devastation upon all who attempt to defy me. Swear your fealty."

"I swear."

Sol lets out a little cry of anguish.

"Drink of me, Brother," the King Toad instructs. "Taste the power of the King of Toads."

Teddy bends his head to the huge body of the King Toad, to where gray sludge seeps from pustules as big as my fist.

My stomach heaves as I watch Teddy's mouth press against one of the pustules. The skin around his lips sizzles and blisters as it makes contact, and I see his Adam's apple bob as he swallows, again and again.

"Good," rumbles the King Toad. "Drink deeply, Brother."

Teddy's body suddenly jerks in a strange paroxysm, and his head snaps backward. The color drains from his cheeks, and he slumps to the floor, convulsing and writhing.

I remember the little natterjack toad from Dr. Veil's desk.

Tetrodotoxin. Can kill you in five minutes, and let me tell you, it's not an easy death.

Teddy's body continues to flail and jerk, the gray toad poison foaming on his lips. His eyes roll back in his head and he is still.

Sol lets out a full-throated wail. "You've *killed* him."

"Silence," mutters Thurmond Boswell. "Have some respect."

A kind of golden haze surrounds Teddy, as if tiny fireflies are sinking slowly into his skin. His lips part and he inhales deeply. His eyes snap open, and he climbs slowly to his feet, every movement carefully controlled.

When he straightens up, he seems taller. His jaw is squarer. His hair seems to flow more fully from his skull, and his eyes glitter with singular purpose. He flexes his biceps, and they ripple and bulge like something from a lurid magazine.

He strides over to the plinth containing Gofannon's Hammer and stretches out a hand. The Hammer seems to leap to his palm, eager and willing. Teddy's fist curls around the shaft, and I see a satisfied smile spread across his lips. It is not *Teddy's* smile, the one I know so well. It's alien on his features. Toadlike.

"Welcome, Brother Howl," says the King Toad. "May you serve me long and well."

Teddy bows his head in acknowledgment. "Thank you, sire, for this greatest of gifts."

"I'm going to kill you," I tell the King Toad, my voice shaking with fury. "I swear it."

The King Toad rumbles a laugh. "You can try."

I wish I had . . . something. A sword. An axe. A heavy-bottomed saucepan. I want to destroy him. To make him pay for everything he's taken from me.

"I am old, Little Fox," the King Toad says to me. "Older than the Eagle of Gwenarbwy. Older than the Salmon of Glyn Llifon. I was old when the Fenlanders first came to Deeping Fen and made me their king. I have devoured the strings of men for a thousand years. Their life-force flows through my veins, keeping me strong. There is nothing you can do that could hurt me. No weapon you can turn upon me. I am too powerful. It is not just my little collection here . . ." And he turns to face the wall of toadstones, running his vast witch tongue over them with relish, tasting the mettle of every fool who has pledged himself a Toad-man. "Can you imagine how many stones have been gifted to me over the centuries?"

He reaches out to a wooden chest and flips it open with a casual movement. The chest is full to the brim with glittering toadstones. The King Toad scoops a hand into the chest and withdraws a fistful. He watches me smugly as he pops one into his mouth, just as he did with my stone.

"Delicious," he says as he swallows another.

He eats the entire fistful like a child guzzling sherbet drops on Hollantide, not breaking eye contact with me.

"You gave the witches their stones back, didn't you?" he says, his giant mouth curved in a hideous smile. "I'm sure you thought you were doing a kind thing. A generous thing. But all you did was give my Brother Ghost here a way of finding them. They will all be brought back to me. Every single one. They are so delicious, you know. I can taste the fury in their mettle. The *rage*."

He shudders with anticipation, his flesh rippling with pleasure.

Then he turns to Caraway, who is still standing immobile, strangled by Toad mettle. "You have been a great disappointment to your father, young tadpole," he says. "And to me. I think perhaps you do not understand the honor that you bear." He gestures to Caraway's toad eye.

"It's no honor," says Caraway, his chin raised. "It's a curse."

"Caraway," says Thurmond Boswell, a warning tone in his voice.

"You do not wish to be gifted my eye?" says the King Toad with mock surprise.

"I hate it more than anything," Caraway spits.

372

"Sire," says Thurmond Boswell, stepping forward. "My son is a wayward colt. Some time under your tutelage will bring him to the fold."

The King Toad swallows another toadstone. "Perhaps," he says. "But in the meantime, he does not deserve to bear my great gift."

He looks around at us, considering something. Then he crooks a long, knobbly finger at Teddy, who steps forward, the Hammer still clutched in one hand. "This Toadman understands how to serve his king," he tells Caraway. "He obeys my every command, do you see?"

Teddy moves to stand before Caraway, his jaw tight.

"My new brother deserves the honor of my eye far more than you do, tadpole," the King Toad says. "What do you think, shall we give it to him?"

"*No!*" I cry out, but all that emerges is a muffled yell around the stone bridle.

Teddy hesitates, his eyes darting sideways.

"Don't be afraid, Brother," the King Toad murmurs, and clenches his long gnarled fingers into fists. "Take it."

Teddy reaches a hand up to Caraway's face. I fight against my restraints, but it is no good. There's nothing I can do but watch, horrified, as Teddy's fingers rise, forming a claw shape, and plunge down into Caraway's face, digging in sharply.

Caraway screams.

Then Teddy—beautiful, funny, brave Teddy, my best friend who I love so very, very dearly—scoops out Caraway's toad eye and holds it aloft, his fingers bright with blood. The eye is glistening and wet in the yellow light cast by the bone chandeliers.

"It is yours now," the king declares. "Eat it."

Bile rises in my throat as Teddy raises Caraway's toad eye to his lips and slides it into his mouth. His jaw works at it once, twice, and then he swallows, his expression unchanging.

"How was it, Brother?" asks the king. "A little bitter, I expect."

Teddy doesn't respond, just stares grimly down at the Hammer.

Caraway slumps to the ground with a whimper, his hand pressed over the place where his toad eye was.

"Sire," says Thurmond Boswell, and for the first time I hear a tremble in his voice, see an urgency in his outstretched hand. "Caraway is my son. My heir. I *will* bring him to heel. He will serve you as faithfully as I have."

The King Toad's huge yellow eye flickers to Teddy. "Perhaps my brothers should no longer be chosen by blood." He glances at me and his giant lamplike eyes narrow. "I hear change is a good thing."

"Sire, please." Thurmond Boswell sinks to one knee again. "Give him a chance. He is strong. He will be a fine Ghost Toad."

"He must prove himself," the King Toad declares.

"Of course, sire," says Thurmond Boswell.

The King Toad considers this. The mettle holding Caraway in place dissolves, and he lets his hand fall, revealing the gaping bloody socket where the toad eye was, then moves both hands in a complicated gesture, spinning his mettle into a silvery net. He's focused entirely on the giant toad before him.

The King Toad turns his yellow eyes back to Thurmond Boswell. "He *is* bold, isn't he? And he has power. But he lacks *discipline.*"

The King Toad's eyes bulge, and a massive wave of mettle emanates from him. Caraway's body tenses, and he lets out a grunt of pain as he collapses to the ground.

"Get up, tadpole."

Thurmond Boswell is watching, impassive, as Caraway writhes on the ground, crying out in pain. I struggle once more against my restraints but am unable to move.

"I said get *up*."

Caraway rises suddenly, his movements jerky, like a marionette. Thick brown Toad mettle wraps around him like a second skin, pulsing with energy. The King Toad is using the mettle to move him, like a puppet. Caraway is trying to resist. His teeth are clenched, sweat pouring from his brow.

"I can make him do anything, you know," the King Toad says lazily.

Caraway starts to dance a jig, with graceless, stiff movements.

"Anything," the King Toad repeats smugly, and Caraway balls his hand into a fist and punches himself right in his own hollow and bleeding eye socket.

I struggle against my restraints.

"Now, how shall I get you to prove your worthiness?" the King Toad muses. "Perhaps you could kill this consort, who is of no use to me."

He points a long finger at Sol, who lifts his chin in defiance.

"I shall make you kill him," the king says to Caraway. "But restore you to yourself at the very moment you drive the knife into his heart. Too late to stop, of course. But so you will see and feel exactly what you have done while you watch the light fade from his eyes."

I notice Teddy's grip shift on the Hammer. Caraway's face is stricken as he takes a step toward Sol, a knife glinting in his fist.

I try to yell at Sol, tell him to run, but my mouth is too full of stone. Sol doesn't move, though. Just gazes calmly at Caraway.

"Don't do it," he says. "Fight him."

Veins stand out on Caraway's neck. I try to reach out with my own mettle, to gift him some of my own strength, but I'm no witch. I don't know how to do it.

The King Toad laughs, a deep, low rumble. "You are strong, boy. But not strong enough to resist me."

Caraway's face is turning purple, his breath blowing in and out of his cheeks in desperate, ragged gasps. He's close enough to strike Sol now.

Sol doesn't flinch away. Doesn't stagger back. Just stares at Caraway, seemingly unafraid.

"Father, please!" Caraway gasps.

But the Ghost Toad just watches.

Teddy doesn't. He stares down at the ground, his cheeks blowing in and out as he tries to suppress his feelings.

"Do it," the King Toad instructs. "Strike him down, and I will make you a king among men."

Caraway's whole body is shaking from the effort of holding himself back. "Go fuck yourself," he grinds out through clenched teeth.

A flicker of annoyance passes over the King Toad's vast face. "Very well, then," he says. "If you will not bend to me, you are of no use."

Sol steps backward as Caraway spins, his wrist twisting, the knife point reversing and moving downward, driving straight toward his own heart.

"Sire," Thurmond Boswell protests, raising his hands. "The boy is young. He will learn. He—"

"The blood bond you share makes you weak, Brother," the King Toad interrupts. "If this were any other man, you would have struck him down yourself. He is an obstacle standing in the way of your giving yourself wholly to your king."

Caraway's breath shudders. His face is gray from exhaustion. He doesn't have much strength left.

"What a shame," the King Toad says with mock sincerity. "You're almost completely drained. It only took a few moments. Think, you could have had so much power." He gestures to Teddy, who has looked up again now that Sol is out of immediate danger. "Like my new brother here. I have gifted him strength beyond his wildest imaginings. It could have been yours too. Instead, all I can offer you now is death."

Caraway's eyes meet mine, and I try to tell him everything with my eyes. Everything I should have said earlier but didn't, because I was too proud, too oblivious, too scared. I see his shoulders soften slightly as he stops resisting the King Toad and accepts his fate.

"*No.*"

It's Thurmond Boswell, the silver needle flashing in his hand.

"Do you defy your king?" the King Toad asks, his voice dangerously quiet.

"Let me do it, sire," says the Ghost Toad. "You are right. The boy is my weakness. Let me prove my loyalty to you and strike him down myself."

The King Toad hesitates. "Very well," he says at last.

The knife Caraway is holding clatters to the ground as he regains control over his body. His breath is ragged as he stares at his father, his face that of a little boy.

The Ghost Toad approaches his son, the silver needle held high.

"Father," Caraway whispers.

Thurmond Boswell leans forward and places a kiss on Caraway's cheek. I see his lips move, forming the words *I'm sorry.*

Then he reverses the point and plunges the needle into his own heart.

Caraway lets out a strangled cry, reaching out to catch his father as he slumps to the ground. Blood spills from Thurmond Boswell's chest, painting Caraway crimson. A faint glow surrounds the bright splashes, tiny starlike fragments rising slowly from the blood, making the air around them shimmer and glitter. The hazy glow surrounds Caraway, just as it surrounded Teddy mere minutes ago. The grayness fades from Caraway's features, and his gaze sharpens.

Thurmond Boswell lies motionless in Caraway's arms, life and power drained from him completely.

Caraway smooths his father's brow, then lays him gently on the ground, standing up to regard his king with one baleful eye.

The new Ghost Toad.

"Thanks for that," he says calmly. "I feel much better now."

"Hmmm," rumbles the King Toad. "How very disappointing." He gestures at Teddy. "Brother Howl, please deal with this."

Caraway sweeps a hand down in a smooth movement and

slides the silver needle from his father's chest, gripping it tightly in his fist.

Teddy steps forward to face him, hefting Gofannon's Hammer.

"I don't want to hurt you," Caraway says to Teddy in a low voice.

Teddy throws back his head and laughs. "As if you could."

He swings the Hammer at Caraway, who ducks and rolls out of the way just in time. The Hammer goes crashing down on one of the marble plinths, which explodes under the impact of the blow. Caraway weaves in and out of Teddy's path, darting forward to slash at Teddy's cheek with the needle. A bright line of blood appears.

"We don't have to do this," Caraway pants.

Teddy swings again, and another marble plinth shatters. Teddy wheels around once more and raises his hammer.

"Teddy, stop!" Sol cries out, and rushes forward to place himself between Caraway and the swinging hammer.

Teddy hesitates, one enormous arm raised to strike.

"Don't do this," Sol whispers. "I know you're still in there. I know you still love me."

I see a flicker of . . . something, pass over Teddy's face. But he shakes his head and reaches out to Sol, not with the hand holding the Hammer, but the other one, pushing Sol to the side and sending him stumbling against a marble plinth bearing an ancient-looking wooden harp. Then Teddy turns back to Caraway.

"Kill him," the King Toad demands, his tone growing impatient. "Crush him beneath your boot like the worm he is."

Teddy advances, as steady and implacable as a mountain.

Caraway feints with the needle and ducks away once more. He's holding back. He doesn't want to hurt Teddy, and I love him for that, but I'm not sure there's any other way for this to end.

The Hammer swings down again, barely missing Caraway's skull. Gold coins go skittering in all directions, winking and flashing in the candlelight. One inch to the left, and Caraway would be dead now. I glance down at Thurmond Boswell's body, limp and lifeless on the stone floor. How many more will die today, and is there anything I can do to stop it?

Improbably, I hear Sweetpea's voice echoing in my mind.

Holler if you need anything.

But how can I holler, down here in the belly of Deeping Fen, trapped in a cage of stone?

Another blow of the Hammer makes a marble bust explode into powder, Caraway stumbling and sliding away from it. He's no longer trying to fight back; it's taking all his energy just to avoid the inexorable rain of blows from Teddy's hammer.

Then a ripple of music washes through the great cavern. It's Sol, the ancient harp balanced on his knee, his head bent over the strings as his fingers dance back and forth. The sound that emerges is so beautiful it makes my heart ache. In every note is Sol's love for Teddy. His unshakable faith in him. His trust.

Teddy freezes, and I see a tremble in his shoulder as his eyes drift toward Sol. Caraway scrambles backward, out of the Hammer's range.

"No more interference," rumbles the King Toad, and more rivers of liquid stone rise up to trap Sol in place. The harp falls to the floor, and every one of its strings snaps and curls up on itself with a series of discordant twangs.

Teddy shakes his head as if to clear it and raises his hammer once more. Blow after blow rains down as Caraway scuttles backward, each one coming closer and closer to taking his life. His one remaining eye is wide and desperate as he stares death in the face.

But Sol is not done. He raises his head and begins to sing, pure and sweet. He sings about home, about the ringing of Teddy's hammer in the forge. About lazy afternoons by the Mira. He sings the story of how they fell in love, and of the bond between them that will withstand any distance, any fight, any obstacle.

Tears start to roll down Teddy's cheeks, but still the Hammer swings. Caraway scrambles away from the blows, trying to avoid Teddy's inexorable advances, backing up against the corpse of his father.

An iron bridle snakes around Sol's cheeks and drives into his mouth, but he keeps singing without words, the warm honey tones of his voice promising sweetness and love and home.

"Stop," Teddy pleads, and I can't tell whether he's talking to Sol, to Caraway, or to the King Toad, who is forcing him to keep fighting.

Caraway's heel slides in a pool of his father's blood, and his legs go out from under him. He raises himself up onto his elbows to face his fate as Teddy moves to stand over him, one leg planted on either side of Caraway's body, raising his hammer high to take one final, fatal blow.

Sol doesn't stop singing.

I struggle against my stone cage, but I can't get free.

The King Toad rumbles a smug laugh of pure satisfaction.

Teddy swings his hammer in a wide arc at the same moment as Sol's voice soars up to the high vaulted ceiling of the cavernous space, making every inch of it ring with beauty and longing. Tears slip down my own cheeks.

I can't look away.

Gofannon's Hammer does not sink into Caraway's skull.

Instead, with a grunt and a massive display of strength, Teddy twists and drives the blow upward toward the wall of toadstones.

The King Toad's eyes bulge.

A hundred stones are instantly pulverized beneath the weight of the Hammer. The force of the blow spreads out like a shock wave on the wall, each stone popping and shattering, one after another, radiating out until every single stone on the wall has fractured and burst into a million glittering fragments, like diamond dust raining down from the sky.

I feel a surge of hope as I watch the wall of toadstones disintegrate. Every single Toadman released from their bondage to the king. I imagine the lightening of shoulders all over Anglyon as that connection is severed. And I know that others will stagger, without the power of the Toadmen to fill the void of their missing strings.

Teddy swings the Hammer once more, and it connects with the bars of my cage with a joyous ringing noise. The stone shatters into fragments as well, and I'm finally free. Sweat streams down Teddy's face as he swings the Hammer one more time, and Sol's cage dissolves into stone shards.

"Teddy!" I scream. "The vial!"

He grits his teeth and swings, and the ornate cradle containing the slimy Toad mettle shatters, along with the Fox Bride's toadstone.

Teddy staggers backward, still clutching the Hammer, and Sol leaps forward to catch him in his arms.

"I'm so sorry," Teddy says, his voice breaking in a sob.

"Shhh." Sol strokes his cheek and presses his lips to Teddy's brow.

The King Toad watches all this, expressionless. I'm a bit disappointed, really. I want him to be gnashing his teeth and cursing us all the way to next Tuesday.

The Fox Bride lets out a rasping, feeble noise, and I run to kneel by her side.

She is dying, her lungs struggling to draw breath.

"It's okay," I murmur to her. "It's nearly over."

"Surrender," says Caraway, who has managed to get to his feet. He looks like he could pass out at any minute. The blank socket where his toad eye once was is starting to weep some kind of thick dark fluid.

The King Toad chuckles. "Me? Surrender? I don't think so. You think that breaking my trinkets will stop me? I have consumed thousands of toadstones, over hundreds of years. Thousands of strings. I am more powerful than you can possibly imagine." He reaches out and drags another chest of toadstones toward him, shoveling them into his mouth by the fistful. "I have no shortage, as you can see."

He places a huge hand on his stomach. "And I still have *her* stone," he says jeeringly, pointing at me. "Tucked away all safe and sound. Whole and perfect."

Caraway raises the silver needle. "I will cut it from your belly."

The King Toad laughs. "You? A tadpole with a knitting needle?"

"No." Caraway shakes his head. "The Ghost Toad."

"And the Howling Toad," says Teddy, who has gotten to his

feet once more, raising the Hammer threateningly. He glances over at me, and my heart soars because the real Teddy is back.

The King Toad spreads his arms wide. "Do your worst, my brothers."

Together, Caraway and Teddy charge toward the King Toad, weapons raised.

But it is for naught. The Hammer bounces off the King Toad's flesh as if it were a child's rubber mallet, and the needle cannot pierce his skin, bending away from it like a cheap spoon.

The rumble of the King Toad's laugh makes the floor under my feet shake.

"You are foolish enough to attack me with my own weapons? The Hammer and the needle were *my* gifts to the Howling Toad and the Ghost Toad. They cannot harm me. No weapon forged by man can harm the King of Toads."

And he lashes out with one great arm.

Teddy and Caraway go flying, their bodies soaring through the air to land with sickening crunches against mounds of treasure. Neither of them gets up again.

Sol snatches up the white-hilted sword from one of the marble plinths and rushes toward the King Toad, but the great beast swipes once more, and Sol crumples to the ground as well.

I gently take the Fox Bride's hand. Her eyes, sunken and clouded, turn to mine, and I know what she needs from me.

"I'm sorry," I tell her. "For all of it. You can be at peace now."

I slide the ring from her finger, disconnecting her from the tide of mettle. Without it to sustain her, the life drains from her eyes, and her heart stills.

I kiss her papery cheek and stand up.

I'm ready.

"It is just you and I, now, Little Fox," the great monster rumbles. "Just as it once was."

I look directly at him, and perhaps I see a tinge of sorrow in his giant yellow eyes. "It's true, then," I say. "You are the original toad. The one from the story."

"The very same. The bramble-frog of Morgendagh. Slayer of beasts. Stronger than any knight, cleverer than any fox."

"Is it all true?" I ask. "The Fox Bride and everything?"

The King Toad shrugs, a gesture like the moving of mountains. "Every tale has its share of truth. And an equal share of lies."

I think back to the story Caraway told me in the Purple Menace. A great Beast threatened the people of Deepdene. The Green Knight went into Deeping Fen but was defeated. But the clever toad defeated the Beast and claimed the hand of the Fox Bride.

I think back to the rhyme the Toadmen recited at Sol's door on Whitsuntide Eve.

About one toad the bards do sing

So bold and brave they made him king

"There never was a Beast, was there?" I say. "*You* were the Beast all along."

The King Toad chuckles. "For centuries I devoured the creatures of the fen," he says. "Gobbled up their hearts, their minds, their strings. Then humans came and oh, Little Fox! Humans are more delicious than any marsh crake or fenworm. Humans taste of jealousy. Of bitterness. Of spite and malice and greed. But humans are clever, and they fight back with iron spears and eagle-fletched arrows. I wondered to myself . . . what if there was a way to trick the humans? To turn their fears and their greed back against them, so that they would *give* me their delicious strings? And so I started to whisper of a great Beast in the fen. I stole their children away in the dead of night and sucked their bones dry. I laid traps for their warriors and drowned them facedown in the fen."

"So they called on the Green Knight," I say.

The King Toad licks his lips. "The Green Knight was the most delicious of all. He was strong and tasted of vanity and hubris. With their hero slain, the humans reeked of despair. It was nothing to convince them that *I* had slain the Beast. They begged me to be their king, and everyone bowed down before my might."

"But it was never *your* might, was it?" I ask. "It was all her. The Fox Bride."

"She was young and greedy. And clever. Even cleverer than you. We made a deal, deep in the Fen. She agreed to let me share in her power, and in return I would give her everything her heart desired. For a time she was happy to live as my queen, to reap the benefits of her position. I kept her in riches. The finest gowns, the largest jewels. In return I took her mettle, her energy, and I spun it into toad magic. But she was still human. She was still riddled with greed and spite and doubt, just as a dog is riddled with fleas. I could taste the treachery on her, long before she made her move against me. I knew she would betray me, but I was sorry to eat her. She was a fighter, and no mistake."

"So you found another one."

"It was easy. Witches are as common as marsh flies."

I thought you had some fight in you, says Sweetpea in my head. *Stop feeling sorry for yourself and try to find a way out of here.*

But how? I can't fight the King Toad. What was it he said?

No weapon forged by man can harm the King of Toads.

But perhaps I don't need a weapon. Perhaps I have everything I need.

I hear a groan from where Caraway lies crumpled on the ground. He raises his head, just a little, to look at me. I feel a little spark when my eyes meet his, and suddenly I'm in the Purple Menace, flying down country roads with my head out the window, singing "Little Lights" at the top of my lungs.

Big love
Little lights combine
You and I ignite

"I'm not a witch, though," I tell the King Toad, and hold up the golden ring. "Are you sure I'm worthy to be your queen?"

He chuckles. "I *do* like you," he says, winking at me. "You've been such a spirited guest. I would have liked to see you try to kill me."

Everything balances for a moment, on a knife edge.

I knew you were a fighter, says Sweetpea in my head.

"Then I have great news," I tell the King Toad, winking back. "You *did* get to see me try to kill you. Better yet, you saw me succeed. You're already dead."

The King Toad laughs heartily at this, but I notice a slight wariness in his expression. He looks down at the pile of toadstones in his fist and shakes them away as if he's just realized they are spiders. They go skittering and bouncing across the floor like marbles.

I let my lips curl into a smile and am gratified to see the uneasiness spread throughout the vast mass of the King Toad.

"Have you ever wondered what might happen," I say conversationally, "if you channeled the power of, say, a few hundred witches into a single toadstone?"

The uncanny double eyelids of the King Toad narrow. "You talk big, Little Fox. But I have tasted your mettle. You are no witch."

"No," I agree. "I'm not."

But I'm not completely powerless.

I turn witch-eyed.

The great river of witch mettle rises up from the body of the Fox Bride. With her ring removed and her toadstone destroyed, there is nowhere for it to go, the silvery threads swirling around her body. I search through the threads until I find one that is familiar, that pulses more strongly than the others.

I race along it, my consciousness speeding up and out of Deeping Fen, over forests and fields and rivers and up the mountain to Ruddock Farm.

She is there, the Spitalwick Hag.

We've been waiting for you, she says as she lets me into her mind.

It's dark and vicious and wise in there.

She opens her eyes and I look through them, and see the other witches, ready.

I see Sweetpea—Winnie, her fierceness burning hot and bright. With the insight of the Spitalwick Hag, I see her differently. She's older than she seems, and somehow I know that she's died before—many times.

The Hag opens herself to me, and together we spread our

388

awareness to the other resistance witches. I feel each of them open up to us as I use my gift, my mettle-tracking ability, to see through the eyes of a hundred witches—two hundred, and more. Not just the witches from Ruddock Farm, but every witch on every farm who wears a Toad wedding ring. Together we pierce the rosy glow of the ring and feel the witches awaken, struggling against their enchantment.

I see through the eyes of a thousand witches, each of us standing with our hands by our sides, our hair blown back by an invisible wind. I feel the sharp spikes of our rage. The energy that throbs in our veins, and in the mettle threads of a thousand toadstones.

A billion little lights
A multitude
Can make a sun

I show them what I need, letting my mind flow into theirs so they can see through my eyes, just as I can see through theirs.

I am no witch. But I understand mettle. I can follow it. Track it. Travel along it and pour my consciousness into a witch's mind.

It's time, I tell them.

And I slide the Fox Bride's ring onto my finger.

Everything is fine.

Rosy clouds envelop me and I'm floating. I grasp for the threads of consciousness, but they slip through my fingers, and I'm carried away into soft contentment.

I don't remember what I was so worried about.

None of it matters anymore.

Except . . .

There's something else, in among the rosiness.

A little spark.

Then another.

And another.

And gradually the rosiness makes way for something else. A galaxy of little lights, a whirling vortex of energy. Of witch consciousness.

Their power ripples through the network of Toad mettle, crackling and pulsing and fizzing with energy.

I remember the Spitalwick Hag, standing before us, the ruins of Ruddock Farm at her back.

A lightning bolt might do it. Or a really focused surge of mettle.

A surge of mettle. The fury and rage of a thousand witches, channeled through me, the Fox Bride, through the ring forged by the King Toad himself, and into . . .

My toadstone, deep in the King Toad's belly.

The stone cannot contain the sheer force of it. It shudders, blurring with vibration, and the enormous, bulging eyes of the King of Toads snap to mine.

"You fool," he gasps. "This doesn't end with me."

And then he explodes.

20.

I HAVE BITS OF TOADFLESH IN MY HAIR.

The King Toad is no more, but he's also everywhere, a layer of his remains coating all the treasure, the marble statues. The floor is slick with it. The air stinks of blood and the thick muddy scent of the fen.

I stand amid it all, my fists clenched at my sides. I am the only person standing in this room.

The King Toad is dead.

The brown Toad mettle is disintegrating, splitting and dissolving into the air. I feel the connection between me and the other witches growing weaker, but I pour my gratitude into them before it severs, and I feel an exhausted surge of satisfaction in return. Their toadstones have all been destroyed too—the energy surge rebounded back along the mettle threads and turned every single stone to dust. The King Toad's power has gone, absorbed into the depths of the fen, and the stones of the Deeping Court, which shudder under my feet.

Teddy is crouched on the floor, his head between his knees

and his arms folded over his head, like a child. His back heaves with sobs.

Sol picks his way through globs of toadflesh and crouches down next to him, laying a tentative hand on Teddy's back. Teddy flinches at his touch.

"Go away," I hear him mumble. "Don't look at me."

"But I *want* to look at you," Sol says. "I like looking at you."

Teddy looks up, his face streaked with tears and sweat and blood. "I did such terrible things."

"You were enchanted."

"I *betrayed* you. And Merry and everyone."

Sol touches a gentle finger to his cheek. "But you came back," he says. "When it really, really mattered, you chose me. Chose us."

Teddy starts to cry again. "I'm so sorry," he says as Sol enfolds him in an embrace.

"Shh," Sol says, laying his cheek against Teddy's golden curls. "It's okay. We're going to be okay."

Caraway groans and rises to a sitting position, and I hurry to his side. The gaping, bloody hole where his eye once was is puffing up, bruised and gory.

"Does it hurt?" I ask him.

He grimaces. "It's starting to."

"We need to get you to a doctor."

"We're in a giant magical fortress," Caraway says dryly. "I expect we can locate a healing potion or two."

There is another deep, rumbling aftershock, and bits of earth and dirt rain down from the cavernous ceiling.

"Or we could just leave?" I suggest.

Caraway's eyes stray down to his father's body.

"I'm sorry," I say.

Caraway nods slowly, his brow creasing in a frown. "Yeah. I . . . I don't really know what to feel."

I'm not sure I do either. The fizzing energy from my connection with the witches is fading, and I feel a bone-numbing exhaustion sinking in. We did what we set out to do—all three Toads of Deeping Fen are dead. The centuries-old power beneath the Deeping Court has been snuffed out. Caraway is free. So is Teddy, and all the witches.

Not Da, though.

Da will never return home from here. Never watch an egg hatch again. Never smile his Da smile.

There's another tremor under my feet, and suddenly the wall that used to contain toadstones cracks, right down the middle.

"We need to get out of here," Sol says, his voice raised over the groaning of shifting stone.

I look up at the blackness overhead. Far above us is the Great Hall, but I have no idea how to get up there again. I glance at Caraway and see that neither does he.

"Get on the platform," I tell everyone. "There's got to be a way to get it moving."

"There's a lever!" Sol shouts, and points to a plinth near where the King Toad used to be. And he's right. An enormous, rusty metal lever. That's got to be it.

But who's going to pull it?

"I'll stay behind," Caraway offers.

"No," I say. "Nobody stays behind. We leave together."

"Could we throw something at it?" Sol asks doubtfully.

I shake my head. "It's too far. And that lever looks heavy."

Caraway casts around for inspiration. "Maybe if we could find a rope?" he suggests. "We could tie it around the lever and pull—"

"I can throw the Hammer," Teddy says suddenly.

His shoulders are set, his expression determined. I know how much this costs him. The Hammer was his dream. One of the most powerful artifacts in the history of Anglyon, and he was powerful enough to wield it. With it, he would be as powerful as Gofannon himself. A god.

There's a moment of silence.

"Are you sure?" Sol asks.

Teddy frowns at him. "Of course I'm sure. It's just a thing. You're much more important."

But I can see the tension in his jaw. This is a choice he's making, and while it may be an easy choice, it's still an important one.

Teddy hefts the Hammer. Touches the black head to his own forehead and closes his eyes for a moment.

So much could go wrong here. Teddy could miss. The lever could do something completely different. Or maybe it just won't work at all, now that the Toad mettle is disintegrating all around us, along with the giant cavern that once held the King Toad.

Teddy takes a deep breath to steady himself as a huge chunk of rock falls from the ceiling and obliterates an enormous marble statue of the blind druid Mug Ruith. Then Teddy's biceps bulge as he draws his arm back, swinging the Hammer around in a full arc before opening his eyes and letting go.

Gofannon's Hammer flies true. It arcs across the great chamber, over piles of jewels spattered with bits of toadflesh and rubble. It smashes into the plinth holding the lever, which cranks forward with an ancient-sounding metallic groan.

And the ground beneath us starts to move, rising up to the blackness above as more great hunks of rock fall and shatter. The ground where we stood not moments ago sunders in a great, wide crack, and brown water gushes in, stinking of decay and musky peat.

We clutch each other, Caraway, Sol, Teddy and I, huddling in the center of our platform, as a huge stone hits the edge of it and it tilts dangerously to once side. We're high enough now that if we fall, we will certainly die.

We continue our slow ascent as the groan and crack of stone intensify, falling all around us to splash into the swiftly rising water below.

The Deeping Court is sinking.

Finally, we reach the top and scramble off the platform. The Great Hall is shuddering and quaking too—one of the torches has fallen from its sconce and set the huge velvet drapes alight, and the room is full of smoke and dust.

"Come on!" Caraway shouts, and leads the way down the aisle and into the corridor. I'm glad he knows his way around the Deeping Court, because as usual it all looks the same to me. We pelt down one corridor, only to discover it's blocked by rubble. We head back the way we came and try a different route, holding our sleeves over our mouths to protect ourselves from the acrid black smoke that seems to be everywhere. The stones quake under our feet, and I hear the crunch and slide of stone on stone.

"The whole place is going to collapse!" I yell, and realize as I say it that this is entirely obvious to everyone present.

We skid around another corner and down a flight of stairs, then up another, finally arriving in the undercover dock, where we hustle onto one of the barges. The water of the fen seems to boil with movement, heaving and surging like an ocean. Teddy, Sol, Caraway and I each take up an oar, and together we row the barge out between the huge pillars and twisting roots of the Deeping Court, finally emerging into the thin gray evening light of the fen.

"Keep going," Teddy says through gritted teeth.

My arms and shoulders are screaming from rowing so hard, but I keep at it, the great Toad fortress behind us, until finally we pause, turning to see the entire structure collapsing in on itself, sending a huge wave surging through the fen that picks up our little barge and washes us away from the destruction. Water closes over the top of ancient mossy stones, great bubbles of air rising and boiling to the surface.

We clutch the sides of our barge so as not to topple over, watching until the water stills and there is nothing left of the Deeping Court but a lake of brown, muddy water.

EPILOGUE

GOLDEN AFTERNOON SUN WARMS THE BACKS OF MY eyelids. I can taste ambrosia on my tongue, and my fingers are stained purple with damson plum juice. The air is sweet with the scent of honeysuckle and wild lotus, and of crushed grass beneath me.

Somewhere nearby, Sol is noodling away on his crwth, plucking strings and humming little snatches of melody. The sound of it mingles with the spirited song of a nearby mistle thrush and the liquid sounds of the Mira as it flows gently by.

We've had a busy couple of weeks, and there will be many more to come. But in this moment, I have absolutely nowhere to be, and nothing to do.

I may not have had the summer of my dreams, but I do have this one perfect afternoon, and I am not taking it for granted.

IT WAS STRANGE, RETURNING to Candlecott and finding everything unchanged.

The Frater House had been continuing as normal, with no idea that the entire Toad operation had collapsed. But Caraway marched in there with all the haughty authority he could muster and confiscated the black iron hook that they used to sever people from their mettle strings. He told them that the Toadmen were over, and that it was time for change. Dr. Gower protested, and Teddy banished him for good. But the rest of the Candlecott Toadmen are, at their hearts, good people. Free from the influence of Toad mettle, they were quite amenable to the idea. They're keeping the Frater House but renaming themselves the Candlecott Social Society, and last week Goody Bhreagh and Peggy Ross were welcomed as their first female members. Goody Bhreagh is teaching Creepy Glen how to knit.

I open my eyes and stare up into the endless blue of the sky. In the distance, I can hear splashing and a shout of victory from Teddy, who must have caught a fish. We'll roast it over a campfire tonight with butter and wild garlic, firelight dancing in our eyes as the stars wheel overhead.

The chickens all miss Da, and I am a poor substitute. I've organized for Peggy Ross to take them. The Whitsuntide competition is being renamed the Alain Morgan Poultry Prize in Da's honor.

It's hard to be in the house without him, but at least it made the decision to leave easy.

Caraway and I talked a lot about Staunton. We wondered if it was worth going, whether it would be better to team up with the Hag and Winnie and the other resistance witches and try to get to doing good work straightaway. But Caraway pointed out that a university is a great place to meet other young people. People who can be recruited to our cause. There'll be other junior Toadmen there, and we can find them and help them to spread the word about the end of all things Toad. Candlecott is just one Frater House. We need to find the others and spread the word all over Anglyon. And that's just the beginning.

We know, now, that the Toadmen weren't the root of the cancer that's eating through the magic of Anglyon.

This doesn't end with me, the King Toad said before he died. There are more secrets to be uncovered. I've been in touch with Winnie, who is investigating rumors about Ilium's CEO, as well as the two other big magic corporations, Moracle and Welch.

We've got a plan, but we can't do it alone. We need other bright young things to join us.

Plus Staunton has an excellent physics program, and free tacos on Thursday afternoons. And that oak tree is calling my name.

Caraway and I are driving up next week in the Purple Menace to check it all out. It still feels weird being out in the world again—I was a bit afraid I was a wanted felon after my escape from Ruddock Farm, but it seems like Ilium and the auditors want to keep the whole thing a secret. I guess it doesn't make them look great, letting hundreds of dangerous resistance witches go free. And with Thurmond Boswell and Dr. Veil gone, I suspect the folks at Ilium have plenty on their plates to keep them busy. Still, I'm keeping my head down. For now.

There are still many other innocent people imprisoned in so-called recovery centers and mettle farms. There's plenty more injustice here in Anglyon, and elsewhere.

Winnie said I could make a difference, and she was right. I can. But change takes time. And it takes people.

Caraway flops down on the grass beside me, his cheeks pink from exertion. His ruined eye is covered with a neat patch made of sky-blue linen. The doctor suggested a glamour that would make it look as if his eye were still there, but Caraway refused. He's done with glamours.

He's wearing jeans and a flannel shirt, but even in flannel Caraway looks like a prince. But not an ice prince. Not anymore. Now he's just a standard handsome prince, slumming it with the country folk, his fingers as purple-stained as mine, his bergamot-and-leather scent now mixed with woodsmoke and sorrel. He went to the city to see his mother after we left Deeping Fen, but now he's back in Candlecott. He's still processing what happened. It'll take time. He's determined to undo some of the harm his father did. To expose some of the hypocrisies of those in power. To stand up for the powerless.

I'm so proud of him. Of us.

"Did you catch anything?" I ask, stretching lazily. He and Teddy have been fishing upstream, where the fattest trout like to sun their bellies.

"Teddy did," Caraway says. "I was really just there for the snacks."

He winds his fingers into mine, his thumb brushing over my wrist. The golden glow of the afternoon feels a little more beautiful, now that he's here. I turn onto my side to face him and see the softening in his expression as we gaze at each other. My stomach does a little flip.

I used to think I knew what my future held. It was a comfortable future, free of surprises. A single frozen image, a beautiful watercolor hanging on a wall.

But life isn't just one still image. Life is messy and complicated. Sometimes it's comfortable, sometimes it isn't. I don't know what my life is going to be like. But I know what I want it to be *for.* I want to do some good in the world. Like Winnie said, I may not be a witch, but I'm not powerless either. There are people out there who have had too much power for too long, and it's time for change.

I hear Teddy's and Sol's voices, low and fond. Teddy has decided he's going to Habasah with Sol. They've been pretty much inseparable since we killed the King Toad. Teddy is still haunted by his enchantment, and the things he did. But Sol is kind and patient, and they both love each other so much. I know they'll be okay.

Caraway pulls me close to him, until we are nose to nose. "Are you ready?" he says in a low voice.

I tilt my head toward his until our lips just brush. "Yeah," I whisper. "I'm ready."

Sol's fingers pick out the melody of "Little Lights" on his crwth, and Caraway and I smile at each other.

A billion little lights—a multitude—can make a sun.

Here we are to save the world.

ACKNOWLEDGMENTS

It's funny how movies and video games have long credit sequences detailing everyone who was involved, and books . . . don't. It's an incredible deception, really. The implication that a book springs from the author's mind fully formed, and doesn't need any help to make its way into the world. Total codswallop.

Here are my credits. Stay to the end for a secret postcredits Easter egg.

Thank you to the Council—Amie, Ellie, Eliza, Kate, Liz, Nicole, Pete, and Skye. You are my daily accountability, my sounding board, my safe space. I love you all to bits. And bonus extra thanks to Amie Kaufman, who suggested the title on a writers retreat, to Liz Barr for her clever prison break ideas, and to Nicole Hayes for being a thoughtful and generous early reader.

Thank you to Fourth Floor Collapse for allowing me to use the lyrics to "Little Lights." I strongly recommend that you go find their stuff on your music platform of choice, and I'm not just saying that because I'm married to one of them.

Thank you to my wonderful agent, Katelyn Detweiler, for

being my biggest cheerleader. You are unfailingly supportive and have been there throughout this whole process, and somehow managed to have an actual human baby at the same time. Extraordinary. Thanks also to the others at Jill Grinberg Literary Management who have helped out, especially Denise Page, Sam Farkas, and Sophia Seidner.

Thank you to my US editors, Krista Marino and Lydia Gregovic at Delacorte Press. You ask the best questions, gently steer me toward better decisions, and love all the best bits. I couldn't ask for better supporters and collaborators. Thanks also to Beverly Horowitz, Barbara Marcus, Colleen Fellingham, Tamar Schwartz, Angela Carlino, Cynthia Lliguichuzhca, and the RHCB Marketing and Publicity teams.

Thank you to my Aussie publisher and editor Jodie Webster at Allen & Unwin. Jodie, you're my rock. I can't imagine publishing a YA novel without you. Thanks also to Hilary Reynolds, Reem Galal, Simon Panagaris, Susannah Chambers, Deb Lum, Carolyn Walsh, and the sales team.

Thanks to all the booksellers who have put my books in the hands of readers. You make magic happen.

Thank you to my parents for all of their support, and for never once suggesting that I get a real job.

Thank you to Michael for coming with me on my creative journeys, and for inviting me on yours. Thank you for being my partner. Thank you for the music. Thank you for loving me.

Thank you to Banjo for being the best kid a mum could ever hope for. I love your creative brain and am so proud of you.

And thank you to Mags, as always. Faithful hound and muse.

And I guess thank you to my chickens, as well? You befoul my back deck, but your eggs are tasty.

Are you still here? Thank *you*. For buying or borrowing this book, for reading it (if you did), for sticking around. I'm so glad you exist.

As promised . . .

CARAWAY'S EYES WIDEN AS I plop a yellow ball of fluff into his cupped hands.

"I don't know what to do!" he says. "What if I break it?"

"You won't *break* it," I say. "Just give it a pat."

"Does it have a name?"

"Not yet. You can pick one, if you like."

Caraway carefully examines the chick, who peeps indignantly at him. "Ceridwen," he says at last. "Goddess and keeper of the cauldron of knowledge."

"He's a boy."

"Barnabas."

"Barnabas?"

Caraway shrugs. "He was born in a barn." He strokes the chick's downy feathers.

"Don't get too attached," I say. "We already have enough roosters. Once he's old enough, I'm sending him off to the butcher."

"Monster."

I shrug. "It's how things are."

Caraway turns, shielding the chick with his body. "Don't listen to her, Barnabas," he mutters to the chick. "I won't let anything happen to you."

I can feel Da everywhere. In every cluck and cheep, every piece of straw. Every rough wooden board and cobweb. It hurts, knowing that he won't appear in the doorway to the barn with a sack of scratch mix over his shoulder. But it feels good, too. To be close to him again.

Caraway is watching me, like he knows exactly what I'm thinking. Still cupping the chick gently in one hand, he reaches out the other to take mine.

He smiles at me, and my insides turn to golden syrup.

"Come on," he says. "It's breakfast time."

"Eggs?" I ask, looking around at all the chickens.

The smile stretches into a grin. His eyes twinkle. "Eggs."

ABOUT THE AUTHOR

Lili Wilkinson is the author of nineteen novels published in Australia, including *Green Valentine*, *The Boundless Sublime*, and *After the Lights Go Out*. She established the Inky Awards at the Centre for Youth Literature, State Library of Victoria. Lili has a PhD in creative writing from the University of Melbourne and spends most of her time reading and writing books for teenagers. Her fantasy novels include *A Hunger of Thorns* and *Deep Is the Fen*.

liliwilkinson.com.au